Honoré de Balzac, Ellen Marriage

Country Parson

Le Curé de Village & Albert Savaron - De Savarus

Honoré de Balzac, Ellen Marriage

Country Parson
Le Curé de Village & Albert Savaron - De Savarus

ISBN/EAN: 9783337227579

Printed in Europe, USA, Canada, Australia, Japan

Cover: Foto ©Andreas Hilbeck / pixelio.de

More available books at **www.hansebooks.com**

H. DE BALZAC

THE

COUNTRY PARSON

(LE CURÉ DE VILLAGE)

AND

ALBERT SAVARON

(DE SAVARUS)

TRANSLATED BY

ELLEN MARRIAGE

AND

CLARA BELL

WITH A PREFACE BY

GEORGE SAINTSBURY

PHILADELPHIA

THE GEBBIE PUBLISHING CO., Ltd.

1898

CONTENTS

LIST OF ILLUSTRATIONS.

PREFACE.

PERHAPS in no instance of Balzac's work is his singular fancy for pulling that work about more remarkably instanced and illustrated than in the case of "The Country Parson." The double date, 1837–1845, which the author attached to it, in his usual conscientious manner, to indicate these revisions, has a greater signification than almost anywhere else. When the book, or rather its constituent parts, first appeared in the *Presse* for 1839, having been written the winter before, not only was it very different in detail, but the order of the parts was altogether dissimilar. Balzac here carried out his favorite plan—a plan followed by many other authors no doubt, but always, as it seems to me, of questionable wisdom—that of beginning in the middle and then "throwing back" with a long retrospective and explanatory digression.

In this version the story of Tascheron's crime and its punishment came first; and it was not till after the execution that the early history of Véronique (who gave her name to this part as to a "Suite du Curé de Village") was introduced. This history ceased at the crisis of her life; and when it was taken up in a third part, called "Véronique au Tombeau," only the present conclusion of the book, with her confession, was given. The long account of her sojourn at Montégnac, of her labors there, of the episode of Farrabesche, and so forth, did not appear till 1841, when the whole book, with the inversions and insertions just indicated, appeared in such a changed form that even the indefatigable M. de Lovenjoul dismisses as "impossible" the idea of exhibiting a complete picture of the various changes made. Nor was the author even yet contented; for in 1845, before establishing it in its place in the "Comédie," he not only, as was his wont, took out the chapter-headings, leaving five divisions only, but introduced other alterations, resulting in the present condition of the book.

As the book stands it may be said to consist of three parts united rather by identity of the personages who act in them than by exact dramatic connection. There is, to take the title-part first (though it is by no means the most really important or pervading) the picture of "The Country Parson," which is almost an exact, and beyond doubt a designed, pendant to that of "The Country Doctor." The Abbé Bonnet indeed is not able to carry out economic ameliorations, as Dr. Benassis is, personally, but by inducing Véronique to do so he brings about the same result, and on an even larger scale. His personal action (with the necessary changes for his profession) is also tolerably identical, and on the whole the two portraits may fairly be hung together as Balzac's ideal representations of the good man in soul-curing and body-curing respectively. Both are largely conditioned by his eighteenth century fancy for "playing Providence," and by his delight in extensive financial-commercial schemes. But the beauty of the portraiture of the "Curé" is nearly, if not quite equal, to that of the doctor, though the institution of celibacy has prevented Balzac from giving a key to the conduct of Bonnet quite as sufficient as that which he furnished for the conduct of Benassis.

The second part of the book is the crime—episodic as regards the criminal, cardinal as regards other points—of Tascheron. Balzac was very fond of "his crimes;" and it is quite worth while in connection with his handling of the murder here to study the curious story of his actual interference in the famous Peytel case, which also interested Thackeray so much in his Paris days. The Tascheron case itself (which from a note appears to have been partly suggested by some actual affair) no doubt has interests for those who like such

things, and the picture of the criminal in prison is very striking. But we see and know so very little of Tascheron himself, and even to the very last (which is long afterwards) we
are left so much in the dark as to his love for Véronique,
that the thing has an extraneous air. It is like a short story
foisted in.

This objection connects itself at once with a similar one to
the delineation of Véronique. There is nothing in her conduct intrinsically impossible, or even improbable. A girl of
her temperament, at once, as often happens, strongly sensual
and strongly devotional, deprived of her good looks by illness,
thrown into the arms of a husband physically repulsive, and
after a short time not troubling himself to be amiable in any
other way, might very well take refuge in the substantial, if
not ennobling, consolations offered by a good-looking and
amiable young fellow of the lower class. Her conduct at the
time of the crime (her exact complicity in which is, as we
have said, rather imperfectly indicated) is also fairly probable, and to her repentance and amendment of life no exception can be taken. But only in this last stage do we really
see anything of the inside of Véronique's nature ; and even
then we do not see it completely. The author's silence on
the details of the actual *liaison* with Tascheron has its advantages, but it also has its defects.

Still, the book is one of great attraction and interest, and
takes, if I may judge by my own experience, a high rank for
enchaining power among that class of Balzac's books which
cannot be put exactly highest. If the changes made in it by
its author have to some extent dislocated it as a whole, they
have resulted in very high excellence for almost all the parts.

As something has necessarily been said already about the
book-history of the " Country Parson," little remains but to
give exact dates and places of appearance. The *Presse* published the (original) first part in December–January, 1838–39,
the original second (" Véronique ") six months later, and the

third ("Véronique au Tombeau") in August. All had chapters and chapter-titles. As a book it was in its first complete form published by Souverain in 1841, and was again altered when it took rank in the "Comédie" six years later.

"Albert Savaron," with its enshrined story of "L'Ambitieux par Amour" (something of an oddity for Balzac, who often puts a story within a story, but less formally than this) contains various appeals, and shows not a few of its author's well-known interests in politics, in affairs, in newspapers, not to mention the enumerations of *dots* and fortunes which he never could refuse himself. The affection of Savaron for the Duchesse d'Argaiolo may interest different persons differently. It seems to me a little *fade*. But the character of Rosalie de Watteville is in a very different rank. Here only, except, perhaps, in the case of Mademoiselle de Verneuil, whose unlucky experiences had emancipated her, has Balzac depicted a girl full of character, individuality, and life. It was apparently necessary that Rosalie should be made not wholly amiable in order to obtain this accession of wits and force, and to be freed from the fatal gift of *candeur*, the curse of the French *ingénue*. Her creator has also thought proper to punish her further, and cruelly, at the end of the book. Nevertheless, though her story may be less interesting than either of theirs, it is impossible not to put her in a much higher rank as a heroine than either Eugénie or Ursule, and not to wish that Balzac had included the conception of her in a more important structure of fiction.

Albert Savaron appeared in sixty headed chapters in the *Siècle* for May and June, 1842, and then assumed its place in the "Comédie." But though left there, it also formed part of a two-volume issue by Souverain in 1844, in company with "La Muse du Department." "Rosalie" was at first named "Philomène."

G. S.

THE COUNTRY PARSON.

(Le Curé de Village.)

I.

VÉRONIQUE.

At the lower end of Limoges, at the corner of the Rue de la Vieille-Poste and the Rue de la Cité, there stood, some thirty years back, an old-fashioned shop of the kind that seems to have changed in nothing since the middle ages. The great stone paving-slabs, riven with countless cracks, were laid upon the earth; the damp oozed up through them here and there; while the heights and hollows of this primitive flooring would have tripped up those who were not careful to observe them. Through the dust on the walls it was possible to discern a sort of mosaic of timber and bricks, iron and stone, a heterogeneous mass which owed its compact solidity to time, and perhaps to chance. For more than two centuries the huge rafters of the ceiling had bent without breaking beneath the weight of the upper stories, which were constructed of wooden framework, protected from the weather by slates arranged in a geometrical pattern; altogether, it was a quaint example of a burgess' house in olden times. Once there had been carved figures on the wooden window-frames, but sun and rain had destroyed the ornaments, and the windows themselves stood all awry; some bent outwards, some bent in, yet others were minded to part company, and one and all carried a little soil deposited (it would be hard to say how) in crannies hollowed by the rain, where a few shy creeping plants and thin weeds grew to break into meagre blossom

*(1)

in the spring.   Velvet mosses covered the roof and the window-sills.

The pillar which supported the corner of the house, built though it was of composite masonry, that is to say, partly of stone, partly of brick and flints, was alarming to behold by reason of its curvature; it looked as though it must give way some day beneath the weight of the superstructure whose gable projected fully six inches.   For which reason the local authorities and the board of works bought the house and pulled it down to widen the street.   The venerable corner pillar had its charms for lovers of old Limoges; it carried a pretty sculptured shrine and a mutilated image of the Virgin, broken during the Revolution.   Citizens of an archæological turn could discover traces of the stone sill meant to hold candlesticks and to receive wax-tapers and flowers and votive offerings of the pious.

Within the shop a wooden staircase at the further end gave access to the two floors above and to the attics in the roof.   The house itself, packed in between two neighboring dwellings, had little depth from back to front, and no light save from the windows which gave upon the street, the two rooms on each floor having a window apiece, one looking out into the Rue de la Vieille-Poste and the other into the Rue de la Cité.   In the middle ages no artisan was better housed.   The old corner shop must surely have belonged to some armorer or cutler, or master of some craft which could be carried on in the open air, for it was impossible for its inmates to see until the heavily-ironed shutters were taken down and air as well as light freely admitted.   There were two doors (as is usually the case where a shop faces into two streets), one on either side the pillar.   But for the interruption of the white thres-hold stones, hollowed by the wear of centuries, the whole shop front consisted of a low wall which rose to elbow height. Along the top of this wall a groove had been contrived, and a similar groove ran the length of the beam above, which supported the weight of the house wall. Into these grooves slid the heavy shutters, secured by huge iron bolts and bars ; and when the doorways had been made fast in like manner, the artisan's workshop was as good as a fortress.

For the first twenty years of this present century the Limousins had been accustomed to see the interior filled up with old iron and brass, cart-springs, tires, bells, and every sort of metal from the demolition of houses ; but the curious in the *débris* of the old town discovered, on a closer inspection, the traces of a forge in the place and a long streak of soot, signs which confirmed the guesses of archæologists as to the original purpose of the dwelling. On the second floor there was a living room and a kitchen, two more rooms on the third, and an attic in the roof, which was used as a warehouse for goods more fragile than the hardware tumbled down pell-mell in the shop.

The house had been first let and then sold to one Sauviat, a hawker, who from 1792 till 1796 traveled in Auvergne for a distance of fifty leagues round, bartering pots, plates, dishes, and glasses, all the gear, in fact, needed by the poorest cottagers, for old iron, brass, lead, and metal of every sort and description. The Auvergnat would give a brown earthen pipkin worth a couple of sous for a pound weight of lead or a couple of pounds of iron, a broken spade or hoe, or an old cracked saucepan ; and was always judge in his own cause, and gave his own weights. In three years' time Sauviat took another trade in addition, and became a tinman.

In 1793 he was able to buy a château put up for sale by the nation. This he pulled down ; and doubtless repeated a profitable experiment at more than one point in his sphere of operations. After a while these first essays of his gave him an idea ; he suggested a piece of business on a large scale to a fellow-countryman in Paris ; and so it befell that the Black Band, so notorious for the havoc which it wrought among old buildings, was a sprout of old Sauviat's brain, the invention of the hawker whom all Limoges had seen for seven-and-twenty years in his tumble-down shop among his broken bells, flails, chains, brackets, twisted leaden gutters, and heterogeneous old iron. In justice to Sauviat, it should be said that he never knew how large and how notorious the association became; he only profited by it to the extent of the capital which he invested with the famous firm of Brézac.

At last the Auvergnat grew tired of roaming from fair to fair and place to place, and settled down in Limoges, where, in 1797, he had married a wife, the motherless daughter of a tinman, Champagnac by name. When the father-in-law died, he bought the house in which he had, in a manner, localized his trade in old iron, though for some three years after his marriage he had still made his rounds, his wife accompanying him. Sauviat had completed his fiftieth year when he married old Champagnac's daughter, and the bride herself was certainly thirty years old at the least. Champagnac's girl was neither pretty nor blooming. She was born in Auvergne, and the dialect was a mutual attraction; she was, moreover, of the heavy build which enables a woman to stand the roughest work; so she went with Sauviat on his rounds, carried loads of lead and iron on her back, and drove the sorry carrier's van full of the pottery on which her husband made usurious profits, little as his customers imagined it. La Champagnac was sunburned and high-colored. She enjoyed rude health, exhibiting when she laughed a row of teeth large and white as blanched almonds, and, as to physique, possessed the bust and hips of a woman destined by nature to be a mother. Her prolonged spinsterhood was entirely due to her father; he had not read Molière, but he raised Harpagon's cry of "Without portion!" scaring suitors. The "*Sans dot*" did not frighten Sauviat away; he was not averse to receiving the bride without a portion; in the first place, a would-be bridegroom of fifty ought not to raise difficulties; and, in the second, his wife saved him the expense of a servant. He added nothing to the furniture of his room. On his wedding-day it contained a four-post bedstead hung with green serge curtains and a valance with a scalloped edge ; a dresser, a chest of drawers, four easy-chairs, a table, and a looking-glass, all bought at different times and from different places ; and till he left the old house for good, the list remained the same. On the upper shelves of the dresser stood sundry pewter plates and dishes, no two of them alike. After this description of the bedroom, the kitchen may be left to the reader's imagination.

Neither husband nor wife could read, a slight defect of education which did not prevent them from reckoning money to admiration, nor from carrying on one of the most prosperous of all trades, for Sauviat never bought anything unless he felt sure of making a hundred per cent. on the transaction, and dispensed with bookkeeping and counting-house by carrying on a ready-money business. He possessed, moreover, a faculty of memory so perfect that an article might remain for five years in his shop, and at the end of the time both he and his wife could recollect the price they gave for it to a farthing, together with the added interest for every year since the outlay.

Sauviat's wife, when she was not busy about the house, always sat on a rickety wooden chair in her shop-door beside the pillar, knitting, and watching the passers-by, keeping an eye on the old iron, and selling, weighing, and delivering it herself if Sauviat was out on one of his journeys. At daybreak you might hear the dealer in old iron taking down the shutters, the dog was let loose into the street, and very soon Sauviat's wife came down to help her husband to arrange their wares. Against the low wall of the shop in the Rue de la Cité and the Rue de la Vieille-Poste, they propped their heterogeneous collection of broken gun-barrels, cart springs, and harness bells—all the gimcracks, in short, which served as a trade sign and gave a sufficiently poverty-stricken look to a shop which in reality often contained twenty thousand francs worth of lead, steel, and bell metal. The retired hawker and his wife never spoke of their money; they hid it as a male-factor conceals a crime, and for a long while were suspected of clipping gold louis and silver crowns.

When old Champagnac died, the Sauviats made no inven-tory. They searched every corner and cranny of the old man's house with the quickness of rats, stripped it bare as a corpse, and sold the tinware themselves in their own shop. Once every year, when December came round, Sauviat would go to Paris, traveling in a public conveyance; from which premises, observers in the quarter concluded that the dealer in old iron saw to his investments in Paris himself, so that he might keep the amount of his money a secret. It came out in after years that as a lad Sauviat had known one of the most celebrated metal merchants in Paris, a fellow-countryman from Auvergne, and that Sauviat's savings were invested with the prosperous firm of Brézac, the corner-stone of the famous association of the Black Band, which was started, as has been said, by Sauviat's advice, and in which he held shares.

Sauviat was short and stout. He had a weary-looking face and an honest expression, which attracted customers, and was of no little use to him in the matter of sales. The dryness of his affirmations, and the perfect indifference of his manner, aided his pretensions. It was not easy to guess the color of the skin beneath the black metallic grime which covered his curly hair and countenance seamed with the smallpox. His forehead was not without a certain nobility; indeed, he resembled the traditional type chosen by painters for Saint Peter, the man of the people among the apostles, the roughest among their number, and likewise the shrewdest; Sauviat had the hands of an indefatigable worker, rifted by ineffaceable cracks, square-shaped, and coarse and large. The muscular framework of his chest seemed indestructible. All through his life he dressed like a hawker, wearing the thick iron-bound shoes, the blue stockings which his wife knitted for him, the leather gaiters, breeches of bottle-green velveteen, a coat with short skirts of the same material, and a flapped waistcoat, where the copper key of a silver watch dangled from an iron chain, worn by constant friction till it shone like polished steel. Round his neck he wore a cotton handkerchief, frayed by the constant rubbing of his beard. On Sundays and holidays he appeared in a maroon overcoat so carefully kept that he bought a new one but twice in a score of years.

As for their manner of living, the convicts in the hulks might be said to fare sumptuously in comparison; it was a day of high festival indeed when they ate meat. Before La Sauviat could bring herself to part with the money needed for their daily sustenance, she rummaged through the two pockets under her skirt, and never drew forth coin that was not clipped or light weight, eyeing the crowns of six livres and fifty-sous pieces dolorously before she changed one of them. The Sauviats contented themselves, for the most part, with herrings, dried peas, cheese, hard-boiled eggs and salad, and vegetables dressed in the cheapest way. They lived from hand to mouth, laying in nothing except a bundle of garlic now and again, or a rope of onions, which could not spoil, and cost them a mere trifle. As for firewood, La Sauviat bought the few sticks which they required in winter of the faggot-sellers day by day. By seven o'clock in winter and nine in summer the shutters were fastened, the master and mistress in bed, and their huge dog, who picked up his living in the kitchens of the quarter, on guard in the shop; Mother Sauviat did not spend three francs a year on candles.

A joy came into their sober hard-working lives; it was a joy that came in the natural order of things, and caused the only outlay which they had been known to make. In May, 1802, La Sauviat bore a daughter. No one was called in to her assistance, and five days later she was stirring about her house again. She nursed her child herself, sitting on the chair in the doorway, selling her wares as usual, with the baby at her breast. Her milk cost nothing, so for two years she suckled the little one, who was none the worse for it, for little Véronique grew to be the prettiest child in the lower town, so pretty indeed that passers-by would stop to look at her. The neighbors saw in old Sauviat traces of a tenderness of which they had believed him incapable. While the wife made the dinner ready he used to rock the little one in his arms, crooning the refrain of some Auvergnat song; and the workmen as they passed sometimes saw him sitting motionless, gazing at little Véronique asleep on her mother's knee. His gruff voice grew gentle for the child; he would wipe his hands on his trousers before taking her up. When Véronique was learning to walk, her father squatted on his heels four paces away, holding out his arms to her, gleeful smiles puckering the deep wrinkles on the harsh, stern face of bronze; it seemed as if the man of iron, brass, and lead had once more become flesh and blood. As he stood leaning against the pillar motionless as a statue, he would start at a cry from Véronique, and spring over the iron to find her, for she spent her childhood in playing about among the metallic spoils of old châteaux heaped up in the recesses of the shop, and never hurt herself; and if she played in the street or with the neighbors' children, she was never allowed out of her mother's sight.

It is worth while to add that the Sauviats were eminently devout. Even when the Revolution was at its height Sauviat kept Sundays and holidays punctually. Twice in those days he had all but lost his head for going to hear mass said by a priest who had not taken the oath to the Republic. He found himself in prison at last, justly accused of conniving at the escape of a bishop whose life he had saved; but luckily for the hawker, steel files and iron bars were old acquaintances of his, and he made his escape. Whereupon the court finding that he failed to put in an appearance, gave judgment by default, and condemned him to death; and it may be added that, as he never returned to clear himself, he finally died under sentence of death. In his religious sentiments his wife shared; the parsimonious rule of the household was only relaxed in the name of religion. Punctually the two paid their quota for sacramental bread, and gave money for charity. If the curate of Saint-Étienne came to ask for alms, Sauviat or his wife gave without fuss or hesitation what they believed to be their due share towards the funds of the parish. The broken Virgin on their pillar was decked with sprays of box when Easter came round; and so long as there were flowers, the passers-by saw that the blue-glass bouquet-holders were never empty, and this especially after Véronique's birth. Whenever there was a procession the Sauviats never failed to drape their house with hangings and garlands, and contributed to the erection and adornment of the altar—the pride of their street.

So Véronique was brought up in the Christian faith. As soon as she was seven years old she was educated by a gray sister, an Auvergnate, to whom the Sauviats had rendered some little service; for both of them were sufficiently obliging so long as their time or their substance was not in question, and helpful after the manner of the poor, who lend themselves with a certain heartiness. It was the Franciscan sister who taught Véronique to read and write; she instructed her pupil in the History of the People of God, in the Catechism and the Old and New Testaments, and, to a certain small extent, in the rules of arithmetic. That was all. The good sister thought that it would be enough, but even this was too much.

Véronique at nine years of age astonished the quarter by her beauty. Every one admired a face which might one day be worthy of the pencil of some impassioned seeker after an ideal type. "The little Virgin," as they called her, gave promise of being graceful of form and fair of face; the thick, bright hair which set off the delicate outlines of her features completed her resemblance to the Madonna. Those who have seen the divine child-virgin in Titian's great picture of the Presentation in the Temple may know what Véronique was like in these years; she had the same frank innocence of expression, the same look as of a wondering seraph in her eyes, the same noble simplicity, the same queenly bearing.

Two years later, Véronique fell ill of the smallpox, and would have died of it but for Sister Martha, who nursed her. During those two months, while her life was in danger, the quarter learned how tenderly the Sauviats loved their daughter. Sauviat attended no sales and went nowhere. All day long he stayed in the shop, or went restlessly up and down the stairs, and he and his wife sat up night after night with the child. So deep was his dumb grief that no one dared to speak to him; the neighbors watched him pityingly, and asked for news of Véronique of no one but Sister Martha. The days came when the child's life hung by a thread, and neighbors and passers-by saw, for the first and only time in Sauviat's life, the slow tears rising under his eyelids and rolling down his hollow cheeks. He never wiped them away. For hours he sat like one stupefied, not daring to go upstairs to the sick-room, staring before him with unseeing eyes; he might have been robbed, and he would not have noticed it.

Véronique's life was saved, not so her beauty. A uniform tint, in which red and brown were evenly blended, overspread her face; the disease left countless little scars which coarsened the surface of the skin, and wrought havoc with the delicate underlying tissues. Nor had her forehead escaped the ravages of the scourge; it was brown, and covered with dints like the marks of hammer-strokes. No combination is more discordant than a muddy-brown complexion and fair hair; the pre-established harmony of coloring is broken. Deep irregular seams in the surface had spoiled the purity of her features and the delicacy of the outlines of her face; the Grecian profile, the subtle curves of a chin finely moulded as white porcelain, were scarcely discernible between the coars-

ened skin ; the disease had only spared what it was powerless
to injure—the teeth and eyes. But Véronique did not lose
her grace and beauty of form, the full rounded curves of her
figure, nor the slenderness of her waist. At fifteen she was a
graceful girl, and (for the comfort of the Sauviats) a good
girl and devout, hard-working, industrious, always at home.

After her convalescence and first communion, her father and
mother arranged for her the two rooms on the third floor.
Some glimmering notion of what is meant by comfort passed
through old Sauviat's mind ; hard fare might do for him and
his wife, but now a dim idea of making compensation for a
loss which his daughter had not felt as yet crossed his brain.
Véronique had lost the beauty of which these two had been
so proud, and thenceforward became the dearer to them and
the more precious in their eyes.

So one day Sauviat came in, carrying a carpet, a chance
purchase, on his back, and this he himself nailed down on
the floor of Véronique's room. He went to a sale of furniture at a château and secured for her the red damask-curtained
bed of some great lady, and hangings and chairs and easy-
chairs covered with the same stuff. Gradually he furnished
his daughter's rooms with second-hand purchases, in complete
ignorance of the real value of the things. He set pots of
mignonette on the window-sill, and brought back flowers for
her from his wanderings ; sometimes it was a rosebush, sometimes a tree-carnation, and plants of all kinds, doubtless given
to him by gardeners and innkeepers. If Véronique had
known enough of other people to draw comparisons, and to
understand their manners of life and the characters and the
ignorance of her parents, she would have known how great
the affection was which showed itself in these little things ;
but the girl gave her father and mother the love that springs
from an exquisite nature—an instinctive and unreasoning
love.

Véronique must have the finest linen which her mother

could buy, and La Sauviat allowed her daughter to choose her own dresses.   Both father and mother were pleased with her moderation ; Véronique had no ruinous tastes.   A blue-silk gown for holiday wear, a winter dress of coarse merino for working-days, and a striped cotton gown in summer; with these she was content.

On Sunday she went to mass with her father and mother, and walked with them after vespers along the banks of the Vienne or in the neighborhood of the town.   All through the week she stayed in the house, busy over the tapestry-work, which was sold for the benefit of the poor, or the plain sewing for the hospital—no life could be more simple, more innocent, more exemplary than hers.   She had other occupations beside her sewing ; she read to herself, but only such books as the curate of Saint-Étienne loaned to her.   (Sister Martha had introduced the priest to the Sauviat family.)

For Véronique all the laws of the household economy were set aside.   Her mother delighted to cook dainty fare for her, and made separate dishes for her daughter.   Father and mother might continue, as before, to eat the walnuts and the hard bread, the herrings, and the dried peas fried with a little salt butter ; but for Véronique, nothing was fresh enough nor good enough.

"Véronique must be a great expense to you," remarked the hatter who lived opposite.   He estimated old Sauviat's fortune at a hundred thousand francs, and had thoughts of Véronique for his son.

"Yes, neighbor ; yes, neighbor ; yes," old Sauviat answered, "she might ask me for ten crowns, and I should let her have them, I should.   She has everything she wants, but she never asks for anything.   She is as good and gentle as a lamb !"

And, in fact, Véronique did not know the price of anything ; she had no wants ; she never saw a piece of gold till the day of her marriage, and had no money of her own ; her mother bought and gave to her all that she wished, and even for a beggar she drew upon her mother's pockets.

"Then she doesn't cost you much," commented the hatter.

"That is what you think, is it?" retorted Sauviat. "You wouldn't do it on less than forty crowns a year. You should see her room! There is a hundred crowns' worth of furniture in it; but when you have only one girl, you can indulge yourself; and, after all, what little we have will all be hers some day."

"*Little?* You must be rich, Father Sauviat. These forty years you have been in a line of business where there are no losses."

"Oh, they shouldn't cut my ears off for a matter of twelve hundred francs," said the dealer in old iron.

From the day when Véronique lost the delicate beauty which every one had admired in her childish face, old Sauviat had worked twice as hard as before. His business revived again, and prospered so well, that he went to Paris not once, but several times a year. People guessed his motives. If his girl had gone off in looks, he would make up for it in money, to use his own language.

When Véronique was about fifteen another change was wrought in the household ways. The father and mother went up to their daughter's room of an evening, and listened while she read aloud to them from the "Lives of the Saints," or the "Lettres édifiantes," or from some other book loaned by the curate of Saint-Étienne. The lamp was set behind a glass globe full of water, and Mother Sauviat knitted industriously, thinking in this way to pay for the oil. The neighbors opposite could look into the room and see the two old people sitting there, motionless as two carved Chinese figures, listening intently, admiring their daughter with all the power of an intelligence that was dim enough save in matters of business or religion. Doubtless there have been girls as pure as Véronique—there have been none purer nor more modest.

Her confession surely filled the angels with wonder, and glad-
dened the Virgin in heaven. She was now sixteen years old,
and perfectly developed ; you beheld in her the woman she
would be. She was a medium height, neither the father nor
the mother was tall ; but the most striking thing about her
figure was its lissome grace, the sinuous, gracious curves which
nature herself traces so finely, which the artist strives so painfully to render ; the soft contours that reveal themselves to
practiced eyes, for in spite of folds of linen and thickness of
stuff, the dress is always moulded and informed by the body.
Simple, natural and sincere, Véronique set this physical beauty
in relief by her unaffected freedom of movement. She produced her " full and entire effect," if it is permissible to make
use of the forcible legal phrase. She had the full-fleshed arms
of an Auvergnate, the red, plump hands of a buxom inn-
servant, and feet strongly made, but shapely, and in proportion to her height.

Sometimes there was wrought in her an exquisite mysterious
change ; suddenly it was revealed that in this frame dwelt a
woman hidden from all eyes but Love's. Perhaps it was this
transfiguration which awakened an admiration of her beauty
in the father and mother, who astonished the neighbors by
speaking of it as something divine. The first to see it were
the clergy of the cathedral and the communicants at the
table of the Lord. When Véronique's face was lighted up by
impassioned feeling—and the mystical ecstasy which filled her
at such times is one of the strongest emotions in the life of
so innocent a girl—it seemed as if a bright inner radiance
effaced the traces of the smallpox, and the pure, bright face
appeared once more in the first beauty of childhood. Scarcely
obscured by the thin veil of tissues coarsened by the disease, her face shone like some flower in dim places under the
sea, when the sunlight strikes down and invests it with a
mysterious glory. For a few brief moments Véronique was
transfigured, the little Virgin appeared and disappeared like

a vision from heaven. The pupils of her eyes, which possessed in a high degree the power of contracting, seemed at
such seasons to dilate and overspread the blue of the iris,
which diminished till it became nothing more than a slender
ring ; the change in the eyes, which thus grew piercing as the
eagle's, completing the wonderful change in the face. Was it
a storm of repressed and passionate longing, was it some
power which had its source in the depths of her nature, which
made those eyes dilate in broad daylight as other eyes widen
in shadow, darkening their heavenly blue ? Whatever the
cause, it was impossible to look upon Véronique with indifference as she returned to her place after having been made one
with God ; all present beheld her in the radiance of her early
beauty ; at such times she would have eclipsed the fairest
woman in her loveliness. What a charm for a jealous lover in
that veil of flesh which should hide his love from all other
eyes ; a veil which the hand of love could raise to let fall
again upon the rapture of wedded bliss. Véronique's lips,
faultless in their curves, seemed to have been painted scarlet,
so richly were they colored by the pure glow of the blood.
Her chin and the lower part of her face were a little full, in
the sense that painters give to the word, and this heaviness
of contour is, by the unalterable laws of physiognomy, a certain sign of a capacity for almost morbid violence of passion.
Her finely-moulded but almost imperious brow was crowned
by a glorious diadem of thick abundant hair; the gold had
deepened to a chestnut tint.

From her sixteenth year till the day of her marriage
Véronique's demeanor was thoughtful and full of melancholy.
In an existence so lonely she fell, as solitary souls are wont,
to watching the grand spectacle of the life within, the progress of her thoughts, the ever-changing phantasmagoria of
mental visions, the yearnings kindled by her pure life. Those
who passed along the Rue de la Cité on sunny days had only
to look up to see the Sauviats' girl sitting at her window with

a bit of sewing or embroidery in her hand, drawing the needle in and out with a somewhat dreamy air. Her head stood out in sharp contrast against its background among the flowers which gave a touch of poetry to the prosaic, cracked, brown window-sill, and the small leaded panes of her casement. At times a reflected glow from the red damask curtains added to the effect of the face so brightly colored already; it looked like some rosy-red flower above the little skyey garden, which she tended so carefully upon the ledge. So the quaint old house contained something still more quaint—a portrait of a young girl, worthy of Mieris, Van Ostade, Terburg, or Gerard Dow, framed in one of the old, worn, and blackened, and almost ruinous windows which Dutch artists loved to paint. If a stranger happened to glance up at the second floor, and stand agape with wonder at its construction, old Sauviat below would thrust out his head till he could look up the face of the overhanging story. He was sure to see Véronique there at the window. Then he would go in again, rubbing his hands, and say to his wife in the patois of Auvergne:

"Hullo, old woman, there is some one admiring your daughter!";

In 1820 an event occurred in Véronique's simple and uneventful life. It was a little thing, which would have exercised no influence upon another girl, but destined to effect a fatal influence on Véronique's future life. On the day of a suppressed church festival, a working-day for the rest of the town, the Sauviats shut their shop and went first to mass and then for a walk. On their way into the country they passed by a bookseller's shop, and among the books displayed outside Véronique saw one called *Paul et Virginie.* The fancy took her to buy it for the sake of the engraving; her father paid five francs for the fatal volume, and slipped it into the vast pocket of his overcoat.

"Wouldn't it be better to show it to M. le Vicaire?"

asked the mother; for her any printed book was something of an abracadabra, which might or might not be for evil.

"Yes, I thought I would," Véronique answered simply.

She spent that night in reading the book, one of the most touching romances in the French language. The love scenes, half-biblical, and worthy of the early ages of the world, wrought havoc in Véronique's heart. A hand, whether diabolical or divine, had raised for her the veil which hitherto had covered nature. On the morrow the little Virgin within the beautiful girl thought her flowers fairer than on the evening of the day before; she understood their symbolical language, she gazed up at the blue sky with exaltation, causeless tears rose to her eyes.

In every woman's life there comes a moment when she understands her destiny, or her organization, hitherto mute, speaks with authority. It is not always a man singled out by an involuntary and stolen glance who reveals the possession of a sixth sense, hitherto dormant; more frequently it is some sight that comes with the force of a surprise, a landscape, a page of a book, some day of high pomp, some ceremony of the Church; the scent of growing flowers, the delicate brightness of a misty morning, the intimate sweetness of divine music—and something suddenly stirs in body or soul. For the lonely child, a prisoner in the dark house, brought up by parents almost as rough and simple as peasants; for the girl who had never heard an improper word, whose innocent mind had never received the slightest taint of evil; for the angelic pupil of Sister Martha and of the good curate of Saint-Étienne, the revelation of love came through a charming book from the hand of genius. No peril would have lurked in it for any other, but for her an obscene work would have been less dangerous. Corruption is relative. There are lofty and virginal natures which a single thought suffices to corrupt, a thought which works the more ruin because the necessity of combating it is not foreseen.

2

The next day Véronique showed her book to the good priest, who approved the purchase of a work so widely known for its childlike innocence and purity. But the heat of the tropics, the beauty of the land described in *Paul et Virginie*, the almost childish innocence of a love scarcely of this earth, had wrought upon Véronique's imagination. She was captivated by the noble and sweet personality of the author, and carried away towards the cult of the ideal, that fatal religion. She dreamed of a lover, a young man like Paul, and brooded over soft imaginings of that life of lovers in some fragrant island. Below Limoges, and almost opposite the Faubourg Saint-Martial, there is a little island in the Vienne; this, in her childish fancy, Véronique called the Isle of France, and, filled with the fantastic creations of a young girl's dreams, vague shadows endowed with the dreamer's own perfections.

She sat more than ever in the window in those days, and watched the workmen as they came and went. Her parents' humble position forbade her to think of any one but an artisan; yet, accustomed as she doubtless was to the idea of becoming a workingman's wife, she was conscious of an instinctive refinement which shrank from anything rough or coarse. So she began to weave for herself a romance such as most girls weave in their secret hearts for themselves alone. With the enthusiasm which might be expected of a refined and girlish imagination, she seized on the attractive idea of ennobling one of these workingmen, of raising him to the level of her dreams. She made (who knows?) a Paul of some young man whose face she saw in the street, simply that she might attach her wild fancies to some human creature, as the overcharged atmosphere of a winter day deposits dew on the branches of a tree by the wayside, for the frost to transform into magical crystals. How should she escape a fall into the depths? for if she often seemed to return to earth from far-off heights with a reflected glory about her brows, yet oftener she appeared to bring with her flowers gathered on the brink of a torrent-stream which she had followed down into the abyss. On warm evenings she asked her old father to walk out with her, and never lost an opportunity of a stroll by the Vienne. She went into ecstasy at every step over the beauty of the sky and land, over the red glories of the sunset, or the joyous freshness of dewy mornings, and the sense of these things, the poetry of nature, passed into her soul.

She curled and waved the hair which she used to wear in simple plaits about her head ; she thought more about her dress. The young, wild vine which had grown as its nature prompted about the old elm tree was transplanted and trimmed and pruned, and grew upon a dainty green trellis.

One evening in December, 1822, when Sauviat (now seventy years old) had returned from a journey to Paris, the curate dropped in, and after a few commonplaces—

"You must think of marrying your daughter, Sauviat," said the priest. "At your age you should no longer delay the fulfillment of an important duty."

"Why, has Véronique a mind to be married ?" asked the amazed old man.

"As you please, father," the girl answered, lowering her eyes.

"We will marry her," cried portly Mother Sauviat, smiling as she spoke.

"Why didn't you say something about this before I left home, mother?" Sauviat asked. "I shall have to go back to Paris again."

In Jerome-Baptiste Sauviat's eyes plenty of money appeared to be synonymous with happiness. He had always regarded love and marriage in their purely physical and practical aspects ; marriage was a means of transmitting his property (he being no more) to another self; so he vowed that Véronique should marry a well-to-do man. Indeed, for a long while past this had become a fixed idea with him. His neighbor the hatter, who was retiring from business, and had an income of two thousand livres a year, had already asked for Véronique for his son and successor (for Véronique was spoken of in the quarter as a good girl of exemplary life), and had been politely refused.   Sauviat had not so much as mentioned this to Véronique.

The curate was Véronique's director, and a great man in the Sauviats' eyes; so the day after he had spoken of Véronique's marriage as a necessity, old Sauviat shaved himself, put on his Sunday clothes, and went out.   He said not a word to his wife and daughter, but the women knew that the old man had gone out to find a son-in-law.   Sauviat went to M. Graslin.

M. Graslin, a rich banker of Limoges, had left his native Auvergne, like Sauviat himself, without a sou in his pocket. He had begun life as a porter in a banker's service, and from that position had made his way, like many another capitalist, partly by thrift, partly by sheer luck.   A cashier at five-and-twenty, and at five-and thirty a partner in the firm of Perret & Grossetête, he at last bought out the original partners, and became sole owner of the bank.   His two colleagues went to live in the country, leaving their capital in his hands at a low rate of interest.   Pierre Graslin, at the age of forty-seven, was believed to possess six hundred thousand francs at the least.   His reputation for riches had recently increased, and the whole department had applauded his free-handedness when he built a house for himself in the new quarter of the Place des Arbres, which adds not a little to the appearance of Limoges.   It was a handsome house, on the plan of alignment, with a façade like a neighboring public building; but though the mansion had been finished for six months, Pierre Graslin hesitated to furnish it.   His house had cost him so dear, that at the thought of living in it he drew back.   Self-love, it may be, had enticed him to exceed the limits he had prudently observed all his life long; he thought, moreover, with the plain sense of a man of business, that it was only right that the inside of his house should be in keeping with

the programme adopted with the façade. The plate and furniture and accessories needed for the housekeeping in such a
mansion would cost more, according to his computations,
than the actual outlay on the building. So, in spite of the
town gossip, the broad grins of commercial circles, and the
charitable surmises of his neighbors, Pierre Graslin stayed
where he was on the damp and dirty ground-floor dwelling in
the Rue Montantmanigne, where his fortune had been made,
and the great house stood empty. People might talk, but
Graslin was happy in the approbation of his two old sleeping
partners, who praised him for displaying such uncommon
strength of mind.

Such a fortune and such a life as Graslin's is sure to excite
plentiful covetousness in a country town. During the past
ten years more than one proposition of marriage had been
skillfully insinuated. But the estate of a bachelor was eminently suited to a man who worked from morning to night,
overwhelmed with business, and wearied by his daily round, a
man as keen after money as a sportsman after game; so Graslin
had fallen into none of the snares set for him by ambitious
mothers who coveted a brilliant position for their daughters.
Graslin, the Sauviat of a somewhat higher social sphere, did
not spend two francs a day upon himself, and dressed no
better than his second clerk. His whole staff consisted of a
couple of clerks and an office boy, though he went through
an amount of business which might fairly be called immense,
so multitudinous were its ramifications. One of the clerks
saw to the correspondence, the other kept the books; and
for the rest Pierre Graslin was both the soul and body of his
business. He chose his clerks from his family circle; they
were of his own stamp, trustworthy, intelligent, and accustomed to work. As for the office boy, he led the life of a
dray horse.

Graslin rose all the year round before five in the morning,
and was never in bed till eleven o'clock at night. His char-

woman, an old Auvergnate, who came in to do the housework
and to cook his meals, had strict orders never to exceed the
sum of three francs for the total daily expense of the household.   The brown earthenware, the strong coarse tablecloths
and sheets, were in keeping with the manners and customs of
an establishment in which the porter was the man of all work,
and the clerks made their own beds.   The blackened deal
tables, the ragged straw-bottomed chairs with the holes
through the centre, the pigeon-hole writing-desks and ram-
shackle bedsteads, in fact, all the furniture of the counting-
house and the three rooms above it, would not have brought
three thousand francs, even if the safe had been included, a
colossal solid iron structure built into the wall itself, before
which the porter nightly slept with a couple of dogs at his
feet.   It had been a legacy from the old firm to the present
one.

Graslin was not often seen in society, where a great deal
was heard about him.   He dined with the receiver-general
(a business connection) two or three times a year, and he had
been known to take a meal at the prefecture; for, to his own
intense disgust, he had been nominated a member of the
general council of the department.   "He wasted his time
there," he said.   Occasionally, when he had concluded a
bargain with a business acquaintance, he was detained to lunch
or dinner; and, lastly, he was sometimes compelled to call
upon his old partners, who spent the winter in Limoges.   So
slight was the hold which social relations had upon him that
at twenty-five years of age Graslin had not so much as offered
a glass of water to any creature.

People used to say, "That is M. Graslin!" when he passed
along the street, which is to say, "There is a man who came
to Limoges without a farthing, and has made an immense
amount of money."   The Auvergnat banker became a kind
of pattern and example held up by fathers of families to their
offspring—and an epigram which more than one wife cast in

her husband's teeth. It is easy to imagine the motives which induced this principal pivot in the financial machinery of Limoges to repel the matrimonial advances so perseveringly made to him. The daughters of Messieurs Perret and Grossetête had been married before Graslin was in a position to ask for them; but as each of these ladies had daughters in the school-room, people let Graslin alone at last, taking it for granted that either old Perret or Grossetête the shrewd had arranged a match to be carried out some future day, when Graslin should be bridegroom to one of the granddaughters.

Sauviat had watched his fellow-countryman's rise and progress more closely than any one. He had known Graslin ever since he came to Limoges, but their relative positions had changed so much (in appearance at any rate) that the friendship became an acquaintance, renewed only at long intervals. Still, in his quality of fellow-countryman, Graslin was never above having a chat with Sauviat in the Auvergne dialect if the two happened to meet, and in their own language they dropped the formal " you " for the more familiar " thee " and " thou."

In 1823, when the youngest of the brothers Grossetête, the Receiver-General of Bourges, married his daughter to the youngest son of the Comte de Fontaine, Sauviat saw that the Grossetêtes had no mind to take Graslin into their family.

After a conference with the banker, old Sauviat returned in high glee to dine in his daughter's room.

" Véronique will be Madame Graslin," he told the two women.

" *Madame Graslin !* " cried Mother Sauviat, in amazement.

"Is it possible?" asked Véronique. She did not know Graslin by sight, but the name produced much such an effect on her imagination as the word Rothschild upon a Parisian shop-girl.

"Yes. It is settled," old Sauviat continued solemnly. " Graslin will furnish his house very grandly; he will have the finest carriage from Paris that money can buy for our daughter, and the best pair of horses in Limousin. He will buy an estate worth five hundred thousand francs for her, and settle the house on her besides. In short, Véronique will be the first lady in Limoges, and the richest in the department, and can do just as she likes with Graslin."

Véronique's boundless affection for her father and mother, her bringing-up, her religious training, her utter ignorance, prevented her from raising a single objection; it did not so much as occur to her that she had been disposed of without her own consent. The next day Sauviat set out for Paris, and was away for about a week.

Pierre Graslin, as you may imagine, was no great talker; he went straight to the point, and acted promptly. A thing determined upon was a thing done at once. So in February, 1822, a strange piece of news surprised Limoges like a sudden thunderclap. Graslin's great house was being handsomely furnished. Heavy wagon-loads from Paris arrived daily to be unpacked in the courtyard. Rumors flew about the town concerning the good taste displayed in the beautiful furniture, modern and antique. A magnificent service of plate came down from Odiot's by the mail; and (actually) three carriages!—a calèche, a brougham, and a cabriolet—arrived carefully packed in straw as if they had been jewels.

"M. Graslin is going to be married!" The words passed from mouth to mouth, and in the course of a single evening the news filtered through the drawing-rooms of the Limousin aristocracy to the back parlors and shops in the suburbs, till all Limoges, in fact, had heard it. But whom was he going to marry? Nobody could answer the question. There was a mystery in Limoges.

As soon as Sauviat came back from Paris, Graslin made his first nocturnal visit, at half-past nine o'clock. Véronique knew that he was coming. She wore her blue-silk gown, cut square at the throat, and a wide collar of cambric with a deep hem. Her hair she had simply parted into two bandeaux, waved and gathered into a Grecian knot at the back of her head. She was sitting in a tapestry-covered chair near the fire-side, where her mother occupied a great armchair with a carved back and crimson velvet cushions, a bit of salvage from some ruined château. A blazing fire burned on the hearth. Upon the mantel-shelf, on either side of an old clock (whose value the Sauviats certainly did not know), stood two old-fashioned sconces; six wax-candles in the sockets among the brazen vine-stems shed their light on the brown chamber, and on Véronique in her bloom. The old mother had put on her best dress.

In the midst of the silence that reigned in the streets at that silent hour, with the dimly-lit staircase as a background, Graslin appeared for the first time before Véronique—the shy childish girl whose head was still full of sweet fancies of love derived from Bernardin de Saint-Pierre's book. Graslin was short and thin. His thick black hair stood up straight on his forehead like bristles in a brush, in startling contrast with a face red as a drunkard's, and covered with suppurating or bleeding pustules. The eruption was neither scrofula nor leprosy, it was simply a result of an overheated condition of the blood; unflagging toil, anxiety, fanatical application to business, late hours, a life steady and sober to the point of abstemiousness, had induced a complaint which seemed to be related to both diseases. In spite of partners, clerks, and doctors, the banker had never brought himself to submit to a regimen which might have alleviated the symptoms or cured an evil, trifling at first, which was daily aggravated by neglect as time went on. He wished to be rid of it, and sometimes for a few days would take the baths and swallow the doses prescribed; but the round of business carried him away, and he forgot to take care of himself. Now and again he would talk of going away for a short holiday, and trying the waters somewhere or other for a cure, but where is the man in hot pursuit of millions who has been known to stop? In this flushed countenance gleamed two gray eyes, the iris speckled with brown dots and streaked with fine green threads radiating from the pupil—two covetous eyes, piercing eyes that went to the depths of the heart, implacable eyes in which you read resolution and integrity and business faculty. A snub nose, thick blubber lips, a prominent rounded forehead, grinning cheek-bones, coarse ears corroded by the sour humors of the blood—altogether Graslin looked like an antique satyr —a satyr tricked out in a great coat, a black satin waistcoat, and a white neckcloth knotted about his neck. The strong muscular shoulders, which had once carried heavy burdens, stooped somewhat already; the thin legs, which seemed to be imperfectly jointed with the short thighs, trembled beneath the weight of that over-developed torso. The bony fingers covered with hair were like claws, as is often the case with those who tell gold all day long. Two parallel lines furrowed the face from the cheek-bones to the mouth—an unerring sign that here was a man whose whole soul was taken up with material interests; while the eyebrows sloped up towards the temples in a manner which indicated a habit of swift decision. Grim and hard though the mouth looked, there was something there that suggested an underlying kindliness, real good-heartedness, not called forth in a life of money-getting, and choked, it may be, by cares of this world, but which might revive at contact with a woman.

At the sight of this apparition, something clutched cruelly at Véronique's heart. Everything grew dark before her eyes. She thought she cried out, but in reality she sat still, mute, staring with fixed eyes.

"Véronique," said old Sauviat, "this is M. Graslin."

Véronique rose to her feet and bowed, then she sank down into her chair again, and her eyes sought her mother. But La Sauviat was smiling at the millionaire, looking so happy, so very happy, that the poor child gathered courage to hide her violent feeling of repulsion and the shock she had received. In the midst of the conversation which followed, something was said about Graslin's health. The banker looked naïvely at himself in the beveled mirror framed in ebony.

"I am not handsome, mademoiselle," he said, and he explained that the redness of his face was due to his busy life, and told them how he had disobeyed his doctor's orders. He hoped that as soon as he had a woman to look after him and his household, a wife who would take more care of him than he took of himself, he should look quite a different man.

"As if anybody married a man for his looks, mate!" cried the dealer in old iron, slapping his fellow-countryman on the thigh.

Graslin's explanation appealed to instinctive feelings which more or less fill every woman's heart. Véronique bethought herself of her own face, marred by a hideous disease, and in her Christian humility she thought better of her first impression. Just then some one whistled in the street outside, Graslin went down, followed by Sauviat, who felt uneasy. Both men soon returned. The porter had brought the first bouquet of flowers, which had been in readiness for the occasion. At the reappearance of the banker with this stack of exotic blossoms, which he offered to his future bride, Véronique's feelings were very different from those with which she had first seen Graslin himself. The room was filled with the sweet scent, for Véronique it was a realization of her daydreams of the tropics. She had never seen white camellias before, had never known the scent of the Alpine cytisus, the exquisite fragrance of the citronella, the jessamine of the Azores, the verbena and musk-rose, and their sweetness, like a melody in perfume, falling on her senses stirred a vague tenderness in her heart.

Graslin left Véronique under the spell of that emotion; but almost nightly after Sauviat returned home the banker waited till all Limoges was asleep, and then slunk along under the walls to the house where the dealer in old iron lived. He used to tap softly on the shutters, the dog did not bark, the old man came down and opened the door to his fellow-countryman, and Graslin would spend a couple of hours in the brown room where Véronique sat, and Mother Sauviat would serve him up an Auvergnat supper. The uncouth lover never came without a bouquet for Véronique, rare flowers only to be procured in M. Grossetête's hothouse, M. Grossetête being the only person in Limoges in the secret of the marriage. The porter went after dark to bring the bouquet, which old Grossetête always gathered himself.

During those two months Graslin went about fifty times to the house, and never without some handsome present, rings, a gold watch, a chain, a dressing-case, or the like; amazing lavishness on his part, which, however, is easily explained.

Véronique would bring him almost the whole of her father's fortune—she would have seven hundred and fifty thousand francs. The old man kept for himself an income of eight thousand francs, an old investment in the Funds, made when he was in imminent danger of losing his head on the scaffold. In those days he had put sixty thousand francs in assignats (the half of his fortune) into government stock. It was Brézac who advised the investment, and dissuaded him afterwards when he thought of selling out; it was Brézac, too, who in the same emergency had been a faithful trustee for the rest of his fortune—the vast sum of seven hundred gold louis, with which Sauviat began to speculate as soon as he made good his escape from prison. In thirty years' time each of those gold louis had been transmuted into a bill for a thousand francs, thanks partly to the interest on the assignats, partly to the money which fell in at the time of Champagnac's death, partly to trading gains in the business, and the money standing at compound interest in Brézac's concern. Brézac had done honestly by Sauviat, as Auvergnat does by Auvergnat.

And so whenever Sauviat went to take a look at the front of Graslin's great house—

" Véronique shall live in that palace ! '' he said to himself.

He knew that there was not another girl in Limousin who would have seven hundred and fifty thousand francs paid down on her marriage-day, beside two hundred and fifty thousand of expectations. Graslin, the son-in-law of his choice, must therefore inevitably marry Véronique. So every evening Véronique received a bouquet, which daily made her little sitting-room bright with flowers, a bouquet carefully kept out of sight of the neighbors. She admired the beautiful jewels, the rubies, pearls and diamonds, the bracelets, dear to all daughters of Eve, and thought herself less ugly thus adorned. She saw her mother happy over this marriage, and she herself had no standard of comparison ; she had no idea what marriage meant, no conception of its duties ; and finally she heard the curate of Saint-Étienne praising Graslin to her, in his solemn voice, telling her that this was an honorable man with whom she would lead an honorable life. So Véronique consented to receive M. Graslin's attentions. In a lonely and monotonous life like hers, let a single person present himself day by day, and before long that person will not be indifferent ; for either an aversion, confirmed by a deeper knowledge, will turn to hate, and the visitor's presence will be intolerable ; or custom stales (so to speak) the sight of physical defects, and then the mind begins to look for compensations. Curiosity busies itself with the face ; from some cause or other the features light up, there is some fleeting gleam of beauty there ; and at last the nature, hidden beneath the outward form, is discovered. In short, first impressions once overcome, the force with which the one soul is attracted to the other is but so much the stronger, because the discovery of the true nature of the other is all its own. So love invariably begins. Herein lies the secret of the passionate love which beautiful persons entertain for others who are not beautiful in appearance ; affection, looking

deeper than the outward form, sees the form no longer, but a
soul, and thenceforward knows nothing else. Moreover, the
beauty so necessary in a woman takes in a man such a strange
character, that women's opinions differ as much on the subject of a man's good looks as men about the beauty of a
woman.

After much meditation and many struggles with herself,
Véronique allowed the banns to be published, and all Limoges
rang with the incredible news. Nobody knew the secret—
the bride's immense dowry. If that had been bruited abroad,
Véronique might have chosen her husband, but perhaps even
so would have been mistaken. It was a love-match on Graslin's side, people averred.

Upholsterers arrived from Paris to furnish the fine house.
The banker was going to great expense over it, and nothing
else was talked of in Limoges. People discussed the price of
the chandeliers, the gilding of the drawing-room, the mythi-
cal subjects of the timepieces ; and there were well-informed
folk who could describe the flower-stands and the porcelain
stoves, the luxurious novel contrivances. For instance, there
was an aviary built above the ice-house in the garden of the
Hôtel Graslin ; all Limoges marveled at the rare birds in it—
the paroquets, and Chinese pheasants, and strange water-
fowl, there was no one who had not seen them.

M. and Mme. Grossetête, old people much looked up to in
Limoges, called several times upon the Sauviats, Graslin
accompanying them. Mme. Grossetête, worthy woman, congratulated Véronique on the fortunate marriage she was to
make ; so the Church, the family, and the world, together
with every trifling circumstance, combined to bring this
match about.

In the month of April formal invitations were sent to all
Graslin's circle of acquaintance. At eleven o'clock one fine
sunny morning a calèche and a brougham, drawn by Limousin
horses in English harness (old Grossetête had superintended

his colleague's stable), arrived before the poor little shop
where the dealer in old iron lived ; and the excited quarter
beheld the bridegroom's sometime partners and his two
clerks. There was a prodigious sensation, the street was filled
by the crowd eager to see the Sauviats' daughter. The most
celebrated hairdresser in Limoges had set the bride's crown
on her beautiful hair and arranged her veil of priceless Brus-
sels lace ; but Véronique's dress was of simple white muslin.
A sufficiently imposing assembly of the most distinguished
women of Limoges was present at the wedding in the cathedral ; the bishop himself, knowing the piety of the Sauviats,
condescended to perform the marriage ceremony. People
thought the bride a plain-looking girl. For the first time she
entered her hôtel, and went from surprise to surprise. A state
dinner preceded the ball, to which Graslin had invited almost
all Limoges. The dinner given to the bishop, the prefect,
the president of the court of first instance, the public prosecutor, the mayor, the general, and to Graslin's sometime
employers and their wives was a triumph for the bride, who,
like all simple and unaffected people, proved unexpectedly
charming. None of the married people would dance, so that
Véronique continued to do the honors of her house, and won
the esteem and good graces of most of her new acquaintances ; asking old Grossetête, who had taken a great kindness
for her, for information about her guests, and so avoiding
blunders. During the evening the two retired bankers spread
the news of the fortune, immense for Limousin, which the
parents of the bride had given her. At nine o'clock the
dealer in old iron went home to bed, leaving his wife to pre-
side at the ceremony of undressing the bride. It was said in
the town that Mme. Graslin was plain but well shaped.

Old Sauviat sold his business and his house in the town,
and bought a cottage on the left bank of the Vienne, between
Limoges and Le Cluzeau, and ten minutes' walk from the
Faubourg Saint-Martial. Here he meant that he and his

wife should end their days in peace. The two old people had rooms in Graslin's hôtel, and dined there once or twice a week with their daughter, whose walks usually took the direction of their house.

The retired dealer in old iron had nothing to do, and nearly died of leisure. Luckily for him, his son-in-law found him some occupation. In 1823 the banker found himself with a porcelain factory on his hands. He had lent large sums to the manufacturers, which they were unable to repay, so he had taken over the business to recoup himself. In this concern he invested more capital, and by this means, and by his extensive business connections, made of it one of the largest factories in Limoges; so that when he sold it in three years after he took it over, he made a large profit on the transaction. He made his father-in-law the manager of this factory, situated in the very same quarter of Saint-Martial where his house stood; and in spite of Sauviat's seventy-two years, he had done not a little in bringing about the prosperity of a business in which he grew quite young again. The plan had its advantages likewise for Graslin; but for old Sauviat, who threw himself heart and soul into the porcelain factory, he would perhaps have been obliged to take a clerk into partnership and lose part of the profits, which he now received in full; but as it was, he could look after his own affairs in the town, and feel his mind at ease as to the capital invested in the porcelain works.

In 1827 Sauviat met with an accident, which ended in his death. He was busy with the stock-taking, when he stumbled over one of the crates in which the china was packed, grazing his leg slightly. He took no care of himself, and mortification set in; they talked of amputation, but he would not hear of losing his leg, and so he died. His widow made over about two hundred and fifty thousand francs, the amount of Sauviat's estate, to her daughter and son-in-law, Graslin undertaking to pay her two hundred francs a month, an amount amply

sufficient for her needs. She persisted in living on without
a servant in the little cottage; keeping her point with the
obstinacy of old age and in spite of her daughter's entreaties; but, on the other hand, she went almost every day to
the Hôtel Graslin, and Véronique's walks, as heretofore,
usually ended at her mother's house. There was a charming view from the windows of the river and the little island
in the Vienne, which Véronique had loved in the old days,
and called her Isle of France.

The story of the Sauviats has been anticipated partly to save
interruption to the other story of the Graslins' household, partly
because it serves to explain some of the reasons of the retired
life which Véronique Graslin led. The old mother foresaw
how much her child might one day be made to suffer through
Graslin's avarice; for long she held out, and refused to give
up the rest of her fortune, and only gave way when Véronique insisted upon it. Véronique was incapable of imagining circumstances in which a wife desires to have the control
of her property, and acted upon a generous impulse; in this
way she meant to thank Graslin for giving her back her
liberty.

The unaccustomed splendors of Graslin's marriage had been
totally at variance with his habits and nature. The great
capitalist's ideas were very narrow. Véronique had had no
opportunity of gauging the man with whom she must spend the
rest of her life. During those fifty-five evening visits Graslin
had shown but one side of his character—the man of business,
the undaunted worker who planned and carried out large
undertakings, the capitalist who looked at public affairs with
a view to their probable effect on the bank-rate and oppor-
tunities of money-making. And, under the influence of his
father-in-law's million, Graslin had behaved generously in
those days, though even then his lavish expenditure was
made to gain his own ends; he was drawn into expense in
the springtide days of his marriage partly by the possession

3

of the great house, which he called his "Folly," the house
still called the Hôtel Graslin in Limoges.

As he had the horses, the calèche, and brougham, it was
natural to make use of them to pay a round of visits on his
marriage, and to go to the dinner-parties and dances given in
honor of the bride by official dignitaries and wealthy houses.
Acting on the impulses which carried him out of his ordinary
sphere, Graslin was "at home" to callers one day in the
week, and sent to Paris for a cook. For about a year, indeed,
he led the ordinary life of a man who has seventeen hundred
thousand francs of his own, and can command a capital of
three millions. He had come to be the most conspicuous
personage in Limoges. During that year he generously allowed Mme. Graslin twenty-five twenty-franc pieces every
month.

Véronique on her marriage had become a person of great
interest to the rank and fashion of Limoges; she was a kind
of godsend to the idle curiosity which finds such meagre sustenance in the provinces. Véronique who had so suddenly made
her appearance was a phenomenon, the more closely scruti-
nized on that account; but she always maintained the simple
and unaffected attitude of an onlooker who watches manners
and usages unknown to her, and seeks to conform to them.
From the first she had been pronounced to have a good figure
and a plain face, and now it was decided that she was good-
natured, but stupid. She was learning so many things at once,
she had so much to see and to hear, that her manner and talk
gave some color to this accusation. A sort of torpor, moreover, had stolen over her which might well be mistaken for
stupidity. Marriage, that "difficult profession" of wifehood,
as she called it, in which the Church, the Code, and her own
mother bade her practice the most complete resignation and
perfect obedience, under pain of breaking all laws human and
divine, and bringing about irreparable evils; marriage had
plunged her into a bewilderment which grew to the pitch of

vertigo and delirium. While she sat silent and reserved, she heard her own thoughts as plainly as the voices about her. For her "existence" had come to be extremely "difficult," to use the phrase of the dying Fontenelle, and ever more increasingly, till she grew frightened, she was afraid of herself. Nature recoiled from the orders of the soul; the body rebelled against the will. The poor snared creature wept on the bosom of the great Mother of the sorrowful and afflicted; she betook herself to the Church, she redoubled her fervor, she confided to her director the temptations which assailed her, she poured out her soul in prayer. Never at any time in her life did she fulfill her religious duties so zealously. The tempest of despair which filled her when she knew that she did not love her husband flung her at the foot of the altar, where divine comforting voices spoke to her of patience. And she was patient and sweet, living in hope of the joys of motherhood.

"Did you see Mme. Graslin this morning?" the women asked among themselves. "Marriage does not agree with her; she looked quite ghastly."

"Yes; but would you have given a daughter of yours to a man like M. Graslin? Of course, if you marry such a monster, you suffer for it."

As soon as Graslin was fairly married, all the mothers who had assiduously hunted him for the past ten years directed spiteful speeches at him. Véronique grew thin, and became plain in good earnest. Her eyes were heavy, her features coarsened, she looked shamefaced and embarrassed, and wore the dreary, chilling expression so repellent in bigoted devotees. A grayish tint overspread her complexion. She dragged herself languidly about during the first year of her marriage, usually the heyday of a woman's life. Before very long she sought for distraction in books, making use of her privilege as a married woman to read everything. She read Scott's novels, Byron's poems, the works of Schiller and Goethe, literature ancient and modern. She learned to ride, to dance, and draw. She made sepia drawings and sketches in water-color, eager to learn every device which women use to while away the tedium of solitary hours; in short, that second education which a woman nearly always undertakes for a man's sake and with his guidance, she undertook alone and for herself.

In the loftiness of a nature frank and free, brought up, as it were, in the desert, but fortified by religion, there was a wild grandeur, cravings which found no satisfaction in the provincial society in which she moved. All the books described love; she looked up from her books on life, and found no traces of passion there. Love lay dormant in her heart like the germs which wait for the sun. Through a profound melancholy, caused by constant brooding over herself, she came by dim and winding ways back to the last bright dreams of her girlhood. She dwelt more than once on the old romantic imaginings, and became the heroine and the theatre of the drama. Once again she saw the island bathed in light, full of blossom and sweet scents, and all things grateful to her soul.

Not seldom her sad eyes wandered over her rooms with searching curiosity; the men she saw were all like Graslin; she watched them closely, and seemed to turn questioningly from them to their wives; but on the women's faces she saw no sign of her own secret trouble, and sadly and wearily she returned to her starting-point, uneasy about herself. Her highest thoughts met with a response in the books which she read of a morning, their wit pleased her; but in the evening she heard nothing but commonplace thoughts, which no one attempted to disguise by giving a witty turn to them; the talk around her was vapid and empty, or ran upon gossip and local news, which had no interest for her. She wondered sometimes at the warmth of discussions in which there was no question of sentiment, for her the very core of life. She was often seen gazing before her with fixed, wide eyes, thinking, doubtless, of hours which she had spent, while still a girl ignorant of life, in the room where everything had been in keeping with her fancies, and now laid in ruins, like Véronique's own existence. She shrank in pain from the thought of being drawn into the eddy of petty cares and interests like the other women among whom she was forced to live; her ill-concealed disdain of the littleness of her lot, visible upon her lips and brow, was taken for upstart insolence.

Mme. Graslin saw the coolness upon all faces, and felt a certain bitter tone in the talk. She did not understand the reason, for as yet she had not made a friend sufficiently intimate to enlighten or counsel her. Injustice, under which small natures chafe, compels loftier souls to return within themselves, and induces in them a kind of humility. Véronique blamed herself, and tried to discover where the fault lay. She tried to be gracious, she was pronounced to be insincere; she redoubled her kindliness, and was said to be a hypocrite (her devotion giving color to the slander); she was lavish of hospitality, and gave dinners and dances, and was accused of pride. All Mme. Graslin's efforts were unsuccessful. She was misjudged and repulsed by the petty querulous pride of provincial coteries, where susceptibilities are always upon the watch for offenses; she went no more into society, and lived in the strictest retirement. The love in her heart turned to the Church. The great spirit in its feeble house of flesh saw in the manifold behests of Catholicism but so many stones set by the brink of the precipices of life, raised there by charitable hands to prop human weakness by the way. So every least religious observance was practiced with the most punctilious care.

Upon this, the Liberal party added Mme. Graslin's name to the list of bigots in the town. She was classed among the Ultras, and party spirit strengthened the various grudges which Véronique had innocently stored up against herself, with its periodical exacerbations. But as she had nothing to

lose by this ostracism, she went no more into society, and betook herself to her books, with the infinite resources which
they opened to her.   She thought over her reading, she
compared methods, she increased the amount of her actual
knowledge and her power of acquiring it, and by so doing
opened the gateways of her mind to curiosity.

It was at this period of close and persistent study, while
religion supported her, that she gained a friend in M. Grossetête, an old man whose real ability had not grown so rusty
in the course of a life in a country town but that contact with
a keen intelligence could still draw a few sparks from it.   The
kind soul was deeply interested in Véronique, who, in return
for the mild warmth of the mellowed affection which age alone
can give, put forth all the treasures of her soul ; for him the
splendid powers cultivated in secret first blossomed forth.

A fragment of a letter written at this time to M. Grossetête
will describe the mental condition of a woman who one day
should give proof of a firm temper and lofty nature :

" The flowers which you sent to me for the dance were very
lovely, yet they suggested painful thoughts.   The sight of that
beauty, gathered by you to decorate a festival, and to fade on
my breast and in my hair, made me think of other flowers
born to die unseen in your woods, to shed sweet scent that no
one breathes.   Then I asked myself why I was dancing, why
I had decked myself with flowers, just as I ask God why I
am here in the world.   You see, my friend, that in everything
there lurks a snare for the unhappy, just as the drollest trifles
bring the sick back to their own sufferings.   That is the
worst of some troubles : they press upon us so constantly that
they shape themselves into an idea which is ever present in
our minds.   An ever-present trouble ought surely to be a
hallowed thought.   You love flowers for their own sake ; I
love them as I love beautiful music.   As I once told you,
the secret of a host of things is hidden from me—— You,

my old friend, for instance, have a passion for gardening. When you come back to town, teach me to share in this taste of yours ; send me with a light footstep to my hothouse to feel the interest which you take in watching your plants grow. You seem to me to live and blossom with them, to take a delight in them, as in something of your own creation ; to discover new colors, novel splendors, which come forth under your eyes, the result of your labors. I feel that the emptiness of my life is breaking my heart. For me, my hothouse is full of pining souls. The distress which I force myself to relieve saddens my very soul. I find some young mother without linen for her newborn babe, some old man starving, I make their troubles mine, and even when I have helped them, the feel- ings aroused in me by the sight of misery relieved are not enough to satisfy my soul. Oh! my friend, I feel that I have great powers asserting themselves in me, powers of doing evil, it may be, which nothing can crush—powers that the hardest commandments of religion cannot humble. When I go to see my mother, when I am quite alone among the fields, I feel that I must cry aloud, and I cry. My body is the prison in which one of the evil genii has pent up some moaning crea- ture, until the mysterious word shall be uttered which shatters the cramping cell. But this comparison is not just. In my case it should be reversed. It is the body which is a prisoner, if I may make use of the expression. Does not religion occupy my soul? And the treasures gained by reading are constant food for the mind. Why do I long for any change, even if it comes as suffering—for any break in the enervating peace of my lot? Unless I find some sentiment to uphold me, some strong interest to cultivate, I feel that I shall drift towards the abyss where every idea grows hazy and meaning- less, where character is enervated, where the springs of one's being grow slack and inert, where I shall be no longer the woman nature intended me to be. That is what my cries mean—— But you will not cease to send flowers to me

because of this outcry of mine? Your friendship has been
so sweet and pleasant a thing, that it has reconciled me
with myself for several months. Yes, I feel happy when I
think that you sometimes throw a friendly glance over the
blossoming desert-place, my inner self; that the wanderer,
half-dead after her flight on the fiery steed of a dream, will
meet with a kind word of greeting from you on her return.''

Three years after Véronique's marriage, it occurred to
Graslin that his wife never used the horses, and, a good opportunity offering itself, he sold them. The carriages were
sold at the same time, the coachman was dismissed, and the
cook from Paris transferred to the bishop's establishment. A
woman-servant took his place. Graslin ceased to give his
wife an allowance, saying that he would pay all the bills. He
was the happiest man in the world when he met with no opposition from the wife who had brought him a million. There
was not much merit, it is true, in Mme. Graslin's self-denial.
She knew nothing of money, she had been brought up in
ignorance of it as an indispensable element in life. Graslin
found the sums which he had given to her lying in a corner
of her desk; scarcely any of it had been spent. Véronique
gave to the poor, her trousseau had been so large that as yet
she had had scarcely any expenses for dress. Graslin praised
Véronique to all Limoges as the pattern of wives.

The splendor of the furniture gave him pangs, so he had it
all shrouded in covers. His wife's bedroom, boudoir, and
dressing-room alone escaped this dispensation, an economical
measure which economized nothing, for the wear and tear to
the furniture is the same, covers or no covers.

He next took up his abode on the ground floor, where the
counting-house and office had been established, so he began
his old life again, and was as keen in pursuit of gain as before.
The Auvergnat banker thought himself a model husband because he breakfasted and dined with his wife, who carefully

ordered the meals for him; but he was so extremely unpunctual, that he came in at the proper hour scarce ten times a
month; and though, out of thoughtfulness, he asked her never
to wait for him, Véronique always stayed to carve for him;
she wanted to fulfill her wifely duties in some one visible
manner. His marriage had not been a matter to which the
banker gave much thought; his wife represented the sum of
seven hundred and fifty thousand francs; he had not discovered that that wife shrank from him. Gradually he had left
Mme. Graslin to herself, and became absorbed in business;
and when he took it into his head to have a bed put up for
himself in a room next to his private office, Véronique saw that
his wishes were carried out at once.

So after three years of marriage this ill-assorted couple went
their separate ways as before, and felt glad to return to them.
The capitalist, owner now of eighteen hundred thousand
francs, returned to his occupation of money-making with all
the more zest after the brief interval. His two clerks and the
office-boy were somewhat better lodged and a little better fed
—that was all the difference between the past and the present.
His wife had a cook and a waiting-maid (the two servants
could not well be dispensed with), and no calls were made on
Graslin's purse except for strict necessaries.

And Véronique was happy in the turn things had taken;
she saw in the banker's satisfaction a compensation for a sep-
aration for which she had never asked; it was impossible
that Graslin should shrink from her as she shrank from him.
She was half-glad, half-sorry of this secret divorce; she had
looked forward to motherhood, which should bring a new
interest into her life; but in spite of their mutual resignation, there was no child of the marriage as yet in 1828.

So Mme. Graslin, envied by all Limoges, led as lonely
a life in her splendid home as formerly in her father's
hovel; but the hopes and the childish joys of inexperience
were gone. She lived in the ruins of her "castles in Spain,"

enlightened by sad experience, sustained by a devout faith, busying herself for the poor of the district, whom she loaded with kindnesses. She made baby linen for them; she gave sheets and bedding to those who lay on straw; she went everywhere with her maid—a good Auvergnate whom her mother found for her. This girl attached herself body and soul to her mistress, and became a charitable spy for her, whose mission it was to find out trouble to soothe and distress to relieve. This life of busy benevolence and of punctilious performance of the duties enjoined by the Church was a hidden life, only known by the curés of the town who directed it, for Véronique took their counsel in all that she did, so that the money intended for the deserving poor should not be squandered by vice.

During these years Véronique found another friendship quite as precious to her and as warm as her friendship with old Grossetête. She became one of the flock of the Abbé Dutheil, one of the vicars-general of the diocese. This priest belonged to the small minority among the French clergy who lean towards concession, who would fain associate the Church with the popular cause. By putting evangelical principles in practice, the Church should gain her old ascendency over the people, whom she could then bind to the Monarchy. But the Abbé Dutheil's merits were unrecognized, and he was persecuted. Perhaps he had seen that it was hopeless to attempt to enlighten the Court of Rome and the clerical party; perhaps he had sacrificed his convictions at the bidding of his superiors; at any rate, he dwelt within the limits of the strictest orthodoxy, knowing the while that the mere expression of his convictions would close his way to a bishopric. A great and Christian humility, blended with a lofty character, distinguished this eminent churchman. He had neither pride nor ambition, and stayed at his post, doing his duty in the midst of peril. The Liberal party in the town, who knew nothing of his motives, quoted his opinions in support of their own, and reckoned him as a "patriot," a word which means "a revolutionaire" for good Catholics. He was beloved by those below him, who did not dare to praise his worth; dreaded by his equals, who watched him narrowly; and a thorn in the side of his bishop. He was not exactly persecuted, his learning and virtues were too well known; it was impossible to find fault with him freely, though he criticised the blunders in policy by which the Throne and the Church alternately compromised each other, and pointed out the inevitable results; like poor Cassandra, he was reviled by his own party before and after the fall which he predicted. Nothing short of a revolution was likely to shake the Abbé Dutheil from his place; he was a foundation-stone in the Church, an unseen block of granite on which everything else rests. His utility was recognized, and—he was left in his place, like most of the real power of which mediocrity is jealous and afraid. If, like the Abbé de Lamennais, he had taken up the pen, he would probably have shared his fate; at him, too, the thunderbolts of Rome would have been launched.

In person the Abbé Dutheil was commanding. Something in his appearance spoke of a soul so profound that the surface is always calm and smooth. His height and spare frame did not mar the general effect of the outlines of his figure, which vaguely recalled those forms which Spanish painters loved best to paint for great monastic thinkers and dreamers—forms which Thorvaldsen in our own time has selected for his apostles. His face, with the long, almost austere lines in it, which bore out the impression made by the straight folds of his garments, possessed the same charm which the sculptors of the middle ages discovered and recorded in the mystic figures about the doorways of their churches. His grave thoughts, grave words, and grave tones were all in keeping, and the expression of the Abbé's personality. At the first sight of the dark eyes, which austerity had surrounded with

hollow shadowy circles; the forehead, yellowed like old
marble; the bony outlines of the head and hands, no one
could have expected to hear any voice but his, or any teaching
but that which fell from his lips.   It was this purely physical
grandeur, in keeping with the moral grandeur of his nature,
that gave him a certain seeming haughtiness and aloofness,
belied, it is true, by his humility and his talk, yet unpre-
possessing in the first instance.   In a higher position these
qualities would have been advantages which would have
enabled him to gain a necessary ascendency over the crowd
—an ascendency which it is quick to feel and to recognize;
but he was a subordinate, and a man's superiors never pardon
him for possessing the natural insignia of power, the majesty
so highly valued in an older time, and often so signally
lacking in modern upholders of authority.

His colleague, the Abbé de Grancour, the other vicar-
general of the diocese, a blue-eyed, stout little man with a
florid complexion, worked willingly enough with the Abbé
Dutheil, albeit their opinions were diametrically opposed; a
curious phenomenon, which only a wily courtier will regard
as a natural thing; but, at the same time, the Abbé de Grancour was very careful not to commit himself in any way
which might cost him the favor of his bishop; the little man
would have sacrificed anything (even convictions) to stand
well in that quarter.   He had a sincere belief in his colleague,
he recognized his ability; in private he admitted his doctrines,
while he condemned them in public; for men of his kind
are attracted to a powerful character, while they fear and hate
the superiority whose society they cultivate.   "He would put
his arms round my neck while he condemned me," said the
Abbé Dutheil.   The Abbé de Grancour had neither friends
nor enemies, and was likely to die a vicar-general.   He gave
out that he was drawn to Véronique's house by a wish to give
a woman so benevolent and so devout the benefit of his
counsels, and the bishop signified his approval; but, in

reality, he was only too delighted to spend an evening now and then in this way with the Abbé Dutheil.

From this time forward both priests became pretty constant visitors in Véronique's house; they used to bring her a sort of general report of any distress in the district, and talk over the best means of benefiting the poor morally and materially; but year by year M. Graslin drew the purse-strings closer and closer; for, in spite of ingenious excuses devised by his wife and Aline the maid, he suspected that all the money was not required for expenses of dress and housekeeping. He grew angry at last when he reckoned up the amount which his wife gave away. He himself would go through the bills with the cook, he went minutely into the details of their expenditure, and showed himself the great administrator that he was by demonstrating conclusively from his own experience that it was possible to live in luxury on three thousand francs per annum. Whereupon he compounded the matter with his wife by allowing her a hundred francs a month, to be duly accounted for, pluming himself on the royal bounty of the grant. The garden, now handed over to him, was "done up" of a Sunday by the porter, who had a liking for gardening. After the gardener was dismissed, the conservatory was turned to account as a warehouse, where Graslin deposited the goods left with him as security for small loans. The birds in the aviary above the ice-house were left to starve, to save the expense of feeding them; and when at length a winter passed without a single frost, he took that opportunity of declining to pay for ice any longer. By the year 1828 every article of luxury was curtailed, and parsimony reigned undisturbed in the Hôtel Graslin.

During the first three years after Graslin's marriage, with his wife at hand to make him follow out the doctor's instructions, his complexion had somewhat improved; now it inflamed again, and became redder and more florid than in the past. So largely, at the same time, did his business increase, that the porter was promoted to be a clerk (as his master had been before him), and another Auvergnat had to be found to do the odd jobs of the Hôtel Graslin.

After four years of married life the woman who had so much wealth had not three francs to call her own. To the niggardliness of her parents succeeded the no less niggardly dispensation of her husband; and Mme. Graslin, whose benevolent impulses were checked, felt the need of money for the first time.

In the beginning of the year 1828 Véronique had recovered the bloom of health which had lent such beauty to the innocent girl who used to sit at the window in the old house in the Rue de la Cité. She had read widely since those days; she had learned to think and to express her thoughts; the habit of forming accurate judgments had lent profundity to her features. The little details of social life had become familiar to her, she wore a fashionable toilet with the most perfect ease and grace. If chance brought her into a drawing-room at this time, she found, not without surprise, that she was received with something like respectful esteem; this way of regarding her, like her reception, was due to the two vicars-general and old Grossetête. The bishop and one or two influential people, hearing of Véronique's unwearying benevolence, had talked about this fair life hidden from the world, this violet perfumed with virtues, this blossom of unfeigned piety. So, all unknown to Mme. Graslin, a revolution had been wrought in her favor; one of those reactions so much the more lasting and sure because they are slowly affected. With this right-about-face in opinion Véronique became a power in the land. Her drawing-room was the resort of the luminaries of Limoges; the practical change · was brought about by this means:

The young Vicomte de Granville came to the town at the end of that year, preceded by the ready-made reputation which awaits a Parisian on his arrival in the provinces. He had been appointed deputy public prosecutor to the Court of Limoges. A few days after his arrival he said, in answer to a sufficiently silly question, that Mme. Graslin was the cleverest, most amiable, and most distinguished woman in the city, and this at the prefect's "At Home," and before a whole room full of people.

"And the most beautiful as well, perhaps?" suggested the receiver-general's wife.

"There I do not venture to agree with you," he answered; "when you are present I am unable to decide. Mme. Graslin's beauty is not of a kind which should inspire jealousy in you, she never appears in broad daylight. Mme. Graslin is only beautiful for those whom she loves ; you are beautiful for all eyes. If Mme. Graslin is deeply stirred, her face is transformed by its expression. It is like a landscape, dreary in winter, glorious in summer. Most people only see it in winter ; but if you watch her while she talks with her friends on some literary or philosophical subject, or upon some religious question which interests her, her face lights up, and suddenly she becomes another woman, a woman of wonderful beauty."

This declaration, a recognition of the same beautiful transfiguration which Véronique's face underwent as she returned to her place from the communion table, made a sensation in Limoges, for the new substitute (destined, it was said, to be attorney-general one day) was the hero of the hour. In every country town a man a little above the ordinary level becomes for a shorter or longer time the subject of a craze, a sham enthusiasm to which the idol of the moment falls a victim. To these freaks of the provincial drawing-room we owe the local genius and the person who suffers from the chronic complaint of unappreciated superiority. Sometimes it is native talent which women discover and bring into fashion, but more frequently it is some outsider ; and for once, in the case of the Vicomte de Granville, the homage was paid to genuine ability,

The Parisian found that Mme. Graslin was the only woman with whom he could exchange ideas or carry on a sustained and varied conversation ; and a few months after his arrival, as the charm of her talk and manner gained upon him, he suggested to some of the prominent men in the town, and to the Abbé Dutheil among them, that they might make their party at whist of an evening in Mme. Graslin's drawing-room. So Véronique was at home to her friends for five nights in the week (two days she wished to keep free, she said, for her own concerns) ; and when the cleverest men in the town gathered about Mme. Graslin, others were not sorry to take brevet rank as wits by spending their evenings in her society. Véronique received the two or three distinguishèd military men stationed in the town or on the garrison staff. The entire freedom of discussion enjoyed by her visitors, the absolute discretion required of them, tacitly and by the adoption of the manners of the best society, combined to make Véronique exclusive and very slow to admit those who courted the honor of her society to her circle. Other women saw not without jealousy that the cleverest and pleasantest men gathered round Mme. Graslin, and her power was the more widely felt in Limoges because she was exclusive. The four or five women whom she accepted were strangers to the district, who had accompanied their husbands from Paris, and looked on provincial tittle-tattle with disgust. If some one chanced to call who did not belong to the inner *cénacle,* the conversation underwent an immediate change, and with one accord all present spoke of indifferent things.

So the Hôtel Graslin became a sort of oasis in the desert where a chosen few sought relief in each other's society from the tedium of provincial life, a house where officials might discuss politics and speak their minds without fear of their opinions being reported, where all things worthy of mockery were fair game for wit and laughter, where every one laid aside his professional uniform to give his natural character free play.

In the beginning of that year 1828, Mme. Graslin, whose
girlhood had been spent in the most complete obscurity, who
had been pronounced to be plain and stupid and a complete
nullity, was now looked upon as the most important person
in the town, and the most conspicuous woman in society.
No one called upon her in the morning, for her benevolence
and her punctuality in the performance of her duties of religion were well known. She almost invariably went to the first
mass, returning in time for her husband's early breakfast. He
was the most unpunctual of men, but she always sat with him,
for Graslin had learned to expect this little attention from his
wife. As for Graslin, he never let slip an opportunity of
praising her; he thought her perfection. She never asked
him for money; he was free to pile up silver crown on silver
crown, and to expand his field of operations. He had opened
an account with the firm of Brézac; he had set sail upon a
commercial sea, and the horizon was gradually widening out
before him ; his over-stimulated interest, intent upon the great
events of the green table called very superficially Speculation,
kept him perpetually in the cold, frenzied intoxication of the
gambler.

During this happy year, and indeed until the beginning
of the year 1829, Mme. Graslin's friends watched a strange
change passing in her, under their eyes; her beauty became
really extraordinary, but the reasons of the change were never
discovered. Her eyes seemed to be bathed in a soft liquid
light, full of tenderness, the blue iris widened like an expand-
ing flower as the dark pupils contracted. Memories and happy
thoughts seemed to light up her brow, which grew whiter,
like some ridge of snow in the dawn, her features seemed to
regain their purity of outline in some refining fire within.
Her face lost the feverish brown color which threatens inflam-
mation of the liver, the malady of vigorous temperaments of
troubled minds and thwarted affections. Her temples grew
adorably fresh and youthful. Frequently her friends saw

4

glimpses of the divinely fair face which a Raphael might have painted, the face which disease had covered with an ugly film, such as time spreads over the canvas of the great master. Her hands looked whiter, there was a delicate fulness in the rounded curves of her shoulders, and her quick dainty movements displayed to the very full the lissome grace of her form.

The women said that she was in love with M. de Granville, who, for that matter, paid assiduous court to her, though Véronique raised between them the barriers of a pious resistance. The deputy public prosecutor professed a respectful admiration for her which did not impose upon frequenters of her house. Clearer-sighted observers attributed to a different cause this change, which made Véronique still more charming to her friends. Any woman, however devout, could not but feel in her inmost soul that it was sweet to be so courted, to know the satisfaction of living in a congenial atmosphere, the delight of exchanging ideas (so great a relief in a tedious life), the pleasure of the society of well-read and agreeable men, and of sincere friendships, which grew day by day. It needed, perhaps, an observer still more profound, more acute, or more suspicious than any of those who came to the Hôtel Graslin to divine the untamed greatness, the strength of the woman of the people pent up in the depths of Véronique's nature. Now and again they might surprise her in a torpid mood, overcast by gloomy or merely pensive musings, but all her friends knew that she carried many troubles in her heart; that, doubtless, in the morning she had been initiated into many sorrows, that she penetrated into dark places where vice is appalling by reason of its unblushing front. Not seldom, indeed, the Vicomte, soon promoted to be advocate-general, scolded her for some piece of blind benevolence discovered by him in the course of his investigations. Justice complained that Charity had paved the way to the police court.

"Do you want money for some of your poor people?" old

"DO YOU WANT MONEY FOR SOME OF YOUR POOR PEOPLE?"

.

Grossetête had asked on this, as he took her hand in his. "I will share the guilt of your benefactions."

"It is impossible to make everybody rich," she answered, heaving a sigh.

An event occurred at the beginning of this year which was to change the whole current of Véronique's inner life, as well as the wonderful expression of her face, which henceforward became a portrait infinitely more interesting to a painter's eyes.

Graslin grew rather fidgety about his health, and to his wife's great despair left his ground-floor quarters and returned to her apartment to be tended. Soon afterwards Mme. Graslin's condition became a matter of town gossip; she was about to become a mother. Her evident sadness, mingled with joy, filled her friends' thoughts; they then divined that, in spite of her virtues, she was happiest when she lived apart from her husband. Perhaps she had had hopes for better things since the day when the Vicomte de Granville had declined to marry the richest heiress in Limousin, and still continued to pay court to her. Ever since that event the profound politicians who exercise the censorship of sentiments, and settle other people's business in the intervals of whist, had suspected the lawyer and young Mme. Graslin of basing hopes of their own on the banker's failing health—hopes which were brought to nothing by this unexpected development. It was a time in Véronique's life when deep distress of mind was added to the apprehensions of a first confinement, always more perilous, it is said, when a woman is past her first youth, but all through those days her friends showed themselves more thoughtful for her; there was not one of them but made her feel in innumerable small ways what warmth there was in these friendships of hers, and how solid they had become.

II

TASCHERON.

It was in the same year that Limoges witnessed the terrible spectacle and strange tragedy of the Tascheron case, in which the young Vicomte de Granville displayed the talents which procured him the appointment of public prosecutor at a later day.

An old man living in a lonely house on the outskirts of the Faubourg Saint-Étienne was murdered. A large orchard isolates the dwelling on the side of the town, on the other there is a pleasure garden, with a row of unused hothouses at the bottom of it; then follow the open fields. The bank of the . Vienne in this place rises up very steeply from the river, the little front garden slopes down to this embankment, and is bounded by a low wall surmounted by an open fence. Square stone posts are set along it at even distances, but the painted wooden railings are there more by way of ornament than as a protection to the property.

The old man, Pingret by name, a notorious miser, lived quite alone save for a servant, a countrywoman whom he employed in the garden. He trained his espaliers and pruned his fruit trees himself, gathering his crops and selling them in the town, and excelled in growing early vegetables for the market. The old man's niece and sole heiress, who had married a M. des Vanneaulx, a man of small independent means, and lived in Limoges, had many a time implored her uncle to keep a man as protection to the place, pointing out to him that he would be able to grow more garden produce in several borders planted with standard fruit trees beneath which he now sowed millet and the like; but it was of no use, the old man would not hear of it. This contradiction in a miser gave rise to all sorts of conjectures in the houses where the Vanneaulx spent their evenings. The most divergent opinions had more than once divided parties at boston. Some knowing folk came to the conclusion that there was a treasure hidden under the growing luzern.

"If I were in Mme. des Vanneaulx's place," remarked one pleasant gentleman, "I would not worry my uncle, I know. If somebody murders him, well and good; somebody will murder him. I should come in for the property."

Mme. des Vanneaulx, however, thought differently. As a manager at the Théâtre-Italien implores the tenor who "draws" a full house to be very careful to wrap up his throat, and gives him his cloak when the singer has forgotten his overcoat, so did Mme. des Vanneaulx try to watch over her relative. She had offered little Pingret a magnificent yard dog, but the old man sent the animal back again by Jeanne Malassis his servant.

"Your uncle has no mind to have one more mouth to feed up at our place," said the handmaid to Mme. des Vanneaulx.

The event proved that his niece's fears had been but too well founded. Pingret was murdered one dark night in the patch of luzern, whither he had gone, no doubt, to add a few louis to a pot full of gold. The servant, awakened by the sounds of the struggle, had the courage to go to the old man's assistance, and the murderer found himself compelled to kill her also, lest she should bear witness against him. This calculation of probable risks, which nearly always prompts a man guilty of one murder to add another to his account, is one unfortunate result of the capital sentence which he beholds looming in the distance.

The double crime was accompanied by strange circumstances, which told as strongly for the defense as for the prosecution. When the neighbors had seen nothing of Pingret nor of the servant for the whole morning; when, as they came and went, they looked through the wooden railings and saw that the doors and windows (contrary to wont) were still barred and fastened, the thing began to be bruited abroad

through the Faubourg Saint-Étienne, till it reached Mme. des
Vanneaulx in the Rue des Cloches. Mme. des Vanneaulx,
whose mind always ran on horrors, sent for the police, and the
doors were broken open. In the four patches of luzern there
were four gaping holes in the earth, surrounded by rubbish,
and strewn with broken shards of the pots which had been
full of gold the night before. In two of the holes, which
had been partly filled up, they found the bodies of old Pingret
and Jeanne Malassis, buried in their clothes; she, poor thing,
had run out barefooted in her night-dress.

While the public prosecutor, the commissary, and the examining magistrate took down all these particulars, the unlucky
des Vanneaulx collected the scraps of broken pottery, put
them together, and calculated the amount the jars should have
held. The authorities, perceiving the common-sense of this
proceeding, estimated the stolen treasure at a thousand pieces
per pot; but what was the value of those coins? Had they
been forty or forty-eight franc-pieces, twenty-four or twenty
francs? Every creature in Limoges who had expectations
felt for the des Vanneaulx in this trying situation. The sight
of those fragments of crockery-ware which once held gold
gave a lively stimulus to Limousin imaginations. As for little
Pingret, who often came to sell his vegetables in the market
himself, who lived on bread and onions, and did not spend
three hundred francs in a year, who never did anybody a good
turn, nor any harm either, no one regretted him in the least—
he had never done a pennyworth of good to the Faubourg
Saint-Étienne. As for Jeanne Malassis, her heroism was considered to be ill-timed; the old man, if he had lived, would
have grudged her reward; altogether, her admirers were few
compared with the number of those who remarked, " I should
have slept soundly in her place, I know ! "

Then the curious and the next-of-kin were made aware of
the inconsistencies of certain misers. The police, when they

came to draw up the report, could find neither pen nor ink in
the bare, cold, dismal, tumble-down house. The little old
man's horror of expense was glaringly evident : in the great
holes in the roof, which let in rain and snow as well as light ;
in the moss-covered cracks which rent the walls ; in the rotting
doors ready to drop from their hinges at the least shock ; in the
unoiled paper which did duty as glass in the windows. There
was not a window curtain in the house, not a looking-glass
over the mantel-shelves ; the grates were chiefly remarkable
for the absence of fire-irons and the accumulation of damp
soot, a sort of varnish over the handful of sticks or the log
of wood which lay on the hearth. And as to the furniture—
a few crippled chairs and maimed armchairs, two beds, hard
and attenuated (Time had adorned old Pingret's bed-curtains
with open-work embroidery of a bold design), one or two
cracked pots and riveted plates, a worm-eaten bureau, where
the old man used to keep his garden seeds, household linen
thick with darns and patches—the furniture, in short, consisted of a mass of rags, which had only a sort of life kept in
them by the spirit of their owner, and now that he was gone,
they dropped to pieces and crumbled to powder. At the
first touch of the brutal hands of the police officers and
infuriated next-of-kin they evaporated, heaven knows how,
and came to nameless ruin and an indefinable end. They
were not. Before the terrors of a public auction they vanished
away.

For a long time the greater part of the inhabitants of the
capital of Limousin continued to take an interest in the hard
case of the worthy des Vanneaulx, who had two children ;
but as soon as justice appeared to have discovered the perpetrator of the crime, this person absorbed all their attention,
he became the hero of the day, and the des Vanneaulx were
relegated to the obscurity of the background.

Towards the end of the month of March, Mme. Graslin
had already felt the discomforts incidental to her condition,

which could no longer be concealed. By that time inquiries were being made into the crime committed in the Faubourg Saint-Étienne, but the murderer was still at large. Véronique received visitors in her bedroom, whither her friends came for their game of whist. A few days later Mme. Graslin kept her room altogether. More than once already she had been seized with the unaccountable fancies commonly attributed to women with child. Her mother came almost every day to see her; the two spent whole hours in each other's society.

It was nine o'clock. The card-tables were neglected, every one was talking about the murder and the des Vanneaulx, when the Vicomte de Granville came in.

"We have caught the man who murdered old Pingret!" he cried in high glee.

"And who is it?" The question came from all sides.

"One of the workmen in a porcelain factory, a man of exemplary conduct, and in a fair way to make his fortune. He is one of your husband's old workmen," he added, turning to Mme. Graslin.

"Who is it?" Véronique asked faintly.

"Jean-François Tascheron."

"The unfortunate man!" she exclaimed. "Yes. I remember seeing him several times. My poor father recommended him to me as a valuable hand——"

"He left the place before Sauviat died," remarked old Mme. Sauviat; "he went over to the MM. Philippart to better himself. But is my daughter well enough to hear about this?" she added, looking at Mme. Graslin, who was as white as the sheets.

After that evening old Mother Sauviat left her house, and in spite of her seventy years, installed herself as her daughter's nurse. She did not leave Véronique's room. No matter at what hour Mme. Graslin's friends called to see her, they found the old mother sitting heroically at her post by the bedside, busied with her eternal knitting, brooding over her Véronique as in the days of the smallpox, answering for her child, and sometimes denying her to visitors. The love between the mother and daughter was so well known in Limoges that people took the old woman's ways as a matter of course.

A few days later, when the Vicomte de Granville began to give some of the details of the Tascheron case, in which the whole town took an eager interest, thinking to interest the invalid, La Sauviat cut him short by asking if he meant to give Mme. Graslin bad dreams again, but Véronique begged M. de Granville to go on, fixing her eyes on his face. So it fell out that Mme. Graslin's friends heard in her house the result of the preliminary examination, soon afterwards made public, at first-hand from the *avocat général.* Here, in a condensed form, is the substance of the indictment which was being drawn up by the prosecution :

Jean-François Tascheron was the son of a small farmer burdened with a large family, who lived in the township of Montégnac. Twenty years before the perpetration of this crime, whose memory still lingers in Limousin, Canton Montégnac bore a notoriously bad character. It was alleged in the criminal court of Limoges that fifty out of every hundred convictions came from the Montégnac district. Since 1816, two years after the arrival of the new curé, M. Bonnet, Montégnac lost its old reputation, and no longer sent up its contingent to the assizes. The change was generally set down to M. Bonnet's influence in the commune, which had once been a perfect hotbed of bad characters who gave trouble in all the country round about. Jean-François Tascheron's crime suddenly restored Montégnac to its former unenviable pre-eminence. It happened, singularly enough, that the Tascherons had been almost the only family in the countryside which had not departed from the old exemplary traditions and religious habits now fast dying out in country places. In them the curé had found a moral support and basis of operations, and naturally he thought a great deal of them. The whole family were hard workers, remarkable for their honesty and the strong affection that bound them to each other; Jean-François Tascheron had had none but good examples set before him at home. A praiseworthy ambition had brought him to Limoges. He meant to make a little fortune honestly by a handicraft, and left the township, to the regret of his relations and friends, who were very much attached to him.

His conduct during his two years of apprenticeship was admirable; apparently no irregularity in his life had foreshadowed the hideous crime for which he forfeited his life. The leisure which other workmen wasted in the wineshop and debauches, Tascheron spent in study.

Justice in the provinces has plenty of time on her hands, but the most minute investigation threw no light whatever on the secrets of his existence. The landlady of Jean François' humble lodging, skillfully questioned, said that she had never had such a steady young man as a lodger. He was pleasant-spoken and good-tempered, almost gay, as you might say. About a year ago a change seemed to come over him. He would stop out all night several times a month, and often for several nights at a time. She did not know whereabouts in the town he spent those nights. Still, she had sometimes thought, judging by the mud on his boots, that her lodger had been somewhere out in the country. He used to wear pumps, too, instead of hobnailed boots, although he was going out of the town, and before he went he used to shave and scent himself, and put on clean clothes.

The examining magistrate carried his investigation to such a length that inquiries were made in houses of ill-fame and among licensed prostitutes, but no one knew anything of Jean-François Tascheron; other inquiries made among the class of factory operatives and shop-girls met with no better success; none of those whose conduct was light had any relations with the accused.

A crime without any motive whatever is inconceivable, especially when the criminal's bent was apparently towards self-improvement, while his ambitions argued higher ideals and sense superior to that of other workmen. The whole criminal department, like the examining magistrate, were fain to find a motive for the murder in a passion for play on Tascheron's part; but after minute investigation, it was proved that the accused had never gambled in his life.

From the very first Jean-François took refuge in a system of denial which could not but break down in the face of circumstantial evidence when his case should come before a jury; but his manner of defending himself suggested the intervention of some person well acquainted with the law, or gifted with no ordinary intelligence. The evidence of his guilt, as in most similar cases, was at once unconvincing and yet too strong to be set aside. The principal points which told against Tascheron were four—his absence from home on the night of the murder (he would not say where he spent that night, and scorned to invent an *alibi*); a shred of his blouse, torn without his knowledge during the struggle with the poor servant-girl, and blown by the wind into the tree where it was found; the fact that he had been seen hanging about the house that evening by people in the suburb, who would not have remembered this but for the crime which followed; and, lastly, a false key which he had made to fit the lock of the garden-gate, which was entered from the fields. It had been hidden rather ingeniously in one of the holes, some two feet below the surface. M. des Vanneaulx had come upon it while digging to see whether by chance there might be a second hoard beneath the first. The police succeeded in finding out the man who supplied the steel, the vise, and the key-file. This had been their first clue, it put

them on Tascheron's track, and finally they arrested him on
the limits of the department in a woods where he was waiting
for the diligence. An hour later, and he would have been on
his way to America. Moreover, in spite of the care with
which the footprints had been erased in the trampled earth
and on the muddy road, the rural policeman had found the
marks of thin shoes, clear and unmistakable, in the soil.
Tascheron's lodgings were searched, and a pair of pumps
were found which exactly corresponded with the impress, a
fatal coincidence which confirmed the curious observations
of his landlady.

Then the criminal investigation department saw another
influence at work in the crime, and a second and perhaps a
prime mover in the case. Tascheron must have had an
accomplice, if only for the reason that it was impossible for
one man to take away such a weight of coin. No man, however strong, could carry twenty-five thousand francs in gold
very far. If each of the pots had held so much, he must
have made four journeys. Now, a singular accident determined the very hour when the deed was done. Jeanne
Malassis, springing out of bed in terror at her master's
shrieks, had overturned the table on which her watch lay
(the one present which the miser had made her in five years).
The fall had broken the mainspring, and stopped the hands
at two o'clock.

In mid-March, the time of the murder, the sun rises between five and six in the morning. So on the hypothesis
traced out by the police and the department, it was clearly
impossible that Tascheron should have carried off the money
unaided and alone, even for a short distance, in the time.
The evident pains which the man had taken to erase other
footprints to the neglect of his own, also indicated an unknown assistant.

Justice, driven to invent some reason for the crime, decided
on a frantic passion for some woman, and, as she was not to

be found among the lower classes, forensic sagacity looked higher.

Could it be some woman of the bourgeoisie who, feeling sure of the discretion of a lover of so puritanical a cut, had read with him the opening chapters of a romance which had ended in this ugly tragedy? There were circumstances in the case which almost bore out this theory. The old man had been killed by blows from a spade. The murder, it seemed, was the result of chance, a sudden fortuitous development, and not a part of a deliberate plan. The two lovers might, perhaps, have concerted the theft, but not the second crime. Then Tascheron the lover and Pingret the miser had crossed each other's paths, and in the thick darkness of night two inexorable passions met on the same spot, both attracted thither by gold.

Justice devised a new plan for obtaining light on these dark facts. Jean-François had a favorite sister; her they arrested and examined privately, hoping in this way to come by a knowledge of the mysteries of her brother's private life. Denise Tascheron denied all knowledge of his affairs; prudence dictating a system of negative answers which led her questioners to suspect that she really knew the reasons of the crime. Denise Tascheron, as a matter of fact, knew nothing whatever about it, but for the rest of her days she was to be under a cloud in consequence of her detention.

The accused showed a spirit very unusual in a workingman. He was too clever for the cleverest "sheep of the prisons" with whom he came in contact—though he did not discover that he had to do with a spy. The keener intelligences among the magistracy saw in him a murderer through passion, not through necessity, like the common herd of criminals who pass by way of the petty sessions and the hulks to a capital charge. He was shrewdly plied with questions put with this idea; but the man's wonderful discretion left the magistrates much where they were before. The romantic but plausible theory of a passion for a woman of higher rank, once admitted, insidious questions were suddenly asked more than once; but Jean-François discretion issued victorious from all the mental tortures which the ingenuity of an examining magistrate could inflict.

As a final expedient, Tascheron was told that the person for whom he had committed the crime had been discovered and arrested; but his face underwent no change, he contented himself with the ironical retort, "I should be very glad to see that person."

When these details became known, there were plenty of people who shared the magistrate's suspicions, confirmed to all appearance by the behavior of the accused, who maintained the silence of a savage. An all-absorbing interest attached to a young man who had come to be a problem. Every one will understand how the public curiosity was stimulated by the facts of the case, and how eagerly reports of the examination were followed; for, in spite of all the probings of the police, the case for the prosecution remained on the brink of a mystery, which the authorities did not dare to penetrate, beset with dangers as it was. In some cases a half-certainty is not enough for the magistracy. So it was hoped that the buried truth would arise and come to light at the great day of the assizes, an occasion when criminals frequently lose their heads.

It happened that M. Graslin was on the jury empaneled for the occasion, and Véronique could not but hear through him or through M. de Granville the whole story of a trial which kept Limousin, and indeed all France, in excitement for a fortnight. The behavior of the prisoner at the bar justified the romances founded on the conjectures of justice which were current in the town; more than once his eyes were turned searchingly on the bevy of women privileged to enjoy the spectacle of a sensational drama in real life. Every time that the clear impenetrable gaze was turned on the fashionable audience, it produced a flutter of consternation, so greatly did every woman fear lest she might seem to inquisitive eyes in the court to be the prisoner's partner in guilt.

The useless efforts of the criminal investigation department were then made public, and Limoges was informed of the precautions taken by the accused to ensure the complete success of his crime.

Some months before that fatal night, Jean-François had procured a passport for North America. Clearly he had meant to leave France. Clearly, therefore, the woman in the case must be married; for there was, of course, no object to be gained by eloping with a young girl. Perhaps it was a desire to maintain the fair unknown in luxury which had prompted the crime; but, on the other hand, a search through the registers of the administration had discovered that no passport for that country had been made out in a woman's name. The police had even investigated the registers in Paris as well as those of the neighboring perfectures, but fruitlessly.

As the case proceeded, every least detail brought to light revealed profound forethought on the part of a man of no ordinary intelligence. While the most virtuous ladies of Limousin explained the sufficiently inexplicable use of evening shoes for a country excursion on muddy roads and heavy soil, by the plea that it was necessary to spy upon old Pingret; the least coxcombically given of men were delighted to point out how eminently a pair of thin pumps favored noiseless movements about a house, scaling windows, and stealing along corridors.

Evidently Jean-François Tascheron and his mistress, a young, romantic, and beautiful woman (for every one drew a superb portrait of the lady), had contemplated forgery, and the words "and wife" were to be filled in after his name on the passport.

Card-parties were broken up during these evenings by malicious conjectures and comments. People began to cast about

for the names of women who went to Paris during March,
1829; or of others who might be supposed to have made preparations openly or secretly for flight. The trial supplied
Limoges with a second Fualdès case, with an unknown Mme.
Manson by way of improvement on the first. Never, indeed,
was any country town so puzzled as Limoges after the court
rose each day. People's very dreams turned on the trial.
Everything that transpired raised the accused in their eyes;
his answers, skillfully turned over and over, expanded and
edited, supplied a theme for endless argument. One of the
jury asked, for instance, why Tascheron had taken a passport
for America, to which the prisoner replied that he meant to
open a porcelain factory there. In this way he screened his
accomplice without quitting his line of defense, and supplied
conjecture with a plausible and sufficient motive for the crime
in this ambition of his.

In the thick of these disputes, it was impossible that Véronique's friends should not also try to account for Tascheron's
close reserve. One evening she seemed better than usual.
The doctor had prescribed exercise; and that very morning
Véronique, leaning on her mother's arm, had walked out as
far as Mme. Sauviat's cottage, and rested there a while. When
she came home again, she tried to sit up until her husband
returned, but Graslin was late, and did not come back from
the court till eight o'clock; his wife waited on him at dinner after her usual custom, and in this way she could not
help but hear the discussion between her husband and his
friends.

"We should have known more about this if my poor father
were still alive," said Véronique, "or perhaps the man would
not have committed the crime—— But I notice that you
have all of you taken one strange notion into your heads!
You will have it that there is a woman at the bottom of this
business (as far as that goes I myself am of your opinion), but
why do you think that she is a married woman? Why cannot

he have loved some girl whose father and mother refused to listen to him?"

"Sooner or later a young girl might have been legitimately his," returned M. de Granville. "Tascheron is not wanting in patience; he would have had time to make an independence honestly; he could have waited until the girl was old enough to marry without her parents' consent."

"I did not know that such a marriage was possible," said Mme. Graslin. "Then how is it that no one had the least suspicion of it, here in a place where everybody knows the affairs of everybody else, and sees all that goes on in his neighbor's house? Two people cannot fall in love without at any rate seeing each other or being seen of each other! What do you lawyers think?" she continued, looking the *avocat général* full in the eyes.

"We all think that the woman must be the wife of some tradesman, a man in business."

"I am of a totally opposite opinion," said Mme. Graslin. "That kind of woman has not sentiments sufficiently lofty," a retort which drew all eyes upon her. Every one waited for the explanation of the paradox.

"At night," she said, "when I do not sleep, or when I lie in bed in the daytime, I cannot help thinking over this mysterious business, and I believe I can guess Tascheron's motives. These are my reasons for thinking that it is a girl, and not a woman in the case. A married woman has other interests, if not other feelings; she has a divided heart in her, she cannot rise to the full height of the exaltation inspired by a love so passionate as this. She must never have borne a child if she is to conceive a love in which maternal instincts are blended with those which spring from desire. It is quite clear that some woman who wished to be a sustaining power to him has loved this man. That unknown woman must have brought to her love the genius which inspires artists and poets, aye, and women also, but in another form, for it

5

is a woman's destiny to create, not things, but men. Our creations are our children, our children are our pictures, our books and statues. Are we not artists when we shape their lives from the first? So I am sure that if she is not a girl, she is not a mother; I would stake my head upon it. Lawyers should have a woman's instinct to apprehend the infinite subtle touches which continually escape them in so many cases.

"If I had been your substitute," she continued, turning to M. de Granville, "we should have discovered the guilty woman, always supposing that she is guilty. I think, with M. l'Abbé Dutheil, that the two lovers had planned to go to America, and to live there on poor Pingret's money, as they had none of their own. The theft, of course, led to the murder, the usual fatal consequence of the fear of detection and death. And it would be worthy of you," she added, with a suppliant glance at the young lawyer, "to withdraw the charge of malice aforethought; you would save the miserable man's life. He is so great in spite of his crime, that he would perhaps expiate his sins by some magnificent repentance. The works of repentance should be taken into account in the deliberations of justice. In these days there are no better ways of atoning an offense than by the loss of a head, or by founding, as in olden times, a Milan cathedral?"

"Madame, your ideas are sublime," returned the lawyer; "but if the averment of malice aforethought were withdrawn, Tascheron would still be tried for his life; and it is a case of aggravated theft, it was committed at night, the walls were scaled, the premises broken into——"

"Then, do you think he will be condemned?" she asked, lowering her eyelids.

"I do not doubt it. The prosecution has the best of it."

A light shudder ran through Mme. Graslin. Her dress rustled.

"I feel cold," she said.

She took her mother's arm and went to bed.

"She is much better to-day," said her friends.

The next morning Véronique was at death's door. She smiled at her doctor's surprise at finding her in an almost dying state.

"Did I not tell you that the walk would do me no good?" she said.

Ever since the opening of the trial there had been no trace of either swagger or hypocrisy in Tascheron's attitude. The doctor, always with a view to diverting his patient's mind, tried to explain this attitude out of which the counsel for the defense made capital for his client. The counsel's cleverness, the doctor opined, had dazzled the accused, who imagined that he should escape the capital sentence. Now and then an expression crossed his face which spoke plainly of hopes of some coming happiness greater than mere acquittal or reprieve. The whole previous life of this man of twenty-three was such a flat contradiction to the deeds which brought it to a close that his champions put forward his behavior as a conclusive argument. In fact, the clues spun by the police into a stout hypothesis fit to hang a man dwindled so pitiably when woven into the romance of the defense, that the prisoner's counsel fought for his client's life with some prospect of success. To save him he shifted the ground of the combat, and fought the battle out on the question of malice aforethought. It was admitted, without prejudice, that the robbery had been planned beforehand, but contended that the double murder had been the result of an unexpected resistance in both cases. The issue looked doubtful; neither side had made good their case.

When the doctor went, the *avocat général* came in as usual to see Véronique before he went to the court.

"I have read the counsel's speeches yesterday," she told

him. "To-day the other side will reply. I am so very much interested in the prisoner that I should like him to be saved. Could you not forego a triumph for once in your life? Let the counsel for the defense gain the day. Come, make me a present of this life, and—perhaps—some day mine shall be yours——   There is a doubt after that fine speech of Tascheron's counsel; well, then, why not——"

"Your voice is quivering——" said the Vicomte, almost taken by surprise.

"Do you know why?" she asked. "My husband has just pointed out a coincidence—hideous for a sensitive nature like mine—a thing that is likely to cause me my death. You will give the order for his head to fall just about the time when my child will be born."

"Can I reform the Code?" asked the public prosecutor.

"There, go! You do not know how to love!" she answered, and closed her eyes.

She lay back on her pillow, and dismissed the lawyer with an imperative gesture.

M. Graslin pleaded hard, but in vain, for an acquittal, advancing an argument, first suggested to him by his wife, and taken up by two of his friends on the jury: "If we spare the man's life, the des Vanneaulx will recover Pingret's money." This irresistible argument told upon the jury, and divided them—seven for acquittal as against five. As they failed to agree, the president and assessors were obliged to add their suffrages, and they were on the side of the minority. Jean-François Tascheron was found guilty of murder.

When sentence was passed, Tascheron burst into a blind fury, natural enough in a man full of strength and life, but seldom seen in court when it is an innocent man who is condemned. It seemed to every one who saw it that the drama was not brought to an end by the sentence. So obstinate a struggle (as often happens in such cases) gave rise to two diametrically opposite opinions as to the guilt of the central

figure in it. Some saw oppressed innocence in him, others a
criminal justly punished. The Liberal party felt it incumbent
upon them to believe in Tascheron's innocence; it was not
so much conviction on their part as a desire to annoy those in
office.

"What?" cried they. "Is a man to be condemned because his foot happens to suit the size of a footmark? Because, forsooth, he was not at his lodgings at the time? (As
if any young fellow would not die sooner than compromise a
woman!) Because he borrowed tools and bought steel?—
(for it has not been proved that he made the key). Because
some one finds a blue rag in a tree, where old Pingret very
likely put it himself to scare the sparrows, and it happens to
match a slit made in the blouse? Take a man's life on such
grounds as these! And, after all, Jean-François has denied
every charge, and the prosecution did not produce any witness who had seen him commit the crime."

Then they fell to corroborating, amplifying, and paraphras-
ing the speeches made by the prisoner's counsel and his line
of defense. As for Pingret; what was Pingret? A money-
box which had been broken open; so said the freethinkers.

A few so-called Progressives, who did not recognize the
sacred laws of property (which the Saint-Simonians had
already attacked in the abstract region of economical theory),
went further still.

"Old Pingret," said these, "was the prime author of the
crime. The man was robbing his country by hoarding the
gold. What a lot of businesses that idle capital might have
fertilized! He had thwarted industry; he was properly
punished."

As for the servant-girl, they were sorry for her; and
Denise, who had baffled the ingenuity of the lawyers, the girl
who never opened her mouth at the trial without long pondering over what she meant to say, excited the keenest interest.
She became a figure comparable, in another sense, with Jeanie

Deans, whom she resembled in charm of character, modesty, in her religious nature and personal comeliness. So François Tascheron still continued to excite the curiosity not merely of Limoges, but of the whole department. Some romantic women openly expressed their admiration of him.

"If there is a love for some woman about him at the bottom of all this," said these ladies, "the man is certainly no ordinary man. You will see that he will die bravely!"

Would he confess? Would he keep silence? Bets were taken on the question. Since that outburst of rage with which he received his doom (an outburst which might have had a fatal ending for several persons in court but for the intervention of the police), the criminal threatened violence indiscriminately to all and sundry who came near him, and with the ferocity of a wild beast. The gaoler was obliged to put him in a strait waistcoat; for if he was dangerous to others, he seemed quite as likely to attempt his own life. Tascheron's despair, thus restrained from all overt acts of violence, found a vent in convulsive struggles which frightened the warders, and in language which, in the middle ages, would have been set down to demoniacal possession.

He was so young that women were moved to pity that a life so filled with an all-engrossing love should be cut off. Quite recently, and as if written for the occasion, Victor Hugo's sombre elegy and vain plea for the abolition of the death-penalty (that support of the fabric of society) had appeared, and "The Condemned's Last Day" was the order of the day in all conversations. Then finally, above the boards of the assizes, set, as it were, upon a pedestal, rose the invisible mysterious figure of a woman, standing there with her feet dipped in blood; condemned to suffer heart-rending anguish, yet outwardly to live in unbroken household peace. At her every one pointed the finger—and yet, they almost admired that Limousin Medea with the inscrutable brow and the heart of steel in her white breast. Perhaps she dwelt in

the home of this one or that, and was the sister, cousin, wife,
or daughter of such an one. What a horror in their midst !
It is in the domain of the imagination, according to Napoleon, that the power of the unknown is incalculably great.

As for the des Vanneaulx's hundred thousand francs, all the
efforts of the police had not succeeded in recovering the
money ; and the criminal's continued silence was a strange
defeat for the prosecution. M. de Granville (in the place of
the public prosecutor then absent at the Chamber of Deputies)
tried the commonplace stratagem of inducing the condemned
man to believe that the penalty might be commuted if a full
confession were made. But the lawyer had scarcely showed
himself before the prisoner greeted him with furious yells,
and epileptic contortions, and eyes ablaze with anger and
regret that he could not kill his enemy. Justice could only
hope that the Church might effect something at the last
moment. Again and again the des Vanneaulx applied to the
Abbé Pascal, the prison chaplain. The Abbé Pascal was not
deficient in the peculiar quality which gains a priest a hearing
from a prisoner. In the name of religion, he braved Tascheron's transports of rage, and strove to utter a few words
amidst the storms that convulsed that powerful nature. But
the struggle between spiritual paternity and the tempest of
uncontrolled passions was too much for poor Abbé Pascal ; he
retired from it defeated and worn out.

"That is a man who has found his heaven here on earth,"
the old priest murmured softly to himself.

Then little Mme. des Vanneaulx thought of approaching the
criminal herself, and took counsel of her friends. The Sieur
des Vanneaulx talked of compromise. Being at his wits' end,
he even betook himself to M. de Granville, and suggested
that he (M. de Granville) should intercede with the King for
his uncle's murderer if only, *if only*, the murderer would hand
over those hundred thousand francs to the proper persons.
The *avocat général* retorted that the King's majesty would not

stoop to haggle with criminals. Then the des Vanneaulx tried Tascheron's counsel, offering him twenty per cent. on the total amount as an inducement to recover it for them. This lawyer was the one creature whom Tascheron could see without flying into a fury; him, therefore, the next-of-kin empowered to offer ten per cent. to the murderer, to be paid over to the man's family. But in spite of the mutilations which these beavers were prepared to make in their heritage, in spite of the lawyer's eloquence, Tascheron continued obdurate. Then the des Vanneaulx, waxing wroth, anathematized the condemned man and called down curses upon his head.

"He is not only a murderer, he has no sense of decency!" cried they, in all seriousness, ignorant though they were of the famous *Plaint of Fualdès.* The Abbé Pascal had totally failed, the application for a reversal of judgment seemed likely to succeed no better, the man would go to the guillotine, and then all would be lost.

"What good will our money be to him where he is going?" they wailed. "A murder you can understand, but to steal a thing that is of no use! The thing is inconceivable. What times we live in, to be sure, when people of quality take an interest in such a bandit! He does not deserve it."

"He has very little sense of honor," said Mme. des Vanneaulx.

"Still, suppose that giving up the money should compromise his sweetheart!" suggested an old maid.

"We would keep his secret," cried the Sieur des Vanneaulx.

"But then you would become accessories after the fact," objected a lawyer.

"Oh! the scamp!" This was the Sieur des Vanneaulx's conclusion of the whole matter.

The des Vanneaulx's debates were reported with some amusement to Mme. Graslin by one of her circle, a very clever woman, a dreamer and idealist, for whom everything must be faultless. The speaker regretted the condemned

man's fury ; she would have had him cold, calm, and dignified.

"Do you not see," said Véronique, "that he is thrusting
temptation aside and baffling their efforts. He is deliberately
acting like a wild beast."

"Besides," objected the Parisieune in exile, "he is not a
gentleman, he is only a common man."

"If he had been a gentleman, it would have been all over
with that unknown woman long ago," Mme. Graslin answered.

These events, twisted and tortured in drawing-rooms and
family circles, made to bear endless constructions, picked to
pieces by the most expert tongues in the town, all contributed
to invest the criminal with a painful interest, when, two
months later, the appeal for mercy was rejected by the
Supreme Court. How would he bear himself in his last
moments? He had boasted that he would make so desperate
a fight for his life that it was impossible that he should lose it.
Would he confess? Would his conduct belie his language?
Which side would win their wagers? Are you going to be
there? Are you not going? How are we to go? As a
matter of fact, the distance from the prison of Limoges to the
place of execution is very short, sparing the dreadful ordeal
of a long transit to the prisoner, but also limiting the number
of fashionable spectators. The prison is in the same building
as the Palais de Justice, at the corner of the Rue du Palais
and the Rue du Pont-Hérisson. The Rue du Palais is the direct
continuation of the short Rue de Monte-à-Regret which leads
to the Place d'Aine or des Arênes, where executions take place
(hence, of course, its name). The way, as has been said, is
very short, consequently there are not many houses along it,
and but few windows. What persons of fashion would care
to mingle with the crowd in the square on such an occasion?

But the execution expected from day to day was day after
day put off, to the great astonishment of the town, and for the
following reasons: The pious resignation of the greatest

scoundrels on their way to death is a triumph reserved for the Church, and a spectacle which seldom fails to impress the crowd. Setting the interests of Christianity totally aside (although this is a principle never lost sight of by the Church), the condemned man's repentance is too strong a testimony to the power of religion for the clergy not to feel that a failure on these conspicuous occasions is a heart-breaking misfortune. This feeling was aggravated in 1829, for party spirit ran high and poisoned everything, however small, which had any bearing on politics. The Liberals were in high glee at the prospect of a public collapse of the " priestly party," an epithet invented by Montlosier, a Royalist who went over to the Constitutionals and was carried by his new associates further than he intended. A party, in its corporate capacity, is guilty of disgraceful actions which in an individual would be infamous, and so it happens that when one man stands out conspicuous as the expression and incarnation of that party, in the eyes of the crowd he is apt to become a Robespierre, a Judge Jeffreys, a Laubardemont—a sort of altar of expiation to which others equally guilty attach *ex votos* in secret.

There was an understanding between the episcopal authorities and the police authorities, and still the execution was put off, partly to secure a triumph for religion, but quite as much for another reason—by the aid of religion justice hoped to arrive at the truth. The power of the public prosecutor, however, had its limits ; sooner or later the sentence must be carried out ; and the very Liberals who insisted, for the sake of opposition, on Tascheron's innocence, and had tried to upset the case, now began to grumble at the delay. Opposition, when systematic, is apt to fall into inconsistencies ; for the point in question is not to be in the right, but to have a stone always ready to sling at authority. So towards the beginning of August, the hand of authority was forced by the clamor (often a chance sound echoed by empty heads) called public opinion. The execution was announced.

In this extremity the Abbé Dutheil took it upon himself to suggest a last resource to the bishop. One result of the success of this plan will be the introduction of another actor in the judicial drama, the extraordinary personage who forms a connecting link between the different groups in it ; the greatest of all figures in this *Scène;* the guide who should hereafter bring Mme. Graslin on a stage where her virtues were to shine forth with the brightest lustre ; where she would exhibit a great and noble charity and act the part of a Christian and a ministering angel.

The bishop's palace at Limoges stands on the hillside above the Vienne. The gardens, laid out in terraces supported by solidly-built walls, crowned by balustrades, descend stepwise, following the fall of the land to the river. The sloping ridge rises high enough to give the spectator on the opposite bank the impression that the Faubourg Saint-Étienne nestles at the foot of the lowest terrace of the bishop's garden. Thence, as you walk in one direction, you look out across the river, and in the other along its course through the broad fertile landscape. When the Vienne has flowed westward past the palace gardens, it takes a sudden turn towards Limoges, skirting the Faubourg Saint-Martial in a graceful curve. A little further, and beyond the suburb, it passes a charming country house called the Cluzeau. You can catch a glimpse of the walls from the nearest point of the nearest terrace, a trick of the perspective uniting them with the church towers of the suburb. Opposite the Cluzeau lies the island in the river, with its indented shores, its thickly growing poplars and forest trees, the island which Véronique in her girlhood called the Isle of France. Eastward, the low hills shut in the horizon like the walls of an amphitheatre.

The charm of the situation and the rich simplicity of the architecture of the palace mark it out among the other buildings of a town not conspicuously happy in the choice or employment of its building materials. The view from the

gardens, which attracts travelers in search of the picturesque,
had long been familiar to the Abbé Dutheil.   He had brought
M. de Grancour with him this evening, and went down from
terrace to terrace, taking no heed of the sunset shedding its
crimson and orange and purple over the balustrades along the
steps, the houses on the suburb, and the waters of the river.
He was looking for the bishop, who at that moment sat under
the vines in a corner of the furthest terrace, taking his dessert,
and enjoying the charms of the evening at his ease.

The long shadows cast by the poplars on the island fell like
a bar across the river; the sunlight lit up their topmost crests,
yellowed somewhat already, and turned the leaves to gold.
The glow of the sunset, differently reflected from the different
masses of green, composed a glorious harmony of subdued
and softened color.   A faint evening breeze stirring in the
depths of the valley ruffled the surface of the Vienne into a
broad sheet of golden ripples that brought out in contrast all
the sober hues of the roofs in the Faubourg Saint-Étienne.
The church towers and housetops of the Faubourg Saint-
Martial were blended in the sunlight with the vine-stems of
the trellis.   The faint hum of the country town, half-hidden
in the re-entering curve of the river, the softness of the air—
all sights and sounds combined to steep the prelate in the
calm recommended for the digestion by the authors of every
treatise on that topic.   Unconsciously the bishop fixed his
eyes on the right bank of the river, on a spot where the length-
ening shadows of the poplars in the island had reached the
bank by the Faubourg Saint-Étienne, and darkened the walls
of the garden close to the scene of the double murder of old
Pingret and the servant; and just as his snug felicity of the
moment was troubled by the difficulties which his vicars-general
recalled to his recollection, the bishop's expression grew
inscrutable by reason of many thoughts. The two subordinates
attributed his absence of mind to ennui; but, on the contrary,
the bishop had just discovered in the sands of the Vienne the

key to the puzzle, the clue which the des Vanneaulx and the
police were seeking in vain.

" My lord," began the Abbé de Grancour, as he came up
to the bishop, " everything has failed ; we shall have the sorrow of seeing that unhappy Tascheron die in mortal sin.   He
will bellow the most awful blasphemies ; he will heap insults
on poor Abbé Pascal ; he will spit on the crucifix, and deny
everything, even hell-fire."

" He will frighten the people," said the Abbé Dutheil.
" The very scandal and horror of it will cover our defeat and
our inability to prevent it.   So, as I was saying to M. de
Grancour as we came, may this scene drive more than one
sinner back to the bosom of the Church."

His words seemed to trouble the bishop, who laid down the
bunch of grapes which he was stripping on the table, wiped
his fingers, and signed to his two vicars-general to be seated.

" The Abbé Pascal has managed badly," said he at last.

" He is quite ill after the last scene with the prisoner," said
the Abbé de Grancour.   " If he had been well enough to
come, we should have brought him with us to explain the
difficulties which put all the efforts which your lordship might
command out of our power."

" The condemned man begins to sing obscene songs at the
top of his voice when he sees one of us ; the noise drowns
every word as soon as you try to make yourself heard," said
a young priest who was sitting beside the bishop.

The young speaker leaned his right elbow on the table, his
white hand drooped carelessly over the bunches of grapes as
he selected the reddest berries, with the air of being perfectly
at home.   He had a charming face, and seemed to be either
a table companion or a favorite with the bishop, and was, in
fact, a favorite and the prelate's table-companion.   As the
younger brother of the Baron de Rastignac he was connected
with the bishop of Limoges by the ties of family relationship
and affection.   Considerations of fortune had induced the

young man to enter the Church; and the bishop, aware of
this, had taken his young relative as his private secretary
until such time as advancement might befall him; for the
Abbé Gabriel bore a name which predestined him to the
highest dignities of the Church.

"Then have you been to see him, my son?" asked the bishop.

"Yes, my lord. As soon as I appeared, the miserable man
poured out a torrent of the most disgusting language against
you and me; his behavior made it impossible for a priest to
stay with him. Will you permit me to offer you a piece of
advice, my lord?"

"Let us hear the wisdom which God sometimes puts into
the mouth of babes," said the bishop.

"Did he not cause Balaam's ass to speak?" the young
Abbé de Rastignac retorted quickly.

"According to some commentators, the ass was not very
well aware of what she was saying," the bishop answered,
laughing.

Both the vicars-general smiled. In the first place, it was
the bishop's joke; and, in the second, it glanced lightly on
this young abbé, of whom all the dignitaries and ambitious
churchmen grouped about the bishop were envious.

"My advice would be to beg M. de Granville to put off
the execution for a few days yet. If the condemned man
knew that he owed those days of grace to our intercession, he
would perhaps make some show of listening to us, and if he
listens——"

"He will persist in his conduct when he sees what comes
of it," said the bishop, interrupting his favorite. "Gentlemen," he resumed after a moment's pause, "is the town
acquainted with these details?"

"Where will you find the house where they are not discussed?" answered the Abbé de Grancour. "The condition
of our good Abbé Pascal since his last interview is matter of
common talk at this moment."

"When is Tascheron to be executed?" asked the bishop.

"To-morrow. It is market-day," replied M. de Grancour.

"Gentlemen, religion must not be vanquished," cried the bishop. "The more attention is attracted to this affair, the more determined am I to secure a signal triumph. The Church is passing through a difficult crisis. Miracles are called for here among an industrial population, where sedition has spread itself and taken root far and wide; where religious and monarchical doctrines are regarded with a critical spirit; where nothing is respected by a system of analysis derived from Protestantism by the so-called Liberalism of to-day, which is free to take another name to-morrow. Go to M. de Granville, gentlemen, he is with us heart and soul; tell him that we ask for a few days' respite. I will go to see the unhappy man."

"You, my lord!" cried the Abbé de Rastignac. "Will not too much be compromised if *you* fail? You should only go when success is assured."

"If my lord bishop will permit me to give my opinion," said the Abbé Dutheil, "I think that I can suggest a means of securing the triumph of religion under these melancholy circumstances."

The bishop's response was a somewhat cool sign of assent, which showed how low his vicar-general's credit stood with him.

"If any one has any ascendency over this rebellious soul, and may bring it to God, it is M. Bonnet, the curé of the village where the man was born," the Abbé Dutheil went on.

"One of your protégés," remarked the bishop.

"My lord, M. Bonnet is one of those who recommend themselves by their militant virtues and evangelical labors."

This answer, so modest and simple, was received with a silence which would have disconcerted any one but the Abbé Dutheil. He had alluded to merits which had been over-

looked, and the three who heard him chose to regard the
words as one of the meek sarcasms, neatly put, impossible to
resent, in which churchmen excel, accustomed as they are by
their training to say the thing they mean without transgressing
the severe rules laid down for them in the least particular.
But it was nothing of the kind; the abbé never thought of
himself.   Then—

"I have heard of Saint Aristides for too long," the bishop
made answer, smiling.   "If I were to leave his light under a
bushel, it would be injustice or prejudice on my part.   Your
Liberals cry up your M. Bonnet as if he were one of themselves; I mean to see this rural apostle and judge for myself.
Go to the public prosecutor, gentlemen, and ask him in my
name for a respite; I will await his answer before despatching
our well-beloved Abbé Gabriel to Montégnac to fetch the holy
man for us.   We will put his beatitude in the way of working a miracle——"

The Abbé Dutheil flushed red at these words from the
prelate-noble, but he chose to disregard any slight that they
might contain for him.   Both vicars-general silently took
their leave, and left the greatly perplexed bishop alone with his
young friend.

"The secrets of the confessional which we require lie buried
there, no doubt," said the bishop, pointing to the shadows of
the poplars where they reached a lonely house half-way between the island and the Faubourg Saint-Étienne.

"So I have always thought," Gabriel answered.   "I am
not a judge, and I do not care to play the spy; but if I had
been the examining magistrate, I should know the name of
the woman who is trembling now at every sound, at every
word that is uttered, compelled all the while to wear a smooth,
unclouded brow under pain of accompanying the condemned
man to his death.   Yet she has nothing to fear.   I have seen
the man—he will carry the secret of his passionate love to his
grave."

"Crafty young man!" said the bishop, pinching his secretary's ear, as he pointed out a spot between the island in the
river and the Faubourg Saint-Étienne, lit up by a last red ray
from the sunset. The young priest's eyes had been fixed on
it as he spoke. "Justice ought to have searched there; is it
not so?"

"I went to see the criminal to try the effect of my guess
upon him; but he is watched by spies, and, if I had spoken
audibly, I might have compromised the woman for whom he
is dying."

"Let us keep silent," said the bishop. "We are not concerned with man's justice. One head will fall, and that is
enough. Besides, sooner or later, the secret will return to
the Church."

The perspicacity of the priest, fostered by the habit of meditation, is far keener than the insight of the lawyer and the
detective. After all the preliminary investigations, after the
legal inquiry, and the trial at the assizes, the bishop and his
secretary, looking down from the height of the terrace, had
in truth, by dint of contemplation, succeeded in discovering
details as yet unknown.

M. de Granville was playing his evening game of whist in
Mme. Graslin's house, and his visitors were obliged to wait
for his return. It was near midnight before his decision was
known at the palace, and by two o'clock in the morning the
Abbé Gabriel started out for Montégnac in the bishop's own
traveling carriage, loaned to him for the occasion. The place
is about nine leagues distant from Limoges; it lies under the
mountains of the Corrèze, in that part of Limousin which
borders on the department of the Creuse. All Limoges, when
the abbé left it, was in a ferment of excitement over the execution promised for this day, an expectation destined to be
balked once more.

A

III

THE CURÉ OF MONTÉGNAC.

In priests and fanatics there is a certain tendency to insist upon the very utmost to which they are legally entitled where their interests are concerned. Is this a result of poverty? Is an egoism which favors the development of greed one of the consequences of isolation upon a man's character? Or are shrewd business habits, as well as parsimony, acquired by a course of management of charitable funds? Each temperament suggests a different explanation, but the fact remains the same whether it lurks (as not seldom happens) beneath urbane good-humor, or (and equally often) is openly manifested; and the difficulty of putting the hand in the pocket is evidently increasingly felt on a journey.

Gabriel de Rastignac, the prettiest young gentleman who had bowed his head before the altar of the tabernacle for some time, only gave thirty sous to the postillions, and traveled slowly accordingly. The postillion tribe drive with all due respect a bishop who does but pay twice the amount demanded of ordinary mortals, but, at the same time, they are careful not to damage the episcopal equipage, for fear of getting themselves into trouble. The abbé, traveling alone for the first time in his life, spoke mildly at each relay—

"Just drive on a little faster, can't you?"

"You can't get the whip to work without a little palm oil," an old postillion replied, and the young abbé, much mystified, fell back in a corner of the carriage. He amused himself by watching the landscape through which they were traveling, and walked up a hill now and again on the winding road from Bordeaux to Lyons.

Five leagues beyond Limoges the country changes. You have left behind the charming low hills about the Vienne and the fair meadow slopes of Limousin, which sometimes (and this particularly about Saint-Léonard) put you in mind of Switzerland. You find yourself in a wilder and sterner district. Wide moors, vast steppes without grass or herds of horses, stretch away to the mountains of the Corrèze on the horizon. The far-off hills do not tower above the plain, a grandly, rent wall of rock like the Alps in the south ; you look in vain for the desolate peaks and glowing gorges of the Apennine, or for the majesty of the Pyrenees—the curving wave-like swell of the hills of the Corrèze bears witness to their origin, to the peaceful slow subsidence of the waters which once overwhelmed this country.

These undulations, characteristic of this, and, indeed, of most of the hill districts of France, have perhaps, contributed quite as much as the climate to gain for the land its title of "the kindly," which Europe has confirmed. But it is a dreary transition country which separates Limousin from the provinces of Marche and Auvergne. In the mind of the poet and thinker who crosses it, it calls up visions of the Infinite (a terrible thought for certain souls) ; a woman looking out on its monotonous sameness is driven to muse ; and to those who must dwell with the wilderness, nature shows herself stubborn, peevish, and barren ; 'tis a churlish soil that covers these wide gray plains.

Only the neighborhood of a great capital can work such a miracle as transformed Brie during the last two centuries. Here there is no large settlement which sometimes puts life into the waste lands which the agricultural economist regards as blanks in creation, spots where civilization groans aghast, and the tourist finds no inns and a total absence of that picturesqueness in which he delights.

But to lofty spirits the moors, the shadows needed in the vast picture of nature, are not repellent. In our own day, Fenimore Cooper, owner of so melancholy a talent, has set forth the mysterious charm of great solitudes magnificently in

"The Prairie." But the wastes shunned by every form of plant life, the barren soil covered with loose stones and waterborne pebbles, the "bad lands" of the earth, are so many challenges to civilization. France must face her difficulties and find a solution for them, as the British are doing; their patient heroism is turning the most barren heather-land in Scotland into productive farms. Left to their primitive desolation, these fallows produce a crop of discouragement, of idleness, of poor physique from insufficient food, and crime, whenever want grows too clamorous. In these few words, you have the past history of Montégnac.

What is there to be done when a waste on so vast a scale is neglected by the administration, deserted by the nobles, execrated by workers? Its inhabitants declare war against a social system which refuses to do its duty, and so it was in former times with the folk of Montégnac. They lived, like Highlanders, by murder and rapine. At sight of that country, a thoughtful observer could readily imagine how that only twenty years ago the people of the village were at war with society at large.

The wide plateau, cut away on one side by the Vienne, on another by the lovely valleys of Marche, bounded by the Auvergne to the east, and shut in by the mountains of the Corrèze on the south, is very much like (agriculture apart) the uplands of Beauce, which separate the basin of the Loire from the basin of the Seine, or the plateaux of Touraine or of Berri, or many others of these facets, as it were, on the surface of France, so numerous that they demand the careful attention of the greatest administrators.

It is an unheard-of thing that while people complain that the masses are discontented with their condition, and constantly aspiring towards social elevation, a government cannot find a remedy for this in a country like France, where statistics show that there are millions of acres of land lying idle, and in some cases (as in Berri) covered with leaf mold seven or eight feet thick! A good deal of this land which should support whole villages, and yield a magnificent return to culti-vation, is the property of pig-headed communes which refuse to sell to speculators because, forsooth, they wish to preserve the right of grazing some hundred cows upon it. Impotence is writ large over all these lands without a purpose. Yet every bit of land will grow some special thing, and neither arms nor will to work are lacking, but administrative ability and conscience.

Hitherto the upland districts of France have been sacrificed to the valleys. The government has given its fostering protec-tion to districts well able to take care of themselves. But most of these unlucky wastes have no water supply, the first requisite for cultivation. The mists which might fertilize the gray dead soil by depositing their oxides are swept across them by the wind. There are no trees to arrest the clouds and suck up their nourishing moisture. A few plantations here and there would be a godsend in such places. The poor folk who live in these wilds, at a practically impossible distance from the nearest large town, are without a market for their produce—if they have any. Scattered about on the edges of a forest left to nature, they pick up their firewood and eke out a precarious existence by poaching; in the winter starvation stares them in the face. They have not capital enough to grow wheat, for so poor are they that ploughs and cattle are beyond their means; and they live on chestnuts. If you have wandered through some Natural History Museum and felt the indescribable depression which comes on after a prolonged study of the unvarying brown hues of the European specimens, you will perhaps understand how the perpetual contemplation of the gray plains must affect the moral conditions of the people who live face to face with such disheartening ster-ility. There is no shadow, nor contrast, nor coolness; no sight to stir associations which gladden the mind. One could hail a stunted crab-tree there as a friend.

The high-road forked at length, and a cross-road branched off towards the village a few leagues distant. Montégnac lying (as its name indicates) at the foot of a ridge of hill is the chief village of a canton on the borders of Haute-Vienne. The hillside above belongs to the township which encircles hill country and plain; indeed, the commune is a miniature Scotland, and has its highlands and its lowlands. Only a league away, at the back of the hill which shelters the township, rises the first peak of the chain of the Corrèze, and all the country between is filled by the great forest of Montégnac, crowning the slope above the village, covering the little valleys and bleak undulating land (left bare in patches here and there), climbing the peak itself, stretching away to the north in a long narrow strip which ends abruptly in a point on a steep bank above the Aubusson road. That bit of steep bank rises above a deep hollow through which the high-road runs from Lyons to Bordeaux. Many a time coaches and foot-passengers have been stopped in the darkest part of the dangerous ravine; and the robberies nearly always went without punishment. The situation favored the highwaymen, who escaped by paths well known to them into their forest fastnesses. In such a country the investigations of justice find little trace. People accordingly shunned that route.

Without traffic neither commerce nor industry can exist; the exchange of intellectual and material wealth becomes impossible. The visible wonders of civilization are in all cases the result of the application of ideas as old as man. A thought in the mind of man—that is from age to age the starting-point and the goal of all our civilization. The history of Montégnac is a proof of this axiom of social science. When the administration found itself in a position to consider the pressing practical needs of the country, the strip of forest was felled, gendarmes were posted to accompany the diligence through the two stages; but, to the shame of the gendarmerie be it said, it was not the sword but a voice, not Corporal Chervin but Parson Bonnet, who won the battle of civilization by reforming the lives of the people. The curé, seized with pity and compassion for those poor souls, tried to regenerate them, and persevered till he gained his end.

After another hour's journey across the plains where flints succeed to dust, and dust to flints, and flocks of partridges abode in peace, rising at the approach of the carriage with a heavy whirring sound of their wings, the Abbé Gabriel, like most other travelers who pass that way, hailed the sight of the roofs of the township with a certain pleasure. As you enter Montégnac you are confronted by one of the queer posthouses, not to be found out of France. The signboard, nailed up with four nails above a sorry empty stable, is a rough oaken plank on which a pretentious postillion has carved an inscription, darkening the letters with ink : "Poast hosses," it runs. The door is nearly always wide open. The threshold is a plank set up edgewise in the earth to keep the rain-water out of the stable, the floor being below the level of the road outside. Within, the traveler sees, to his sorrow, the harness, worn, mildewed, mended with string, ready to give way at the first tug. The horses are probably not to be seen ; they are at work on the land, or out at grass, anywhere and everywhere but in the stable. If by any chance they are within they are feeding. If the horses are ready, the postillion has gone to see his aunt or his cousin, or gone to sleep, or he is getting in his hay. Nobody knows where he is ; you must wait while somebody goes to find him. He does not stir until he has a mind ; and when he comes, it takes him an eternity to find his waistcoat or his whip, or to rub down his cattle. The buxom dame in the door-way fidgets about even more restlessly than the traveler, and forestalls any outburst on his part by bestirring herself a good deal more quickly than the horses. She personates the post-mistress whose husband is out in the fields.

It was in such a stable as this that the bishop's favorite left his traveling carriage. The walls looked like maps ; the

thatched roof, as gay with flowers as a garden bed, bent under
the weight of its growing house-leeks.   He asked the woman
of the place to have everything in readiness for his departure
in an hour's time, and inquired of her his way to the parsonage.   The good woman pointed out a narrow alley between
two houses.   That was the way to the church, she said, and
he would find the parsonage hard by.

While the abbé climbed the steep path paved with cobble-
stones between the hedgerows on either side, the postmistress
fell to questioning the postboy.   Every postboy along the
road from Limoges had passed on to his brother whip the
surmises of the first postillion concerning the bishop's intentions.   So while Limoges was turning out of bed and talking
of the execution of old Pingret's murderer, the country-folk
all along the road were spreading the news of the pardon
procured by the bishop for the innocent prisoner, and prattling
of supposed miscarriages of justice, insomuch that when Jean-
François came to the scaffold at a later day, he was likely to be
regarded as a martyr.

The Abbé Gabriel went some few paces along the footpath,
red with autumn leaves, dark with blackberries and sloes;
then he turned and stood, acting on the instinct which
prompts us to make a survey of any strange place, an instinct
which we share with the horse and dog.   The reason of the
choice of the site of Montégnac was apparent ; several streams
broke out of the hillside, and a small river flowed along by
the departmental road which leads from the township to the
prefecture.   Like the rest of the villages in this plateau,
Montégnac is built of blocks of clay, dried in the sun ; if a
fire broke out in a cottage, it is possible that it might find it
earth and leave it brick.   The roofs are of thatch ; altogether,
it was a poor-looking place that the bishop's messenger saw.
Below Montégnac lay fields of rye, potatoes, and turnips,
land won from the plain.   In the meadows on the lowest
slope of the hillside, watered by artificial channels, were

some of the celebrated breed of Limousin horses ; a legacy
(so it is said) of the Arab invaders of France, who crossed
the Pyrenees to meet death from the battle-axes of Charles
Martel's Franks, between Poitiers and Tours.   Up above on
the heights the soil looked parched.   Now and again the
reddish scorched surface, burnt bare by the sun, indicated the
arid soil which the chestnuts love.   The water, thriftily distributed along the irrigation channels, was only sufficient to
keep the meadows fresh and green ; on these hillsides grows
the fine short grass, the delicate sweet pasture that builds you
up a breed of horses delicate and impatient of control, fiery,
but not possessed of much staying-power ; unexcelled in their
native district, but apt to change their character when they
change their country.

Some young mulberry trees indicated an intention of growing silk.   Like most villages, Montégnac could only boast a
single street, to wit, the road that ran through it ; but there
was an Upper and Lower Montégnac on either side of it,
each cut in two by a little pathway running at right angles to
the road.   The hillside below a row of houses on the ridge
was gay with terraced gardens which rose from a level of
several feet above the road, necessitating flights of steps,
sometimes of earth, sometimes paved with cobble-stones.   A
few old women, here and there, who sat spinning or looking
after the children, put some human interest into the picture,
and kept up a conversation between Upper and Lower Montégnac by talking to each other across the road, usually quiet
enough.   In this way news traveled pretty quickly from one
end of the township to the other.   The gardens were full of
fruit trees, cabbages, onions, and potherbs ; beehives stood
in rows along the terraces.

A second parallel row of cottages lay below the road, their
gardens sloping down towards the little river which flowed
through fields of thick-growing hemp, the fruit trees which
love damp places marking its course.   A few cottages, the

posthouse among them, nestled in a hollow, a situation well adapted for the weavers who lived in them, and almost every house was overshadowed by the walnut trees, which flourish best in heavy soil.   At the further end of Montégnac, and on the same side of the road, stood a house larger and more carefully kept than the rest; it was the largest of a group equally neat in appearance, a little hamlet, in fact, separated from the township by its gardens, and known then, as to-day, by the name of "Tascherons.'" The commune was not much in itself, but some thirty outlying farms belonged to it.   In the valley several "water-lanes" like those in Berri and Marche marked out the course of the little streams with green fringes.   The whole commune looked like a green ship in the midst of a wide sea.

Whenever a house, a farm, a village, or a district passes from a deplorable state to a more satisfactory condition of things, though as yet scarcely to be called strikingly prosperous, the life there seems so much a matter of course, so natural, that at first sight a spectator can never guess how much toil went to the founding of that not extraordinary prosperity; what an amount of effort, vast in proportion to the strength that undertook it ; what heroic persistence lies there buried and out of sight, effort and persistence without which the visible changes could not have taken place.   So the young abbé saw nothing unusual in the pleasant view before his eyes ; he little knew what that country had been before M. Bonnet came to it.

He turned and went a few paces further up the path, and soon came in sight of the church and parsonage, about six hundred feet above the gardens of Upper Montégnac.   Both buildings, when first seen in the distance, were hard to distinguish among the ivy-covered stately ruins of the old Castle of Montégnac, a stronghold of the Navarreins in the twelfth century.   The parsonage house had every appearance of being built in the first instance for a steward or a head gamekeeper.

It stood at the end of a broad terrace planted with lime trees, and overlooked the whole countryside. The ravages of time bore witness to the antiquity of the flight of steps and the walls which supported the terrace, the stones had been forced out of place by the constant imperceptible thrusting of plant life in the crevices, until tall grasses and wild flowers had taken root among them. Every step was covered with a dark-green carpet of fine close moss. The masonry, solid though it was, was full of rifts and cracks, where wild plants of the pellitory and camomile tribe were growing ; the maiden-hair fern sprang from the loopholes in thick masses of shaded green. The whole face of the wall, in fact, was hung with the finest and fairest tapestry, damasked with bracken fronds, purple snap-dragons with their golden stamens, blue borage, and brown fern and moss, till the stone itself was only seen by glimpses here and there through its moist, cool covering.

Up above, upon the terrace, the clipped box borders formed geometrical patterns in a pleasure garden framed by the parsonage house, and behind the parsonage rose the crags, a pale background of rock, on which a few drooping, feathery trees struggled to live. The ruins of the castle towered above the house and the church.

The parsonage itself, built of flints and mortar, boasted a single story and garrets above, apparently empty, to judge by the dilapidated windows on either gable under the high-pitched roof. A couple of rooms on the ground floor, separated by a passage with a wooden staircase at the farther end of it, two more rooms on the second floor, and a little lean-to kitchen built against the side of the house in the yard, where a stable and coach-house stood perfectly empty, useless, abandoned— this was all. The kitchen garden lay between the house and the church ; a ruinous covered passage led from the parsonage to the sacristy.

The young abbé's eyes wandered over the place. He noted the four windows with their leaded panes, the brown

moss-grown walls, the rough wooden door, so full of splits
and cracks that it looked like a bundle of matches, and the
adorable quaintness of it all by no means took his fancy. The
grace of the plant life which covered the roofs, the wild
climbing flowers that sprang from the rotting wooden sills
and cracks in the wall, the trails and tendrils of the vines,
covered with tiny clusters of grapes, which found their way
in through the windows, as if they were fain to carry merri-
ment and laughter into the house—all this he beheld, and
thanked his stars that his way led to a bishopric, and not to a
country parsonage.

The house, open all day long, seemed to belong to every
one. The Abbé Gabriel walked into the dining-room, which
opened into the kitchen. The furniture which met his eyes
was poor—an old oak table with four twisted legs, an easy-
chair covered with tapestry, a few wooden chairs, and an old
chest, which did duty as a sideboard. There was no one in
the kitchen except the cat, the sign of a woman in the house.
The other room was the parlor ; glancing round it, the young
priest noticed that the easy-chairs were made of unpolished
wood, and covered with tapestry. The paneling of the walls,
like the rafters, was of chestnut-wood, and black as ebony.
There was a timepiece in a green case painted with flowers, a
table covered with a worn green cloth, one or two chairs, and
on the mantle-shelf an Infant Jesus in wax under a glass shade
set between two candlesticks. The hearth, surrounded by a
rough wooden moulding, was hidden by a paper screen representing the Good Shepherd with a sheep on his shoulder. In
this way, doubtless, one of the family of the mayor, or of the
justice of the peace, endeavored to express his acknowledg-
ments of the care bestowed on his training.

The state of the house was something piteous. The walls,
which had once been lime-washed, were discolored here and
there, and rubbed and darkened up to the height of a man's
head. The wooden staircase, with its heavy balustrades,

neatly kept though it was, looked as though it must totter if any one set foot on it.   At the end of the passage, just oppo-site the front door, another door stood open, giving the Abbé Gabriel an opportunity of surveying the kitchen garden, shut in by the wall of the old rampart, built of the white crumb-ling stone of the district.   Fruit trees in full bearing had been trained espalier-fashion along this side of the garden, but the long trellises were falling to pieces, and the vine-leaves were covered with blight.

The abbé went back through the house, and walked along the paths in the front garden.   Down below the magnificent wide view of the valley was spread out before his eyes, a sort of oasis on the edge of the great plain, which, in the light morning mists, looked something like a waveless sea.   Behind, and rather to one side, the great forest stretched away to the horizon, the bronzed mass making a contrast with the plains, and on the other hand the church and the castle perched on the crag stood sharply out against the blue sky.   As the Abbé Gabriel paced the tiny paths among the box-edged diamonds, circles, and stars, crunching the gravel beneath his boots, he looked from point to point at the scene ; over the village, where already a few groups of gazers had formed to stare at him, at the valley in the morning light, the quick-set hedges that marked the ways, the little river flowing under its willows, in such contrast with the infinite of the plains. Gradually his impressions changed the current of his thoughts. He admired the quietness, he felt the influences of the pure air, of the peace inspired by a glimpse of a life of biblical simplicity ; and with these came a dim sense of the beauty of that life.   He went back again to look at its details with a more serious curiosity.

A little girl, left in charge of the house no doubt, but busy pilfering in the garden, came back at the sound of a man's shoes creaking on the flagged pavement of the ground-floor rooms.   In her confusion at being caught with fruit in her

hand and between her teeth, she made no answer whatever to
the questions put to her by this abbé—young, handsome,
daintily arrayed. The child had never believed it possible
that such an abbé could exist—radiant in fine lawn, neat as a
new pin, and dressed in fine black cloth without a speck or a
crease.   ,

"M. Bonnet?" she echoed at last. "M. Bonnet is saying
mass, and Mlle. Ursule is gone to the church."

The covered passage from the house to the sacristy had
escaped the Abbé Gabriel's notice; so he went down the path
again to enter the church by the principal door. The church
porch was a sort of pent-house facing the village, set at the
top of a flight of worn and disjointed steps, overlooking a
square below; planted with the great elm trees which date
from the time of the Protestant Sully, and full of channels
washed by the rains.

The church itself, one of the poorest in France, where
churches are sometimes very poor, was not unlike those huge
barns which boast a roof above the door, supported by brick
pillars or tree-trunks. Like the parsonage house, it was built
of rubble, the square tower being roofed with round tiles; but
nature had covered the bare walls with the richest tracery
mouldings, and made them fairer still with color and light and
shade, carving her lines and disposing her masses, showing
all the craftsman's cunning of a Michel Angelo in her work.
The ivy clambered over both sides, its sinewy stems clung to
the walls till they were covered, beneath the green leaves, with
as many veins as any anatomical diagram. Under this mantle,
wrought by time to hide the wounds which time had made,
damasked by autumn flowers that grew in the crevices, nestled
the singing birds. The rose window in the west front was
bordered with blue harebells, like the first page of some richly-
painted missal. There were fewer flowers on the north side,
which communicated with the parsonage, though even there
there were patches of crimson moss on the gray stone, but

the south wall and the apse were covered with many-colored blossoms ; there were a few saplings rooted in the cracks, notably an almond-tree, the symbol of hope. Two giant firs grew up close to the wall of the apse, and served as lightning-conductors. A low ruinous wall repaired and maintained at elbow height with fallen fragments of its own masonry ran round the churchyard. In the midst of the space stood an iron cross mounted on a stone pedestal, strewn with sprigs of box blessed at Easter, a reminder of a touching Christian rite, now fallen into disuse except in country places. Only in little villages and hamlets does the priest go at Eastertide to bear to his dead the tidings of the Resurrection—" You will live again in happiness." Here and there above the grass-covered graves rose a rotten wooden cross.

The inside was in every way in keeping with the picturesque neglect outside of the poor church, where all the ornament had been given by time, grown charitable for once. Within, your eyes turned at once to the roof. It was lined with chestnut-wood and sustained at equal distances by strong king-posts set on cross-beams ; age had imparted to it the richest tones which old woods can take in Europe. The four walls were lime-washed and bare of ornament. Poverty had made unconscious iconoclasts of these worshipers.

Four pointed windows in the side walls let in the light through their leaded panes ; the floor was of brick ; the seats, wooden benches. The tomb-shaped altar bore for ornament a great crucifix, beneath which stood a tabernacle in walnut-wood (its mouldings brightly polished and clean), eight candlesticks (the candles thriftily made of painted wood), and a couple of china vases full of artificial flowers, things that a broker's man would have declined to look at, but which must serve for God. The lamp in the shrine was simply a floating-light, like a night-light, set in an old silver-plated holy water stoup, hung from the ceiling by silken cords brought from the wreck of some château. The baptismal fonts were of wood like the pulpit, and a sort of cage where the church-wardens sat—the patricians of the place. The shrine in the Lady Chapel offered to the admiration of the public two colored lithographs framed in a narrow gilded frame. The altar had been painted white, and adorned with artificial flowers planted in gilded wooden flower-pots set out on a white altar-cloth edged with shabby yellowish lace.

But at the end of the church a long window covered with a red cotton curtain produced a magical effect. The lime-washed walls caught a faint rose-tint from that glowing crimson ; it was as if some thought divine shone from the altar to fill the poor place with warmth and light. On one wall of the passage which led into the sacristy the patron saint of the village had been carved in wood and painted—a St. John the Baptist and his sheep, an execrable daub. Yet, in spite of the bareness and poverty of the church, there was about the whole a subdued harmony which appeals to those whose spirits have been finely touched, a harmony of the visible and invisible emphasized by the coloring. The rich dark-brown tints of the wood made an admirable relief to the pure white of the walls, and both blended with the triumphant crimson of the chancel window, an austere trinity of color which recalled the great doctrine of the Catholic Church.

If surprise was the first feeling called forth by the sight of this miserable house of God, pity and admiration followed quickly upon it. Did it not express the poverty of those who worshiped there ? Was it not in keeping with the quaint simplicity of the parsonage ? And it was clean and carefully kept. You breathed, as it were, an atmosphere of the simple virtues of the fields ; nothing within spoke of neglect. Primitive and homely though it was, it was clothed in prayer ; a soul pervaded it which you felt, though you could not explain how.

The Abbé Gabriel slipped in softly, so as not to interrupt the meditations of two groups on the front benches before the

high-altar, which was railed off from the nave by a balustrade
of the inevitable chestnut-wood, roughly made enough, and
covered with a white cloth for the communion. Just above
the space hung the lamp. Some score of peasant-folk on
either side were so deeply absorbed in passionate prayer, that
they paid no heed to the stranger as he walked up the church
in the narrow gangway between the rows of benches. As the
Abbé Gabriel stood beneath the lamp, he could see into the
two chancels which completed the cross of the ground-plan;
one of them led to the sacristy, the other to the churchyard.
It was in this latter, near the graves, that a whole family clad
in black were kneeling on the brick floor, for there were no
benches in this part of the church. The abbé bent before
the altar on the step of the balustrade and knelt to pray,
giving a side glance at this sight, which was soon explained.
The Gospel was read; the curé took off his chasuble and
came down from the altar towards the railing; and the abbé,
who had foreseen this, slipped away and stood close to the
wall before M. Bonnet could see him. The clock struck ten.

"My brethren," said the curé in a faltering voice, "even
at this moment, a child of this parish is paying his forfeit to
man's justice by submitting to its extreme penalty. We offer
the holy sacrifice of the mass for the repose of his soul. Let
us all pray together to God to beseech Him not to forsake
that child in his last moments, to entreat that repentance here
on earth may find in heaven the mercy which has been refused
to it here below. The ruin of this unhappy child, on whom
we had counted most surely to set a good example, can only
be attributed to a lapse from religious principles——"

The curé was interrupted by the sound of sobbing from the
group of mourners in the transept; and by the paroxysm of
grief the young priest knew that this was the Tascheron family,
though he had never seen them before. The two foremost
among them were old people of seventy years at least. Their
faces, swarthy as a Florentine bronze, were covered with deep

7

impassive lines. Both of them, in their old patched garments,
stood like statues close against the wall; evidently this was
the condemned man's grandfather and grandmother. Their
red glassy eyes seemed to shed tears of blood; the old arms
trembled so violently that the sticks on which they leaned
made a faint sound of scratching on the bricks. Behind them
the father and mother, their faces hidden in their handker-
chiefs, burst into tears. About the four heads of the family
knelt two married daughters with their husbands, then three
sons, stupefied with grief. Five kneeling little ones, the oldest
not more than seven years of age, understood nothing probably of all that went on, but looked and listened with the
apparently torpid curiosity, which in the peasant is often a
process of observation carried (so far as the outward and visible is concerned) to the highest possible pitch. Last of all
came the poor girl Denise, who had been imprisoned by justice, the martyr to sisterly love; she was listening with an
expression which seemed to betoken incredulity and straying
thoughts. To her it seemed impossible that her brother should
die. Her face was a wonderful picture of another face, that of
one among the three Marys who could not believe that Christ
was dead, though she had shared the agony of His passion.
Pale and dry-eyed, as is the wont of those who have watched
for many nights, her freshness had been withered more by
sorrow than by work in the fields; but she still kept the
beauty of a country-girl, the full plump figure, the shapely
red arms, a perfectly round face, and clear eyes, glittering at
that moment with the light of despair in them. Her throat,
firm-fleshed and white below the line of sunburned brow, indicated the rich tissue and fairness of the skin beneath the
stuff. The two married daughters were weeping; their husbands, patient tillers of the soil, were grave and sad. None
of the three sons in their sorrow raised their eyes from the
ground.

Only Denise and her mother showed any sign of rebellion

in the harrowing picture of resignation and despairing anguish.
The sympathy and sincere and pious commiseration felt by
the rest of the villagers for a family so much respected had
lent the same expression to all faces, an expression which became a look of positive horror when they gathered from the
curé's words that even in that moment the knife would fall.
All of them had known the young man from the day of his
birth, and doubtless all of them believed him to be incapable
of committing the crime laid to his charge. The sobbing
which broke in upon the simple and brief address grew so
vehement that the curé's voice suddenly ceased, and he invited those present to fervent prayer.

There was nothing in this scene to surprise a priest, but
Gabriel de Rastignac was too young not to feel deeply moved
by it. He had not as yet put priestly virtues in practice; he
knew that a different destiny lay before him; that it would
never be his duty to go forth into the social breaches where
the heart bleeds at the sight of suffering on every side; his
lot would be cast among the upper ranks of the clergy which
keep alive the spirit of sacrifice, represent the highest intelligence of the Church, and, when occasion calls for it, display
these same virtues of the village curé on the largest scale, like
the great bishops of Marseilles and Meaux, the archbishops of
Arles and Cambrai. The poor peasants were praying and
weeping for one who (as they believed) was even then going
to his death in a great public square, before a crowd of people
assembled from all parts to see him die, the agony of death
made intolerable for him by the weight of shame; there was
something very touching in this feeble counterpoise of sympathy and prayer from a few, opposed to the cruel curiosity of
the rabble and the curses, not undeserved. The poor church
heightened the pathos of the contrast.

The Abbé Gabriel was tempted to go over to the Tascherons and cry, "Your son, your brother has been reprieved!"
but he shrank from interrupting the mass; he knew, more-

over, that it was only a reprieve, the execution was sure to take place sooner or later. But he could not follow the service; in spite of himself, he began to watch the pastor of whom the miracle of conversion was expected.

Out of the indications in the parsonage house, Gabriel de Rastignac had drawn a picture of M. Bonnet in his own mind: He would be short and stout, he thought, with a red, powerful face, a rough workingman, almost like one of the peasants themselves, and tanned by the sun. The reality was very far from this; the Abbé Gabriel found himself in the presence of an equal. M. Bonnet was short, slender, and weakly-looking; yet it was none of these characteristics, but an impassioned face, such a face as we imagine for an apostle, which struck you at a first glance. In shape it was almost triangular; starting from the temples on either side of a broad forehead, furrowed with wrinkles, the meagre outlines of the hollow cheeks met at a point in the chin. In that face, overcast by an ivory tint like the wax of an altar candle, blazed two blue eyes, full of the light of faith and the fires of a living hope. A long, slender, straight nose divided it into two equal parts. The wide mouth spoke even when the full, resolute lips were closed, and the voice which issued thence was one of those which go to the heart. The chestnut hair, thin, smooth, and fine, denoted a poor physique, poorly nourished. The whole strength of the man lay in his will. Such were his personal characteristics. In any other such short hands might have indicated a bent towards material pleasures; perhaps he too, like Socrates, had found evil in his nature to subdue. His thinness was ungainly, his shoulders protruded too much, and he seemed to be knock-kneed; his bust was so over-developed in comparison with his limbs that it gave him something of the appearance of a hunchback without the actual deformity; altogether, to an ordinary observer, his appearance was not prepossessing. Only those who know the miracles of thought and faith and art can recognize and reverence the light that burns in a martyr's eyes, the pallor of steadfastness, the voice of love—all traits of the Curé Bonnet. Here was a man worthy of that early Church which no longer exists save in the pages of the "Martyrology" and in pictures of the sixteenth century; he bore unmistakably the seal of human greatness which most nearly approaches the divine; conviction had set its mark on him, and a conviction brings a salient indefinable beauty into faces made of the commonest human clay; the devout worshiper at any shrine reflects something of its golden glow; even as the glory of a noble love shines like a sort of light from a woman's face. Conviction is human will come to its full strength; and being at once the cause and the effect, conviction impresses the most indifferent, it is a kind of mute eloquence which gains a hold upon the masses.

As the curé came down from the altar, his eyes fell on the Abbé Gabriel, whom he recognized; but when the bishop's secretary appeared in the sacristy, he found no one there but Ursule. Her master had already given his orders. Ursule, a woman of canonical age, asked the Abbé de Rastignac to follow her along the passage through the garden.

"Monsieur le Curé told me to ask you whether you had breakfasted, sir," she said. "You must have started out from Limoges very early this morning to be here by ten o'clock, so I will set about getting breakfast ready. Monsieur l'Abbé will not find the bishop's table here, but we will do our best. M. Bonnet will not be long; he has gone to comfort those poor souls—the Tascherons. Something very terrible is happening to-day to one of their sons."

"But where do the poor people live?" the Abbé Gabriel put in at length. "I must take M. Bonnet back to Limoges with me at once by the bishop's orders. The unhappy man is not to be executed to-day; his lordship has obtained a reprieve——"

"Ah!" cried Ursule, her tongue itching to spread the

news. " There will be plenty of time to take that comfort to
the poor things whilst I am getting breakfast ready. The
Tascherons live at the other end of the village. You follow
the path under the terrace, that will take you to the house."

As soon as the Abbé Gabriel was fairly out of sight, Ursule
went down herself to take the tidings to the village, and to
obtain the things needed for breakfast.

The curé had learned, for the first time, at the church of a
desperate resolve on the part of the Tascherons, made since
the appeal had been rejected.   They would leave the district;
they had already sold all they had, and that very morning the
money was to be paid down.   Formalities and unforeseen
delays had retarded the sale; they had been forced to stay in
the countryside after Jean-François was condemned, and every
day had been for them a cup of bitterness to drink.   The
news of the plan, carried out so secretly, had only transpired
on the eve of the day fixed for the execution.   The Tascherons
had meant to leave the place before the fatal day; but the
purchaser of their property was a stranger to the canton, a
Corrèzien to whom their motives were indifferent, and he on
his own part had found some difficulty in getting the money
together.   So the family had endured the utmost of their
misery.   So strong was the feeling of their disgrace in these
simple folk who had never tampered with conscience, that
grandfather and grandmother, daughters and sons-in-law,
father and mother, and all who bore the name of Tascheron,
or were connected with them, were leaving the place.   Every
one in the commune was sorry that they should go, and the
mayor had gone to the curé, entreating him to use his influence with the poor mourners.

As the law now stands, the father is no longer responsible
for his son's crime, and the father's guilt does not attach to
his children, a condition of things in keeping with other
emancipations which have weakened the paternal power, and
contributed to the triumph of that individualism which is

eating the heart of society in our days. The thinker who looks to the future sees the extinction of the spirit of the family; those who drew up the new code have set in its place equality and independent opinion. The family will always be the basis of society; and now the family, as it used to be, exists no longer, it has come of necessity to be a temporary arrangement, continually broken up and reunited only to be separated again; the links between the future and the past are destroyed, the family of an older time has ceased to exist in France. Those who proceeded to the demolition of the old social edifice were logical when they decided that each member of the family should inherit equally, lessening the authority of the father, making of each child the head of a new household, suppressing great responsibilities; but is the social system thus re-edified as solid a structure, with its laws of yesterday unproved by long experience, as the old monarchy was in spite of its abuses? With the solidarity of the family, society has lost that elemental force which Montesquieu discovered and called "honor." Society has isolated its members the better to govern them, and has divided in order to weaken. The social system reigns over so many units, an aggregation of so many ciphers, piled up like grains of wheat in a heap. Can the general welfare take the place of the welfare of the family? Time holds the answer to this great enigma. And yet—the old order still exists, it is so deeply rooted that you find it most alive among the people. It is still an active force in remote districts where "prejudice," as it is called, likewise exists; in old-world nooks where all the members of a family suffer for the crime of one, and the children for the sins of their fathers.

It was this belief which made their own countryside intolerable to the Tascherons. Their profoundly religious natures had brought them to the church that morning, for how was it possible to stay away when the mass was said for their son, and prayer offered that God might bring him to a repentance

which should reopen eternal life to him? and, moreover, must
they not take leave of the village altar? But, for all that,
their plans were made; and when the curé, who followed
them, entered the principal house, he found the bundles made
up, ready for the journey. The purchaser was waiting with
the money. The notary had just made out the receipt. Out
in the yard, in front of the house, stood a country cart ready
to take the old people and the money and Jean-François'
mother. The rest of the family meant to set out on foot that
night.

The young abbé entered the room on the ground floor
where the whole family were assembled, just as the curé of
Montégnac had exhausted all his eloquence. The two old
people seemed to have ceased to feel from excess of grief;
they were crouching on their bundles in a corner of the room,
gazing round them at the old house, which had been a family
possession from father to son, at the familiar furniture, at the
man who had bought it all, and then at each other, as who
should say, "Who would have thought that we should ever
have come to this?" For a long time past the old people
had resigned their authority to their son, the prisoner's father;
and now, like old kings after their abdication, they played the
passive part of subjects and children. Tascheron stood
upright listening to the curé, to whom he gave answers in a
deep voice by monosyllables. He was a man of forty-eight
or thereabouts, with a fine face, such as served Titian for his
apostles. It was a trustworthy face, gravely honest and
thoughtful; a severe profile, a nose at right angles with the
brows, blue eyes, a noble forehead, regular features, dark,
crisped, stubborn hair, growing in the symmetrical fashion
which adds a charm to a visage bronzed by a life of work in
the open air—this was the present head of the house. It was
easy to see that the curé's arguments were shattered against
that resolute will.

Denise was leaning against the bread hutch, watching the

notary, who used it as a writing-table; they had given him the grandmother's armchair. The man who had bought the place sat beside the scrivener. The two married sisters were laying the cloth for the last meal which the old folk would offer or partake of in the old house and in their own country before they set out to live beneath alien skies. The men of the family half-stood, half-sat, propped against the large bedstead with the green serge curtains, while Tascheron's wife, their mother, was whisking an omelette by the fire. The grandchildren crowded about the doorway, and the pur- chaser's family were outside.

Out of the window you could see the garden, carefully cul- tivated, stocked with fruit trees; the two old people had planted them—every one. Everything about them, like the old smoke-begrimed room with its black rafters, seemed to share in the pent-up sorrow, which could be read in so many different expressions on the different faces. The meal was being prepared for the notary, the purchaser, the children, and the men; neither the father, nor mother, nor Denise, nor her sisters cared to satisfy their hunger, their hearts were too heavily oppressed. There was a lofty and heart-rending resignation in this last performance of the duties of country hospitality—the Tascherons, men of an ancient stock, ended as people usually begin, by doing the honors of their house.

The bishop's secretary was impressed by the scene, so simple and natural, yet so solemn, which met his eyes as he came to summon the curé of Montégnac to do the bishop's bidding.

"The good man's son is still alive," Gabriel said, address- ing the curé.

At the words, which every one heard in the prevailing silence, the two old people sprang to their feet as if the trumpet had sounded for the last judgment. The mother dropped her frying-pan into the fire. A cry of joy broke from Denise. All the others seemed to be turned to stone in their dull amazement.

"*Jean-François is pardoned!*"   The cry came at that moment as from one voice from the whole village, who rushed up to the Tascherons' house. "It is his lordship the bishop."

"I was *sure* of his innocence !" exclaimed the mother.

"The purchase holds good all the same, doesn't it?" asked the buyer, and the notary answered him by a nod.

In a moment the Abbé Gabriel became the point of interest, all eyes were fixed on him; his face was so sad that it was suspected that there was some mistake, but he could not bear to correct it, and went out with the curé.   Outside the house he dismissed the crowd by telling those who came round about him that there was no pardon, only a reprieve, and a dismayed silence at once succeeded to the clamor.   Gabriel and the curé turned into the house again, and saw a look of anguish on all the faces—the sudden silence in the village had been understood.

"Jean-François has not received his pardon, my friends," said the young abbé, seeing that the blow had been struck, "but my lord bishop's anxiety for his soul is so great that he has put off the execution that your son may not perish to all eternity at least."

"Then is he living?" cried Denise.

The abbé took the curé aside and told him of his parishioner's impiety, of the consequent peril to religion, and what it was that the bishop expected of the curé of Montégnac.

"My lord bishop requires my death," returned the curé. "Already I have refused to go to this unhappy boy when his afflicted family asked me.   The meeting and the scene *there* afterwards would shatter me like glass.   Let every man do his work.   The weakness of my system, or rather the oversensitiveness of my nervous organization, makes it out of the question for me to fulfill these duties of our ministry.   I am still a country parson that I may serve my like, in a sphere where nothing more is demanded of me in a Christian life than I can accomplish.   I thought very carefully over this

"AH! SAVE HIS SOUL AT LEAST!"

matter, and tried to satisfy these good.Tascherons and to do my duty towards this poor boy of theirs ; but at the bare thought of mounting the cart with him, the mere idea of being present while the preparations for death were being made, a deadly chill runs through my veins. No one would ask it of a mother ; and remember, sir, he is a child of my poor church——"

"Then you refuse to obey the bishop's summons?" asked the Abbé Gabriel.

M. Bonnet looked at him.

"His lordship does not know the state of my health," he said, "nor does he know that my nature rises in revolt against——"

"There are times when, like Belzunce at Marseilles, we are bound to face a certain death," the Abbé Gabriel broke in.

Just at that moment the curé felt that a hand pulled his cassock ; he heard sobs, and, turning, saw the whole family on their knees. Old and young, parents and children, men and women, held out their hands to him imploringly ; all the voices united in one cry as he showed his flushed face.

"Ah ! save his soul at least ! "

It was the old grandmother who had caught at the skirt of his cassock and was bathing it with tears.

"I will obey, sir——" No sooner were the words uttered than the curé was forced to sit down ; his knees trembled under him. The young secretary explained the nature of Jean-François' frenzy.

"Do you think that the sight of his younger sister might shake him?" he added, as he came to an end.

"Yes, certainly," returned the curé. "Denise, you will go with us."

"So shall I," said the mother.

"No!" shouted the father. "That boy is dead to us. You know that. Not one of us shall see him."

"Do not stand in the way of his salvation," said the

young abbé. "If you refuse us the means of softening him, you take the responsibility of his soul upon yourself. In his present state his death may reflect more discredit on his family than his life."

"She shall go," said the father. "She always interfered when I tried to correct my son, and this shall be her punishment."

The Abbé Gabriel and M. Bonnet went back together to the parsonage. It was arranged that Denise and her mother should be there at the time when the two ecclesiastics should set out for Limoges. As they followed the footpath along the outskirts of Upper Montégnac, the younger man had an opportunity of looking more closely than heretofore in the church at this country parson, so highly praised by the vicar-general. He was favorably impressed almost at once by his companion's simple, dignified manners, by the magic of his voice, and by the words he spoke, in keeping with the voice. The curé had been but once to the palace since the bishop had taken Gabriel de Rastignac as his secretary, so that he had scarcely seen the favorite destined to be a bishop some day; he knew that the secretary had great influence, and yet in the dignified kindness of his manner there was a certain independence, as of the curé whom the Church permits to be in some sort a sovereign in his own parish.

As for the young abbé, his feelings were so far from appearing in his face that they seemed to have hardened it into severity; his expression was not chilly, it was glacial.

A man who could change the disposition and manners of a whole countryside necessarily possessed some faculty of observation, and was more or less of a physiognomist; and even had the curé been wise only in well-doing, he had just given proof of an unusually keen sensibility. The coolness with which the bishop's secretary met his advances and responded to his friendliness struck him at once. He could only account for this reception by some secret dissatisfaction on the other's part, and looked back over his conduct, wondering how he could have given offense, and in what the offense lay. There was a short embarrassing silence, broken by the Abbé de Rastignac.

"You have a very poor church, Monsieur le Curé," he remarked, aristocratic insolence in his tones and words.

"It is too small," answered M. Bonnet. "For great church festivals the old people sit on benches round the porch, and the younger ones stand in a circle in the square down below; but they are so silent that those outside can hear."

Gabriel was silent for several moments.

"If the people are so devout, why do you leave the church so bare?" he asked at length.

"Alas! sir, I cannot bring myself to spend money on the building when the poor need it. The poor are the church. Besides, I should not fear a visitation from my lord bishop at the Fête-Dieu! Then the poor give the church such things as they have! Did you notice the nails along the walls? They fix a sort of wire trellis work to them, which the women cover with bunches of flowers; the whole church is dressed in flowers, as it were, which keep fresh till the evening. My poor church, which looked so bare to you, is adorned like a bride, and fragrant with sweet scents; the ground is strewn with leaves, and a path in the midst for the passage of the Holy Sacrament is carpeted with rose petals. For that one day I need not fear comparison with Saint Peter's at Rome. The Holy Father has his gold, and I my flowers; to each his miracle. Ah! the township of Montégnac is poor, but it is Catholic. Once upon a time they used to rob travelers, now any one who passes through the place might drop a bag full of money here, and he would find it when he returned home."

"Such a result speaks strongly in your praise," said Gabriel.

"I have had nothing to do with it," answered the curé, flushing at this incisive epigram. "It has been brought about by the Word of God and the sacramental bread."

"Bread somewhat brown," said the Abbé Gabriel, smiling.

"White bread is only suited to the rich," said the curé humbly.

The abbé took both M. Bonnet's hands in his and grasped them cordially.

"Pardon me, Monsieur le Curé," he said ; and in a moment the reconciliation was completed by a look in the beautiful blue eyes that went to the depths of the curé's soul.

"My lord bishop recommended me to put your patience and humility to the proof, but I can go no farther. After this little while I see how greatly you have been wronged by the praises of the Liberal party."

Breakfast was ready. Ursule had spread the white cloth, and set new-laid eggs, butter, honey and fruit, cream and coffee, among bunches of flowers on the old-fashioned table in the old-fashioned sitting-room. The window that looked out upon the terrace stood open, framed about with green leaves. Clematis grew about the ledge—white starry blossoms, with tiny sheaves of golden crinkled stamens at their hearts to relieve the white. Jessamine climbed up one side of the window, and nasturtiums on the other ; above it, a trail of vine, turning red even now, made a rich setting, which no sculptor could hope to render, so full of grace was that lace-work of leaves outlined against the sky.

"You will find life here reduced to its simplest terms," said the curé, smiling, though his face did not belie the sadness of his heart. "If we had known that you were coming—and who could have foreseen the events which have brought you here ?—Ursule would have had some trout for you from the torrent ; there is a trout-stream in the forest, and the fish are excellent ; but I am forgetting that this is August, and that the Gabou will be dry ! My head is very much confused——"

"Are you very fond of this place?" asked the abbé.

"Yes. If God permits, I shall die curé of Montégnac. I could wish that other and distinguished men, who have thought to do better by becoming lay philanthropists, had taken this way of mine. Modern philanthropy is the bane of society; the principles of the Catholic religion are the one remedy for the evils which leaven the body social. Instead of describing the disease and making it worse by jeremiads, each one should have put his hand to the plough and entered God's vineyard as a simple laborer. My task is far from being ended here, sir; it is not enough to have raised the moral standard of the people, who lived in a frightful state of irreligion when I first came here; I would fain die among a generation fully convinced."

"You have only done your duty," the younger man retorted drily; he felt a pang of jealousy in his heart.

The other gave him a keen glance.

"Is this yet another test?" he seemed to say—but aloud he answered humbly, "Yes. I wish every hour of my life," he added, "that every one in the kingdom would do his duty."

The deep underlying significance of those words was still further increased by the tone in which they were spoken. It was clear that here, in this year 1829, was a priest of great intellectual power, great likewise in the simplicity of his life; who, though he did not set up his own judgment against that of his superiors, saw none the less clearly whither the church and the monarchy were going.

When the mother and daughter had come, the abbé left the parsonage and went down to see if the horses had been put in. He was very impatient to return to Limoges. A few minutes later he returned to say that all was in readiness for their departure, and the four set out on their journey. Every creature in Montégnac stood in the road about the posthouse to see them go. The condemned man's mother and sister said not a word; and as for the two ecclesiastics, there were so many topics to be avoided that conversation was difficult, and they could neither appear indifferent nor try to take a cheerful tone. Still endeavoring to discover some neutral ground for their talk as they traveled on, the influences of the great plain seemed to prolong the melancholy silence.

"What made you accept the position of an ecclesiastic?" Gabriel asked at last out of idle curiosity, as the carriage turned into the high-road.

"I have never regarded my office as a 'position,'" the curé answered simply. "I cannot understand how any one can take holy orders for any save the one indefinable and all-powerful reason—a vocation. I know that not a few have become laborers in the great vineyard with hearts worn out in the service of the passions; men who have loved without hope, or whose hopes have been disappointed; men whose lives were blighted when they laid the wife or the woman they loved in the grave; men grown weary of life in a world where in these times nothing, not even sentiments, are stable and secure, where doubt makes sport of the sweetest certainties, and belief is called superstition.

"Some leave political life in times when to be in power seems to be a sort of expiation, when those who are governed look on obedience as an unfortunate necessity; and very many leave a battlefield without standards where powers, by nature opposed, combine to defeat and dethrone the right. I am not supposing that any man can give himself to God for what he may gain. There are some who appear to see in the clergy a means of regenerating our country; but, according to my dim lights, the patriot priest is a contradiction in terms. The priest should belong to God alone.

"I had no wish to offer to our Father, who yet accepts all things, a broken heart and an enfeebled will; I gave myself to Him whole and entire. It was a touching fancy in the old pagan religion which brought the victim crowned with flowers to the temple of the gods for sacrifice. There is something in that custom that has always appealed to me. A sacrifice is nothing unless it is made graciously. So the story of my life is very simple, there is not the least touch of romance in it. Still, if you would like to hear a full confession, I will tell you all about myself.

" My family are well-to-do and almost wealthy. My father, a self-made man, is hard and inflexible ; he deals the same measure to himself as to his wife and children. I have never seen the faintest smile on his lips. With a hand of iron, a brow of bronze, and an energetic nature at once sullen and morose, he crushed us all—wife and children, clerks and servants, beneath a savage tyranny. I think (I speak for myself alone) that I could have borne the life if the pressure brought to bear on us had been even ; but he was crotchety and changeable, and this fitfulness made it unbearable. We never knew whether we had done right or wrong, and the horrible suspense in which we lived at home becomes intolerable in domestic life. It is pleasanter to be out in the streets than in the house. Even as it was, if I had been alone at home, I could have borne all this without a murmur ; but there was my mother, whom I loved passionately ; the sight of her misery and the continual bitterness of her life broke my heart ; and if, as sometimes happened, I surprised her in tears, I was beside myself with rage. I was sent to school ; and those years, usually a time of hardship and drudgery, were a sort of golden age for me. I dreaded the holidays. My mother herself was glad to come to see me at the school.

" When I had finished my humanities, I went home and entered my father's office, but I could only stay there a few months ; youth was strong in me, my mind might have given way.

" One dreary autumn evening my mother and I took a walk by ourselves along the Boulevard Bourdon, then one of the most depressing spots in Paris, and there I opened my

8

heart to her. I said that I saw no possible life for me save in
the church. So long as my father lived I was bound to be
thwarted in my tastes, my ideas, even in my affections. If I
adopted the priest's cassock, he would be compelled to
respect me, and in this way I might become a tower of
strength to the family should occasion call for it. My mother
cried bitterly. At that very time my older brother had
enlisted as a common soldier, driven out of the house by the
causes which had decided my vocation. (He became a
general afterwards, and fell in the battle of Leipsic.) I
pointed out to my mother as a way of salvation for her that
she should marry my sister (as soon as she should be old
enough to settle in life) to a man with plenty of character,
and look to this new family for support.

"So in 1807, under the pretext of escaping the conscription without expense to my father, and at the same time de-
claring my vocation, I entered the Seminary of Saint-Sulpice
at the age of nineteen. Within those famous old walls I
found happiness and peace, troubled only by thoughts of
what my mother and sister must be enduring. Things had
doubtless grown worse and worse at home, for when they came
to see me they upheld me in my determination. Initiated,
it may be, by my own pain into the secret of charity, as the
great apostle has defined it in his sublime epistle, I longed to
bind the wounds of the poor and suffering in some out-of-the-
way spot; and thereafter to prove, if God deigned to bless my
efforts, that the Catholic religion, as put in practice by man,
is the one true, good, and noble civilizing agent on earth.

"During those last days of my diaconate, grace doubtless
enlightened me. Fully and freely I forgave my father, for I
saw that through him I had found my real vocation. But my
mother—in spite of a long and tender letter, in which I explained this, and showed how the trace of the finger of God
was visible throughout—my mother shed many tears when she
saw my hair fall under the scissors of the church; for she

knew how many joys I was renouncing, and did not know the
hidden glories to which I aspired. Women are so tender-
hearted. When at last I was God's, I felt an infinite peace.
All the cravings, the vanities, and cares-that vex so many ⌐
souls fell away from me. I thought that heaven would have
a care for me as for a vessel of its own. I went forth into a
world from which all fear was driven out, where the future
was sure, where everything is the work of God—even the
silence. This quietness of soul is one of the gifts of grace.
My mother could not imagine what it was to take a church for
a bride ; nevertheless, when she saw that I looked serene and
happy, she was happy. After my ordination I came to pay a
visit to some of my father's relatives in Limousin, and one of
these by accident spoke of the state of things in the Montégnac district. With a sudden illumination like lightning
the thought flashed through my inmost soul—'Behold thy
vine ! ' And I came here. So, as you see, sir, my story is
quite simple and uninteresting."

As he spoke, Limoges appeared in the rays of the sunset,
and at the sight the two women could not keep back their
tears.

' Meanwhile the young man whom love in its separate guises
had come to find, the object of so much outspoken curiosity,
hypocritical sympathy, and very keen anxiety, was lying on
his prison mattress in the condemned cell. A spy at the door
was on the watch for any words that might escape him waking
or sleeping, or in one of his wild fits of fury ; so bent was
justice upon coming at the truth, and on discovering Jean-
François' accomplice as well as the stolen money, by every
means that the wit of man could devise.

The des Vanneaulx had the police in their interest ; the
police spies watched through the absolute silence. Whenever
the man told off for this duty looked through the hole made
for the purpose, he always saw the prisoner in the same atti-

tude, bound in his strait waistcoat, his head tied up by a leather strap to prevent him from tearing the stuff and the thongs with his teeth. Jean-François lay staring at the ceiling with a fixed desperate gaze, his eyes glowed, and seemed as if they were reddened by the full-pulsed tide of life sent surging through him by terrible thoughts. It was as if an antique statue of Prometheus had become a living man, with the thought of some lost joy gnawing his heart; so when the second *avocat général* came to see him, the visitor could not help showing his surprise at a character so dogged. At sight of any human being admitted into his cell, Jean-François flew into a rage which exceeded everything in the doctor's experience of such affections. As soon as he heard the key turn in the lock or the bolts drawn in the heavily-ironed door, a light froth came to his lips.

In person, Jean-François Tascheron, twenty-five years of age, was short but well made. His hair was stiff and crisp, and grew rather low on his forehead, signs of great energy. The clear, brilliant, yellow eyes, set rather too close together, gave him something the look of a bird of prey. His face was of the round dark-skinned type common in Central France. One of his characteristics confirmed Lavater's assertion that the front teeth overlap in those predestined to be murderers; but the general expression of his face spoke of honesty, of simple warm-heartedness of disposition—it would have been nothing extraordinary if a woman had loved such a man passionately. The lines of the fresh mouth, with its dazzling white teeth, were gracious; there was that peculiar shade in the scarlet of the lips which indicates ferocity held in check, and frequently a temperament which thirsts for pleasure and demands free scope for indulgence. There was nothing of the workman's coarseness about him. To the women who watched his trial it seemed evident that it was a woman who had brought flexibility and softness into the fibre inured to toil, the look of distinction into the face of a son of the fields, and grace into his bearing. Women recognize the traces of love in a man, and men are quick to see in a woman whether (to use a colloquial phrase), "love has passed that way."

That evening Jean-François heard the sound as the bolts were withdrawn and the key was thrust into the lock; he turned his head quickly with the terrible smothered growl with which his fits of fury began; but he trembled violently when through the soft dusk he made out the forms of his mother and sister, and behind the two dear faces another—the curé of Montégnac.

"So this is what those barbarous wretches held in store for me!" he said, and closed his eyes.

Denise, with her prison experience, was suspicious of every least thing in the room; the spy had hidden himself, meaning, no doubt, to return; she fled to her brother, laid her tear-stained face against his, and said in his ear, "Can they hear what we say?"

"I should rather think they can, or they would not have sent you here," he answered aloud. "I have asked as a favor this long while that I might not see any of my family."

"What a way they have treated him!" cried the mother, turning to the curé. "My poor boy! my poor boy!" She sank down on the foot of the mattress, and hid her face in the priest's cassock. The curé stood upright beside her. "I cannot bear to see him bound and tied up like that and put into that sack——"

"If Jean will promise me to be good and make no attempt on his life, and to behave well while we are with him, I will ask for leave to unbind him; but I shall suffer for the slightest infraction of his promise."

"I have such a craving to stretch myself out and move freely, dear M. Bonnet," said the condemned man, his eyes filling with tears, "that I give you my word I will do as you wish."

The curé went out, the gaoler came, and the strait waist-coat was taken off.

"You are not going to kill me this evening, are you?" asked the turnkey.

Jean made no answer.

"Poor brother!" said Denise, bringing out a basket, which had been strictly searched, "there are one or two things here that you are fond of; here, of course, they grudge you every morsel you eat."

She brought out fruit gathered as soon as she knew that she might see her brother in prison, and a cake which her mother had put aside at once. This thoughtfulness of theirs, which recalled old memories, his sister's voice and movements, the presence of his mother and the curé—all combined to bring about a reaction in Jean. He burst into tears, and for a moment was completely overcome.

"Ah! Denise," he said, "I have not made a meal these six months past; I have eaten because hunger drove me to eat, that is all."

Mother and daughter went out and returned, and came and went. The housewifely instinct of seeing to a man's comfort put heart into them, and at last they set supper before their poor darling. The people of the prison helped them in this, having received orders to do all in their power compatible with the safe custody of the condemned man. The des Vanneaulx, with unkindly kindness, had done their part towards securing the comfort of the man in whose power their heritage lay. So Jean by these means was to know a last gleam of family happiness—happiness overshadowed by the sombre gloom of the prison and death.

"Was my appeal rejected?" he asked M. Bonnet.

"Yes, my boy. There is nothing left to you now but to make an end worthy of a Christian. This life of ours is as nothing compared with the life which awaits us; you must think of your happiness in eternity. Your account with men

is settled by the forfeit of your life, but God requires more, a
life is too small a thing for Him."

"Forfeit my life?—— Ah, you do not know all that I
must leave behind."

Denise looked at her brother, as if to remind him that prudence was called for even in matters of religion.

"Let us say nothing of that," he went on, eating fruit with
an eagerness that denoted a fierce and restless fire within.
"When must I——?"

"*No ! no !* nothing of that before me !" cried the mother.

"I should be easier if I knew," he said in a low voice,
turning to the curé.

"The same as ever !" exclaimed M. Bonnet, and he bent
to say in Jean's ear—"If you make your peace with God to-
night, and your repentance permits me to give you absolution,
it shall be to-morrow." Aloud he added, "We have already
gained something by calming you."

At these last words, Jean grew white to the lips, his eyes
contracted with a heavy scowl, his features quivered with the
coming storm of rage.

"What, am I calm?" he asked himself. Luckily his eyes
met the tearful eyes of his sister Denise, and he regained the
mastery over himself.

"Ah, well," he said, looking at the curé, "I could not
listen to any one but you. They knew well how to tame me,"
and he suddenly dropped his head on his mother's shoulder.

"Listen, dear," his mother said, weeping, "our dear M.
Bonnet is risking his own life by undertaking to be with you
on the way to"—she hesitated, and then finished—"to
eternal life."

And she lowered Jean's head and held it for a few moments
on her heart.

"Will he go with me?" asked Jean, looking at the curé,
who took it upon himself to bow his head. "Very well, I will
listen to him. I will do everything that he requires of me."

"Promise me that you will," said Denise, "for your soul must be saved; that is what we are all thinking of. And then—would you have it said in Limoges and all the country round that a Tascheron could not die like a man? After all, just think that all that you lose here you may find again in heaven, where forgiven souls will meet again."

This preternatural effort parched the heroic girl's throat. Like her mother, she was silent, but she had won the victory. The criminal, hitherto frantic that justice had snatched away his cup of bliss, was thrilled with the sublime doctrine of the Catholic Church, expressed so artlessly by his sister. Every woman, even a peasant-girl like Denise Tascheron, possesses at need this tender tact; does not every woman love to think that love is eternal? Denise had touched two responsive chords. Awakened pride roused other qualities numbed by such utter misery and stunned by despair. Jean took his sister's hand in his and kissed it, and held her to his heart in a manner profoundly significant; tenderly, but in a mighty grasp.

"There," he said, "everything must be given up! That was my last heart-throb, my last thought—intrusted to you, Denise." And he gave her such a look as a man gives at some solemn moment, when he strives to impress his whole soul on another soul.

A whole last testament lay in the words and the thoughts; the mother and sister, the curé and Jean, understood so well that these were mute bequests to be faithfully executed and loyally demanded that they turned away their faces to hide their tears and the thoughts that might be read in their eyes. Those few words, spoken in the death-agony of passion, were the farewell to fatherhood and all that was sweetest on earth —the earnest of a Catholic renunciation of the things of earth. The curé, awed by the majesty of human nature, by all its greatness even in sin, measured the force of this mysterious passion by the enormity of the crime, and raised his eyes as

if to entreat God's mercy. In that action the touching con-
solation—the infinite tenderness of the Catholic faith—was
revealed—a religion that shows itself so human, so loving, by
the hand stretched down to teach mankind the laws of a
higher world, so awful, so divine, by the hand held out to
guide him to heaven. It was Denise who had just discovered
to the curé, in this mysterious manner, the spot where the
rock would yield the streams of repentance. Suddenly Jean
uttered a blood-curdling cry, like some hyena caught by the
hunters. Memories had awakened.

"No! no! no!" he cried, falling upon his knees. "I
want to live! Mother, take my place. Change clothes with
me. I could escape! Have pity! Have pity. Go to the
King and tell him——"

He stopped short, a horrible sound like the growl of a wild
beast broke from him; he clutched fiercely at the curé's
cassock.

"Go," M. Bonnet said in a low voice, turning to the two
women, who were quite overcome by this scene. Jean heard
the word, and lifted his head. He looked up at his mother
and sister, and kissed their feet.

"Let us say good-bye," he said. "Do not come back any
more. Leave me alone with M. Bonnet; and do not be
anxious about me now," he added, as he clasped his mother
and sister in a tight embrace, in which he seemed as though
he would fain put all the life that was in him.

"How can any one go through all this and live?" asked
Denise as they reached the wicket.

It was about eight o'clock in the evening when they separated. The Abbé de Rastignac was waiting at the gate of
the prison, and asked the two women for news.

"He will make his peace with God," said Denise. "If he
has not repented already, repentance is near at hand."

A few minutes later the bishop learned that the Church
would triumph in this matter, and that the condemned man

would go to his execution with the most edifying religious sentiments. The public prosecutor was with his lordship, who expressed a wish to see the curé. It was midnight before M. Bonnet came. The Abbé Gabriel, who had been going to and fro between the palace and the prison, considered that the bishop's carriage ought to be sent for him, for the poor man was so exhausted that he could scarcely stand. The thought of to-morrow's horrible journey, the anguish of soul which he had witnessed, the full and entire repentance of this member of his flock, who broke down completely at last when the great forecast of eternity was put before him—all these things had combined to wear out M. Bonnet's strength, for with his nervous temperament and electric swiftness of apprehension, he was quick to feel the sorrows of others as if they were his own.

Souls like this beautiful soul are so open to receive the impressions, the sorrows, passions, and sufferings of those towards whom they are drawn, that they feel the pain as if it were in very truth their own, and this in a manner which is torture ; for their clearer eyes can measure the whole extent of the misfortune in a way impossible to those blinded by the egoism of love or paroxysms of grief. In this respect such a confessor as M. Bonnet is an artist who feels, instead of an artist who judges.

In the drawing-room at the palace, where the two vicars-general, the public prosecutor, and M. de Granville, and the Abbé de Rastignac were waiting, it dawned upon M. Bonnet that he was expected to bring news.

"Monsieur le Curé," the bishop began, "have you obtained any confessions with which you may in confidence enlighten justice without failing in your duty ? "

" Before I gave absolution to that poor lost child, my lord, I was not content that his repentance should be as full and entire as the Church could require ; I still further insisted on the restitution of the money."

"I came here to the palace about that restitution," said the public prosecutor. "Some light will be thrown on obscure points in the case by the way in which it is made. He certainly has accomplices——"

"With the interests of man's justice I have no concern," the curé said. "I do not know how or where the restitution will be made, but made it will be. When my lord bishop summoned me here to one of my own parishioners, he replaced me in the exact conditions which give a curé in his own parish the rights which a bishop exercises in his diocese —ecclesiastical obedience and discipline apart."

"Quite right," said the bishop. "But the point is to obtain a voluntary confession before justice from the condemned man."

"My mission was simply to bring a soul to God," returned M. Bonnet.

M. de Grancour shrugged his shoulders slightly, and the Abbé Dutheil nodded approval.

"Tascheron, no doubt, wants to screen some one whom a restitution would identify," said the public prosecutor.

"Monsieur," retorted the curé, "I know absolutely nothing which might either confirm or contradict your conjecture; and, moreover, the secrets of the confessional are inviolable."

"So the restitution will be made?" asked the man of law.

"Yes, monsieur," answered the man of God.

"That is enough for me," said the public prosecutor. He relied upon the cleverness of the police to find and follow up any clue, as if passion and personal interest were not keener-witted than any detective.

Two days later, on a market-day, Jean-François Tascheron went to his death in a manner which left all pious and politic souls nothing to desire. His humility and piety were exemplary; he kissed with fervor the crucifix which M. Bonnet held out to him with trembling hands. The unfortunate

man was closely scanned; all eyes were on the watch to
see the direction his glances might take; would he look up
at one of the houses, or gaze on some face in the crowd?
His discretion was complete and inviolable. He met his
death like a Christian, penitent and forgiven.

The poor curé of Montégnac was taken away unconscious
from the foot of the scaffold, though he had not so much as
set eyes on the fatal machine.

The next day at nightfall, three leagues away from Limoges,
out on the high-road, and in a lonely spot, Denise Tascheron
suddenly stopped. Exhausted though she was with physical
weariness and sorrow, she begged her father to allow her to
go back to Limoges with Louis-Marie Tascheron, one of her
brothers.

" What more do you want to do in that place ? " her father
asked sharply, raising his eyebrows, and frowning.

" We have not only to pay the lawyer, father," she said in
his ear; " there is something else. The money that he hid
must be given back."

" That is only right," said the rigorously honest man,
fumbling in a leather purse which he carried about him.

" No," Denise said swiftly, " he is your son no longer; and
those who blessed, not those who cursed him, ought to pay the
lawyer's fees."

" We will wait for you at Havre ? " her father said.

Denise and her brother crept into the town again before it
was day. Though the police learned later on that two of the
Tascherons had come back, they never could discover their
lodging. It was near four o'clock when Denise and her
brother went to the higher end of the town, stealing along
close to the walls. The poor girl dared not look up, lest the
eyes which should meet hers had seen her brother's head fall.
First of all, she had sought out M. Bonnet, and he, unwell
though he was, had consented to act as Denise's father and

guardian for the time being. With him they went to the
barrister, who lived in the Rue de la Comédie.

"Good-day, poor children," the lawyer began, with a bow
to M. Bonnet. "How can I be of use to you? Perhaps you
want me to make application for your brother's body."

"No, sir," said Denise, her tears flowing at the thought,
which had not occurred to her; "I have come to pay our
debt to you, in so far as money can repay an eternal debt."

"Sit down a moment," said the lawyer, seeing that Denise
and the curé were both standing. Denise turned away to draw
from her stays two notes of five hundred francs, pinned to her
shift. Then she sat down and handed over the bills to her
brother's counsel. The curé looked at the lawyer with a light
in his eyes, which soon filled with tears.

"Keep it," the barrister said; "keep the money yourself,
my poor girl. Rich people do not pay for a lost cause in this
generous way.

"I cannot do as you ask, sir, it is impossible," said Denise.

"Then the money does not come from you?" the barrister
asked quickly.

"Pardon me," she replied, with a questioning glance at
M. Bonnet—would God be angry with her for that lie?

The curé kept his eyes lowered.

"Very well," said the barrister, and, keeping one of the
notes in his hand, he gave the other to the curé, "then I will
divide it with the poor. And now, Denise, this is certainly
mine"—he held out the note as he spoke—"will you give me
your velvet ribbon and gold cross in exchange for it? I will
hang the cross above my chimney-piece in memory of the
purest and kindest girl's heart which I shall every meet with,
I doubt not, in my career."

"There is no need to buy it," cried Denise, "I will give
it you," and she took off her gilt cross and handed it to the
lawyer.

"Very well, sir," said the curé, "I accept the five hundred

francs to pay the expenses of exhuming and removing the poor boy's body to the churchyard at Montégnac. Doubtless God has forgiven him; Jean will rise again with all my flock at the Last Day, when the righteous as well as the penitent sinner will be summoned to sit at the Father's right hand."

"So be it," said the barrister. He took Denise's hand and drew her towards him to put a kiss on her forehead, a movement made with another end in view.

"My child," he said, "nobody at Montégnac has such a thing as a five-hundred franc-note; they are rather scarce in Limoges; people don't take them here without asking something for changing them. So this money has been given to you by somebody; you are not going to tell me who it was, and I do not ask you, but listen to this : if you have anything left to do here which has any reference to your poor brother, mind how you set about it. M. Bonnet and you and your brother will all three of you be watched by spies. People know that your family have gone away. If anybody recognizes you here, you will be surrounded before you suspect it."

"Alas!" she said, "I have nothing left to do here."

"She is cautious," said the lawyer to himself, as he went to the door with her. "She has been warned, so let her extricate herself."

It was late September, but the days were as hot as in the summer. The bishop was giving a dinner-party. The local authorities, the public prosecutor, and the first *avocat général* were among the guests. Discussions were started, which grew lively in the course of the evening, and it was very late before they broke up. Whist and backgammon, that game beloved of bishops, were the order of the day. It happened that about eleven o'clock the public prosecutor stepped out upon the upper terrace, and from the corner where he stood saw a light on the island, which the Abbé Gabriel and the bishop had already fixed upon as the central spot and clue to the inexplicable tangle about Tascheron's crime—on Véronique's

Isle of France in fact. There was no apparent reason why anybody should kindle a fire in the middle of the Vienne at that time of night—then, all at once, the idea which had struck the bishop and his secretary flashed-upon the public prosecutor's brain, with a light as sudden as that of the fire which shot up out of the distant darkness.

"What a set of great fools we have all been!" cried he, "but we have the accomplices now."

He went up to the drawing-room again, found out M. de Granville, and said a word or two in his ear; then both of them vanished. But the Abbé de Rastignac, courteously attentive, watched them go out, saw that they went towards the terrace, and noticed too that fire on the shore of the island.

"It is all over with her," thought he.

The messengers of justice arrived on the spot—too late. Denise and Louis-Marie (whom his brother Jean had taught to dive) were there, it is true, on the bank of the Vienne at a place pointed out by Jean; but Louis-Marie had already dived four times, and each time had brought up with him twenty thousand francs in gold. The first installment was secured in a bandana with the four corners tied up. As soon as the water had been wrung from the handkerchief, it was thrown on a great fire of dry sticks, kindled beforehand. A shawl contained the second, and the third was secured in a lawn handkerchief. Just as Denise was about to fling the fourth wrapper into the fire the police came up, accompanied by a commissary, and pounced upon a very important clue, as they thought, which Denise suffered them to seize without the slightest emotion. It was a man's pocket-handkerchief, which still retained some stains of blood in spite of its long immersion. Questioned forthwith as to her proceedings, Denise said that she had brought the stolen money out of the river, as her brother bade her. To the commissary, inquiring why she had burned the wrappings, she answered that she was following out her brother's instructions. Asked what the wrappings were, she replied boldly and with perfect truth, "A bandana handkerchief, a lawn handkerchief, and a shawl."

The handkerchief which had just been seized belonged to her brother.

This fishing expedition and the circumstances accompanying it made plenty of talk in Limoges. The shawl in particular confirmed the belief that there was a love affair at the bottom of Tascheron's crime.

"He is dead, but he shields her still," commented one lady, when she heard these final revelations, so cleverly rendered useless.

"Perhaps there is some married man in Limoges who will find that he is a bandana short, but he will perforce hold his tongue," said the public prosecutor, smilingly.

"Little mistakes in one's wardrobe have come to be so compromising, that I shall set about verifying mine this very evening," said old Mme. Perret, smiling too.

"Whose are the dainty little feet that left the footmarks, so carefully erased?" asked M. de Granville.

"Pshaw! perhaps they belong to some ugly woman," returned the *avocat général.*

"She has paid dear for her slip," remarked the Abbé de Grancour.

"Do you know what all this business goes to prove?" put in the *avocat général.* "It just shows how much women have lost through the Revolution, which obliterated social distinctions. Such a passion is only to be met with nowadays in a man who knows that there is an enormous distance between him and the woman he loves."

"You credit love with many vanities," returned the Abbé Dutheil.

"What does Mme. Graslin think?" asked the prefect.

"What would you have her think? She was confined, as she told me she would be, on the day of the execution, and has seen nobody since; she is dangerously ill," said M. de Granville.

Meanwhile, in another room in Limoges, an almost comic scene was taking place. The des Vanneaulx's friends were congratulating them upon the restitution of their inheritance.

"Well, well," said Mme. des Vanneaulx, "they ought to have let him off, poor man. It was love, and not mercenary motives, that brought him to it; he was neither vicious nor wicked."

"He behaved like a thorough gentleman," said the Sieur des Vanneaulx. "*If I knew where his family was, I would do something for them;* they are good people, those Tascherons."

When Mme. Graslin was well enough to rise, towards the end of the year 1829, after the long illness which followed her confinement, and obliged her to keep her bed in absolute solitude and quiet, she heard her husband speak of a rather considerable piece of business which he wanted to conclude. The Navarreins family thought of selling the forest of Montégnac and the waste lands which they owned in the neighborhood. Graslin had not yet put into execution a clause in his wife's marriage settlement, which required that her dowry should be invested in land; he had preferred to put her money out at interest through the bank, and already had doubled her capital. On this, Véronique seemed to recollect the name of Montégnac, and begged her husband to carry out the contract by purchasing the estate for her.

M. Graslin wished very much to see M. Bonnet, to ask for information concerning the forest and lands which the Duc de Navarreins thought of selling. The Duc de Navarreins, be it said, foresaw the hideous struggle which the Prince de Polignac had made inevitable between the Liberals and the Bourbon dynasty; and augured the worst, for which reasons he was one of the boldest opponents of the Coup d'État. The Duke had sent his man of business to Limoges with instructions to sell, if a bidder could be found for so large a sum of money, for his grace recollected the Revolution of 1789 too well not

9

to profit by the lessons then taught to the aristocracy. It was this man of business who, for more than a month, had been at close quarters with Graslin, the shrewdest old fox in Limousin, and the only man whom common report singled out as being able to pay down the price of so large an estate on the spot.

At a word sent by the Abbé Dutheil, M. Bonnet hastened to Limoges and the Hôtel Graslin. Véronique would have prayed the curé to dine with her; but the banker only allowed M. Bonnet to go up to his wife's room after he had kept him a full hour in his private office, and obtained information which satisfied him so well, that he concluded his purchase out of hand, and the forest and domain of Montégnac became his (Graslin's) for five hundred thousand francs. He acquiesced in his wife's wish, stipulating that this purchase and any outlay relating thereto should be held to accomplish the clause in her marriage contract as to her fortune. Graslin did this the more willingly because the piece of honesty now cost him nothing.

At the time of Graslin's purchase the estate consisted of the forest of Montégnac, some thirty thousand acres in extent, but too inaccessible to bring in any money, the ruined castle, the gardens, and some five thousand acres in the uncultivated plains under Montégnac. Graslin made several more purchases at once, so as to have the whole of the first peak of the Corrèzien range in his hands, for there the vast forest of Montégnac came to an end. Since the taxes had been levied upon it, the Duc de Navarreins had not drawn fifteen thousand francs a year from the manor, formerly one of the richest tenures in the kingdom. The lands had escaped sale when put up under the Convention, partly because of their barrenness, partly because it was a recognized fact that nothing could be made of them.

When the curé came face to face with the woman of whom he had heard, a woman whose cleverness and piety were well

known, he started in spite of himself. At this time Véronique
had entered upon the third period of her life, a period in
which she was to grow greater by the exercise of the loftiest
virtues, and become a totally different-woman. To the
Raphael's Madonna, hidden beneath the veil of smallpox
scars, a beautiful, noble, and impassioned woman had succeeded,
a woman afterwards laid low by inward sorrows, from which
a saint emerged. Her complexion had taken the sallow tint
seen in the austere faces of abbesses of ascetic life. A
yellowish hue had overspread the temples, grown less imperious
now. The lips were paler, the red of the opening pomegranate
flower had changed into the paler crimson of the Bengal rose.
Between the nose and the corners of the eyes sorrow had worn
two pearly channels, down which many tears had coursed in
secret ; much weeping had worn away the traces of smallpox.
It was impossible not to fix your eyes on the spot where a network of tiny blue veins stood out swollen and distended with
the full pulses that throbbed there, as if they fed the source
of many tears. The faint brownish tinge about the eyes alone
remained, but there were dark circles under them now, and
wrinkles in the eyelids which told of terrible suffering. The
lines in the hollow cheeks bore record of solemn thoughts.
The chin, too, had shrunk, it had lost its youthful fulness of
outline, and this scarcely to the advantage of a face which
wore an expression of pitiless austerity, confined, however,
solely to Véronique herself. At twenty-nine years of age her
hair, one of her greatest beauties, had faded and grown scanty ;
she had been obliged to pull out a large quantity of white
hair, bleached during her confinement. Her thinness was
shocking to see. In spite of the doctor's orders, she had persisted in nursing the child herself; and the doctor was not
disposed to let people forget this when all his evil prognosti-
cations were so thoroughly fulfilled.

"See what a difference a single confinement has made in a
woman !" said he. "And she worships that child of hers ;

but I have always noticed that the more a child costs the
mother, the dearer it is."

All that remained of youth in Véronique's face lay in her
eyes, wan though they were.   An untamed fire flashed from
the dark blue iris; all the life that had deserted the cold impassive mask of a face, expressionless now save for the charitable look which it wore when her poorer neighbors were
spoken of, seemed to have taken refuge there.   So the curé's
first dismay and surprise abated somewhat as he went on to
explain to her how much good a resident landowner might effect
in Montégnac, and for a moment Véronique's face grew beautiful, lighted up by this unexpected hope which began to shine
in upon her.

"I will go there," she said.   "It shall be my property.   I
will ask M. Graslin to put some funds at my disposal, and I
will enter into your charitable work with all my might.
Montégnac shall be cultivated; we will find water somewhere
to irrigate the waste land in the plain.   You are striking the
rock, like Moses, and tears will flow from it!"

The curé of Montégnac spoke of Mme. Graslin as a saint
when his friends in Limoges asked him about her.

The very day after the purchase was completed, Graslin
sent an architect to Montégnac.   He was determined to restore
the castle, the gardens, terraces, and park, to reclaim the
forest by a plantation, putting an ostentatious activity into all
that he did.

Two years later a great misfortune befell Mme. Graslin.
Her husband, in spite of his prudence, was involved in the
commercial and financial disasters of 1830.   The thought of
bankruptcy, or of losing three millions, the gains of a lifetime of toil, were both intolerable to him.   The worry and
anxiety aggravated the inflammatory disease, always lurking
in his system, the result of impure blood.   He was compelled
to take to his bed.   In Véronique a friendly feeling towards
Graslin had developed during her pregnancy, and dealt a fatal

blow to the hopes of her admirer, M. de Granville.   By careful nursing she tried to save her husband's life, but only succeeded in prolonging a suffering existence for a few months.
This respite, however, was very useful to Grossetête, who,
foreseeing the end, consulted with his old comrade, and made
all the necessary arrangements for a prompt realization.

In April, 1831, Monsieur Graslin died, and his widow's despairing grief only sobered down into Christian resignation.
From the first Véronique had wished to give up her whole
fortune to her husband's creditors ; but M. Graslin's estate
proved to be more than sufficient.   It was Grossetête who
wound up his affairs, and two months after the settlement
Mme. Graslin found herself the mistress of the domains of
Montégnac and of six hundred and sixty thousand francs, all
her own ; and no blot rested on her son's name.   No one
had lost anything through Graslin—not even his wife ; and
Francis Graslin had about a hundred thousand francs.

Then M. de Granville, who had reason to know Véronique's
nature and loftiness of soul, came forward as a suitor ; but, to
the amazement of all Limoges, Mme. Graslin refused the
newly-appointed public prosecutor, on the ground that second
marriages were discountenanced by the Church.   Grossetête,
a man of unerring forecast and sound sense, advised Véronique to invest the rest of M. Graslin's fortune and her own
in the Funds, and effected this himself for her at once, in the
month of July, when the three per cents. stood at fifty.   So
Francis had an income of six thousand livres, and his mother
about forty thousand.   Véronique's was still the greatest fortune in the department.

All was settled at last, and Mme. Graslin gave out that she
meant to leave Limoges to live nearer to M. Bonnet.   Again
she sent for the curé, to consult him about his work at Montégnac, in which she was determined to share ; but he generously tried to dissuade her, and to make it clear to her that
her place was in society.

"I have sprung from the people, and I mean to return to them," said she.

The curé's great love for his own village resisted the more feebly when he learned that Mme. Graslin had arranged to make over her house in Limoges to M. Grossetête. Certain sums were due to the banker, and he took the house at its full value in settlement.

Mme. Graslin finally left Limoges towards the end of August, 1831. A troop of friends gathered about her, and went with her as far as the outskirts of the town; some of them went the whole first stage of the journey. Véronique traveled in a calèche with her mother; the Abbé Dutheil, recently appointed to a bishopric, sat opposite them with old M. Grossetête. As they went through the Place d'Aine, Véronique's emotion was almost uncontrollable; her face contracted; every muscle quivered with the pain; she snatched up her child, and held him tightly to her in a convulsive grasp, while La Sauviat tried to cover her emotion by following her example— it seemed that La Sauviat was not unprepared for something of this kind.

Chance so ordered it that Mme. Graslin caught a glimpse of the house where her father had lived; she clutched Mme. Sauviat's hand, great tears filled her eyes and rolled down her cheeks. When Limoges was fairly left behind, she turned and took a last farewell glance; and all her friends noticed a certain look of happiness in her face. When the public prosecutor, the young man of five-and-twenty whom she had declined to marry, came up and kissed her hand with lively expressions of regret, the newly-made bishop noticed something strange in Véronique's eyes: the dark pupils dilated till the blue became a thin ring about them. It was unmistakable that some violent revulsion took place within her.

"Now I shall never see him again," she said in her mother's ear, but there was not the slightest trace of feeling in the impassive old face as Mme. Sauviat received that confidence.

Grossetête, the shrewd old banker, sitting opposite, watching the women with keen eyes, had not discovered that Véronique hated this man, whom for that matter she received as a visitor. In things of this kind a churchman is far clearer-sighted than other men, and the bishop surprised Véronique by a glance that revealed an ecclesiastic's perspicacity.

"You have no regret in leaving Limoges?" the bishop said to Mme. Graslin.

"You are leaving the town," she replied. "And M. Grossetête scarcely ever comes among us now," she added, with a smile for her old friend as he said good-bye.

The bishop went the whole of the way to Montégnac with Véronique.

"I ought to have made this journey in mourning," she said in her mother's ear as they walked up the hill near Saint-Léonard.

The old woman turned her crabbed, wrinkled face, and laid her finger on her lips; then she pointed to the bishop, who was giving the child a terrible scrutiny. Her mother's gesture first, and yet more the significant expression in the bishop's eyes, made Mme. Graslin shudder. The light died out of her face as she looked out across the wide gray stretch of plain before Montégnac, and melancholy overcame her. All at once she saw the curé coming to meet her, and made him take a seat in the carriage.

"This is your domain," said M. Bonnet, indicating the level waste.

IV

MADAME GRASLIN AT MONTÉGNAC.

In a few moments the township of Montégnac came in sight; the hillside and the conspicuous new buildings upon it shone golden in the light of the sunset; it was a lovely landscape like an oasis in the desert, with a picturesque charm of its own, due to the contrast with its setting. Mme. Graslin's eyes began to fill with tears. The curé pointed out a broad white track like a scar on the hillside.

"That is what my parishioners have done to show their gratitude to their lady of the manor," he said. "We can drive the whole way to the château. The road is finished now, and has not cost you a sou; we shall put in a row of trees beside it in two months' time. My lord bishop can imagine how much toil, thought, and devotion went to the making of such a change."

"And they have done this themselves!" said the bishop.

"They would take nothing in return, my lord. The poorest lent a hand, for they all knew that one who would be like a mother to them was coming to live among us."

There was a crowd at the foot of the hill, all the village was there. Guns were fired off, and mortars exploded, and then the two prettiest girls of Montégnac, in white dresses, came to offer flowers and fruit to Mme. Graslin.

"That I should be welcomed here like this!" she cried, clutching M. Bonnet's hand as if she felt that she was falling over a precipice.

The crowd went up as far as the great iron gateway, whence Mme. Graslin could see her château. At first sight the splendor of her dwelling was a shock to her. Stone for building is scarce in this district, for the native granite is

(136)

hard and exceedingly difficult to work; so Graslin's architect had used brick for the main body of the great building, there being plenty of brick earth in the forest of Montégnac, and wood for the felling. All the woodwork and stone, in fact, came also from the forest and the quarries in it. But for these economies, Graslin must have been put to a ruinous expense; but as it was, the principal outlay was for wages, carriage, and salaries, and the money circulating in the township had put new life into it.

At a first glance the château stood up a huge red mass, scored with dark lines of mortar, and outlined with gray, for the facings and quoins and the string courses along each story were of granite, each block being cut in facets diamond fashion. The surface of the brick walls round the courtyard (a sloping oval like the courtyard of Versailles) was broken by slabs of granite surrounded by bosses, and set at equal distances. Shrubs had been planted under the walls, with a view to obtaining the contrasts of their various foliage. Two handsome iron gateways gave access on the one hand to the terrace which overlooked Montégnac, and on the other to a farm and outbuildings. The great gateway at the summit of the new road, which had just been finished, had a neat lodge on either side, built in the style of the sixteenth century.

The façade of the château fronted the courtyard and faced the west. It consisted of three towers, the central tower being connected with the one on either side of it by two wings. The back of the house was precisely similar, and looked over the gardens towards the east. There was but one window in each tower on the side of the courtyard and gardens, each wing having three. The centre tower was built something after the fashion of a campanile, the corner-stones were vermiculated, and here some delicate sculptured work had been sparingly introduced. Art is timid in the provinces; and though in 1829 some progress had been made in architectural ornament (thanks to certain writers), the owners of houses shrank at that time from an expense which lack of competition and scarcity of craftsmen rendered somewhat formidable.

The tower at either end (three windows in depth) was crowned by a high-pitched roof, with a granite balustrade by way of decoration ; each angle of the pyramid was sharply cut by an elegant balcony lined with lead, and surrounded by cast-iron railings, and an elegantly sculptured window occupying each side of the roof. All the door and window cornices on each story were likewise ornamented with carved work copied from Genoese palace fronts. The three side windows of the southern tower looked out over Montégnac, the northern gave a view of the forest.

From the eastern windows you could see beyond the gardens that part of Montégnac where the Tascherons had lived, and far down below in the valley the road which led to the chief town in the arrondissement. From the west front, which faced towards the courtyard, you saw the wide map of the plain stretching away on the Montégnac side to the mountains of the Corrèze, and elsewhere to the circle of the horizon, where it blended with the sky.

The wings were low, the single story being built in the mansard roof, in the old French style, but the towers at either end rose a story higher. The central tower was crowned by a sort of flattened dome like the clock towers of the Tuileries or the Louvre ; the single room in the turret was a sort of belvedere, and fitted with a turret-clock. Ridge tiles had been used for economy's sake ; the massive balks of timber from the forest readily carried the enormous weight of the roof.

Graslin's " folly," as he called the château, had brought five hundred thousand francs into the commune. He had planned the road before he died, and the commune out of gratitude had finished it. Montégnac had, moreover, grown considerably. Behind the stables and outbuildings, on the north side of the hill where it slopes gradually down into the plain, Graslin had begun to build the steadings of a farm on a large scale, which showed that he had meant to turn the waste land in the plain to account. The plantations considered indispensable by M. Bonnet were still proceeding under the direction of a head gardener with six men, who were lodged in the outbuildings.

The whole ground floor of the château, taken up by sitting-rooms, had been splendidly furnished, but the second story was rather bare, M. Graslin's death having suspended the upholsterer's operations.

"Ah! my lord," said Mme. Graslin, turning to the bishop, after they had been through the château, "I had thought to live here in a thatched cottage. Poor M. Graslin committed many follies——"

"And you——" the bishop added, after a pause, and Mme. Graslin's light shudder did not escape him—"*you* are about to do charitable deeds, are you not?"

She went to her mother, who held little Francis by the hand, laid her hand on the old woman's arm, and went with the two as far as the long terrace which rose above the church and the parsonage ; all the houses in the village, rising stepwise up the hillside, could be seen at once. The curé took possession of M. Dutheil, and began to point out the various features of the landscape ; but the eyes of both ecclesiastics soon turned to the terrace, where Véronique and her mother stood motionless as statues ; the older woman took out a handkerchief and wiped her eyes, her daughter leaned upon the balustrade, and seemed to be pointing out the church below.

"What is the matter, madame?" the Curé Bonnet asked, turning to La Sauviat.

"Nothing," answered Mme. Graslin, coming towards the two priests and facing them. "I did not know that the churchyard would be right under my eyes——"

"You can have it removed ; the law is on your side."

" *The law !* " the words broke from her like a cry of pain.

Again the bishop looked at Véronique. But she—tired of meeting that sombre glance, which seemed to lay bare the soul and discover her secret in its depths, a secret buried in a grave in that churchyard—cried out—

"Very well, then—*yes !* "

The bishop laid his hand over his eyes, so overwhelmed by this, that for some moments he stood lost in thought.

"Hold her up," cried the old mother; "she is turning pale."

"The air here is so keen, I have taken a chill," murmured Mme. Graslin, and she sank fainting as the two ecclesiastics caught her in their arms. They carried her into the house, and when she came to herself again she saw the bishop and the curé kneeling in prayer for her.

"May the angel which has visited you ever stay beside you !" the bishop said, as he gave her his blessing. "Adieu, my daughter."

Mme. Graslin burst into tears at the words.

"Is she really saved?" cried the old mother.

"In this world and in the next," the bishop turned to answer, as he left the room.

Mme. Graslin had been carried by her mother's orders to a room on the first floor of the southern tower; the windows looked out upon the churchyard and the south side of Montégnac. Here she chose to remain, and installed herself there as best she could with her maid Aline, and little Francis. Mme. Sauviat's room naturally was near her daughter's.

It was some days before Mme. Graslin recovered from the cruel agitation which prostrated her on the day of her arrival, and, moreover, her mother insisted that she must stay in bed in the morning. In the evening, however, Véronique came to sit on a bench on the terrace, and looked down on the church and parsonage and into the churchyard. In spite of mute opposition on Mme. Sauviat's part, Véronique contracted a habit of always sitting in the same place and giving way to melancholy broodings; it was almost a mania.

"Madame is dying," Aline said to the old mother.

At last the two women spoke to the curé; and he, good man, who had shrunk from intruding himself upon Mme. Graslin, came assiduously to see her when he learned that she was suffering from some malady of the soul, carefully timing his visits so that he always found Véronique and the child, both in mourning, out on the terrace. The country was already beginning to look dreary and sombre in the early days of October.

When Véronique first came to the château, M. Bonnet had seen at once that she was suffering from some hidden wound, but he thought it better to wait until his future penitent should give him her confidence. One evening, however, he saw an expression in Mme. Graslin's eyes that warned him to hesitate no longer—the dull apathy of a mind brooding over the thought of death. He set himself to check the progress of this cruel disease of the mind.

At first there was a sort of struggle between them, a fence of empty words, each of them striving to disguise their thoughts. The evening was chilly, but for all that Véronique sat out on the granite bench with little Francis on her knee. She could not see the churchyard, for Mme. Sauviat, leaning against the parapet, deliberately shut it out from sight. Aline stood waiting to take the child indoors. It was the seventh time that the curé had found Véronique there on the terrace. He spoke—

"I used to think that you were merely sad, madame, but," and he lowered his voice and spoke in her ear, "this is despair. Despair, Madame Graslin, is neither Christian nor is it Catholic."

"Oh!" she exclaimed, with an intent glance at the sky, and a bitter smile stole over her lips, "what would the church leave to a damned soul, if not despair?"

Her words revealed to the curé how far this soul had been laid waste.

"Ah! you are making for yourself a hell out of this hillside, when it should rather be a calvary whence your soul might lift itself up towards heaven."

"I am too humble now," she said, "to put myself on such a pedestal," and her tone was a revelation of the depth of her self-scorn.

Then a sudden light flashed across the curé—one of the inspirations which come so often and so naturally to noble and pure souls who live with God. He took up the child and kissed him on the forehead. "Poor little one!" he said, in a fatherly voice, and gave the child to the nurse, who took him away. Mme. Sauviat looked at her daughter, and saw how powerfully those words had wrought on her, for Véronique's eyes, long dry, were wet with tears. Then she too went, with a sign to the priest.

"Will you take a walk on the terrace?" suggested M. Bonnet when they were alone. "You are in my charge; I am accountable to God for your sick soul," and they went towards the end of the terrace above "Tascherons'."

"Leave me to recover from my prostration," she said.

"Your prostration is the result of pernicious broodings."

"Yes," she said, with the naïveté of pain, too sorely troubled to fence any longer.

"I see," he answered; "you have sunk into the depths of indifference. If physical pain passes a certain point it extinguishes modesty, and so it is with mental anguish, it reaches a degree when the soul grows faint within us; I know."

Véronique was not prepared for this subtle observation and tender pity in M. Bonnet; but as has been seen already, the quick sympathies of a heart unjaded by emotion of its own had taught him to detect and feel the pain of others among his flock with the maternal instinct of a woman. This apostolic tenderness, this *mens divinior*, raises the priest above his fellow-men and makes of him a being divine. Mme. Graslin had not as yet looked deep enough into the curé's nature to discover the beauty hidden away in that soul, the source of its grace and freshness and its inner life.

"Ah! monsieur——" she began, and a glance and a gesture, such a gesture and glance as the dying give, put her secret into his keeping.

"I understand!" he answered. "But what then? What is to be done?"

Silently they went along the terrace towards the plain. To the bearer of good-tidings, the son of Christ, the solemn moment seemed propitious.

"Suppose that you stood now before the Throne of God," he said, and his voice grew low and mysterious, "what would you say to Him?"

Mme. Graslin stopped short as if thunderstruck; a light shudder ran through her.

"I should say to Him as Christ said, 'My Father, Thou hast forsaken me!'" she answered simply. The tones of her voice brought tears to the curé's eyes.

"Oh Magdalen, those are the very words I was waiting to hear!" he exclaimed, unable to refuse his admiration. "You see, you appeal to God's justice! Listen, madame, religion is the rule of God before the time. The church reserves the right of judgment in all that concerns the soul. Man's justice is but the faint image of God's justice, a pale shadow of the eternal adapted to the temporal needs of society."

"What do you mean?"

"You are not judge in your own cause, you are amenable to God; you have no right to condemn nor to pardon yourself. God is the great reviser of judgments, my daughter."

"Ah!" she cried.

"He *sees* to the origin of all things, while we only see the things themselves."

Again Véronique stopped. These ideas were new to her.

"To a soul as lofty as yours," he went on courageously, "I do not speak as to my poor parishioners; I owe it to you to use a different language. You who have so cultivated your mind can rise to the knowledge of the spirit of the Catholic religion, which words and symbols must express and make visible to the eyes of babes and the poor. Follow what I am about to say carefully, for it refers to you; and if the point of view which I take for the moment seems wide, it is none the less your own case which I am considering, and now about to make clear to your understanding.

"Justice, devised for the protection of society, is based upon a theory of the equality of individuals. Society, which is nothing but an aggregation of facts, is based on *inequality*. So there is a fundamental discrepancy between justice and fact. Should the law exercise a restraining or encouraging influence on the progress of society? In other words, should the law oppose itself to the internal tendency of society, so as to maintain things as they are; or, on the other hand, should the law be more flexible, adapt itself, and keep pace with the tendency so as to guide it? No maker of laws since men began to live together has taken it upon himself to decide that problem. All legislators have been content to analyze facts, to indicate those which seemed to them to be blameworthy or criminal, and to prescribe punishments or rewards. Such is law as man has made it. It is powerless to prevent evil-doing; powerless no less to prevent offenders who have been punished from offending again.

"Philanthropy is a sublime error. Philanthropy vainly applies severe discipline to the body, while it cannot find the balm which heals the soul. Philanthropy conceives projects, sets forth theories, and leaves mankind to carry them out by means of silence, work, and discipline—dumb methods, with no virtue in them. Religion knows nought of these imperfections; for her, life extends beyond this world; for religion, we are all of us fallen creatures in a state of degradation, and it is this very view of mankind which opens out to us an inexhaustible treasure of indulgence. All of us are on the way to our complete regeneration, some of us are farther advanced, and some less, but none of us are infallible; the church is prepared for sins, aye, and even for crimes. In a criminal, society sees an individual to be cut off from its midst, but the church sees in him a soul to be saved. And more, far more!—— Inspired by God, whose dealings with man she watches and ponders, the church admits our inequality as human beings, and takes the disproportionate burden into account, and we who are so unequal in heart, in body or mind, in courage or aptitude, are made equal by repentance. In this, madame, equality is no empty word ; we can be, and are, all equal through our sentiments.

"One idea runs through all religions, from the uncouth fetichism of the savage to the graceful imaginings of the Greek and the profound and ingenious doctrines of India and Egypt, an idea that finds expression in all cults joyous or gloomy, a conviction of man's fall and of his sin, whence, everywhere, the idea of sacrifice and redemption.

"The death of the Redeemer, who died for the whole human race, is for us a symbol ; this, too, we must do for ourselves ; we must redeem our errors !—redeem our sins !—redeem our crimes ! There is no sin beyond redemption—all Catholicism lies in that. It is the wherefore of the holy sacraments which assist in the work of grace and sustain the repentant sinner. And though one should weep, madame, and sigh like the Magdalen in the desert, this is but the beginning—an action is the end. The monasteries wept, but acted too ; they prayed, but they civilized ; they were the active practical spreaders of our divine religion. They built, and planted, and tilled Europe ; they rescued the treasures of learning for us ; to them we owe the preservation of our jurisprudence, our traditions of statecraft and art. The sites of those centres of light will be for ever remembered in Europe

10

with gratitude.   Most modern towns sprang up about a monastery.

"If you believe that God is to judge you, the church, using my voice, tells you that there is no sin beyond redemption through the good works of repentance.   The evil we have wrought is weighed against the good that we have done by the great hands of God.   Be yourself a monastery here ; it is within your power to work miracles once more.   For you, work must be prayer.   Your work should be to diffuse happiness among those above whom you have been set by your fortune and your intellect, and in all ways, even by your natural position, for the height of your château above the village is a visible expression of your social position."

They were turning towards the plains as he spoke, so that the curé could point out the village on the lower slopes of the hill and the château towering above it.   It was half-past four in the afternoon.   A shaft of yellow sunlight fell across the terrace and the gardens ; it lighted up the château and brought out the pattern of the gleaming gilt scroll-work on the corner balconies high up on the towers ; it lit the plain which stretched into the distance divided by the road, a sober gray ribbon with no embroidery of trees as yet to outline a waving green border on either side.   Véronique and M. Bonnet passed the end of the château and came into the court-yard, beyond which the stables and barn buildings lay in sight, and farther yet, the forest of Montégnac ; the sunlight slid across the landscape like a lingering caress.   Even when the last glow of the sunset had faded except from the highest hills, it was still light enough in the plain below to see all the chance effects of color in the splendid tapestry of an autumn forest spread between Montégnac and the first peak of the chain of the Corrèze.   The oak trees stood out like masses of Florentine bronze among the verdigris greens of the walnuts and chestnuts ; the leaves of a few trees, the first to change, shone like gold among the others ; and all these different shades of color were emphasized by the gray patches of bare earth. The trunks of leafless trees looked like pale columns; and every tint, red, tawny, and gray, picturesquely blended in the pale October sunshine, made a harmony of color with the fertile lowland, where the vast fallows were green as stagnant water. Not a tree stirred, not a bird—death in the plain, silence in the forest; a thought in the priest's mind, as yet unuttered, was to be the sole comment on that dumb beauty. A streak of smoke rose here and there from the thatched roofs of the village. The château seemed sombre as its mistress' mood, for there is a mysterious law of uniformity, in virtue of which the house takes its character from the dominant nature within it, a subtle presence which hovers throughout. The sense of the curé's words had reached Mme. Graslin's brain; they had gone to her heart with all the force of conviction; the angelic resonance of his voice had stirred her tenderness; she stopped suddenly short. The curé stretched his arm out towards the forest; Véronique looked at him.

"Do you not see a dim resemblance between this and the life of humanity? His own fate for each of us! And what unequal lots there are among that mass of trees. Those on the highest ground have poorer soil and less water; they are the first to die——"

"And some are *cut down in the grace of their youth by some woman* gathering wood!" she said bitterly.

"Do not give way to those feelings again," he answered firmly, but with indulgence in his manner. "The forest has not been cut down, and that has been its ruin. Do you see something yonder there among the dense forest?"

Véronique could scarcely distinguish between the usual and unusual in a forest, but she obediently looked in the required direction, and then timidly at the curé.

"Do you not observe," he said, seeing in that glance that Véronique did not understand, "that there are strips where all the trees of every kind are still green?"

" Oh, so there are ! " she cried.   "How is it ?"

" In those strips of green lies a fortune for Montégnac and for you—a vast fortune, as I pointed out to M. Graslin. You can see three furrows; those are three valleys, the streams there are lost in the torrent-bed of the Gabou.   The Gabou is the boundary line between us and the next commune. All through September and October it is dry, but when November comes it will be full.   All that water runs to waste ; but it would be easy to make one or two weirs across from side to side of the valley to keep back the water (as Riquet did at Saint-Ferréol, where there are huge reservoirs which supply the Languedoc canal); and it would be easy to increase the volume of the water by turning several little streams in the forest into the river.   Wisely distributing it as required, by means of sluices and irrigation trenches, the whole plain can be brought into cultivation, and the overflow, besides, could be turned into our little river.

"You will have fine poplars along all the channels, and you will raise cattle in the finest possible meadows.   What is grass but water and sun ?   You could grow corn in the plain, there is quite enough depth of earth ; with so many trenches there will be moisture to enrich the soil ; the poplar trees will flourish along the channels and attract the rain-clouds, and the fields will absorb the principles of the rain : these are the secrets of the luxuriant greenness of the valleys.   Some day you will see life and joy and stir instead of this prevailing silence and barren dreariness.   Will not this be a noble prayer?   Will not these things occupy your idleness better than melancholy broodings?"

Véronique grasped the curé's hand, and made but a brief answer, but that answer was grand—

"It shall be done, monsieur."

"You have a conception of this great thing," he began again, " but you will not carry it out yourself.   Neither you nor I have knowledge enough for the realization of a thought

which might occur to any one, but that raises immense practical difficulties ; for simple and almost invisible as those difficulties are, they call for the most accurate skill of science.
So to-morrow begin your search for the human instruments
which, in a . dozen years' time, will contrive that the six
thousand acres thus brought into cultivation shall yield you
an income of six or seven thousand louis d'or. The undertaking will make Montégnac one of the richest communes in
the department some day. The forest brings in nothing as
yet ; but sooner or later buyers will come here for the splendid
timber, treasures slowly accumulated by time, the only treasures which man cannot procure save by patient waiting,
and cannot do without. Perhaps some day (who knows)
the government will take steps to open up ways of transporting
timber grown here to its dockyards ; but the government will
wait until Montégnac is ten times its present size before giving '
its fostering aid ; for the government, like fortune, gives only
to those who have. By that time this estate will be one of
the finest in France ; it will be the pride of your grandson,
who may possibly find the château too small in proportion to
his income."

" That is a future for me to live for," said Véronique.

" Such a work might redeem many errors," said the curé.

Seeing that he was understood, he endeavored to send a
last shaft home by way of her intelligence ; he had divined
that in the woman before him the heart could only be reached
through the brain ; whereas, in other women, the way to the
brain lies through the heart.

" Do you know what a great mistake you are making ? "
he asked, after a pause.

She looked at him with frightened eyes.

" Your repentance as yet is only the consciousness of a
defeat. If there is anything fearful, it is the despair of Satan ;
and perhaps man's repentance was like this before Jesus Christ
came on earth. But for us Catholics, repentance is the horror

which seizes on a soul hurrying on its downward course, and in that shock God reveals Himself. You are like a Pagan Orestes; become a Saint Paul!"

"Your words have just wrought a complete change in me," she cried. "Now, oh! I want to live!"

"The spirit has overcome," the humble priest said to himself, as he went away, glad at heart. He had found food for the secret despair which was gnawing Mme. Graslin, by giving to her repentance the form of a good and noble deed.

The very next day, therefore, Véronique wrote to M. Grossetête, and in answer to her letter three saddle-horses arrived from Limoges for her in less than a week. M. Bonnet made inquiries, and sent the postmaster's son to the château; the young fellow, Maurice Champion by name, was only too pleased to put himself at Mme. Graslin's disposal, with a chance of earning some fifty crowns. Véronique took a liking for the lad—round-faced, black-eyed, and black-haired, short, and well built—and he was at once installed as groom; he was to ride out with his mistress and to take charge of the horses.

The head forester at Montégnac was a native of Limoges, an old quartermaster in the Royal Guard. He had been transferred from another estate when the Duc de Navarreins began to think of selling the Montégnac lands, and wanted information to guide him in the matter; but in Montégnac forest Jerome Colorat only saw waste land, never likely to come under cultivation, timber valueless for lack of means of transport, gardens run wild, and a castle in ruins, calling for a vast outlay if it was to be set in order and made habitable. He saw wide rock-strewn spaces and conspicuous gray patches of granite even in the forest, and the honest but unintelligent servant took fright at these things. This was how the property had come into the market.

Mme. Graslin sent for this forester.

"Colorat," she said, "I shall most probably ride out to-

morrow morning and every following day. You should know
the different bits of outlying land which M. Graslin added to
the estate, and you must point them out to me; I want to see
everything for myself."

The servants at the château were delighted at this change
in Véronique's life. Aline found out her mistress' old black
riding habit, and mended it, without being told to do so, and
next morning, with inexpressible pleasure, Mme. Sauviat saw
her daughter dressed for a riding excursion. With Champion
and the forester as her guides, Mme. Graslin set herself first
of all to climb the heights. She wanted to understand the
position of the slopes and the glens, the natural roadways
cleft in the long ridge of the mountain. She would measure
her task, study the course of the streams, and see the rough
material of the curé's schemes. The forester and Champion
were often obliged to consult their memories, for the mountain paths were scarcely visible in that wild country. Colorat
went in front, and Champion followed a few paces from
her side.

So long as they kept in the denser forest, climbing and
descending the continual undulations of a French mountain
district, its wonders filled Véronique's mind. The mighty
trees which had stood for centuries amazed her, until she saw
so many that they ceased to be a surprise. Then others succeeded, full grown and ready for felling; or in a forest clearing some single pine risen to giant height; or, stranger still,
some common shrub, a dwarf growth elsewhere, here risen,
under some unusual conditions, to the height of a tree nearly
as old as the soil in which it grew. The wreaths of mist
rolling over the bare rocks filled her with indescribable feelings. Higher yet, pale furrows cut by the melting snows
looked like scars far up on the mountain sides; there were
bleak ravines in which no plant grew, hillside slopes where
the soil had been washed away, leaving bare the rock-clefts,
where the hundred-year-old chestnuts grew straight and tall as

pines in the Alps; sometimes they went by vast shifting sands, or boggy places where the trees are few; by fallen masses of granite, overhanging crags, dark glens, wide stretches of burnt grass or moor, where the heather was still in bloom, arid and lonely spots where the caper grows and the juniper, then through meadows covered with fine short grass, where the rich alluvial soil had been brought down and deposited century after century by the mountain torrents; in short, this rapid ride gave her something like a bird's-eye view of the land, a glimpse of the dreariness and grandeur, the strength and sweetness of nature's wilder moods in the mountain country of midland France.   And by dint of gazing at these pictures so various in form, but instinct with the same thought, the deep sadness expressed by the wild ruined land in its barrenness and neglect passed into her own thoughts, and found a response in her secret soul.   As, through some gap in the woods, she looked down on the gray stretch of plain below, or when their way led up some parched ravine where a few stunted shrubs starved among the boulders and the sand, by sheer reiteration of the same sights she fell under the influence of this stern scenery; it called up new ideas in her mind, stirred to a sense of the significance underlying these outward and visible forms.   There is no spot in a forest but has this inner sense, not a clearing, not a thicket, but has an analogy in the labyrinth of the human thought.

Who is there with a thinking brain or a wounded heart that can pass through a forest and find the forest dumb?   Before you are aware its voice is in your ears, a soothing or an awful voice, but more often soothing than awful.   And if you were to examine very closely into the causes of this sensation, this solemn, incomplex, subduing, and mysterious forest-influence that comes over you, perhaps you will find its source in the sublime and subtle effect of the presence of so many creatures all obedient to their destinies, immovable in submission.   Sooner or later the overwhelming sense of the abidingness of nature fills your heart and stirs deeper feelings, until at length you grow restless to find God in it. And so it was that the silence of the mountain heights about her, out in the pure clear air with the forest scents in it, Véronique recovered, as she told M. Bonnet in the evening, the certainty of Divine mercy. She had glimpses of the possibility of an order of things above and beyond that in which her musings had hitherto revolved. She felt something like happiness. For a long time past she had not known such peace. Could it have been that she was conscious of a certain likeness between this country and the waste and dried-up places in her own soul? Did she look with a certain exultation on the troubles of nature with some thought that matter was punished here for no sin? Certain it is that her inner self was strongly stirred.

More than once Colorat and Champion looked at her, and then at each other, as if for them she was transfigured. One spot in particular that they reached in the steep bed of a dry torrent seemed to Véronique to be unspeakably arid. It was with a certain surprise that she found herself longing to hear the sound of falling water in those scorching ravines.

"Always to love!" she thought. The words seemed like a reproach spoken aloud by a voice. In confusion she urged her horse blindly up towards the summit of the mountain of the Corrèze, and in spite of her guides dashed up to the top (called the Living Rock), and stood there alone. For several moments she scanned the whole country below her. She had heard the secret voices of so many existences asking to live, and now something took place within her that determined her to devote herself to this work with all the perseverance which she had already displayed to admiration. She tied her horse's bridle to a tree and sat down on a slab of rock. Her eyes wandered over the land where nature showed herself so harsh a step-dame, and felt within her own heart something of the mother's yearning which she had felt over her child. Her half-unconscious meditations, which, to use her own beautiful metaphor, "had sifted her heart," had prepared her to receive the sublime teaching of the scene that lay before her.

"It was then," she told the curé, "that I understood that our souls need to be tilled quite as much as the land."

The pale November sunlight shone over the wide landscape, but already a few gray clouds were gathering, driven across the sky by a cold west wind. It was now about three o'clock. Véronique had taken four hours to reach the point; but, as is the wont of those who are gnawed by profound inward misery, she gave no heed to anything without. At that moment her life shared the sublime movement of nature and dilated within her.

"Do not stay up there any longer, madame," said a man's voice, and something in its tone thrilled her. "You cannot reach home again in any direction if you do, for the nearest house lies a couple of leagues away, and it is impossible to find your way through the forest in the dark. And even those risks are nothing compared with the risk you are running where you are; in a few moments it will be deadly cold on the peak; no one knows the why or wherefore, but it has been the death of many a one before now."

Mme. Graslin, looking down, saw a face almost black with sunburn, and two eyes that gleamed from it like tongues of fire. A shock of brown hair hung on either side of the face, and a long pointed beard wagged beneath it. The owner of the face respectfully raised one of the great broad-brimmed hats which the peasantry wear in the midland districts of France, and displayed a bald but magnificent brow, such as sometimes in a poor man compels the attention of passers-by. Véronique felt not the slightest fear; for a woman in such a position as hers, all the petty considerations which cause feminine tremors have ceased to exist.

"How did you come there?" she asked him.

"I live here, hard by," the stranger answered.

"And what do you do in this out-of-the-way place?" asked Véronique.

"I live in it."

"But how, and on what do you live?"

"They pay me a trifle for looking after this part of the forest," he said, pointing to the slopes of the peak opposite the plains of Montégnac. As he moved, Mme. Graslin caught sight of a game-bag and the muzzle of a gun, and any mis-givings she might have entertained vanished forthwith.

"Are you a keeper?"

"No, madame. You can't be a keeper until you have been sworn, and you can't take the oath unless you have all your civic rights——"

"Then, who are you?"

"I am Farrabesche," said the man, in deep humility, with his eyes on the ground.

The name told Mme. Graslin nothing. She looked at the man before her. In an exceedingly kindly face there were signs of latent savagery; the uneven teeth gave an ironical turn, a suggestion of evil hardihood to the mouth and blood-red lips. In person he was of middle height, broad in the shoulders, short in the neck, which was very full and deeply sunk. He had the large hairy hands characteristic of violent-tempered people capable of abusing their physical advantages. His last words suggested some mystery, and his bearing, face, and figure all combined to give to that mystery a terrible interpretation.

"So you are in my employ?" Véronique said gently.

"Then have I the honor of speaking to Mme. Graslin?" asked Farrabesche.

"Yes, my friend," said she.

Farrabesche vanished with the speed of some wild creature after a frightened glance at his mistress. Véronique hastily mounted and went down to her two servants; the men were growing uneasy about her, for the inexplicable unwholesome-

ness of the Living Rock was well known in the country.
Colorat begged her to go down a little valley into the plain.
"It would be dangerous to return by the higher ground," he
said ; "the tracks were hard to find, and crossed each other,
and in spite of his knowledge of the country, he might lose
himself."

Once in the plain, Véronique slackened the pace of her
horse.

"Who is this Farrabesche whom you employ?" she asked,
turning to the head forester.

"Did madame meet him?" exclaimed Colorat.

"Yes, but he ran away."

"Poor fellow! Perhaps he does not know how kind
madame is."

"But, after all, what has he done?"

"Why, madame, Farrabesche is a murderer," Champion
blurted out.

"Then, of course, he was pardoned, was he not?" Véronique asked in a tremulous voice.

"No, madame,"! Colorat answered. "Farrabesche was
tried at the assizes, and condemned to ten years' penal servitude; but he only did half his time, for they let him off the
rest of the sentence; he came back from the hulks in 1827.
He owes his life to M. le Curé, who persuaded him to give
himself up. Judged by default, and sentenced to death, they
would have caught him sooner or later, and he would have
been in a bad way. M. Bonnet went out to look for him at
the risk of his life. Nobody knows what he said to Farrabesche; they were alone for a couple of days; on the third
he brought Farrabesche back to Tulle, and there he gave himself up. M. Bonnet went to see a clever lawyer, and got him
to take up Farrabesche's case; and Farrabesche came off with
ten years in jail. M. le Curé used to go to see him while he
was in prison; and that fellow yonder, who was a terror to
the whole countryside, grew as meek as any maid, and let

them take him off to prison quietly. When he came out again, he settled down hereabouts under M. le Curé's direction. People mind what they say to him; he always goes on Sundays and holidays to the services and to mass. He has a seat in the church along with the rest of us, but he always keeps by himself close to the wall. He takes the sacrament from time to time, but at the communion-table he keeps apart too."

" And this man has killed another man ! "

" *One ?* " asked Colorat ; " he has killed a good many, he has ! But he is not a bad sort for all that."

" Is it possible ? " cried Véronique, and in her amazement she let the bridle fall on the horse's neck.

The head forester asked nothing better than to tell the tale.

" You see, madame," he said, " Farrabesche maybe was in the right at bottom. He was the last of the Farrabesches, an old family in the Corrèze ; aye, yes! His eldest brother, Captain Farrabesche, was killed just ten years before in Italy, at Montenotte; only twenty-two he was, and a captain ! That is what you might call bad luck, now, isn't it ? And he had a little book-learning too ; he could read and write, and he had made up his mind to be a general. They were sorry at home when he died, as well they might be, indeed ! I was in the army with *The Other** then ; and I heard talk of his death. Oh ! Captain Farrabesche fell gloriously ; he saved the army, he did, and the Little Corporal ! I was serving at that time under General Steingel, a German—that is to say, an Alsatian—a fine soldier he was, but shortsighted, and that was how he came by his end, some time after Captain Farrabesche's. The youngest boy, that is, the one yonder, was just six years old when he heard them talking about his big brother's death. The second brother went into the army too, but he went as a private soldier ; and died a sergeant, first regiment of the Guard, a fine post, at the battle of Austerlitz,

* *L'Autre,* viz., Napoleon.

where, you see, madame, they manœuvred us all as smoothly as if it had been review day at the Tuileries. I was there myself. Oh! I was lucky; I went through it all, and never came in for a single wound. Well, then, our Farrabesche, the youngest, brave though he was, took it into his head that he would not go for a soldier. And 'tis a fact, the army did not suit that family. When the sub-prefect wanted him in 1811, he took to the woods; a 'refractory conscript,' eh! that's what they used to call them. Thereupon a gang of *chauffeurs* got hold of him by fair means or foul, and he took to warming people's feet at last! You understand that no one except M. le Curé knows what he did along with those rascals, asking their pardon! Many a brush he had with the gendarmes, and the regular troops as well! First and last he has seen seven skirmishes.''

"People say that he killed two soldiers and three gendarmes!" put in Champion.

"Who is to know how many?" Colorat answered. "He did not tell them. At last, madame, all the others were caught; but he, an active young fellow, knowing the country as he did, always got away. That gang of *chauffeurs* used to hang on the outskirts of Brives and Tulle, and they would often come over here to lie low, because Farrabesche knew places where they could hide easily. After 1814 nobody troubled about him any more, the conscription was abolished; but he had to spend the year 1815 in the woods. As he could not sit down with his arms folded and live, he helped once more to stop a coach down below yonder in the ravine; but in the end he took M. le Curé's advice, and gave himself up. It was not easy to find witnesses; nobody dared give evidence against him. Then M. le Curé and his lawyer worked so hard for him that they let him off with ten years. He was lucky after being a *chauffeur*, for a *chauffeur* he was.''

"But what is a *chauffeur*?"

"If you like, madame, I will just tell you the sort of thing they did, by all that I can make out from one and another, for you will understand that I was never a *chauffeur* myself. It was not nice, but necessity knows no law. It was like this: if they suspected some farmer or landowner of having money in his possession, seven or eight of them would drop in in the middle of the night, and they would light a fire and have supper there and then ; when supper was over, if the master of the house would not give them as much money as they asked, they would tie his feet up to the pot-hook at the back of the fire, and would not let him go until they had what they asked for. That was all. They came in masks. With so many expeditions, there were a few mishaps. Lord ! yes ; there are obstinate folk and stingy people everywhere. There was a farmer once, old Cochegrue, a regular skinflint he was, he let them burn his feet ; and, well, the man died of it. There was M. David's wife too, not far from Brives ; she died afterwards of the fright they gave her, simply seeing them tie her husband's feet. ' Just give them what you have ! ' she said to him as she went. He would not, and she showed them the hiding-place. For five years the *chauffeurs* were the terror of the countryside ; but get this well into your pate—I beg pardon, madame !—that more than one of them belonged to good families, and that sort of people are not the ones to let themselves be nabbed."

Mme. Graslin listened and made no reply. There was a moment's pause ; then young Champion, eager to interest his mistress in his turn, was anxious to tell what he knew of Farrabesche.

"Madame ought to hear the whole truth of the matter. Farrabesche has not his match on horseback or afoot. He will fell an ox with a blow of his fist ! He can carry seven-hundred weight, that he can ! and there is not a better shot anywhere. When I was a little chap they used to tell me tales about Farrabesche. One day he and three of his comrades were surprised ; they fought till one was killed and two

were wounded; well, and good, Farrabesche saw that he was
caught; bah! he jumps on a gendarme's horse behind the
man, claps spurs to the animal, which bolts off at a furious
gallop and is out of sight, he gripping that gendarme round
the waist all the time; he hugged the man so tight that after
a while he managed to fling him off and ride single in the
saddle, so he escaped and came by a horse. And he had the
impudence to sell it directly afterwards ten leagues on the
other side of Limoges. He lay in hiding for three months
after that exploit, and no one could find him. They offered a
reward of a hundred louis to any one who would betray him."

"Another time," added Colorat, " as to those hundred
louis put on his head by the prefect at Tulle, Farrabesche put
a cousin of his in the way of earning it—Giriex it was, over
at Vizay. His cousin denounced him, and seemed as if he
meant to give him up. Oh! he actually gave him up; and
very glad the gendarmes were to take him to Tulle. But he
did not go far; they had to put him in the prison at Lubersac,
and he got away the very first night, by way of a hole made
by one of the gang, one Gabilleau, a deserter from the 17th,
executed at Tulle, who was moved away the night before he
expected to escape. A pretty character Farrabesche gained
by these adventures. The troop had trusty friends, you know.
And, besides, people liked the *chauffeurs*. Lord, they were
quite different then from what they are nowadays, jolly fellows
every one of them, that spent their money like princes.
Just imagine it, madame; finds the gendarmes on his track
one evening, does he? Well, he slipped through their fingers
that time by lying twenty-four hours in a pond in a farmyard,
drawing his breath through a hole in the straw at the edge of
a dung-heap. What did a little discomfort like that matter to
him when he had spent whole nights up among the little
branches at the very top of a tree where a sparrow could
hardly hold, watching the soldiers looking for him, passing
and repassing below. Farrabesche was one of the five or six

chauffeurs whom they never could catch; for as he was a fellow-countryman, and joined the gang perforce (for, after all, he only took to the woods to escape the conscription), all the women took his part, and that counts for much."

"So Farrabesche has really killed several men," Mme. Graslin said again.

"Certainly," Colorat replied; "they even say that it was he who murdered the traveler in the coach in 1812; but the courier and postillion, the only witnesses who could have identified him, were dead when he came up for trial."

"And the robbery?" asked Mme. Graslin.

"Oh! They took all there was; but the five-and-twenty thousand francs which they found belonged to the government."

For another league Mme. Graslin rode on in silence. The sun had set, and in the moonlight the gray plain looked like the open sea. Once or twice Champion and Colorat looked at Mme. Graslin, for her silence made them uneasy, and both were greatly disturbed to see that her eyes were red with much weeping and full of tears, which fell drop by drop and glittered on her cheeks.

"Oh! don't be sorry for him, madame," said Colorat. "The fellow led a jolly life, and has had pretty sweethearts. And if the police keep an eye on him now, he is protected by M. le Curé's esteem and friendship; for he repented, and in the convict's prison behaved in the most exemplary way. Everybody knows that he is as good as the best among us; only he is so proud, he has no mind to lay himself open to any slight, but he lives peaceably and does good after his fashion. Over the other side of the Living Rock he has ten acres or so of young saplings of his own planting; and when he sees a place for a tree in the forest, he will stick one of them in. Then he lops off the dead branches, and collects the wood, and does it up in faggots ready for poor people. And the poor people, knowing that they can have firewood all ready

11

for the asking, go to him instead of helping themselves and damaging your woods. So if he still ' warms people's feet,' as you may say, it does them good now. Farrabesche is fond of your forest ; he looks after it as if it were his own."

"And yet he lives !—— quite alone." Mme. Graslin hastily added the last two words.

"Asking your pardon, madame, no. He is bringing up a little lad ; going fifteen now he is," said Maurice Champion.

"Faith, yes, that he is," Colorat remarked, "for La Curieux had that child a good while before Farrabesche gave himself up."

"Is it his son ?" asked Mme. Graslin.

"Well, every one thinks so."

"And why did he not marry the girl ?"

"Why? Because they would have caught him ! And, besides, when La Curieux knew that he was condemned, she left the neighborhood, poor thing."

"Was she pretty ?"

"Oh, my mother says that she was very much like—dear me ! another girl who left the place too—very much like Denise Tascheron."

"Was he loved ?" asked Mme. Graslin.

"Bah ! yes, because he was a *chauffeur !*" said Colorat. "The women always fall in love with anything out of the way. But for all that, nothing astonished people hereabouts so much as this love affair. Catherine Curieux was a good girl who lived like a virgin saint ; she was looked on as a paragon of virtue in her neighborhood over at Vizay, a large village in the Corrèze, on the boundary of two departments. Her father and mother were tenants of M. Brézac's. Catherine Curieux was quite seventeen years old at the time of Farrabesche's sentence. The Farrabesches were an old family out of the same district, but they settled on the Montégnac lands ; they had the largest farm in the village. Farrabesche's father and mother are dead now, and La Curieux's three sisters are married; one lives at Aubusson, one at Limoges, and one at Saint-Léonard."

"Do you think that Farrabesche knows where Catherine is?" asked Mme. Graslin.

"If he knew, he would break his bounds. Oh! he would go to her—— As soon as he came back he asked her father and mother (through M. Bonnet) for the child. La Curieux's father and mother were taking care of the child; M. Bonnet persuaded them to give him up to Farrabesche."

"Does nobody know what became of her?"

"Bah!" said Colorat. "The lass thought herself ruined, she was afraid to stop in the place! She went to Paris. What does she do there? That is the rub. As for looking for her in Paris, you might as well try to find a marble among the flints there in the plain."

Colorat pointed to the plain of Montégnac as he spoke. By this time Mme. Graslin was only a few paces from the great gateway of the château. Mme. Sauviat, in anxiety, was waiting there for her with Aline and the servants; they did not know what to think of so long an absence.

"Well," said Mme. Sauviat, as she helped her daughter to dismount, "you must be horribly tired."

"No, dear mother," Mme. Graslin answered, in an unsteady voice, and Mme. Sauviat, looking at her daughter, saw that she had been weeping for a long time.

Mme. Graslin went into the house with Aline, her confidential servant, and shut herself into her room. She would not see her mother; and when Mme. Sauviat tried to enter, Aline met the old Auvergnate with "Madame is asleep."

The next morning Véronique set out on horseback, with Maurice as her sole guide. She took the way by which they had returned the evening before, so as to reach the Living Rock as quickly as might be. As they climbed up the ravine which separates the last ridge in the forest from the actual summit of the mountain (for the Living Rock, seen from the plain, seems to stand alone), Véronique bade Maurice show her the way to Farrabesche's cabin and wait with the horses until she came back.   She meant to go alone.   Maurice went with her as far as a pathway which turned off towards the opposite side of the Living Rock, farthest from the plain, and pointed out the thatched roof of a cottage half-hidden on the mountain side ; below it lay the nursery-ground of which Colorat had spoken.

It was almost noon.   A thin streak of smoke rising from the cottage chimney guided Véronique, who soon reached the place, but would not show herself at first.   At the sight of the little dwelling, and the garden about it, with its fence of dead thorns, she stood for a few moments lost in thoughts known to her alone.   Several acres of grass land, enclosed by a quickset hedge, wound away beyond the garden ; the low-spreading branches of apple and pear and plum trees were visible here and there in the field.   Above the house, on the sandier soil of the high mountain slopes, there rose a splendid grove of tall chestnut trees, their topmost leaves turned yellow and sere.

Mme. Graslin pushed open the crazy wicket which did duty as a gate, and saw before her the shed, the little yard, and all the picturesque and living details of the dwellings of the poor. Something surely of the grace of the open fields hovers about them.   Who is there that is not moved by the revelation of lowly, almost vegetative lives—the clothes drying on the hedge, the rope of onions hanging from the roof, the iron cooking pots set out in the sun, the wooden bench hidden among the honeysuckle leaves, the houseleeks that grow on the ridges of almost every thatched hovel in France ?

Véronique found it impossible to appear unannounced in her keeper's cottage, for two fine hunting-dogs began to bark as soon as they heard the rustle of her riding habit on the dead leaves ; she gathered up her skirts on her arm, and went towards the house. Farrabesche and the boy were sitting on a wooden bench outside. Both rose to their feet and uncovered respectfully, but without a trace of servility.

" I have been told that you are seeing after my interests," said Véronique, with her eyes fixed on the lad ; " so I determined to see your cottage and nursery of saplings for myself, and to ask you about some improvements."

" I am at your service, madame," replied Farrabesche.

Véronique was admiring the lad. It was a charming face ; somewhat sunburned and brown, but in shape a faultless oval ; the outlines of the forehead were delicately fine, the orange-colored eyes exceedingly bright and alert ; the long dark hair, parted on the forehead, fell upon either side of the brow. Taller than most boys of his age, he was very nearly five feet high. His trousers were of the same coarse brown linen as his shirt ; he wore a threadbare waistcoat of rough blue cloth with horn buttons, a short jacket of the material facetiously described as "Maurienne velvet," in which Savoyards are wont to dress, and a pair of iron-bound shoes on his otherwise bare feet to complete the costume. His father was dressed in the same fashion ; but instead of the little lad's brown woolen cap, Farrabesche wore the wide-brimmed peasant's hat. In spite of its quick intelligence, the child's face bore the look of gravity (evidently unforced) peculiar to young creatures brought up in solitude ; he must have put himself in harmony with the silence and the life of the forest. Indeed, in both Farrabesche and his son the physical side of their natures seemed to be the most highly developed ; they possessed the peculiar faculties of the savage—the keen sight, the alertness, the complete mastery of the body as an instrument, the quick hearing, the signs of activity and intelligent skill. No sooner did the boy's eyes turn to his father than Mme. Graslin divined that here was the limitless affection in which the promptings of natural instinct and deliberate thought were confirmed by the most effectual happiness.

" Is this the child of whom I have heard?" asked Véronique, indicating the lad.

" Yes, madame."

Véronique signed to Farrabesche to come a few paces away.
"But have you taken no steps towards finding his mother?"
she asked.

" Madame does not know, of course, that I am not allowed
to go beyond the bounds of the commune where I am living——"

" And have you never heard of her?"

" When my time was out," he said, "the commissary paid
over to me the sum of a thousand francs, which had been
sent me, a little at a time, every quarter; the rules would not
allow me to have it until I came out.   I thought that no one
but Catherine would have thought of me, as it was not M.
Bonnet who sent it; so I am keeping the money for Benjamin."

" And how about Catherine's relations?"

" They thought no more about her after she went away. Besides, they did their part by looking after the child."

Véronique turned to go towards the house.

" Very well, Farrabesche," she said; " I will have inquiry
made, so as to make sure that Catherine is still living, and
where she is, and what kind of life she is leading——"

" Madame, whatever she may be, I shall look upon it as
good fortune to have her for my wife," the man cried in a
softened tone.   " It is for her to show reluctance, not for me.
Our marriage will legitimate the poor boy, who has no suspicion yet of how he stands."

The look in the father's eyes told the tale of the life these
two outcasts led in their voluntary exile; they were all in all
to each other, like two fellow-countrymen in the midst of a
desert.

" So you love Catherine?" asked Véronique.

" It is not so much that I love her, madame," he answered,

" as that, placed as I am, she is the one woman in the world for me."

Mme. Graslin turned swiftly, and went as far as the chestnut trees, as if some pang had shot through her. The keeper thought that this was some whim of hers, and did not venture to follow. For nearly a quarter of an hour she sat, apparently engaged in looking out over the landscape. She could see all that part of the forest which lay along the side of the valley, with the torrent in the bottom ; it was dry now, and full of boulders, a sort of huge ditch shut in between the forest-covered mountains above Montégnac and another parallel range, these last hills being steep though low, and so bare that there was scarcely so much as a starveling tree here and there to crown the slopes, where a few rather melancholy-looking birches, juniper bushes, and briars were trying to grow. This second range belonged to a neighboring estate, and lay in the department of the Corrèze ; indeed, the cross-road which meanders along the winding valley is the boundary line of the *arrondissement* of Montégnac, and also of the two estates. The opposite side of the valley beyond the torrent was quite unsheltered and barren enough. It was a sort of long wall with a slope of fine woodland behind it, and a complete contrast in its bleakness to the side of the mountain on which Farrabesche's cottage stood. Gnarled and twisted forms on the one side, and on the other shapely growths and delicate curving lines ; on the one side the dreary, unchanging silence of a sloping desert, held in place by blocks of stone and bare, denuded rocks, and on the other, the contrasts of green among the trees. Many of them were leafless now, but the fine variegated tree-trunks stood up straight and tall on each ledge, and the branches waved as the wind stirred through them. A few of them, the oaks, elms, beeches, and chestnuts which held out longer against the autumn than the rest, still retained their leaves—golden, or bronze, or purple.

In the direction of Montégnac the valley opens out so

widely that the two sides describe a vast horsehoe. Véronique, with her back against a chestnut tree, could see glen after glen arranged like the stages of an amphitheatre, the topmost crests of the trees rising one above the other in rows like the heads of spectators.   On the other side of the ridge lay her own park, in which, at a later time, this beautiful hillside was included.   Near Farrabesche's cottage the valley grew narrower and narrower, till it closed in as a gully scarce a hundred feet across.

The beauty of the view over which Mme. Graslin's eyes wandered, heedlessly at first, soon recalled her to herself. She went back to the cottage, where the father and son were standing in silence, making no attempt to explain the strange departure of their mistress. Véronique looked at the house. It was more solidly built than the thatched roof had led her to suppose; doubtless it had been left to go to ruin at the time when the Navarreins ceased to trouble themselves about the estate.   No sport, no gamekeepers.   But though no one had lived in it for a century, the walls held good in spite of the ivy and climbing plants which clung about them on every side.   Farrabesche himself had thatched the roof when he received permission to live there; he had laid the stone-flags on the floor, and brought in such furniture as there was.

Véronique went inside the cottage.   Two beds, such as the peasants use, met her eyes; there was a large cupboard of walnut-wood, a hutch for bread, a dresser, a table, three chairs, a few brown earthen platters on the shelves of the dresser; in fact, all the necessary household gear.   A couple of guns and a game-bag hung above the mantle-shelf.   It went to Véronique's heart to see how many things the father had made for the little one; there was a toy man-of-war, a fishing smack, and a carved wooden cup, a chest wonderfully ornamented, a little box decorated with mosaic work in straw, a beautifully-wrought crucifix and rosary.   The rosary was made of plum-stones; on each a head had been carved with wonderful skill—Jesus Christ, the Apostles, the Madonna, St. John the Baptist, St. Anne, the two Magdalens.

"I did it to amuse the child during the long winter evenings," he said, with something of apology in his tone.

Jessamine and climbing roses covered the front of the house, and broke into blossom about the upper windows. Farrabesche used the first floor as a storeroom; he kept poultry, ducks, and a couple of pigs, and bought nothing but bread, salt, sugar, and such groceries as they needed. Neither he nor the lad drank wine.

"Everything that I have seen and heard of you," Mme. Graslin said at last, turning to Farrabesche, "has led me to take an interest in you which shall not come to nothing."

"This is M. Bonnet's doing, I know right well!" cried Farrabesche with touching fervor.

"You are mistaken; M. le Curé has said nothing to me of you as yet; chance or God, it may be, has brought it all about."

"Yes, madame, it is God's doing; God alone can work wonders for such a wretch as I."

"If your life has been a wretched one," said Mme. Graslin, in tones so low that they did not reach the boy (a piece of womanly feeling which touched Farrabesche), "your repentance, your conduct, and M. Bonnet's good opinion should go far to retrieve it. I have given orders that the buildings on the large farm near the château which M. Graslin planned are to be finished; you shall be my steward there; you will find scope for your energies and employment for your son. The public prosecutor at Limoges shall be informed of your case, and I will engage that the humiliating restrictions which make your life a burden to you shall be removed."

Farrabesche dropped down on his knees as if thunderstruck at the words which opened out a prospect of the realization of hopes hitherto cherished in vain. He kissed the hem of Mme. Graslin's riding habit; he kissed her feet. Benjamin saw the tears in his father's eyes, and began to sob without knowing why.

"Do not kneel, Farrabesche," said Mme. Graslin ; "you do not know how natural it is that I should do for you these things that I have promised to do—— Did you not plant those trees?" she added, pointing to one or two pitch-pines, Norway pines, firs, and larches at the base of the arid, thirsty hillside opposite.

"Yes, madame."

"Then is the soil better just there?"

"The water is always wearing the rocks away, so there is a little light soil washed down on to your land, and I took advantage of it, for all the valley down below the road belongs to you ; the road is the boundary line."

"Then does a good deal of water flow down the length of the valley?"

"Oh ! in a few days, madame, if the weather sets in rainy, you will maybe hear the roaring of the torrent over at the château ! but even then it is nothing compared with what it will be when the snow melts. All the water from the whole mountain side there at the back of your park and gardens flows into it ; in fact, all the streams hereabouts flow down to the torrent, and the water comes down like a deluge. Luckily for you, the tree-roots on your side of the valley bind the soil together, and the water slips off the leaves, for the fallen leaves here in autumn are like an oilcloth cover for the land, or it would all be washed down into the valley bottom, and the bed of the torrent is so steep that I doubt whether the soil would stop there."

"What becomes of all the water?" asked Mme. Graslin.

Farrabesche pointed to the gully which seemed to shut in the valley below his cottage.

"It pours out over a chalky bit of level ground that separates Limousin from the Corrèze, and there it lies for several months in stagnant green pools, sinking slowly down into the soil. That is how the common came to be so unhealthy that no one lives there, and nothing can be done with it. No kind of cattle will pasture on the reeds and rushes in those brackish pools. Perhaps there are three thousand acres of it altogether; it is the common land of three parishes ; but it is just like the plain of Montégnac, you can do nothing with it. And down in your plain there is a certain amount of sand and a little soil among the flints, but here there is nothing but the bare tufa.''

''Send for the horses ; I mean to see all this for myself.''

Mme. Graslin told Benjamin where she had left Maurice, and the lad went forthwith.

''They tell me that you know every yard of this country,'' Mme. Graslin continued ; ''can you explain to me how it happens that no water flows into the plain of Montégnac from my side of the ridge? there is not the smallest torrent there even in rainy weather or in the time of the melting of the snows.''

''Ah! madame,'' Farrabesche answered, ''M. le Curé, who is always thinking of the prosperity of Montégnac, guessed the cause, but had not proof of it. Since you came here, he told me to mark the course of every runnel in every little valley. I had been looking at the lay of the land yesterday, and was on my way back when I had the honor of meeting you at the base of the Living Rock. I heard the sound of horsehoofs, and I wanted to know who was passing this way. Madame, M. Bonnet is not only a saint, he is a man of science. 'Far-rabesche,' said he (I being at work at the time on the road which the commune finished up to the château for you)— 'Farrabesche, if no water from this side of the hill reaches the plain below, it must be because nature has some sort of drainage arrangement for carrying it off elsewhere.' Well, madame, the remark is so simple that it looks downright trite, as if any child might have made it. But nobody since Mon-tégnac was Montégnac, neither great lords, nor stewards, nor keepers, nor rich, nor poor, though the plain lay there before their eyes with nothing growing on it for want of water, not one of them ever thought of asking what became of the water in the Gabou. The stagnant water gives them the fever in three communes, but they never thought of looking for the remedy; and I myself never dreamed of it; it took a man of God to see that——"

Farrabesche's eyes filled with tears as he spoke.

" The discoveries of men of genius are all so simple, that every one thinks he could have found them out," said Mme. Graslin; and to herself she added, " But there is this grand thing about genius, that while it is akin to all others, no one resembles it."

" At once I saw what M. Bonnet meant," Farrabesche went on. " He had not to use a lot of long words to explain my job to me. To make the thing all the queerer, madame, all the ridge above your plain (for it all belongs to you) is full of pretty deep cracks, ravines, and gullies, and whatnot; but all the water that flows down the valleys, clefts, ravines, and gorges, every channel, in fact, empties itself into a little valley a few feet lower than the level of your plain, madame. I know the cause of this state of things to-day, and here it is: There is a sort of embankment of rock (*schist*, M. Bonnet calls it) twenty or thirty feet thick, which runs in an unbroken line all round the bases of the hills between Montégnac and the Living Rock. The earth being softer than the stone, has been worn away and been hollowed out; so, naturally the water all flows round into the Gabou, eating its passage out of each valley. The trees and thickets and brushwood hide the lay of the land; but when you follow the streams and track their passage, it is easy to convince yourself of the facts. In this way both hillsides drain into the Gabou, all the water from this side that we see, and the other over the ridge where your park lies, as well as from the rocks opposite. M. le Curé thinks that this state of things would work its own cure when the water-courses on your side of the ridge are blocked up at the mouth by the rocks and soil washed down from above, so that they raise barriers between themselves and the Gabou. When that time comes your plain will be flooded in turn like the common land you are just about to see ; but it would take hundreds of years to bring that about. And, besides, is it a thing to wish for, madame? Suppose that your plain of Montégnac should not suck up all that water, like the common land here, there would be some more standing pools there to poison the whole country."

"So the places M. le Curé pointed out to me a few days ago, where the trees are still green, must mark the natural channels through which the water flows down into the Gabou?"

"Yes, madame. There are three hills between the Living Rock and Montégnac, and consequently there are three water-courses, and the streams that flow down them, banked in by the schist barrier, turn to the Gabou. That belt of wood still green, round the base of the hills, looks as if it were part of your plain, but it marks the course of the channel which was there, as M. le Curé guessed it would be."

"The misfortune will soon turn to a blessing for Montégnac," said Mme. Graslin, with deep conviction in her tones. "And since you have been the first instrument, you shall share in the work; you shall find active and willing workers, for hard work and perseverance must make up for the money which we lack."

Mme. Graslin had scarcely finished the sentence when Benjamin and Maurice came up; she caught at her horse's bridle, and, by a gesture, bade Farrabesche mount Maurice's horse.

"Now bring me to the place where the water drowns the common land," she said.

"It will be so much the better that you should go, madame, since that the late M. Graslin, acting on M. Bonnet's advice, bought about three hundred acres of land at the mouth of the gully where the mud has been deposited by the torrent, so that over a certain area there is some depth of rich soil. Madame will see the other side of the Living Rock ; there is some magnificent timber there, and doubtless M. Graslin would have had a farm on the spot. The best situation would be a place where the little stream that rises near my house sinks into the ground again ; it might be turned to advantage.''

Farrabesche led the way, and Véronique followed down a steep path towards a spot where the two sides of the gully drew in, and then separated sharply to east and west, as if divided by some earthquake shock. The gully was about sixty feet across. Tall grasses were growing among the huge boulders in the bottom. On the one side the Living Rock, cut to the quick, stood up a solid surface of granite without the slightest flaw in it ; but the height of the uncompromising rock-wall was crowned with the overhanging roots of trees, for the pines clutched the soil with their branching roots, seeming to grasp the granite as a bird clings to a bough ; but on the other side the rock was yellow and sandy, and hollowed out by the weather : there was no depth in the caverns, no boldness in the hollows of the soft crumbling ochre-tinted rock. A few prickly-leaved plants, burdocks, reeds, and water-plants at its base were sufficient signs of a north aspect and poor soil. Evidently the two ranges, though parallel, and as it were blended at the time of the great cataclysm which changed the surface of the globe, were composed of entirely different materials—an inexplicable freak of nature, or the result of some unknown cause which waits for genius to discover it. In this place the contrast between them was most strikingly apparent.

Véronique saw in front of her a vast dry plateau. There was no sign of plant-life anywhere ; the chalky soil explained the infiltration of the water, only a few stagnant pools remained here and there where the surface was incrusted. To the right stretched the mountains of the Corrèze, and to the

left the eye was arrested by the huge mass of the Living Rock,
the tall forest trees that clothed its sides, and two hundred
acres of grass below the forest, in strong contrast with the
ghastly solitude about them.

" My son and I made the ditch that you see down yonder,"
said Farrabesche ; " you can see it by the line of tall grass ; it
will be connected shortly with the ditch that marks the edge
of your forest. Your property is bounded on this side by a
desert, for the first village lies a league away."

Véronique galloped into the hideous plain, and her keeper
followed. She cleared the ditch and rode at full speed across
the dreary waste, seeming to take a kind of wild delight in the
vast picture of desolation before her. Farrabesche was right.
No skill, no human power could turn that soil to account, the
ground rang hollow beneath the horse's hoofs. This was a
result of the porous nature of the tufa, but there were cracks
and fissures no less through which the flood-water sank out of
sight, doubtless to feed some far-off springs.

"And yet there are souls like this!" Véronique exclaimed
within herself as she reined in her horse, after a quarter of an
hour's gallop.

She mused a while with the desert all about her ; there was
no living creature, no animal, no insect ; birds never crossed
the plateau. In the plain of Montégnac there were at any rate
the flints, a little sandy or clayey soil, and crumbled rock to
make a thin crust of earth a few inches deep as a beginning for cultivation ; but here the ungrateful tufa, which
had ceased to be earth, and had not become stone, wearied
the eyes so cruelly that they were absolutely forced to turn
for relief to the illimitable ether of space. Véronique
looked along the boundary of her forests and at the meadow
which her husband had added to the estate, then she went
slowly back towards the mouth of the Gabou. She came
suddenly upon Farrabesche, and found him looking into a
hole, which might have suggested that some one of a specu-

lative turn had been probing this unlikely spot, imagining that
nature had hidden some treasure there.

"What is it?" asked Véronïque, noticing the deep sadness
of the expression on the manly face.

"Madame, I owe my life to this trench here, or, more
properly, I owe to it a space for repentance and time to redeem my faults in the eyes of men——"

The effect of this explanation of life was to nail Mme.
Graslin to the spot. She reined in her horse.

"I used to hide here, madame. The ground is so full of
echoes, that if I laid my ear to the earth I could catch the
sound of the horses of the gendarmerie or the tramp of soldiers (an unmistakable sound that!) more than a league away.
Then I used to escape by way of the Gabou. I had a horse
ready in a place there, and I always put five or six leagues
between myself and them that were after me. Catherine used
to bring me food of a night. If she did not find any sign
of me, I always found bread and wine left in a hole covered
over by a stone."

These recollections of his wild vagrant life, possibly un-
wholesome recollections for Farrabesche, stirred Véronique's
most indulgent pity, but she rode rapidly on towards the
Gabou, followed by the keeper. While she scanned the gap,
looking down the long valley, so fertile on one side, so forlorn
on the other, and saw, more than a league away, the hillside
ridges, tier on tier, at the back of Montégnac, Farrabesche
said, "There will be famous waterfalls here in a few days."

"And by the same day next year, not a drop of water will
ever pass that way again. I am on my own property on
either side, so I shall build a wall solid enough and high
enough to keep the water in. Instead of a valley which is
doing nothing, I shall have a lake, twenty, thirty, forty, or
fifty feet deep, and about a league across—a vast reservoir for
the irrigation channels that shall fertilize the whole plain of
Montégnac."

"M. le Curé was right, madame, when he told us, as
we were finishing your road, that we were working for
our mother; may God give his blessing to such an enterprise."

"Say nothing about it, Farrabesche," said Mme. Graslin;
"it is M. Bonnet's idea."

Véronique returned to Farrabesche's cottage, found Maurice, and went back at once to the château. Her mother and
Aline were surprised at the change in her face; the hope of
doing good to the country had given it a look of something
like happiness. Mme. Graslin wrote to M. Grossetête; she
wanted him to ask M. de Granville for complete liberty for
the poor convict, giving particulars as to his good conduct,
which was further vouched for by the mayor's certificate and
a letter from M. Bonnet. She also sent other particulars concerning Catherine Curieux, and entreated Grossetête to interest
the public prosecutor in her kindly project, and to cause a
letter to be written to the prefecture of police in Paris with a
view to discovering the girl. The mere fact that Catherine
had remitted sums of money to the convict in prison should
be a sufficient clue by which to trace her. Véronique had set
her heart on knowing the reason why Catherine had failed to
come back to her child and to Farrabesche. Then she told
her old friend of her discoveries in the torrent bed of the
Gabou, and laid stress on the necessity of finding the clever
man for whom she had already asked him.

The next day was Sunday. For the first time since Véronique took up her abode in Montégnac, she felt able to go to
church for mass. She went and took possession of her pew
in the Lady Chapel. Looking round her, she saw how bare ·
the poverty-stricken church was, and determined to set by a
certain sum every year for repairs and the decoration of the
altars. She heard the words of the priest, tender, gracious,
and divine; for the sermon, couched in such simple language
that all present could understand it, was in truth sublime.

12

The sublime comes from the heart; it is not to be found by effort of the intellect; and religion is an inexhaustible source of sublime thoughts with no false glitter of brilliancy, for the catholicism which penetrates and changes hearts is wholly of the heart. M. Bonnet found in the epistle a text for his sermon, to the effect that soon or late God fulfills his promises, watches over his own, and encourages the good. He made it clear that great things would be the result of the presence of a rich and charitable resident in the parish, by pointing out that the duties of the poor towards the beneficent rich were as extensive as those of the rich towards the poor, and that the relation should be one of mutual help.

Farrabesche had spoken to some of those who were glad to see him (one consequence of the spirit of Christian charity which M. Bonnet had infused into practical action in his parish), and had told them of Mme. Graslin's kindness to him. All the commune had talked this over in the square below the church, where, according to country custom, they gathered together before mass. Nothing could more completely have won the good-will of these folk, who are so readily touched by any kindness shown to them; and when Véronique came out of church she found almost all the parish standing in a double row. All hats went off respectfully and in deep silence as she passed. This welcome touched her, though she did not know the real reason of it. Among the last of all she saw Farrabesche, and spoke to him.

"You are a good sportsman; do not forget to send us some game."

A few days after this Véronique walked with the curé in that part of the forest nearest her château; she determined to descend the ridges which she had seen from the Living Rock, ranged tier on tier on the other side of the hill. With the curé's assistance she would ascertain the exact position of the higher affluents of the Gabou. The result was the discovery by the curé of the fact that the streams which water Upper

Montégnac really rose in the mountains of the Corrèze. These ranges were united to the mountain by the arid rib of hill which ran parallel to the chain of the Living Rock. The curé came back from that walk with boyish glee ; he saw, with the *naïveté* of a poet, the prosperity of the village that he loved. And what is a poet but a man who realizes his dreams before the time ? M. Bonnet reaped his harvests as he looked down from the terrace at the barren plain.

Farrabesche and his son came up to the château next morning loaded with game. The keeper had brought a cup for Francis Graslin ; it was nothing less than a masterpiece—a battle-scene carved on a cocoanut shell. Mme. Graslin happened to be walking on the terrace, on the side that overlooked " Tascherons." She sat down on a garden seat, and looked long at that fairy's work. Tears came into her eyes from time to time.

" You must have been very unhappy," she said, addressing Farrabesche after a silence.

" What could I do, madame ? " he answered. " I was there without the hope of escape, which makes life bearable to almost all the convicts——"

" It is an appalling life ! " she said, and her look and compassionate tones invited Farrabesche to speak.

In Mme. Graslin's convulsive tremor and evident emotion Farrabesche saw nothing but the overwrought interest excited by pitying curiosity. Just at that moment Mme. Sauviat appeared in one of the garden walks, and seemed about to join them, but Véronique drew out her handkerchief and motioned her away. " Let me be, mother," she cried, in sharper tones than she had ever before used to the old Auvergnate.

" For five years I wore a chain riveted here to a heavy iron ring, madame," Farrabesche said, pointing to his leg. " I was fastened to another man. I have had to live like that with three convicts first and last. I used to lie on a wooden camp bedstead, and I had to work uncommonly hard to get a thin mattress, called a *serpentin.* There were eight hundred men in each ward. Each of the beds (*tolards,* they called them) held twenty-four men, all chained together two and two, and nights and mornings they passed a long chain called the ' bilboes string,' in and out of the chains that bound each couple together, and made it fast to the *tolard,* so that all of us were fastened down by the feet. Even after a couple of years of it, I could not get used to the clank of those chains; every moment they said, ' You are in a convicts' prison ! ' If you dropped off to sleep for a minute, some rogue or other would begin to wrangle or turn himself round, and put you in mind of your plight. You had to serve an apprenticeship to learn how to sleep. I could not sleep at all, in fact, unless I was utterly exhausted with a heavy day's work.

"After I managed to sleep, I had, at any rate, the night when I could forget things. Forgetfulness—that is something, madame ! Once a man is there, he must learn to satisfy his needs after a manner fixed by the most pitiless rules. You can judge, madame, what sort of effect this life was like to have on me, a young fellow who had always lived in the woods, like the wild goats and the birds ! Ah ! if I had not eaten my bread cooped up in the four walls of a prison for six months beforehand, I should have thrown myself into the sea at the sight of my mates, for all the beautiful things M. Bonnet said, and (I may say it) he has been the father of my soul. I did pretty well in the open air ; but when once I was shut up in the ward to sleep or eat (for we ate our food there out of troughs, three couples to each trough), it took all the life out of me ; the dreadful faces and the language of the others always sickened me. Luckily, at five o'clock in the summer, and half-past seven in winter, out we went in spite of heat or cold or wind or rain, in the ' jail gang '—that means to work. So we were out of doors most of our time, and the open air seems very good to you when you come out of a place where eight hundred convicts herd together. The air, you must always remember, is sea-air ! You enjoy the breeze, the sun is like a friend, and you watch the clouds pass over, and look for hopeful signs of a beautiful day. For my own part, I took an interest in my work."

Farrabesche stopped, for two great tears rolled down Véronique's cheeks.

"Oh ! madame, these are only the roses of that existence ! " he cried, taking the expression on Mme. Graslin's face for pity of his lot. " These are the dreadful precautions the government takes to make sure of us, the inquisition kept up by the warders, the inspection of fetters morning and evening, the coarse food, the hideous clothes that humiliate you at every moment, the constrained position while you sleep, the frightful sound of four hundred double chains clanking in an echoing ward, the prospect of being mowed down with grapeshot if half-a-dozen scoundrels take it into their heads to rebel—all these horrible things are nothing, they are the roses of that life, as I said before. Any respectable man unlucky enough to be sent there must die of disgust before very long. You have to live day and night with another convict ; you have to endure the company of five more at every meal, and twenty-three at night ; you have to listen to their talk.

" The convicts have secret laws among themselves, madame ; if you make an outlaw of yourself, they will murder you ; if you submit, you become a murderer. You have your choice— you must be either victim or executioner. After all, if you die at a blow, that would put an end to you and your troubles ; but they are too cunning in wickedness, it is impossible to hold out against their hatred : any one whom they dislike is completely at their mercy, they can make every moment of his life one constant torture worse than death. Any man who repents and tries to behave well is the common enemy, and more particularly they suspect him of tale-telling.

They will take a man's life on a mere suspicion of tale-telling. Every ward has its tribunal, where they try crimes against the convicts' laws. It is an offense not to conform to their customs, and a man may be punished for that. For instance, everybody is bound to help the escape of a convict; every convict has his chance of escape in turn, when the whole prison is bound to give him help and protection. It is a crime to reveal anything done by a convict to further his escape. I will not speak of the horrible moral tone of the prison; strictly speaking, it has nothing to do with the subject. The prison authorities chain men of opposite dispositions together, so as to neutralize any attempt at escape or rebellion; and always put those who either could not endure each other, or were suspicious of each other, on the same chain."

"What did you do?" asked Mme. Graslin.

"Oh! it was like this, I had luck," said Farrabesche; "the lot never fell to me to kill a doomed man; I never voted the death of anybody, no matter whom; I was never punished, no one took a dislike to me, and I lived comfortably with the three mates they gave me one after another—all three of them feared and liked me. But then I was well known in the prison before I got there, madame. A *chauffeur!* for I was supposed to be one of those brigands. I have seen them do it," Farrabesche went on in a low voice, after a pause, "but I never would help to torture folk, nor take any of the stolen money. I was a 'refractory conscript,' that was all. I used to help the rest, I was scout for them, I fought, I was forlorn sentinel, rearguard, what you will, but I never shed blood except in self-defense. Oh! I told M. Bonnet and my lawyer everything, and the judges knew quite well that I was not a murderer. But, all the same, I am a great criminal; the things that I have done are all against the law.

"Two of my old comrades had told them about me before I came. I was a man of whom the greatest things might be

expected, they said.   In the convicts' prison, you see, madame,
there is nothing like a character of that kind ; it is worth even
more than money.   A murder is a passport in this republic of
wretchedness ; they leave you in peace.⁻ I did nothing to
destroy their opinion of me.   I looked gloomy and resigned ;
it was possible to be misled by my face, and they were misled.
My sullen manner and my silence were taken for signs of
ferocity.   Every one there, convicts and warders, young and
old, respected me.   I was president of my ward.   I was never
tormented at night, nor suspected of tale-telling.   I lived
honestly according to their rules ; I never refused to do any
one a good turn ; I never showed a sign of disgust ; in short,
I 'howled with the wolves,' to all appearance, and in my
secret soul I prayed to God.   My last mate was a soldier, a
lad of two-and-twenty, who had stolen something, and then
deserted in consequence ; I had him for four years.   We were
friends, and wherever I may be I can reckon on *him* when he
comes out.   The poor wretch, Guépin they called him, was
not a rascal, he was only a harebrained boy; his ten years
will sober him down.   Oh ! if the rest had known that it was
religion that reconciled me to my fate ; that when my time
was up I meant to live in some corner without letting them
know where I was, to forget those fearful creatures, and never
to be in the way of meeting one of them again, they would
very likely have driven me mad."

"But, then, suppose that some unhappy, sensitive boy had
been carried away by passion, and—pardoned so far as the
death penalty is concerned——? "

"Madame, a murderer is never fully pardoned.   They begin by commuting the sentence for twenty years of penal servitude.   But for a decent young fellow it is a thing to shudder
at !   It is impossible to tell you about the life in store for him ;
it would be a hundred times better for him that he should
die !   Yes, for such a death on the scaffold is good fortune."

"I did not dare to think it," said Mme. Graslin.

Véronique had grown white as wax. She leaned her fore
head against the balustrade to hide her face for several moments. Farrabesche did not know whether he ought to go
or stay. Then Mme. Graslin rose to her feet, and with an
almost queenly look she said, to Farrabesche's great astonishment, "Thank you, my friend!" in tones that went to his
heart. Then after a pause—"Where did you draw courage
to live and suffer as you did?" she asked.

"Ah, madame, M. Bonnet had set a treasure in my soul!
That is why I love him more than I have ever loved any one
else in this world."

"More than Catherine?" asked Mme. Graslin, with a
certain bitterness in her smile.

"Ah, madame, almost as much."

"How did he do it?"

"Madame, the things that he said and the tones of his
voice subdued me. It was Catherine who showed him the
way to the hiding-place in the chalk-land which I showed you
the other day. He came to me quite alone. He was the new
curé of Montégnac, he told me; I was his parishioner, I was
dear to him, he knew that I had only strayed from the path,
that I was not yet lost; he did not mean to betray me, but to
save me; in fact, he said things that thrill you to the very
depths of your nature. And you see, madame, he can make
you do right with all the force that other people take to make
you do wrong. He told me, poor dear man, that Catherine
was a mother; I was about to give over two creatures to shame
and neglect. 'Very well,' said I, 'then they will be just as
I am; I have no future before me.' He answered that I had
two futures before me, and both of them bad—one in this
world, the other in the next—unless I desisted and reformed.
Here below I was bound to die on the scaffold. If I were
caught, my defense would break down in a court of law.
On the other hand, if I took advantage of the mildness of the
new government towards 'refractory conscripts' of many

years' standing, and gave myself up, he would strain every nerve to save my life. He would find me a clever advocate who would pull me through with ten years' penal servitude. After that M. Bonnet talked to me of another life. Catherine cried like a Magdalen at that. There, madame,'' said Farrabesche, holding out his right hand, '' she laid her face against *this*, and I felt it quite wet with her tears. She prayed me to live ! M. le Curé promised to contrive a quiet and happy lot for me and my child, even in this district, and undertook that no one should cast up the past to me. In short, he lectured me as if I had been a little boy. After three of those nightly visits I was as pliant as a glove. Do you care to know why, madame?''

Farrabesche and Mme. Graslin looked at each other, and neither of them to their secret souls explained the real motive of their mutual curiosity.

'' Very well,'' the poor ticket-of-leave man continued, '' the first time when he had gone away, and Catherine went, too, to show him the way back, and I was left alone, I felt a kind of freshness and calm happiness such as I had not known since I was a child. It was something like the happiness I had felt with poor Catherine. The love of this dear man, who had come to seek me out, the interest that he took in me, in my future, in my soul—it all worked upon me and changed me. It was as if a light arose in me. So long as he was with me and talked, I held out. How could I help it ? He was a priest, and we bandits do not eat their bread. But when the sound of his footsteps and Catherine's died away—oh ! I was, as he said two days later, ' enlightened by grace.'

'' From that time forwards God gave . me strength to endure everything—the jail, the sentence, the putting on of the irons, the journey, the life in the convicts' prison. I reckoned upon M. Bonnet's promise as upon the truth of the Gospel ; I looked on my sufferings as a payment of arrears. Whenever things grew unbearable, I used to see, at the end

of the ten years, this house in the woods, and my little Benjamin and Catherine there.   Good M. Bonnet, he kept his
promise; but some one else failed me.   Catherine was not at
the prison-door when I came out, nor yet at the trysting-place
on the common lands.   She must have died of grief.   That is
why I am always sad.   Now, thanks to you, madame, I shall
have work to do that needs doing; I shall put myself into it
body and soul, so will my boy for whom I live——"

"You have shown me how it was that M. le Curé could
bring about the changes in his parish——"

"Oh! nothing can resist him," said Farrabesche.

"No, no.   I know that," Véronique answered briefly, and
she very kindly dismissed the grateful Farrabesche with a sign
of farewell.

Farrabesche went.   Most of that day Véronique spent in
pacing to and fro along the terrace, in spite of the drizzling
rain that fell till evening came on.   She was gloomy and sad.
When Véronique's brows were thus contracted, neither her
mother nor Aline dared to break in on her mood; she did not
see her mother talking in the dusk with M. Bonnet, who,
seeing that she must be roused from this appalling dejection,
sent the child to find her.   Little Francis went up to his
mother and took her hand, and Véronique suffered herself to
be led away.   At the sight of M. Bonnet she started with
something almost like dismay.   The curé led the way back to
the terrace.

"Well, madame," he said, "what can you have been talking about with Farrabesche?"

Véronique did not wish to lie nor to answer the question;
she replied to it by another—

"Was he your first victory?"

"Yes," said M. Bonnet.   "If I could win him, I felt sure
of Montégnac; and so it proved."

Véronique pressed M. Bonnet's hand.

"From to-day I am your penitent, M. le Curé," she said,

with tears in her voice; "to-morrow I will make you a general confession."

The last words plainly spoke of a great inward struggle and a hardly-won victory over herself. The cure led the way back to the château without a word, and stayed with her till dinner, talking over the vast improvements to be made in Montégnac.

"Agriculture is a question of time," he said. "The little that I know about it has made me to understand how much may be done by a well-spent winter. Here are the rains beginning, you see; before long the mountains will be covered with snow, and your operations will be impossible; so hurry M. Grossetête."

M. Bonnet exerted himself to talk, and drew Mme. Graslin into the conversation; gradually her thoughts were forced to take another turn, and by the time he left her she had almost recovered from the day's excitement. But even so, Mme. Sauviat saw that her daughter was so terribly agitated that she spent the night with her.

Two days later a messenger sent by M. Grossetête arrived with the following letters for Mme. Graslin:

Grossetête to Mme. Graslin.

"My dear Child:—Horses are not easily to be found, but I hope that you are satisfied with the three which I sent you. If you need draught-horses or plough-horses, they must be looked for elsewhere. It is better in any case to use oxen for ploughing and as draught animals. In all districts where they use horses on the land, they lose their capital as soon as the animal is past work, while an ox, instead of being a loss, yields a profit to the farmer.

"I approve of your enterprise in every respect, my child; you will find in it an outlet for the devouring mental energy which was turned against yourself and wearing you out. But when you asked me to find you, over and above the horses, a

man able to second you, and more particularly to enter into
your views, you ask me for one of those rare birds that we
rear it is true in the provinces, but which we in no case keep
among us.   The training of the noble animal is too lengthy
and too risky a speculation for us to undertake, and, besides,
we are afraid of these very clever folk—'eccentrics,' we call
them.

"As a matter of fact, too, the men who are classed in the
scientific category in which you are fain to find a co-operator
are, as rule, so prudent and so well provided for, that I hardly
liked to write to tell you how impossible it would be to come
by such a prize.   You ask me for a poet, or, if you prefer
it, a madman ; but all our madmen betake themselves to Paris.
I did speak to one or two young fellows engaged on the land
survey and assessments, contractors for embankments, or foremen employed on canal cuttings ; but none of them thought
it worth their while to entertain your proposals.   Chance all at
once threw in my way the very man you want, a young man
whom I thought to help; for you will see by his letter that
one ought not to set about doing a kindness in a happy-go-
lucky fashion, and, indeed, an act of kindness requires more
thinking about than anything else on this earth.   You can
never tell whether what seemed to you to be right at the time
may not do harm by and by.   By helping others we shape our
own destinies ; I see that now——"

As Mme. Graslin read those words, the letter dropped from
her hands.   For some moments she sat deep in thought.
"Oh, God," she cried, "when wilt Thou cease to smite
me by every man's hand?"
Then she picked up the letters and read on—

"Gérard seems to me to have plenty of enthusiasm and a
cool head ; the very man for you !   Paris is in a ferment just
now with this leaven of new doctrine, and I shall be delighted

if the young fellow keeps out of the snares spread by ambitious spirits, who work upon the instincts of the generous youth of France. The rather torpid existence of the provinces is not altogether what I like for him, but neither do I like the idea of the excitement of the life in Paris, and the enthusiasm for renovating, which urges youngsters into the new ways. You, and you only, know my opinions; to me it seems that the world of ideas revolves on its axis much as the material world does. Here is this poor protégé of mine wanting impossibilities. No power on earth could stand before ambitions so violent, imperious, and absolute. I have a liking myself for a jog trot; I like to go slowly in politics, and have but very little taste for the social topsy-turvydom which all these lofty spirits are minded to inflict upon us. To you I confide the principles of an old and trusted supporter of the Monarchy, for you are discreet. I hold my tongue here among these good folk, who believe more and more in progress the farther they get into a mess; but for all that it hurts me to see the irreparable damage done already to our dear country.

"So I wrote and told the young man that a task worthy of him was waiting for him here. He is coming to see you; for though his letter (which I enclose) will give you a very fair idea of him, you would like to see him as well, would you not? You women can tell so much from the look of people; and, besides, you ought not to have any one, however insignificant, in your service unless you like him. If he is not the man you want, you can decline his services; but if he suits you, dear child, cure him of his flimsily-disguised ambitions, induce him to adopt the happy and peaceful life of the fields, a life in which beneficence is perpetual, where all the qualities of a great and strong nature are continually brought into play, where the products of nature are a daily source of new wonder, and a man finds worthy occupation in making a real advance and practical improvements. I do not in any way overlook the fact that great deeds come of great ideas—great theories;

but as ideas of that kind are seldom met with, I think that, for the most part, practical attainments are worth more than ideas. A man who brings a bit of land into cultivation or a tree or fruit to perfection, who makes grass grow where grass would not grow before, ranks a good deal higher than the seeker after formulas for humanity. In what has Newton's science changed the lot of the worker in the fields? Ah! my dear, I loved you before, but to-day, appreciating to the full the task which you have set before you, I love you far more. You are not forgotten here in Limoges. and every one admires your great resolution of improving Montégnac. Give us our little due, in that we have the wit to admire nobility when we see it, and do not forget that the first of your admirers is also your earliest friend.

"F. Grossetête."

Gérard to Grossetête.

"I come to you, monsieur, with sad confidences, but you have been like a father to me, when you might have been simply a patron. So to you alone, who have made me any-thing that I am, can I make them. I have fallen a victim to a cruel disease, a disease, moreover, not of the body; I am conscious that I am completely unfitted by my thoughts, feel-ings, and opinions, and by the whole bent of my mind, to do what is expected of me by the government and by society. Perhaps this will seem to you to be a piece of ingratitude, but it is simply and solely an indictment that I address to you.

"When I was twelve years old you saw the signs of a certain aptitude for the exact sciences, and a precocious ambition to succeed, in a workingman's son, and it was through you, my generous godfather, that I took my flight towards higher spheres; but for you I should be following out my original destiny, I should be a carpenter like my poor father, who did not live to rejoice in my success. And most surely, monsieur, you did me a kindness; there is no day on which I do not bless you ; and so, perhaps, it is I who am in the wrong. But whether right or wrong, I am unhappy ; and does not the fact that I pour out my complaints to you set you very high ? Is it not as if I made of you a supreme judge, like God ? In any case, I trust to your indulgence.

" I studied the exact sciences so hard between the ages of sixteen and eighteen that I made myself ill, as you know. My whole future depended on my admission to the École Polytechnique. The work I did at that time was a disproportionate training for the intellect ; I all but killed myself ; I studied day and night ; I exerted myself to do more than I was perhaps fit for. I was determined to pass my examinations so well that I should be sure not only of admittance into the École, but of a free education there, for I wanted to spare you the expense, and I succeeded !

" It makes me shudder now to think of that appalling conscription of brains yearly made over to the government by family ambition ; a conscription which demands such severe study at a time when a lad is almost a man, and growing fast in every way, cannot but do incalculable mischief ; many precious faculties which later would have developed and grown strong and powerful are extinguished by the light of the student's lamp. Nature's laws are inexorable ; they are not to be thrust aside by the schemes nor at the pleasure of society ; and the laws of the physical world, the laws which govern the nature without, hold good no less of human nature—every abuse must be paid for. If you must have fruit out of season, you have it from a forcing house either at the expense of the tree or of the quality of the fruit. La Quintinie killed the orange trees that Louis XIV. might have a bouquet of orange blossoms every morning throughout the year. Any heavy demand made on a still-growing intellect is a draft on its future.

" The pressing and special need of our age is the spirit of the lawgiver. Europe has so far seen no lawgiver since Jesus

Christ; and Christ, who gave us no vestige of a political code, left His work incomplete. For example, before technical schools were established, and the present means of filling them with scholars was adopted, did they call in one of the great thinkers who hold in their heads the immensity of the sum of the relations of the institution to human brain-power; who can balance the advantages and disadvantages, and study in the past the laws of the future? Was any inquiry made into the after-lives of men who, for their misfortune, knew the circle of the sciences at too early an age? Was any estimate of their rarity attempted? Was their fate ascertained? Was it discovered how they contrived to endure the continual strain of thought? How many of them died like Pascal, prematurely, worn out by science? Some, again, lived to old age; when did these begin their studies? Was it known then, is it known now as I write, what conformation of the brain is best fitted to stand the strain and to cope prematurely with knowledge? Is it so much as suspected that this is before all things a physiological question?

"Well, I think myself that the general rule is that the vegetative period of adolescence should be prolonged. There are exceptions; there are some so constituted that they are capable of this effort in youth, but the result is the shortening of life in most cases. Clearly the man of genius who can stand the precocious exercise of his faculties is bound to be an exception among exceptions. If medical testimony and social data bear me out, our way of recruiting for the technical schools in France works as much havoc among the best human specimens of each generation as La Quintinie's process among the orange trees.

"But to continue (for I will append my doubts to each series of facts), I began my work anew at the École, and with more enthusiasm than ever. I meant to leave it as successfully as I had entered it. Between the ages of nineteen and one-and-twenty I worked with all my might, and developed

my faculties by their constant exercise. Those two years set
the crown on the three which came before them, when I was
only preparing to do great things. And then, what pride did
I not feel when I had won the privilege of choosing the career
most to my mind? I might be a military or marine engineer,
might go on the staff of the artillery, into the mines department, or the roads and bridges. I took your advice, and
became a civil engineer.

"Yet where I triumphed, how many fell out of the ranks!
You know that from year to year the government raises the
standard of the École. The work grows harder and more
trying from time to time. The course of preparatory study
through which I went was nothing compared with the work at
fever-heat in the École, to the end that every physical science—
mathematics, astronomy, and chemistry, and the terminologies
of each—may be packed into the heads of so many young men
between the ages of nineteen and twenty-one. The government here in France, which in so many ways seems to aim at
taking the place of the paternal authority, has in this respect
no bowels—no father's pity for its children; it makes its
experiments *in anima vili*. The ugly statistics of the mischief
it has wrought have never been asked for; no one has troubled
to inquire how many cases of brain fever there have been
during the last thirty-six years; how many explosions of despair among those young lads; no one takes account of the
moral destruction which decimates the victims. I lay stress
on this painful aspect of the problem because it occurs by the
way and before the final result; for a few weaklings the
result comes soon instead of late. You know, besides, that
these victims, whose minds work slowly, or who, it may be,
are temporarily stupefied with overwork, are allowed to stay
for three years instead of two at the École, but the way these
are regarded there has no very favorable influence on their
capacity. In fact, it may chance that young men, who at a
later day will show that they have something in them, may

13

leave the École without an appointment at all, because at the final examination they do not exhibit the amount of knowledge required of them. These are 'plucked,' as they say, and Napoleon used to make sub-lieutenants of them. In these days the 'plucked' candidate represents a vast loss of capital invested by families, and a loss of time for the lad himself.

" But, after all, I myself succeeded! At the age of one-and-twenty I had gone over all the ground discovered in mathematics by men of genius, and I was impatient to distinguish myself by going farther. The desire is so natural that almost every student when he leaves the École fixes his eyes on the sun called glory in an invisible heaven. The first thought in all our minds was to be a Newton, a Laplace, or a Vauban. Such are the efforts which France requires of young men who leave the famous École Polytechnique!

" And now let us see what becomes of the men sorted and sifted with such care out of a whole generation. At one-and-twenty we dream dreams, a whole lifetime lies before us, we expect wonders. I entered the School of Roads and Bridges, and became a civil engineer. I studied construction, and with what enthusiasm! You must remember it. In 1826, when I left the school, at the age of twenty-four, I was still only a civil engineer on my promotion, with a government grant of a hundred and fifty francs a month. The worst-paid book-keeper in Paris will earn as much by the time he is eighteen, and with four hours' work in the day. By unhoped-for good luck, it may be because my studies had brought me distinction, I received an appointment as a surveyor in 1828. I was twenty-six years old. They sent me, you know where, into a sub-prefecture with a salary of two thousand five hundred francs. The money matters nothing. My lot is at any rate more brilliant than a carpenter's son has a right to expect ; but what journeyman grocer put into a shop at the age of sixteen will not be fairly on the way to an independence by the time he is six-and-twenty ?

" Then I found out the end to which these terrible displays of intelligence were directed, and why the gigantic efforts, required of us by the government, were made. The government sent me to count paving-stones and measure the heaps of road-material by the waysides. I must repair, keep in order, and occasionally construct runnels and culverts, maintain the ways, clean out, and occasionally open ditches. At the office I must answer all questions relating to the alignment or the planting and felling of trees. These are, in fact, the principal and often the only occupations of an ordinary surveyor. Perhaps from time to time there is some bit of leveling to be done, and that we are obliged to do ourselves, though any of the foremen with his practical experience could do the work a good deal better than we can with all our science.

" There are nearly four hundred of us altogether—ordinary surveyors and assistants—and as there are only some hundred-odd engineers-in-chief, all the subordinates cannot hope for promotion ; there is practically no higher rank to absorb the engineers-in-chief, for twelve or fifteen inspectors-general or divisionaries scarcely count, and their posts are almost as much of sinecures in our corps as colonelcies in the artillery when the battery is united with it. An ordinary civil engineer, like a captain of artillery, knows all that is known about his work ; he ought not to need any one to look after him except an administrative head to connect the eighty-six engineers with each other and the government, for a single engineer with two assistants is quite enough for a department. A hierarchy in such a body as ours works in this way. Energetic minds are subordinated to old effete intelligences, who think themselves bound to distort and alter (they think for the better) the drafts submitted to them ; perhaps they do this simply to give some reason for their existence ; and this, it seems to me, is the only influence exerted on public works in France by the General Council of Roads and Bridges.

"Let us suppose, however, that between the ages of thirty

and forty I become an engineer of the first-class, and am an engineer-in-chief by the time I am fifty. Alas! I foresee my future; it lies before my eyes. My engineer-in-chief is a man of sixty. He left the famous École with distinction, as I did; he has grown gray in two departments over such work as I am doing; he has become the most commonplace man imaginable, has fallen from the heights of attainment he once reached; nay, more than that, he is not even abreast of science. Science has made progress, and he has remained stationary; worse still, has forgotten what he once knew! The man who came to the front at the age of twenty-two with every sign of real ability has nothing of it left now but the appearance. At the very outset of his career his education was especially directed to mathematics and the exact sciences, and he took no interest in anything that was not 'in his line.' You would scarcely believe it, but the man knows absolutely nothing of other branches of learning. Mathematics have dried up his heart and brain. I cannot tell any one but you what a nullity he really is, screened by the name of the École Polytechnique. The label is impressive; and people, being prejudiced in his favor, do not dare to throw any doubt on his ability. But to you I may say that his befogged intellects have cost the department in one affair a million francs, where two hundred thousand should have been ample. I was for protesting, for opening the prefect's eyes, and whatnot; but a friend of mine, another surveyor, told me about a man in the corps who became a kind of black sheep in the eyes of the administration by doing something of this sort. 'Would you yourself be very much pleased, when you are engineer-in-chief, to have your mistakes shown up by a subordinate?' asked he. 'Your engineer-in-chief will be a divisionary inspector before very long. As soon as one of us makes some egregious blunder, the administration (which, of course, must never be in the wrong) withdraws the perpetrator from active service and makes him an inspector.' That is

how the reward due to a capable man becomes a sort of pre-
mium on stupidity.

"All France saw one disaster in the heart of Paris, the
miserable collapse of the first suspension bridge which an
engineer (a member of the Académie des Sciences, moreover)
endeavored to construct, a collapse caused by blunders which
would not have been made by the constructor of the Canal
de Briare in the time of Henri IV., nor by the monk who
built the Pont Royal. Him, too, the administration consoled
by a summons to the Board of the General Council.

"Are the technical schools really manufactories of incom-
petence? The problem requires prolonged observation. If
there is anything in what I say, a reform is needed, at any
rate in the way in which they are carried on, for I do not
venture to question the usefulness of the Écoles. Still, looking back over the past, does it appear that France has ever
lacked men of great ability at need, or the talent she tries to
hatch as required in these days by Monge's method? What
school turned out Vauban save the great school called ' vocation?' Who was Riquet's master? When genius has raised
itself above the social level, urged upwards by a vocation, it
is almost always fully equipped; and in that case your man is
no 'specialist,' but has something universal in his gift. I do
not believe that any engineer who ever left the École could
build one of the miracles of architecture which Leonardo da
Vinci reared; Leonardo at once mechanician, architect, and
painter, one of the inventors of hydraulic science, the indefatigable constructor of canals. They are so accustomed
while yet in their teens to the bald simplicity of geometry,
that by the time they leave the École they have quite lost all
feeling for grace or ornament; a column to their eyes is a
useless waste of material; they return to the point where art
begins—on utility they take their stand, and stay there.

"But this is as nothing compared with the disease which is
consuming me. I feel that a most terrible change is being

wrought in me ; I feel that my energy and faculties, after the exorbitant strain put upon them, are dwindling and growing feeble. The influence of my humdrum life is creeping over me. After such efforts as mine, I feel that I am destined to do great things, and I am confronted by the most trivial task work, such as verifying yards of road-material, inspecting highways, checking inventories of stores. I have not enough to do to fill two hours in the day.

" I watch my colleagues marry and fall out of touch with modern thought. Is my ambition really immoderate? I should like to serve my country. My country required me to give proof of no ordinary powers, and bade me become an encyclopedia of the sciences—and here I am, folding my arms in an obscure corner of a province. I am not allowed to leave the place where I am penned up, to exercise my wits by trying new and useful experiments elsewhere. A vague indefinable grudge is the certain reward awaiting any one of us who follows his own inspirations, and does more than the department requires of him. The most that such a man ought to hope for is that his overweening presumption may be passed over, his talent neglected, while his project receives decent burial in the pigeon-holes at headquarters. What will Vicat's reward be, I wonder ? (Between ourselves, Vicat is the only man among us who has made any real advance in the science of construction.)

" The General Council of Roads and Bridges is partly made up of men worn out by long and sometimes honorable service, but whose remaining brain-power only exerts itself negatively; these gentlemen erase anything that they cannot understand at their age, and act as a sort of extinguisher to be put when required on audacious innovations. The Council might have been created for the express purpose of paralyzing the arm of the generous younger generation, which only asks for leave to work, and would fain serve France.

" Monstrous things happen in Paris. The future of a

province hangs on the signature of these bureaucrats. I have not time to tell you all about the intrigues which balk the best schemes; for them the best schemes are, as a matter of fact, those which open up the best prospects of money-making to the greed of speculators and companies, which knock most abuses on the head, for abuses are always stronger than the spirit of improvement in France. In five years' time my old self-will has ceased to rule. I shall see my ambitions die out in me, and my noble desire to use the faculties which my country bade me display, and then left to rust in my obscure corner.

"Taking the most favorable view possible, my outlook seems to me to be very poor. I took advantage of leave of absence to come to Paris. I want to change my career, to find scope for my energies, knowledge, and activity. I shall send in my resignation, and go to some country where men with my special training are needed, where great things may be done. If none of all this is possible, I will throw in my lot with some of these new doctrines which seem as if they must make some great change in the present order of things, by directing the workers to better purpose. For what are we but laborers without work, tools lying idle in the warehouse? We are organized as if it was a question of shaking the globe, and we are required to do—nothing.

"I am conscious that there is something great in me which is pining away and will perish; I tell you this with mathematical explicitness. But I should like to have your advice before I make a change in my condition. I look on myself as your son, and should never take any important step without consulting you, for your experience is as great as your goodness. I know, of course, that when the government has obtained its specially trained men, it can no more set its engineers to construct public monuments than it can declare war to give the army an opportunity of winning great battles and of finding out which are its great captains. But, then, as the man has never failed to appear when circumstances called for him; as, at the moment when there is much money to be spent and great things to be done, one of these unique men of genius springs up from the crowd; and as, particularly in matters of this kind, one Vauban is enough at a time, nothing could better demonstrate the utter uselessness of the institution. In conclusion, when a picked man's mental energies have been stimulated by all this preparation, how can the government help seeing that he will make any amount of struggle before he allows himself to be effaced? Is it wise policy? What is it but a way of kindling burning ambition? Would they bid all those perfervid heads learn to calculate anything and everything but the probabilities of their own futures?

"There are, no doubt, exceptions among some six hundred young men, some firm and unbending characters, who decline to be withdrawn in this way from circulation. I know some of them; but if the story of their struggles with men and things could be told in full; if it were known how that, while full of useful projects and ideas which would put life and wealth into stagnant country districts, they meet with hindrances put in their way by the very men who (so the government led them to believe) would give them help and countenance, the strong man, the man of talent, the man whose nature is a miracle, would be thought a hundred times more unfortunate and more to be pitied than the man whose degenerate nature tamely resigns himself to the atrophy of his faculties.

"So I would prefer to direct some private commercial or industrial enterprise, and live on very little, while trying to find a solution of some one of the many unsolved problems of industry and modern life, rather than remain where I am. You will say that there is nothing to prevent me from employing my powers as it is; that in the silence of this humdrum life I might set myself to find the solution of one of those problems which presses on humanity. Ah! monsieur, do you not understand what the influence of the provinces is; the enervating effect of a life just sufficiently busy to fill the days with all but futile work, but yet not full enough to give occupation to the powers so fully developed by such a training as ours? You will not think, my dear guardian, that I am eaten up with the ambition of money-making or consumed with a mad desire for fame. I have not learned to calculate to so little purpose that I cannot measure the emptiness of fame. The inevitable activity of life has led me not to think of marriage; and looking at my present prospects, I have not so good an opinion of existence as to give such a sorry present to another self. Although I look upon money as one of the most powerful instruments that can be put in the hands of a civilized man, money is, after all, only a means. My sole pleasure lies in the assurance that I am serving my country. To have employment for my faculties in a congenial atmosphere would be the height of enjoyment for me. Perhaps among your acquaintance in your part of the world, in the circle on which you shine, you might hear of something which · requires some of the aptitude which you know that I possess; I will wait six months for an answer from you.

" These things which I am writing to you, dear patron and friend, others are thinking. I have seen a good many of my colleagues or old scholars at the École caught, as I was, in the snare of a special training; ordnance surveyors, captain-professors, captains in the artillery, doomed (as they see) to be captains for the rest of their days, bitterly regretting that they did not go into the regular army. Again and again, in fact, we have admitted to each other in confidence that we are victims of a long mystification, which we only discover when it is too late to draw back, when the mill-horse is used to the round and the sick man accustomed to his disease.

"After looking carefully into these melancholy results, I have asked myself the following questions, which I send to you, as a man of sense, whose mature wisdom will see all that lies in them, knowing that they are fruit of thought refined by the fires of painful experience.

"What end has the government in view? To obtain the best abilities? If so, the government sets to work to obtain a directly opposite result : if it had hated talent, it could not have had better success in producing respectable mediocrities. Or does it intend to open out a career to selected intelligence? It could not well have given it a more mediocre position. There is not a man sent out by the Écoles who does not regret between fifty and sixty that he fell into the snare concealed by the offers of the government. Does it mean to secure men of genius? What really great man have the Écoles turned out since 1790? Would Cachin, the genius to whom we owe Cherbourg, have existed but for Napoleon? It was imperial despotism which singled him out; the Constitutional Administration would have stifled him. Does the Académie des Sciences number many members who have passed through the technical schools? Two or three, it may be ; but the man of genius invariably appears from outside. In the particular sciences which are studied at these schools, genius obeys no laws but its own ; it only develops under circumstances over which we have no control ; and neither the government nor anthropology knows the conditions. Riquet, Perronet, Leonardo da Vinci, Cachin, Palladio, Brunelleschi, Michel Angelo, Bramante, Vauban, and Vicat all derived their genius from unobserved causes and preparation to which we give the name of chance—the great word for fools to fall back upon. Schools or no schools, these sublime workers have never been lacking in every age. And now, does the government, by means of organizing, obtain works of public utility better done or at a cheaper rate?

"In the first place, private enterprise does very well without professional engineers ; and, in the second, state-directed works are the most expensive of all ; and besides the actual outlay, there is the cost of the maintenance of the great staff of the Roads and Bridges Department. Finally, in other countries where they have no institutions of this kind, in Germany, England, and Italy, such public works are carried out quite as well, and cost less than ours in France. Each of the three countries is well known for new and useful inventions of this kind. I know it is the fashion to speak of our Écoles as if they were the envy of Europe ; but Europe has been watching us these fifteen years, and nowhere will you find the like instituted elsewhere. The English, those shrewd men of business, have better schools among their working classes, where they train practical men, who become conspicuous at once when they rise from practical work to theory. Stephenson and Macadam were not pupils in these famous institutions of ours.

" But where is the use ? When young and clever engineers, men of spirit and enthusiasm, have solved at the outset of their career the problem of the maintenance of the roads of France, which requires hundreds of millions of francs every twenty-five years, which roads are in a deplorable state, it is in vain for them to publish learned treatises and memorials ; everything is swallowed down by the board of direction, everything goes in and nothing comes out of a central bureau in Paris, where the old men are jealous of their juniors, and high-places are refuges for superannuated blunderers.

" This is how, with a body of educated men distributed all over France, a body which is part of the machinery of administrative government, and to whom the country looks for direction and enlightenment on the great questions within their department, it will probably happen that we in France shall still be talking about railways when other countries have finished theirs. Now, if ever France ought to demonstrate the excellence of her technical schools as an institution, should it not be in a magnificent public work of this special kind, destined to change the face of many countries, and to double the length of human life by modifying the laws of time and space? Belgium, the United States, Germany, and England, without an École Polytechnique, will have a network of railways while our engineers are still tracing out the plans, and hideous jobbery lurking behind the projects will check· their execution. You cannot lay a stone in France until half a score of scribblers in Paris have drawn up a driveling report that nobody wants. The government, therefore, gets no good of its technical schools; and as for the individual —he is tied down to a mediocre career, his life is a cruel delusion. Certain it is that with the abilities which he displayed between the ages of sixteen and twenty-five he would have gained more reputation and riches if he had been left to shift for himself than he will acquire in the career to which government condemns him. As a merchant, a scientific man, or a soldier, this picked man would have a wide field before him, his precious faculties and enthusiasm would not have been prematurely and stupidly exhausted. Then where is the advance? Assuredly the individual and the state both lose by the present system. Does not an experiment carried on for half a century show that changes are needed in the way the institution is worked? What priesthood qualifies a man for the task of selecting from a whole generation those who shall hereafter be the learned class of France? What studies should not these high-priests of destiny have made? A knowledge of mathematics is, perhaps, scarcely so necessary · as physiological knowledge; and does it not seem to you that something of that clairvoyance which is the wizardry of great men might be required too? As a matter of fact, the examiners are old professors, men worthy of all honor, grown old in harness; their duty it is to discover the best memories, and there is an end of it; they can do nothing but what is required of them. Truly, their functions should be the most important ones in the state, and call for extraordinary men to fulfill them.

" Do not think, my dear friend and patron, that my censure is confined to the École through which I myself passed ; it applies not only to the institution itself, but also and still more to the methods by which lads are admitted ; that is to say, to the system of competitive examination. Competition is a modern invention, and essentially bad. It is bad not only in learning, but in every possible connection, in the arts, in every election made of men, projects, or things. It is unfortunate that our famous schools should not have turned out better men than any other chance assemblage of lads ; but it is still more disgraceful that among the prizemen at the institute there has been no great painter, musician, architect, or sculptor ; even as for the past twenty years the general elections have swept no single great statesman to the front out of all the shoals of mediocrities. My remarks have a bearing upon an error which is vitiating both politics and education in France. This cruel error is based on the following principle, which organizers have overlooked :

" ' *Nothing in experience or in the nature of things can warrant the assumption that the intellectual qualities of early manhood will be those of maturity.*'

" At the present time I have been brought in contact with several distinguished men who are studying the many moral maladies which prey upon France. They recognize, as I do, the fact that secondary education forces a sort of temporary capacity in those who have neither present work nor future prospects ; and that the enlightenment diffused by primary education is of no advantage to the state, because it is bereft of belief and sentiment.

" Our whole educational system calls for sweeping reform, which should be carried out under the direction of a man of profound knowledge, a man with a strong will, gifted with that legislative faculty which, possibly, is found in Jean-Jacques Rousseau alone of all moderns.

" Then, perhaps, the superfluous specialists might find em-

ployment in elementary teaching; it is badly needed by the
mass of the people. We have not enough patient and devoted
teachers for the training of these classes. The deplorable preva-
lence of crimes and misdemeanors points to a weak spot in our
social system—the one-sided education which tends to weaken
the fabric of society, by teaching the masses to think sufficiently to reject the religious beliefs necessary for their government, yet not enough to raise them to a conception of the
theory of obedience and duty, which is the last word of
transcendental philosophy. It is impossible to put a whole
nation through a course of Kant; and belief and use and
wont are more wholesome for the people than study and argument.

"If I had to begin again from the very beginning, I dare
say I might enter a seminary and incline to the life of a simple
country parson or a village schoolmaster. But now I have
gone too far to be a mere elementary teacher; and, besides, a
wider field of action is open to me than the schoolhouse or
the parish. I cannot go the whole way with the Saint-Simonians, with whom I am tempted to throw in my lot; but with
all their mistakes, they have laid a finger on many weak points
in our social system, the results of our legislation, which will
be palliated rather than remedied—simply putting off the evil
day for France. Good-bye, dear sir; in spite of these observations of mine, rest assured of my respectful and faithful
friendship, a friendship which can only grow with time.

"GRÉGOIRE GÉRARD."

Acting on old business habit, Grossetête had indorsed the
letter with the rough draft of a reply, and written beneath it
the sacramental word "Answered."

"MY DEAR GÉRARD :—It is the more unnecessary to enter
upon any discussion of the observations contained in your
letter, since that chance (to make use of the word for fools)

enables me to make you an offer which will practically extricate you from a position in which you find yourself so ill at ease. Mme. Graslin, who owns the forest of Montégnac, and a good deal of barren land below the long range of hills on which the forest lies, has a notion of turning her vast estates to some account, of exploiting the woods and bringing the stony land into cultivation. Small pay and plenty of work! A great result to be brought about by insignificant means, a district to be transformed! Abundance made to spring up on the barest rock! Is not this what you wished to do, you who would fain realize a poet's dream? From the sincere ring of your letter, I do not hesitate to ask you to come to Limoges to see me, but do not send in your resignation, my friend, only sever your connection with your corps, explain to the authorities that you are about to make a study of some problems that lie within your province, but outside the limits of your work for the government. In that way you will lose none of your privileges, and you will gain time in which to decide whether this scheme of the curé's at Montégnac, which finds favor in Mme. Graslin's eyes, is a feasible one. If these vast changes should prove to be practicable, I will lay the possible advantages before you by word of mouth, and not by letter. Believe me to be always sincerely your friend,

"GROSSETÊTE."

For all reply Mme. Graslin wrote :

"Thank you, my friend; I am waiting to see your protégé."

She showed the letter to M. Bonnet, with the remark, "Here is one more wounded creature seeking the great hospital!"

The curé read the letter and re-read it, took two or three turns upon the terrace, and handed the paper back to Mme. Graslin.

"It comes from a noble nature, the man has something in him," he said. "He writes that the schools, invented by the spirit of the Revolution, manufacture inaptitude; for my own part, I call them manufactories of unbelief; for if M. Gérard is not an atheist, he is a Protestant——"

"We will ask him," she said, struck with the curé's answer.

A fortnight later, in the month of December, M. Grossetête came to Montégnac, in spite of the cold, to introduce his protégé. Véronique and M. Bonnet awaited his arrival with impatience.

"One must love you very much, my child," said the old man, taking both of Véronique's hands, and kissing them with the old-fashioned elderly gallantry which a woman never takes amiss; "yes, one must love you very much indeed to stir out of Limoges in such weather as this; but I had made up my mind that I must come in person to make you a present of M. Grégoire Gérard. Here he is. A man after your own heart, M. Bonnet," the old banker added with an affectionate greeting to the curé.

Gérard's appearance was not very prepossessing. He was a thick-set man of middle height; his neck was lost in his shoulders, to use the common expression; he had the golden hair and red eyes of an Albino; and his eyelashes and eyebrows were almost white. Although, as often happens in these cases, his complexion was dazzlingly fair, its original beauty was destroyed by the very apparent pits and seams left by an attack of smallpox; much reading had doubtless injured his eyesight, for he wore colored spectacles. Nor when he divested himself of a thick overcoat, like a gendarme's, did his dress redeem these personal defects.

The way in which his clothes were put on and buttoned, like his untidy cravat and crumpled shirt, were distinctive signs of that personal carelessness, laid to the charge of learned men, who are all, more or less, oblivious of their surroundings. His face and bearing, the great development of chest and shoulders, as compared with his thin legs, suggested a sort of physical deterioration produced by meditative habits, not uncommon in those who think much ; but the stout heart and eager intelligence of the writer of the letter were plainly visible on a forehead which might have been chiseled in Carrara marble. Nature seemed to have reserved her seal of greatness for the brow, and stamped it with the steadfastness and goodness of the man. The nose was of the true Gallic type, and blunted. The firm, straight lines of the mouth indicated an absolute discretion and the sense of economy ; but the whole face looked old before its time, and worn with study.

Mme. Graslin turned to speak to the inventor. "We already owe you thanks, monsieur," she said, "for being so good as to come to superintend engineering work in a country which can hold out no inducements to you save the satisfaction of knowing that you can do good."

" M. Grossetête told me enough about you on our way here, madame," he answered, "to make me feel very glad to be of any use to you. The prospect of living near to you and M. Bonnet seemed to be charming. Unless I am driven away, I look to spend my life here."

"We will try to give you no cause for changing your opinion," said Mme. Graslin.

Grossetête took her aside. "Here are the papers which the public prosecutor gave me," he said. "He seemed very much surprised that you did not apply directly to him. All that you have asked has been done promptly and with goodwill. In the first place, your protégé will be reinstated in all his rights as a citizen ; and, in the second, Catherine Curieux will be sent to you in three months' time."

"Where is she ?" asked Véronique.

"At the Hôpital Saint-Louis," Grossetête answered. "She cannot leave Paris until she is recovered."

14

" Ah ! is she ill, poor thing? "

" You will find all that you want to know here," said Grossetête, holding out a packet.

Véronique went back to her guests, and led the way to the magnificent dining-hall on the ground floor, walking between Grossetête and Gérard.   She presided over the dinner without joining them, for she had made it a rule to take her meals alone since she had come to Montégnac.   No one but Aline was in the secret, which the girl kept scrupulously until her mistress was in danger of her life.

The mayor of Montégnac, the justice of the peace, and the doctor had naturally been invited to meet the newcomer.

The doctor, a young man of seven-and-twenty, Roubaud by name, was keenly desirous of making the acquaintance of the great lady of Limousin.   The curé was the better pleased to introduce him at the château since it was M. Bonnet's wish that Véronique should gather some sort of society about her, to distract her thoughts from herself, and to find some mental food.   Roubaud was one of the young doctors perfectly equipped in his science, such as the École de Médecine turns out in Paris, a man who might, without doubt, have looked to a brilliant future in the vast theatre of the capital ; but he had seen something of the strife of ambitions there, and took fright, conscious that he had more knowledge than capacity for scheming, more aptitude than greed ; his gentle nature had inclined him to the narrower theatre of provincial life, where he hoped to win appreciation sooner than in Paris.

At Limoges Roubaud had come into collision with old-fashioned ways and patients not to be shaken in their prejudices ; he had been won over by M. Bonnet, who at sight of the kindly and prepossessing face had thought that here was a worker to co-operate with him.   Roubaud was short and fair-haired, and would have been rather uninteresting looking but for the gray eyes, which revealed the physiologist's sagacity and the perseverance of the student.   Hitherto

Montégnac was fain to be content with an old army surgeon, who found his cellars a good deal more interesting than his patients, and who, moreover, was past the hard work of a country doctor. He happened to die just at that time. Roubaud had been in Montégnac for some eighteen months, and was very popular there; but Desplein's young disciple, one of the followers of Cabanis, was no Catholic in his beliefs. In fact, as to religion, he had lapsed into a fatal indifference, from which he was not to be roused. He was the despair of the curé, not that there was any harm whatever in him, his invariable absence from church was excused by his profession, he never talked on religious topics, he was incapable of making proselytes, no good Catholic could have behaved better than he, but he declined to occupy himself with a problem which, to his thinking, was beyond the scope of the human mind; and the curé once hearing him let fall the remark that Pantheism was the religion of all great thinkers, fancied that Roubaud inclined to the Pythagorean doctrine of the transformation of souls.

Roubaud, meeting Mme. Graslin for the first time, felt violently startled at the sight of her. His medical knowledge enabled him to divine in her face and bearing and worn features unheard-of suffering of mind and body, a preternatural strength of character, and the great faculties which can endure the strain of very different vicissitudes. He, in a manner, read her inner history, even the dark places deliberately hidden away; and more than this, he saw the disease that preyed upon the secret heart of this fair woman; for there are certain tints in human faces that indicate a poison working in the thoughts, even as the color of fruit will betray the presence of the worm at its core. From that time forward M. Roubaud felt so strongly attracted to Mme. Graslin, that he feared to be drawn beyond the limit where friendship ends. There was an eloquence, which men always understand, in Véronique's brows and attitude, and, above all, in her eyes; it was suffi-

ciently unmistakable that she was dead to love, even as other
women with a like eloquence proclaim the contrary. The
doctor became her chivalrous worshiper on the spot. He
exchanged a swift glance with the curé, and M. Bonnet said
within himself—

"Here is the flash from heaven that will change this
poor unbeliever? Mme. Graslin will have more eloquence
than I."

The mayor, an old countryman, overawed by the splendor
of the dining-room, and surprised to be asked to meet one of
the richest men in the department, had put on his best clothes
for the occasion; he felt somewhat uneasy in them, and
scarcely more at ease with his company. Mme. Graslin, too,
in her mourning dress was an awe-inspiring figure; the worthy
mayor was dumb. He had once been a farmer at Saint-
Léonard, had bought the one habitable house in the township,
and cultivated the land that belonged to it himself. He could
read and write, but only managed to acquit himself in his
official capacity with the help of the justice's clerk, who prepared his work for him; so he ardently desired the advent of
a notary, meaning to lay the burden of his public duties on
official shoulders when that day should come; but Montégnac
was so poverty-stricken that a resident notary was hardly
needed, and the notaries of the principal place in the arrondissement found clients in Montégnac.

The justice of the peace, Clousier by name, was a retired
barrister from Limoges. Briefs had grown scarce with the
learned gentleman, owing to a tendency on his part to put in
practice the noble maxim that a barrister is the first judge of
the client and the case. About the year 1809 he obtained
this appointment; the salary was a meagre pittance, but
enough to live upon. In this way he had reached the most
honorable but the most complete penury. Twenty-two years
of residence in the poor commune had transformed the worthy
lawyer into a countryman, scarcely to be distinguished from

any of the small farmers round about, whom he resembled even in the cut of his coat. But beneath Clousier's homely exterior dwelt a clairvoyant spirit, a philosophical politician whose Gallio's attitude was due to his perfect knowledge of human nature and of men's motives. For a long time he had baffled M. Bonnet's perspicacity. The man who, in a higher sphere, might have played the active part of a L'Hôpital, incapable of intrigue, like all deep thinkers, had come at last to·lead the contemplative life of a hermit of olden time. Rich without doubt with all the gains of privation, he was swayed by no personal considerations ; he knew the law, and judged impartially. His life, reduced to the barest necessaries, was regular and pure. The peasants loved and respected M. Clousier for the fatherly disinterestedness with which he settled their disputes and gave advice in even their smallest difficulties. For the last two years " Old Clousier," as every one called him in Montégnac, had had one of his nephews to help him, a rather intelligent young man, who, at a later day, contributed not a little to the prosperity of the commune.

The most striking thing about the old man's face was the broad vast forehead. Two bushy masses of white hair stood out on either side of it. A florid complexion and magisterial portliness might give the impression that (in spite of his real sobriety) he was as earnest a disciple of Bacchus as of Troplong and Toullier. His scarcely audible voice indicated asthmatic oppression of breathing ; possibly the dry air of Montégnac had counted for something in his decision when he made up his mind to accept the post. His little house had been fitted up for him by the well-to-do sabot-maker, his landlord.

Clousier had already seen Véronique at the church, and had formed his own opinion of her, which opinion he kept to himself ; he had not even spoken of her to M. Bonnet, with whom he was beginning to feel at home. For the first time in

his life, the justice of the peace found himself in the company
of persons able to understand him.

When the six guests had taken their places round a hand-
somely-appointed table (for Véronique had brought all her
furniture with her to Montégnac), there was a brief embarrassed pause. The doctor, the mayor, and the justice were
none of them acquainted with Grossetête or with Gérard.
But during the first course the banker's geniality thawed the
ice, Mme. Graslin graciously encouraged M. Roubaud and
drew out Gérard; under her influence all these different
natures, full of exquisite qualities, recognized their kinship.
It was not long before each felt himself to be in a congenial
atmosphere. So that by the time dessert was put on the table,
and the crystal and the gilded edges of the porcelain sparkled,
when choice wines were set in circulation, handed to the
guests by Aline, Maurice Champion, and Grossetête's man,
the conversation had become more confidential, so that the four
noble natures thus brought together by chance felt free to
speak their real minds on the great subjects that men love to
discuss in good faith.

"Your leave of absence coincided with the Revolution of
July," Grossetête said, looking at Gérard in a way that asked
his opinion.

"Yes," answered the engineer. "I was in Paris during
the three famous days; I saw it all; I drew some disheartening conclusions."

"What were they?" M. Bonnet asked quickly.

"There is no patriotism left except under the workman's
shirt," answered Gérard. "Therein lies the ruin of France.
The Revolution of July is the defeat of men who are notable
for birth, fortune, and talent, and a defeat in which they
acquiesce. The enthusiastic zeal of the masses has gained a
victory over the rich and intelligent classes, to whom zeal and
enthusiasm are antipathetic."

"To judge by last year's events," added M. Clousier, "the

change is a direct encouragement to the evil which is devouring us—to individualism. In fifty years' time every generous
question will be replaced by a '*What is that to me?*' the
watchword of independent opinion descended from the spiritual heights where Luther, Calvin, Zwingle, and Knox inaugurated it, till even in political economy each has a right to
his own opinion. *Each for himself! Let each man mind his
own business!*—these two terrible phrases, together with *What
is that to me?* complete a trinity of doctrine for the bourgeoisie and the peasant proprietors. This egoism is the result
of defects in our civil legislation, somewhat too hastily accomplished in the first instance, and now confirmed by the terrible
consecration of the Revolution of July."

The justice relapsed into his wonted silence again with this
speech, which gave the guests plenty to think over.   Then M.
Bonnet ventured yet further, encouraged by Clousier's remarks, and by a glance exchanged between Gérard and
Grossetête.

"Good King Charles X.," said he, " has just failed in the
most provident and salutary enterprise that king ever undertook for the happiness of a nation intrusted to him.   The
Church should be proud of the share she had in his councils.
But it was the heart and brain of the upper classes which failed
him, as they had failed before over the great question of the
law with regard to the succession of the eldest son, the eternal
honor of the one bold statesman of the Restoration—the
Comte de Peyronnet.   To reconstruct the nation on the basis
of the family, to deprive the press of its power to do harm
without restricting its usefulness, to confine the elective chamber to the functions for which it was really intended, to give
back to religion its influence over the people—such were the
four cardinal points of the domestic policy of the House of
Bourbon.   Well, in twenty years' time all France will see the
necessity of that great and salutary course.   King Charles X.
was, moreover, more insecure in the position which he decided

to quit than in the position in which his paternal authority came to an end. The future history of our fair country, when everything shall be periodically called in question, when ceaseless discussion shall take the place of action, when the press shall become the sovereign power and the tool of the basest ambitions, will prove the wisdom of the king who has just taken with him the real principles of government. History will render to him his due for the courage with which he withstood his best friends, when once he had probed the wound, seen its extent, and the pressing necessity for the treatment, which has not been continued by those for whom he threw himself into the breach."

"Well, M. le Curé, you go straight to the point without the slightest disguise," cried M. Gérard, "but I do not say nay. When Napoleon made his Russian campaign he was forty years ahead of his age; he was misunderstood. Russia and England, in 1830, can explain the campaign of 1812. Charles X. was in the same unfortunate position; twenty-five years hence his ordinances may perhaps become law."

"France, too eloquent a country not to babble, too vainglorious to recognize real ability, in spite of the sublime good sense of her language and the mass of her people, is the very last country in which to introduce the system of two deliberating chambers," the justice of the peace remarked. "At any rate, not without the admirable safeguards against these elements in the national character, devised by Napoleon's experience. The representative system may work in a country like England, where its action is circumscribed by the nature of the soil; but the right of primogeniture, as applied to real estate, is a necessary part of it; without this factor, the representative system becomes sheer nonsense. England owes its existence to the quasi-feudal law which transmitted the house and lands to the oldest son. Russia is firmly seated on the feudal system of autocracy. For these reasons, both nations at the present day are making alarming progress. Austria

could not have resisted our invasions as she did, nor declared
a second war against Napoleon, had it not been for the law of
primogeniture, which preserves the strength of the family and
maintains production on the large scale necessary to the state.
The House of Bourbon, conscious that liberalism had relegated
France to the rank of a third-rate power in Europe, determined to regain and keep their place, and the country shook
off the Bourbons when they had all but saved the country. I
do not know how deep the present state of things will sink us."

"If there should be a war," cried Grossetête, "France
will be without horses, as Napoleon was in 1813, when he was
reduced to the resources of France alone, and could not
make use of the victories of Lutzen and Bautzen, and was
crushed at Leipsic! If peace continues, the evil will grow
worse: twenty years hence the number of horned cattle and
horses in France will be diminished by one-half."

"M. Grossetête is right," said Gérard. "So the work
which you have decided to attempt here is a service done to
your country, madame," he added, turning to Véronique.

"Yes," said the justice of the peace, "because Mme.
Graslin has but one son. But will this chance in the succession repeat itself? For a certain time, let us hope, the great
and magnificent scheme of cultivation which you are to
carry into effect will be in the hands of one owner, and therefore will continue to provide grazing land for horses and
cattle. But, in spite of all, a day will come when forest and
field will be either divided up or sold in lots. Division and
subdivision will follow, until the six thousand acres of plain
will count ten or twelve hundred owners; and when that time
comes there will be no more horses nor prize cattle."

"Oh! when that time comes——" said the mayor.

"There is a *What is that to me?*" cried M. Grossetête,
"and M. Clousier sounded the signal for it; he is caught in
the act. But, monsieur," the banker went on gravely,
addressing the bewildered mayor, "the time *has* come!

Round about Paris for a ten-league radius, the land is divided
up into little patches that will hardly pasture sufficient milch
cows.   The commune of Argenteuil numbers thirty-eight
thousand eight hundred and eighty-five plots of land, a good
many of them bringing in less than fifteen centimes a year!
If it were not for high farming and manure from Paris, which
give heavy crops of fodder of different kinds, I do not know
how cow-keepers and dairymen would manage.   As it is, the
animals are peculiarly subject to inflammatory diseases consequent on the heating diet and confinement to cow-sheds.
They wear out their cows round about Paris just as they wear
out horses in the streets.   Then market-gardens, orchards,
nurseries, and vineyards pay so much better than pasture, that
the grazing land is gradually diminishing.   A few years more,
and milk will be sent in by express to Paris, like saltfish, and
what is going on round Paris is happening also about all large
towns.   The evils of the minute subdivision of landed property are extending round a hundred French cities; some day
all France will be eaten up by them.

"In 1800, according to Chaptal, there were about five
million acres of vineyard; exact statistics would show fully
five times as much to-day.   When Normandy is split up into
an infinitude of small holdings, by our system of inheritance
fifty per cent. of the horse and cattle trade there will fall off;
still Normandy will have the monopoly of the Paris milk
trade, for luckily the climate will not permit vine culture.
Another curious thing to notice is the steady rise in the price
of butcher meat.   In 1814, prices ranged from seven to
eleven sous per pound; in 1850, twenty years hence, Paris
will pay twenty sous, unless some genius is raised up to carry
out the theories of Charles X."   .

"You have pointed out the greatest evil in France," said
the justice of the peace.   "The cause of it lies in the chapter
Des Successions in the Civil Code, wherein the equal division
of real estate among the children of the family is required.

That is the pestle which is constantly grinding the country to powder, gives to every one but a life-interest in property which cannot remain as it is after his death. A continuous process of decomposition (for the reverse process is never set up) will end by ruining France. The French Revolution generated a deadly virus, and the Days of July have set the poison working afresh; this dangerous germ of disease is the acquisition of land by peasants. If the chapter *Des Successions* is the origin of the evil, it is through the peasant that it reaches its worst phase. The peasant never relinquishes the land he has won. Let a bit of land once get between the ogre's ever-hungry jaws, he divides and subdivides it until there are but strips of three furrows left. Nay, even there he does not stop! he will divide the three furrows in lengths. The commune of Argenteuil, which M. Grossetête instanced just now, is a case in point. The preposterous value which the peasants set on the smallest scraps of land makes it quite impossible to reconstruct an estate. The law and procedure are made a dead letter at once by this division, and ownership is reduced to absurdity. But it is a comparatively trifling matter that the minute subdivision of the law should paralyze the treasury and the law by making it impossible to carry out its wisest regulations. There are far greater evils than even these. There are actually landlords of property bringing in fifteen and twenty centimes per annum!

"Monsieur has just said something about the falling off of cattle and horses," Clousier continued, looking at Grossetête; "the system of inheritance counts for much in that matter. The peasant proprietor keeps cows, and cows only, because milk enters into his diet; he sells the calves; he even sells butter. He has no mind to raise oxen, still less to breed horses; he has only just sufficient fodder for a year's consumption; and when a dry spring comes and hay is scarce, he is forced to take his cow to market; he cannot afford to keep her. If it should fall out so unluckily that two bad hay harvests came in succession, you would see some strange fluctuations in the price of beef in Paris, and, above all, in veal, when the third year came."

"And how would they do for patriotic banquets then?" asked the doctor, smiling.

"Ah!" exclaimed Mme. Graslin, glancing at Roubaud, "so even here, as everywhere else, politics must be served up with journalistic items."

"In this bad business the bourgeoisie play the part of American pioneers," continued Clousier. "They buy up the large estates, too large for the peasant to meddle with, and divide them. After the bulk has been cut up and triturated, a forced sale or an ordinary sale in lots hands it over sooner or later to the peasant. Everything nowadays is reduced to figures, and I know of none more eloquent than these: France possesses forty-nine million *hectares* of land, for the sake of convenience, let us say forty, deducting something for roads and high-roads, dunes, canals, land out of cultivation, and wastes like the plain of Montégnac, which need capital. Now, out of forty million *hectares* to a population of thirty-two millions, there are a hundred and twenty-five million parcels of land, according to the land-tax returns. I have not taken the fractions into account. So we have outrun the agrarian law, and yet neither poverty nor discord are at an end. Then the next thing will be that those who are turning the land into crumbs and diminishing the output of produce will find mouthpieces for the cry that true social justice only permits the usufruct of the land to each. They will say that ownership in perpetuity is robbery. The Saint-Simonians have begun already."

"There spoke the magistrate," said Grossetête, "and this is what the banker adds to his bold reflections. When landed property became tenable by peasants and small shopkeepers, a great wrong was done to France, though the government does not so much as suspect it. Suppose that we set down the whole mass of the peasants at three million families, after deducting the paupers. Those families all belong to the wage-earning class. Their wages are paid in money instead of in kind——''

''There is another immense blunder in our legislation,'' Clousier cried, breaking in on the banker. ''In 1790 it might still have been possible to pass a law empowering employers to pay wages in kind, but now—to introduce such a measure would be to risk a revolution.''

''In this way,'' Grossetête continued, ''the money of the country passes into the pockets of the proletariat. Now, the peasant has one passion, one desire, one determination, one aim in life—to die a landed proprietor. This desire, as M. Clousier has very clearly shown, is one result of the Revolution—a direct consequence of the sale of the national lands. Only those who have no idea of the state of things in country districts could refuse to admit that each of those three million families annually buries fifty francs as a regular thing, and in this way a hundred and fifty millions of francs are withdrawn from circulation every year. The science of political economy has reduced to an axiom the statement that a five-franc piece, if it passes through a hundred hands in the course of a day, does duty for five hundred francs. Now, it is certain for some of us old observers of the state of things in country districts that the peasant fixes his eyes on a bit of land, keeps ready to pounce upon it, and bides his time—meanwhile he never invests his capital. The intervals in the peasant's land-purchases should, therefore, be reckoned at periods of seven years. For seven years, consequently, a capital of eleven hundred million francs is lying idle in the peasants' hands; and as the lower middle classes do the same thing to quite the same extent, and behave in the same way with regard to land on too large a scale for the peasant to nibble at, in forty-two years France loses the interest on two milliards of francs at least—that is to say, on something like a hundred millions every seven years, or six hundred millions in forty-two years. But this is not the only loss. France has failed to create the worth of six hundred millions in agricultural or industrial produce. And this failure to produce may be taken as a loss of twelve hundred million francs ; for if the market price of a product were not double the actual cost of production, commerce would be at a standstill. The proletariat deprives itself of six hundred million francs of wages. These six hundred millions of initial loss that represent, for an economist, twelve hundred millions of loss of benefit derived from circulation, explain how it is that our commerce, shipping trade, and agriculture compare so badly with the state of things in England. In spite of the differences between the two countries (a good two-thirds of them, moreover, in our favor), England could mount our cavalry twice over, and every one there eats meat. But then, under the English system of land-tenure, it is almost impossible for the working classes to buy land, and so all the money is kept in constant circulation. So besides the evils of the comminution of the land, and the decay of the trade in cattle, horses, and sheep, the chapter *Des Successions* costs us a further loss of six hundred million francs of interest on the capital buried by the peasants and trades-people, or twelve hundred million francs' worth of produce (at the least)—that is to say, a total loss of three milliards of francs withdrawn from circulation every half-century.''

"The moral effect is worse than the material effect!" cried the curé. "We are turning the peasantry into pauper landowners, and half educating the lower middle classes. It will not be long before the canker of *Each for himself! Let each mind his own business !* which did its work last July among the upper classes, will spread to the middle classes. A proletariat of hardened materialists, knowing no God but envy, no zeal but the despair of hunger, with no faith nor belief left, will come to the front, and trample the heart of the country under foot. The foreigner, waxing great under a monarchical government, will find us under the shadow of royalty without the reality of a king, without law under the cover of legality, owners of property but not proprietors, with the right of election but without a government, listless holders of free and independent opinions, equal but equally unfortunate. Let us hope that between now and then God will raise up in France the man for the time, one of those elect who breathe a new spirit into a nation, a man who, whether he is a Sylla or a Marius, whether he comes from the heights or rises from the depths, will reconstruct society."

"The first thing to do will be to send him to the assizes or to the police court," said Gérard. "The judgment of Socrates or of Christ will be given to him, here in 1831, as of old in Attica and at Jerusalem. To-day, as of old, jealous mediocrity allows the thinker to starve. If the great political physicians who have studied the diseases of France, and are opposed to the spirit of the age, should resist to the starvation-point, we ridicule them, and treat them as visionaries. Here in France we revolt against the sovereign thinker, the great man of the future, just as we rise in revolt against the political sovereign."

"But in those old times the Sophists had a very limited audience," cried the justice of the peace; "while to-day, through the medium of the periodical press, they can lead a whole nation astray ; and the press which pleads for common-sense finds no echo ! "

The mayor looked at M. Clousier with intense astonishment. Mme. Graslin, delighted to find a simple justice of the peace interested in such grave problems, turned to her neighbor, M. Roubaud, with, " Do you know M. Clousier ? "

"Not till to-day ! Madame, you are working miracles," he added in her ear. "And yet look at his forehead, how finely shaped it is ! It is like the classical or traditional brow that sculptors gave to Lycurgus and the wise men of

Greece, is it not? Clearly there was an impolitic side to the Revolution of July,," he added aloud, after going through Grossetête's reasonings. He had been a medical student, and perhaps would have lent a hand at a barricade.

"'Twas trebly impolitic," said Clousier. " We have concluded the case for law and finance, now for the government. The royal power, weakened by the dogma of the national sovereignty, in virtue of which the election was made on the 9th of August, 1830, will strive to overcome its rival, a principle which gives the people the right of changing a dynasty every time they fail to apprehend the intentions of their king; so there is a domestic struggle before us which will check progress in France for a long while yet."

"England has wisely steered clear of all these sunken rocks," said Gérard. "I have been in England. I admire the hive which sends swarms over the globe to settle and civilize. In England political debate is a comedy intended to satisfy the people and to hide the action of authority which moves untrammeled in its lofty sphere; election there is not, as in France, the referring of a question to a stupid bourgeoisie. If the land were divided up, England would cease to exist at once. The great landowners and the lords control the machinery of government. They have a navy which takes possession of whole quarters of the globe (and under the very eyes of Europe) to fulfill the exigencies of their trade, and form colonies for the discontented and unsatisfactory. Instead of waging war on men of ability, annihilating and underrating them, the English aristocracy continually seeks them out, rewards and assimilates them. The English are prompt to act in all that concerns the government, and in the choice of men and material, while with us action of any kind is slow; and yet they are slow, and we impatient. Capital with them is adventurous, and always moving; with us it is shy and suspicious. Here is corroboration of M. Grossetête's statements about the loss to industry of the peasants' capital; I can sketch the difference in a few words.   English capital, which is constantly circulating, has created ten milliards of wealth in the shape of expanded manufactures and joint-stock companies paying dividends; while here in France, though we have more capital, it has not yielded one-tenth part of the profit.''

"It is all the more extraordinary," said Roubaud, "since they are lymphatic, and we are generally either sanguine or nervous.''

" Here is a great problem for you to study, monsieur," said Clousier.   " Given a national temperament, to find the institutions best adapted to counteract it.   Truly, Cromwell was a great legislator.   He, one man, made England what she is by promulgating the *Act of Navigation*, which made the English the enemy of all other nations, and infused into them a fierce pride, that has served them as a lever.   But in spite of their garrison at Malta, as soon as France and Russia fully understand the part to be played in politics by the Black Sea and the Mediterranean, the discovery of a new route to Asia by way of Egypt or the Euphrates valley will be a death-blow to England, just as the discovery of the Cape of Good Hope was the ruin of Venice.''

" And nothing of God in all this ! " cried the curé.   " M. Clousier and M. Roubaud are quite indifferent in matters of religion—— and you, monsieur?" he asked questioningly, turning to Gérard.

"A Protestant," said Grossetête.

"You guessed rightly ! " exclaimed Véronique, with a glance at the curé as she offered her hand to Clousier to return to her apartments.

All prejudices excited by M. Gérard's appearance quickly vanished, and the three notables of Montégnac congratulated themselves on such an acquisition.

"Unluckily," said M. Bonnet, " there is a cause for antagonism between Russia and the Catholic countries on the

15

shores of the Mediterranean ; a schism of little real importance divides the Greek Church from the Latin, to the great
misfortune of humanity."

" Each preaches for his saint," said Mme. Graslin, smiling.
" M. Grossetête thinks of lost milliards ; M. Clousier of law
in confusion ; the doctor sees in legislation a question of
temperaments ; M. le Curé sees in religion an obstacle in the
way of a good understanding between France and Russia."

" Please add, madame," said Gérard, " that in the seques-
tration of capital by the peasant and small tradesman, I see
the delay of the completion of railways in France——"

" Then what would you have ? " asked she.

" Oh ! The admirable Councilors of State who devised
laws in the time of the Emperor and the *Corps législatif*, when
those who had brains as well as those who had property had a
voice in the election, a body whose sole function it was to
oppose unwise laws or capricious wars.   The present Chamber
of Deputies is like to end, as you will see, by becoming the
governing body, and legalized anarchy it will be."

" Great heavens ! " cried the curé in an excess of lofty
patriotism, " how is it that minds so enlightened "—he indicated Clousier, Roubaud, and Gérard—" see the evil, and
point out the remedy, and do not begin by applying it to
themselves ?   All of you represent the classes attacked ; all of
you recognize the necessity of passive obedience on the part
of the great masses in the state, an obedience like that of the
soldier in time of war ; all of you desire the unity of authority,
and wish that it shall never be called in question.   But that
consolidation to which England has attained through the development of pride and material interests (which are a sort of
belief) can only be attained here by sentiments induced by
catholicism, and you are not Catholics !   I the priest drop
my character, and reason with rationalists.

" How can you expect the masses to become religious and
to obey if they see irreligion and relaxed discipline around

them? A people united by any faith will easily get the better of men without belief. The law of the interest of all, which underlies patriotism, is at once annulled by the law of individual interest, which authorizes and implants selfishness. Nothing is solid and durable but that which is natural, and the natural basis of politics is the family. The family should be the basis of all institutions. A universal effect denotes a coextensive cause. These things that you notice proceed from the social principle itself, which has no force, because it is based on independent opinion, and the right of private judgment is the forerunner of individualism. There is less wisdom in looking for the blessing of security from the intelligence and capacity of the majority than in depending upon the intelligence of institutions and the capacity of one single man for the blessing of security. It is easier to find wisdom in one man than in a whole nation. The peoples have but a blind heart to guide them; they feel, but they do not see. A government must see; and must not be swayed by sentiments. There is therefore an evident contradiction between the first impulses of the masses and the action of authority which must direct their energy and give it unity. To find a great prince is a great chance (to use your language), but to trust your destinies to any assembly of men, even if they are honest, is madness.

"France is mad at this moment! Alas! you are as thoroughly convinced of this as I. If all men who really believe what they say, as you do, would set the example in their own circle; if every intelligent thinker would set his hand to raising once more the altars of the great spiritual republic, of the one Church which has directed humanity, we might see once more in France the miracles wrought there by our fathers."

"What would you have, M. le Curé?" said Gérard, "if one must speak to you as in the confessional—I look on faith as a lie which you consciously tell yourself, on hope as a lie about the future, and on this charity of yours as a child's trick ; one is a good boy, for the sake of the jam.''

"And yet, monsieur, when hope rocks us we sleep well,'' said Mme. Graslin.

Roubaud, who was about to speak, supported by a glance from Grossetête and the curé, stopped short, however, at the words.

"Is it any fault of ours," said Clousier, "if Jesus Christ had not time to formulate a system of government in accordance with His teaching, as Moses did and Confucius— the two greatest legislators whom the world has seen, for the Jews and the Chinese still maintain their national existence, though the first are scattered all over the earth, and the second an isolated people ?''

"Ah ! you are giving me a task indeed,'' said the curé candidly, "but I shall triumph, I shall convert all of you. You are much nearer the faith than you think. Truth lurks beneath the lie; come forward but a step, and you return ! ''

And with this cry from the curé the conversation took a fresh direction.

The next morning before M. Grossetête went, he promised to take an active share in Véronique's schemes so soon as they should be judged practicable. Mme. Graslin and Gérard rode beside his traveling carriage as far as the point where the cross-road joined the high-road from Bordeaux to Lyons. Gérard was so eager to see the place, and Véronique so anxious to show it to him, that this ride had been planned overnight. After they took leave of the kind old man, they galloped down into the great plain and skirted the hillsides that lay between the château and the Living Rock. The surveyor recognized the rock embankment which Farrabesche had pointed out; it stood up like the lowest course of masonry under the foundations of the hills, in such a manner that when the bed of this indestructible canal of nature's making should be cleared out, and the water-courses regulated so as not to choke it, irrigation would actually be facilitated by that long channel which lay about ten feet above the surface of the plain. The first thing to be done was to estimate the volume of water in the Gabou, and to make certain that the sides of the valley could hold it; no decision could be made till this was known.

Véronique gave a horse to Farrabesche, who was to accompany Gérard and acquaint him with the least details which he himself had observed. After some days of consideration Gérard thought the base of either parallel chains of hill solid enough (albeit of different material) to hold the water.

In the January of the following year, a wet season, Gérard calculated the probable amount of water discharged by the Gabou, and found that, when the three water-courses had been diverted into the torrent, the total amount would be sufficient to water an area three times as great as the plain of Montégnac. The dams across the Gabou, the masonry and engineering works needed to bring the water-supply of the three little valleys into the plain, should not cost more than sixty thousand francs; for the surveyor discovered a quantity of chalky deposit on the common, so that lime would be cheap, and the forest being so near at hand, stone and timber would cost nothing even for transport. All the preparations could be made before the Gabou ran dry, so that when the important work should be begun it should quickly be finished. But the plain was another matter. Gérard considered that there the first preparation would cost at least two hundred thousand francs, sowing and planting apart.

The plain was to be divided into four squares of two hundred and fifty acres each. There was no question of breaking up the waste; the first thing to do was to remove the largest flints. Navvies would be employed to dig a great number of trenches and to line the channels with stone to keep the water in, for the water must be made to flow or to stand as required. All this work called for active, devoted, and painstaking workers. Chance so ordered it that the plain was a straightforward piece of work, a level stretch, and the water with a ten-foot fall could be distributed at will. There was nothing to prevent the finest results in farming the land ; here there might be just such a splendid green carpet as in North Italy, a source of wealth and of pride to Lombardy. Gérard sent to his late district for an old and experienced foreman, Fresquin by name.

Mme. Graslin, therefore, wrote to ask Grossetête to negotiate for her a loan of two hundred and fifty thousand francs on the security of her government stock ; the interest of six years, Gérard calculated, should pay off the debt, capital and interest. The loan was concluded in the course of the month of March ; and by that time Gérard, with Fresquin's assistance, had finished all the preliminary operations, leveling, boring, observations, and estimates. The news of the great scheme had spread through the country and roused the poor people ; and the indefatigable Farrabesche, Colorat, Clousier, Roubaud, and the Mayor of Montégnac, all those, in fact, who were interested in the enterprise for its own sake or for Mme. Graslin's, chose the workers or gave the names of the poor who deserved to be employed.

Gérard bought partly for M. Grossetête, partly on his own account, some thousand acres of land on the other side of the road through Montégnac. Fresquin, his foreman, also took five hundred acres, and sent for his wife and children.

In the early days of April, 1833, M. Grossetête came to Montégnac to see the land purchased for him by Gérard ; but the principal motive of his journey was the arrival of Catherine Curieux. She had come by the diligence from Paris to Limoges, and Mme. Graslin was expecting her. Grossetête found Mme. Graslin about to start for the church. M. Bonnet was to say a mass to ask the blessing of heaven on the work about to begin. All the men, women, and children were present.

M. Grossetête brought forward a woman of thirty or there-abouts, who looked weak and out of health.   "Here is your protégé," he said, addressing Véronique.

"Are you Catherine Curieux?" Mme. Graslin asked.

"Yes, madame."

For a moment Véronique looked at her; Catherine was rather tall, shapely, and pale; the exceeding sweetness of her features was not belied by the beautiful soft gray eyes.   In the shape of her face and the outlines of her forehead there was a nobleness, a sort of grave and simple majesty, sometimes seen in very young girls' faces in the country, a kind of flower of beauty, which field-work, and the constant wear of household cares, and sunburn, and neglect of appearance, wither with alarming rapidity.   From her attitude as she stood it was easy to discern that she would move with the ease of a daughter of the fields and something of an added grace, un-consciously learned in Paris.   If Catherine had never left the Corrèze, she would no doubt have been by this time a wrinkled and withered woman, the bright tints in her face would have grown hard; but Paris, which had toned down the high color, had preserved her beauty; and ill-health, weariness, and sor-row had given to her the mysterious gifts of melancholy and of that inner life of thought denied to poor toilers in the field who lead an almost animal existence.   Her dress likewise marked a distinction between her and the peasants; for it abundantly displayed the Parisian taste which even the least coquettish women are so quick to acquire.   Catherine Curieux, not knowing what might await her, and unable to judge the lady in whose presence she stood, seemed somewhat embarrassed.

"Do you still love Farrabesche?" asked Mme. Graslin, when Grossetête left the two women together for a moment.

"Yes, madame," she answered, flushing red.

"But if you sent him a thousand francs while he was in prison, why did you not come to him when he came out?

Do you feel any repugnance for him? Speak to me as you would to your own mother. Were you afraid that he had gone utterly to the bad? that he cared for you no longer?"

"No, madame; but I can neither read nor write. I was living with a very exacting old lady; she fell ill; we sat up with her of a night, and I had to nurse her. I knew the time was coming near when Jacques would be out of prison, but I could not leave Paris until the lady died. She left me nothing, after all my devotion to her and her interests. I had made myself ill with sitting up with her and the hard work of nursing, and I wanted to get well again before I came back. I spent all my savings, and then I made up my mind to go into the Hôpital Saint-Louis, and have just been discharged as cured."

Mme. Graslin was touched by an explanation so simple.

"Well, but, my dear," she said, "tell me why you left your people so suddenly; what made you leave your child? why did you not send them news of you, or get some one to write——"

For all answer, Catherine wept.

"Madame," she said at last, reassured by the pressure of Véronique's hand, "I daresay I was wrong, but it was more than I could do to stop in the place. It was not that I felt I had done wrong; it was the rest of them; I was afraid of their gossip and talk. So long as Jacques was here in danger, he could not do without me; but when he was gone, I felt as if I could not stop. There was I, a girl with a child and no husband! The lowest creature would have been better than I. If I had heard them say the least word about Benjamin or his father, I do not know what I should have done. I should have killed myself perhaps or gone out of my mind. My own father or mother might have said something hasty in a moment of anger. Meek as I am, I am too irritable to bear hasty words or insult. I have been well punished; I could not see my child, and never a day passed but I thought of him! I wanted to be forgotten, and forgotten I am. Nobody has given me a thought. They thought I was dead, and yet many and many a time I felt I could like to leave everything to have one day here and see my little boy——"

"Your little boy—see, Catherine, here he is!" replied Madame Graslin.

Catherine looked up and saw Benjamin, and something like a feverish shiver ran through her.

"Benjamin," said Mme. Graslin, "come and kiss your mother."

"My mother?" cried Benjamin in amazement. He flung his arms round Catherine's neck, and she clasped him to her with wild energy. But the boy escaped, and ran away crying, "I will find *him!*"

Mme. Graslin, seeing that Catherine's strength was failing, made her sit down; and as she did so her eyes met M. Bonnet's look, her color rose, for in that keen glance her confessor read her heart. She spoke tremulously.

"I hope, M. le Curé," she said, "that you will marry Catherine and Farrabesche at once. Do you not remember M. Bonnet, my child? He will tell you that Farrabesche has behaved himself like an honest man since he came back. Every one in the countryside respects him; if there is a place in the world where you may live happily with the good opinion of every one about you, it is here in Montégnac. With God's will, you will make your fortune here, for you shall be my tenants. Farrabesche has all his citizen's rights again."

"This is all true, my daughter," said the curé.

As he spoke, Farrabesche came in, led by his eager son. Face to face with Catherine in Mme. Graslin's presence, his face grew white, and he was mute. He saw how active the kindness of the one had been for him, and guessed all that the other had suffered in her enforced absence. Véronique turned to go with M. Bonnet, and the curé for his part wished to take Véronique aside. As soon as they were out of hearing,

Véronique's confessor looked full at her and saw her color rise ; she lowered her eyes like a guilty creature.

"You are degrading charity," he said severely.

"And how?" she asked, raising her head.

"Charity," said M. Bonnet, "is a passion as far greater than love, as humanity, madame, is greater than one human creature. All this is not the spontaneous work of disinterested virtue. You are falling from the grandeur of the service of man to the service of a single creature. In your kindness to Catherine and Farrabesche there is an alloy of memories and after-thoughts which spoils it in the sight of God. Pluck out the rest of the dart of the spirit of evil from your heart. Do not spoil the value of your good deeds in this way. Will you ever attain at last to that holy ignorance of the good that you do, which is the supreme grace of man's actions?"

Mme. Graslin turned away to dry her eyes. Her tears told the curé that his words had reached and probed some unhealed wound in her heart. Farrabesche, Catherine, and Benjamin came to thank their benefactress, but she made a sign to them to go away and leave her with M. Bonnet.

"You see how I have hurt them," she said, bidding him see their disappointed faces. And the tender-hearted curé beckoned to them to come back.

"You must be completely happy," she said. "Here is the patent which gives you back all your rights as a citizen, and exempts you from the old humiliating formalities," she added, holding out to Farrabesche a paper which she had kept. Farrabesche kissed Véronique's hand. There was an expression of submissive affection and quiet devotion in his eyes, the devotion which nothing could change, the fidelity of a dog for his master.

"If Jacques has suffered much, madame, I hope that it will be possible for me to make up to him in happiness for the trouble he has been through," said Catherine ; "for whatever he may have done, he is not bad."

Mme. Graslin turned away her head. The sight of their happiness seemed to crush her. M. Bonnet left her to go to the church, and she dragged herself thither on M. Grossetéte's arm.

After breakfast, every one went to see the work begun. All the old people of Montégnac were likewise present. Véronique stood between M. Grossetête and M. Bonnet on the top of the steep slope which the new road ascended, whence they could see the alignment of the four new roads, which served as a deposit for the stones taken off the land. Five navvies were clearing a space of eighteen feet (the width of each road), and throwing up a sort of embankment of good soil as they worked. Four men on either side were engaged in making a ditch, and these also made a bank of fertile earth along the edge of the field. Behind them came two men, who dug holes at intervals, and planted trees. In each division, thirty laborers (chosen from among the poor), twenty women, and forty girls and children, eighty-six workers in all, were busy piling up the stones which the workmen riddled out along the bank so as to measure the quantity produced by each group. In this way all went abreast, and with such picked and enthusiastic workers rapid progress was being made. Grossetête promised to send some trees, and to ask for more, among Mme. Graslin's friends. It was evident that there would not be enough in the nursery plantations at the château to supply such a demand.

Towards the end of the day, which was to finish with a great dinner at the château, Farrabesche begged to speak with Mme. Graslin for a moment. Catherine came with him.

"Madame," he said, "you were so kind as to promise me the home farm. You meant to help me to a fortune when you granted me such a favor, but I have come round to Catherine's ideas about our future. If I did well there, there would be jealousy; a word is soon said; I might find things unpleasant, I am afraid, and, besides, Catherine would never feel comfortable; it would be better for us to keep to ourselves, in fact. So I have come just to ask you if you will give us the land about the mouth of the Gabou, near the common, to farm instead, and a little bit of the wood yonder under the Living Rock. You will have a lot of workmen thereabouts in July, and it would be easy then to build a farmhouse on a knoll in a good situation. We should be very happy. I would send for Guépin, poor fellow, when he comes out of prison; he would work like a horse, and it is likely I might find a wife for him. My man is no do-nothing. No one will come up there to stare at us; we will colonize that bit of land, and it will be my great ambition to make a famous farm for you there. Besides, I have come to suggest a tenant for your great farm—a cousin of Catherine's, who has a little money of his own; he will be better able than I to look after such a big concern as that. In five years' time, please God, you will have five or six thousand head of cattle or horses down there in the plain that they are breaking up, and it will really take a good head to look after it all."

Mme. Graslin recognized the good sense of Farrabesche's request, and granted it.

As soon as a beginning was made in the plain, Mme. Graslin fell into the even ways of a country life. She went to mass in the morning, watched over the education of the son whom she idolized, and went to see her workmen. After dinner she was at home to her friends in the little drawing-room on the first floor of the centre tower. She taught Roubaud, Clousier, and the curé whist—Gérard knew the game already—and when the party broke up towards nine o'clock, every one went home. The only events in the pleasant life were the successes of the different parts of the great enterprise.

June came, the bed of the Gabou was dry, Gérard had taken up his quarters in the old keeper's cottage; for Farrabesche's farmhouse was finished by this time, and fifty masons, obtained from Paris, were building a wall across the valley from side to side. The masonry was twenty feet thick at the base, gradually sloping away to half that thickness at the top, and the whole length of it was embedded in twelve feet of solid concrete. On the side of the valley Gérard added a course of concrete with a sloping surface twelve feet thick at the base, and a similar support on the side nearest the commons, covered with leaf-mold several feet deep, made a substantial barrier which the flood-water could not break through. In case of a very wet season, Gérard contrived a channel at a suitable height for the overflow. Everywhere the masonry was carried down on the solid rock (granite, or tufa), that the water might not escape at the sides. By the middle of August the dam was finished. Meanwhile, Gérard also prepared three channels in the three principal valleys, and all of the undertakings cost less than the estimate. In this way the farm by the château could be put in working order.

The irrigation channels in the plain under Fresquin's superintendence corresponded with the natural canal at the base of the hills ; all the water-courses departed thence. The great abundance of flints enabled him to pave all the channels, and sluices were constructed so that the water might be kept at the required height in them.

Every Sunday after mass Véronique went down through the park with Gérard and the curé, the doctor, and the mayor, to see how the system of water-supply was working. The winter of 1833–1834 was very wet. The water from the three streams had been turned into the torrent, and the flood had made the valley of the Gabou into three lakes, arranged of set design one above the other, so as to form a reserve for times of great drought. In places where the valley widened out, Gérard had taken advantage of one or two knolls to make an island here and there, and to plant them with different trees. This vast engineering operation had completely altered the appearance of the landscape, but it would still be five or six years before it would take its true character.

"The land was quite naked," Farrabesche used to say, "and now madame has clothed it." After all these great changes, every one spoke of Véronique as "madame" in the countryside. When the rains ceased in June, 1834, trial was made of the irrigation system in the part of the plain where seed had been sown; and the green growth thus watered was of the same fine quality as in an Italian *marcita,* or a Swiss meadow. The method in use on farms in Lombardy had been employed; the whole surface was kept evenly moist, and the plain was as even as a carpet. The nitre in the snow, dissolved in the water, doubtless contributed not a little to the fineness of the grass. Gérard hoped that the produce would be something like that of Switzerland, where, as is well known, this substance is an inexhaustible source of riches. The trees planted along the roadsides, drawing water sufficient from the ditches, made rapid progress. So it came to pass that in 1838, five years after Mme. Graslin came to Montégnac, the waste land, condemned as sterile by twenty generations, was a green and fertile plain, the whole of it under cultivation.

Gérard had built houses for five farms, besides the large one at the château; Gérard's farm, like Grossetête's and Fresquin's, received the overflow from Mme. Graslin's estate; they were conducted on the same methods, and laid out on the same lines. Gérard built a charming lodge on his own property.

When all was finished, the township of Montégnac acted on the suggestion of its mayor, who was delighted to resign his office to Gérard, and the surveyor became mayor in his stead.

In 1840 the departure of the first herd of fat cattle sent from Montégnac to the Paris markets was an occasion for a rural fête. Cattle and horses were raised on the farms in the plain; for when the ground was cleared, seven inches of mold were usually found, which were manured by pasturing

cattle on them, and continually enriched by the leaves that
fell every autumn from trees, and, first and foremost, by the
melted snow-water from the reservoirs in the Gabou.

It was in this year that Mme. Graslin decided that a tutor
must be found for her son, now eleven years old. She was
unwilling to part with him, and yet desired to make a well-
educated man of her boy. M. Bonnet wrote to the seminary.
Mme. Graslin, on her side, let fall a few words concerning
her wishes and her difficulty to Monseigneur Dutheil, recently
appointed to an archbisopric. It was a great and serious
matter to make choice of a man who must spend at least nine
months out of twelve at the château. Gérard had offered
already to ground his friend Francis in mathematics, but it
was impossible to do without a tutor; and this choice that
she must make was the more formidable to Mme. Graslin
because she knew that her health was giving way. As the
value of the land in her beloved Montégnac increased, she
redoubled the secret austerities of her life.

Monseigneur Dutheil, with whom Mme. Graslin still corresponded, found her the man for whom she wished. He sent
a schoolmaster named Ruffin from his own diocese. Ruffin
was a young man of five-and-twenty with a genius for private
teaching; he was widely read; in spite of an excessive sensibility, could, when necessary, show himself sufficiently severe
for the education of a child, nor was his piety in any way
prejudicial to his knowledge; finally, he was patient and
pleasant-looking.

"This is a real gift which I am sending you, my dear
daughter," so the archbishop wrote; "the young man is
worthy to be the tutor of a prince, so I count upon you to
secure his future, for he will be your son's spiritual father."

M. Ruffin was so much liked by Mme. Graslin's little circle
of faithful friends that his coming made no change in the

various intimacies of those who grouped about their idol, seized with a sort of jealousy on the hours and moments spent with her.

The year 1843 saw the prosperity of Montégnac increasing beyond all hopes. The farm on the Gabou rivaled the farms on the plain, and the château led the way in all improvements. The five other farms, which by the terms of the lease paid an increasing rent, and would each bring in the sum of thirty thousand francs in twelve years' time, then brought in sixty thousand francs a year all told. The farmers were just beginning to reap the benefits of their self-denial and Mme. Graslin's sacrifices, and could afford to manure the meadows in the plain where the finest crops grew without fear of dry seasons. The Gabou farm paid its first rent of four thousand francs joyously.

It was in this year that a man in Montégnac started a *diligence* between the chief town in the arrondissement and Limoges ; a coach ran either way daily. M. Clousier's nephew sold his clerkship and obtained permission to practice as a notary, and Fresquin was appointed to be tax-collector in the canton. Then the new notary built himself a pretty house in upper Montégnac, planted mulberry trees on his land, and became Gérard's deputy. And Gérard himself, grown bold with success, thought of a plan which was· to bring Mme. Graslin a colossal fortune ; for this year she paid off her loan, and began to receive interest from her investment in the funds. This was Gérard's scheme : He would turn the little river into a canal by diverting the abundant water of the Gabou into it. This canal should effect a junction with the Vienne, and in this way it would be possible to exploit twenty thousand acres of the vast forest of Montégnac. The woods were admirably superintended by Còlorat, but hitherto had brought in nothing on account of the difficulty of transport. With this arrangement it would be possible to fell a thousand acres every year (thus dividing the forest into twenty strips for suc-

cessive cuttings), and the valuable timber for building pur-
poses could be sent by water to Limoges. This had been
Graslin's plan ; he had scarcely listened to the curé's projects
for the plain, he was far more interested in the scheme for
making a canal of the little river.

16

V

VÉRONIQUE LAID IN THE TOMB.

In the beginning of the following year, in spite of Mme.
Graslin's bearing, her friends saw warning signs that death
was near. To all Roubaud's observations, as to the utmost
ingenuity of the most keen-sighted questioners, Véronique
gave but one answer, "She felt wonderfully well." Yet that
spring, when she revisited forest and farms and her rich
meadows, it was with a childlike joy that plainly spoke of
sad forebodings.

Gérard had been obliged to make a low wall of concrete
from the dam across the Gabou to the park at Montégnac
along the base of the lower slope of the hill of the Corrèze ;
this had suggested an idea to him. He would enclose the
whole forest of Montégnac, and throw the park into it. Mme.
Graslin put by thirty thousand francs a year for this purpose.
It would take seven years to complete the wall ; but when it
was finished, the splendid forest would be exempted from the
dues claimed by the government over unenclosed woods and
lands, and the three ponds in the Gabou valley would lie
within the circuit of the park. Each of the ponds, proudly
dubbed "a lake," had its island. This year, too, Gérard,
in concert with Grossetête, prepared a surprise for Mme.
Graslin's birthday ; he had built on the second and largest
island a little *Chartreuse*—a summer-house, satisfactorily rustic
without and perfectly elegant within. The old banker was
in the plot, so were Farrabesche, Fresquin, and Clousier's
nephew, and most of the well-to-do folk in Montégnac. Grossetête sent the pretty furniture. The bell tower, copied from
the tower of Vevay, produced a charming effect in the landscape. Six boats (two for each lake) had been secretly built,

rigged, and painted during the winter by Farrabesche and Guépin, with some help from the village carpenter at Montégnac.

So one morning in the middle of May, after Mme. Graslin's friends had breakfasted with her, they led her out into the park, which Gérard had managed for the last five years as architect and naturalist. It had been admirably laid out, sloping down towards the pleasant meadows in the Gabou valley, where below, on the first lake, two boats were in readiness for them. The meadowland, watered by several clear streams, had been taken in at the base of the great amphitheatre at the head of the Gabou valley. The woods round about them had been carefully thinned and disposed with a view to the effect ; here the shapeliest masses of trees, there a charming inlet of meadow ; there was an air of loneliness about the forest-surrounded place which soothed the soul.

On a bit of rising ground by the lake Gérard had carefully reproduced the chalet which all travelers see and admire on the road to Brieg, through the Rhone valley. This was to be the château, dairy, and cow-shed. From the balcony there was a view over this landscape created by the engineer's art, a view comparable, since the lakes had been made, to the loveliest Swiss scenery.

It was a glorious day. Not a cloud in the blue sky, and on the earth beneath, the myriad gracious chance effects that the fair May month can give. Light wreaths of mist, risen from the lake, still hung like a thin smoke about the trees by the water's edge—willows and weeping willows, ash and alder and abeles, Lombard and Canadian poplars, white and pink hawthorn, birch and acacia, had been grouped about the lake, as the nature of the ground and the trees themselves (all finely grown specimens now ten years old) suggested. The high green wall of forest trees was reflected in the sheet of water, clear as a mirror, and serene as the sky ; their topmost crests, clearly outlined in that limpid atmosphere, stood out in con-

trast with the thicket below them, veiled in delicate green
undergrowth.   The lakes, divided by strongly-built embankments with a causeway along them that served as a short cut
from side to side of the valley, lay like three mirrors, each
with a different reflecting surface, the water trickling from
one to another in musical cascades.   And beyond this, from
the chalet you caught a glimpse of the bleak and barren common lands, the pale chalky soil (seen from the balcony)
looked like a wide sea, and supplied a contrast with the fresh
greenery about the lake.   Véronique saw the gladness in her
friends' faces as their hands were held out to assist her to
enter the larger boat, tears rose to her eyes, and they rowed
on in silence until they reached the first causeway.   Here
they landed, to embark again on the second lake; and Véronique, looking up, saw the summer-house on the island, and
Grossetête and his family sitting on a bench before it.

"They are determined to make me regret life, it seems,"
she said, turning to the curé.

"We want to keep you among us," Clousier said.

"There is no putting life into the dead," she answered;
but at M. Bonnet's look of rebuke, she withdrew into herself
again.

"Simply let me have the charge of your health," pleaded
Roubaud in a gentle voice; "I am sure that I could preserve
her who is the living glory of the canton, the common bond
that unites the lives of all our friends."

Véronique bent her head, while Gérard rowed slowly out
towards the island in the middle of the sheet of water, the
largest of the three.   The upper lake chanced to be too full;
the distant murmur of the weir seemed to find a voice for the
lovely landscape.

"You did well indeed to bring me here to bid farewell to
this entrancing view!" she said, as she saw the beauty of the
trees so full of leaves that they hid the bank on either
side.

The only sign of disapprobation which Véronique's friends permitted themselves was a gloomy silence ; and, at a second glance from M. Bonnet, she sprang lightly from the boat with an apparent gaiety, which she sustained. Once more she be-came the lady of the manor, and so charming was she that the Grossetête family thought that they saw in her the beauti-ful Mme. Graslin of old days.

" Assuredly, you may live yet," her mother said in Véron-ique's ear.

On that pleasant festival day, in the midst of a scene sub-limely transformed by the use of nature's own resources, how should anything wound Véronique ? Yet then and there she received her death-blow.

It had been arranged that the party should return home towards nine o'clock by way of the meadows ; for the roads, quite as fine as any in England or Italy, were the pride of their engineer. There were flints in abundance ; as the stones were taken off the land they had been piled in heaps by the roadside ; and with such plenty of road-material, it was so easy to keep the ways in good order that in five years' time they were in a manner macadamized. Carriages were waiting for the party at the lower end of the valley nearest the plain, almost under the Living Rock. The horses had all been bred in Montégnac. Their trial formed part of the pro-gramme for the day ; for these were the first that were ready for sale, the manager of the stud having just sent ten of them up to the stables of the château. Four handsome animals in light and plain harness were to draw Mme. Graslin's calèche, a present from Grossetête.

After dinner the joyous company went to take coffee on a promontory where a little wooden kiosk had been erected, a copy of one on the shores of the Bosphorus. From this point there was a wide outlook over the lowest lake, stretch-ing away to the great barrier across the Gabou, now covered thickly with a luxuriant growth of green, a charming spot for the eyes to rest upon.   Colorat's house and the old cottage, now restored, were the only buildings in the landscape; Colorat's capacities were scarcely adequate for the difficult post of head forester in Montégnac, so he had succeeded to Farrabesche's office.

From this point Mme. Graslin fancied that she could see Francis near Farrabesche's nursery of saplings; she looked for the child, and could not find him, till M. Ruffin pointed him out playing on the brink of the lake with M. Grossetête's great-grandchildren.   Véronique felt afraid that some accident might happen, and, without listening to remonstrances, sprang into one of the boats, landed on the causeway, and herself hurried away in search of her son.   This little incident broke up the party on the island.   Grossetête, now a venerable great-grandfather, was the first to suggest a walk along the beautiful field-path that wound up and down by the side of the lower lakes.

Mme. Graslin saw Francis a long way off.   He was with a woman in mourning, who had thrown her arms about him. She seemed to be from a foreign country, judging by her dress and the shape of her hat.   Véronique in dismay called her son to her.

"Who is that woman?" she asked of the other children; "and why did Francis go away from you?"

"The lady called him by his name," said one of the little girls.   Mme. Sauviat and Gérard, who were ahead of the others, came up at that moment.

"Who is that woman, dear?" said Mme. Graslin, turning to Francis.

"I do not know," he said, "but no one kisses me like that except you and grandmamma. She was crying," he added in his mother's ear.

"Shall I run and fetch her?" asked Gérard.

"No!" said Mme. Graslin, with a curtness very unusual with her.

With kindly tact, which Véronique appreciated, Gérard took the little ones with him and went back to meet the others; so that Mme. Sauviat, Mme. Graslin, and Francis were left together.

"What did she say to you?" asked Mme. Sauviat, addressing her grandson.

"I don't know. She did not speak French."

"Did you not understand anything she said?" asked Véronique.

"Oh, yes; one thing she said over and over again, that is how I can remember it—*dear brother!* she said."

Véronique leaned on her mother's arm and took her child's hand, but she could scarcely walk, and her strength failed her.

"What is it?—— What has happened?"—— every one asked of Mme. Sauviat.

A cry broke from the old Auvergnate: "Oh! my daughter is in danger!" she exclaimed, in her guttural accent and deep voice.

Mme. Graslin had to be carried to her carriage. She ordered Aline to keep beside Francis, and beckoned to Gérard.

"You have been in England, I believe," she said, when she had recovered herself; "do you understand English? What do these words mean—*dear brother?*"

"That is very simple," said Gérard, and he explained.

Véronique exchanged glances with Aline and Mme. Sauviat; the two women shuddered, but controlled their feelings. Mme. Graslin sank into a torpor from which nothing roused her; she did not heed the gleeful voices as the carriages started, nor the splendor of the sunset light on the meadows, the even pace of the horses, nor the laughter of the friends who followed them on horseback at a gallop. Her mother bade the man drive faster, and her carriage was the first to reach the château. When the rest arrived they were told that Véronique had gone to her room, and would see no one.

"I am afraid that Mme. Graslin must have received a fatal wound," Gérard began, speaking to his friends.

"Where?—— How?" asked they.

"In the heart," answered Gérard.

Two days later Roubaud set out for Paris. He had seen that Mme. Graslin's life was in danger, and to save her he had gone to summon the first doctor in Paris to give his opinion of the case. But Véronique had only consented to see Roubaud to put an end to the importunities of Aline and her mother, who begged her to be more careful of herself; she knew that she was dying. She declined to see M. Bonnet, saying that the time had not yet come; and although all the friends who had come from Limoges for her birthday festival were anxious to stay with her, she entreated them to pardon her if she could not fulfill the duties of hospitality, but she needed the most profound solitude. So, after Roubaud's sudden departure, the guests left the château of Montégnac and went back to Limoges, not so much in disappointment as in despair, for all who had come with Grossetête adored Véronique, and were utterly at a loss as to the cause of this mysterious disaster.

One evening, two days after Grossetête's large family party had left the château, Aline brought a visitor to Mme. Graslin's room. It was Catherine Farrabesche. At first Catherine stood glued to the spot, so astonished was she at this sudden change in her mistress, the features so drawn.

"Good God! madame, what harm that poor girl has done! If only we could have known, Farrabesche and I, we would never have taken her in. She has just heard that madame is ill, and sent me to tell Mme. Sauviat that she should like to speak to her."

"*Here!*" cried Véronique. "Where is she at this moment?"

"My husband took her over to the chalet."

"Good," said Mme. Graslin; "leave us, and tell Farrabesche to go. Tell the lady to wait, and my mother will go to see her."

At nightfall Véronique, leaning on her mother's arm, crept slowly across the park to the chalet. The moon shone with its most brilliant glory, the night air was soft; the two women, both shaken with emotion .that they could not conceal, received in some sort the encouragement of nature. From moment to moment Mme. Sauviat stopped and made her daughter rest; for Véronique's sufferings were so poignant that it was nearly midnight before they reached the path that turned down through the wood to the meadows, where the chalet roof sparkled like silver. The moonlight on the surface of the still water lent it a pearly hue. The faint noises of the night, which travel so far in the silence, made up a delicate harmony of sound.

Véronique sat down on the bench outside the chalet in the midst of the glorious spectacle beneath the starry skies. The murmur of two voices and footfalls on the sands made by two persons still some distance away was borne to her by the water, which transmits every sound in the stillness as faithfully as it reflects everything in its calm surface. There was an exquisite quality in the intonation of one of the voices, by which Véronique recognized the curé, and with the rustle of his cassock was blended the light sound of a silk dress. Evidently there was a woman.

"Let us go in," she said to her mother. Mme. Sauviat and Véronique sat down on a manger in the low, large room built for a cow-shed.

"I am not blaming you at all, my child," the curé was saying; "but you may be the innocent cause of an irreparable misfortune, for she is the life and soul of this wide countryside."

"Oh, monsieur! I will go to-night," the stranger woman's voice answered; "but—I can say this to you—it will be like death to me to leave my country a second time. If I had stayed a day longer in that horrible New York or in the United States, where there is neither hope nor faith nor charity, I should have died without any illness. The air I was breathing hurt my chest, the food did me no good, I was dying though I looked full of life and health. When I stepped on board the suffering ceased; I felt as if I were in France. Ah, monsieur! I have seen my mother and my brother's wife die of grief. And then my grandfather and grandmother Tascheron died—died, dear M. Bonnet, in spite of the unheard-of prosperity of Tascheronville—— Yes. Our father began a settlement, a village in Ohio, and now the village is almost a town. One-third of the land thereabouts belongs to our family, for God has watched over us all along, and the farms have done well, our crops are magnificent, and we are rich— so rich that we managed to build a Catholic church. The whole town is Catholic; we will not allow any other worship, and we hope to convert all the endless sects about us by our example. The true faith is in a minority in that dreary, mercenary land of the dollar, a land which chills one to the soul. Still I would go back to die there sooner than to do the least harm here or give the slightest pain to the mother of our dear Francis. Only take me to the parsonage house to-night, dear M. Bonnet, so that I can pray awhile on *his* grave; it was just that that drew me here, for as I came nearer and nearer the place where *he* lies I felt quite a different being: No, I did not believe I should feel so happy here——"

"Very well," said the curé; "come, let us go. If at some future day you can come back without evil consequences, I will write to tell you, Denise; but perhaps after this visit to your old home you may feel able to live yonder without suffering——"

"Leave this country now when it is so beautiful here! Just see what Mme. Graslin has made of the Gabou!" she added, pointing to the moonlit lake. "And then all this will belong to our dear Francis——"

"You shall not go, Denise," said Mme. Graslin, appearing in the stable doorway.

Jean-François Tascheron's sister clasped her hands at the sight of this ghost who spoke to her; for Véronique's white face in the moonlight looked unsubstantial as a shadow against the dark background of the open stable-door. Her eyes glittered like two stars.

"No, child, you shall not leave the country you have traveled so far to see, and you shall be happy here, unless God should refuse to second my efforts; for God, no doubt, has sent you here, Denise."

She took the astonished girl's hand in hers, and went with her down the path towards the opposite shore of the lake. Mme. Sauviat and the curé, left alone, sat down on the bench.

"Let her have her way," murmured Mme. Sauviat.

A few minutes later Véronique returned alone; her mother and the curé brought her back to the château. Doubtless she had thought of some plan of action which suited the mystery, for nobody saw Denise, no one knew that she had come back.

Mme. Graslin took to her bed, nor did she leave it. Every day she grew worse. It seemed to vex her that she could not rise, for again and again she made vain efforts to get up and take a walk in the park. One morning in early June, some days after that night at the chalet, she made a violent effort and rose and tried to dress herself, as if for a festival. She begged Gérard to lend her his arm; for her friends came daily for news of her, and when Aline said that her mistress meant to go out they all hurried up to the château. Mme. Graslin had summoned all her remaining strength to spend it on this last walk. She gained her object by a violent spasmodic effort of the will, inevitably followed by a deadly reaction.

"Let us go to the chalet—and alone," she said to Gérard. The tones of her voice were soft, and there was something like coquetry in her glance. "This is my last escapade, for I dreamed last night that the doctors had come."

"Would you like to see your woods?" asked Gérard.

"For the last time. But," she added, in coaxing tones, "I have some strange proposals to make to you."

Gérard, by her direction, rowed her across the second lake, when she had reached it on foot. He was at a loss to understand such a journey, but she indicated the summer-house as their destination, and he plied his oars.

There was a long pause. Her eyes wandered over the hill-sides, the water, and the sky; then she spoke.

"My friend, it is a strange request that I am about to make to you, but I think that you are the man to obey me."

"In everything," he said, "sure as I am that you cannot will anything but good."

"I want you to marry," she said; "you will fulfill the wishes of a dying woman, who is certain that she is securing your happiness."

"I am too ugly!" said Gérard.

"*She* is pretty, she is young, she wants to live in Mon-tégnac; and if you marry her, you will do something towards making my last moments easier. We need not discuss her qualities. I tell you this, that she is a woman of a thousand; and as for her charms, youth, and beauty, the first sight will suffice, we shall see her in a moment in the summer-house. On our way back you shall give me your answer, a 'Yes' or a 'No,' in sober earnest."

Mme. Graslin smiled as she saw the oars move more swiftly after this confidence. Denise, who was living out of sight in the island sanctuary, saw Mme. Graslin, and hurried to the door. Véronique and Gérard came in. In spite of herself, the poor girl flushed as she met the eyes that Gérard turned upon her; Denise's beauty was an agreeable surprise to him.

"La Curieux does not let you want for anything, does she?" asked Véronique.

"Look, madame," said Denise, pointing to the breakfast table.

"This is M. Gérard, of whom I have spoken to you," Véronique went on. "He will be my son's guardian, and when I am dead you will all live together at the château until Francis comes of age."

"Oh, madame! don't talk like that."

"Just look at me, child!" said Véronique, and all at once she saw tears in the girl's eyes. "She comes from New York," she added, turning to Gérard.

This by way of putting both on a footing of acquaintance. Gérard asked questions of Denise, and Mme. Graslin left them to chat, going to look out over the view of the last lake on the Gabou. At six o'clock Gérard and Véronique rowed back to the chalet.

"Well?" queried she, looking at her friend.

"You have my word."

"You may be without prejudices," Véronique began, "but you ought to know how it was that she was obliged to leave the country, poor child, brought back by a home-sick longing."

"A slip?"

"Oh, no," said Véronique, "or should I introduce her to you? She is the sister of a workman who died on the scaffold——"

"Oh! Tascheron, who murdered old Pingret——"

"Yes. She is a murderer's sister," said Mme. Graslin, with inexpressible irony in her voice; "you can take back your word."

She went no further. Gérard was compelled to carry her to the bench at the chalet, and for some minutes she lay there unconscious. Gérard, kneeling beside her, said, as soon as she opened her eyes—

"I will marry Denise."

Mme. Graslin made him rise, she took his head in her

hands, and set a kiss on his forehead. Then, seeing that he was astonished to be thus thanked, she grasped his hand and said—

" You will soon know the meaning of this puzzle. Let us try to reach the terrace again, our friends are there. It is very late, and I feel very weak, and yet I should like to bid farewell from afar to this dear plain of mine."

The weather had been intolerably hot all day ; and though the storms, which did so much damage that year in different parts of Europe and in France itself, respected the Limousin, there had been thunder along the Loire, and the air began to grow fresher. The sky was so pure that the least details on the horizon were sharp and clear. What words can describe the delicious concert of sounds, the smothered hum of the township, now alive with workers returning from the fields? It would need the combined work of a great landscape painter and a painter of figures to do justice to such a picture. Is there not, in fact, a subtle connection between the lassitude of nature and the laborer's weariness, an affinity of mood hardly to be rendered ? In the tepid twilight of the dog days, the rarefied air gives its full significance to the least sound made by every living thing.

The women sit chatting at their doors with a bit of work even then in their hands, as they wait for the good man who, probably, will bring the children home. The smoke going up from the roofs is the sign of the last meal of the day and the gayest for the peasants ; after it they will sleep. The stir at that hour is the expression of happy and tranquil thoughts in those who have finished their day's work. There is a very distinct difference between their evening and morning snatches of song ; for in this the village-folk are like the birds, the last twitterings at night are utterly unlike their notes at dawn. All nature joins in the hymn of rest at the end of the day, as in the hymn of gladness at sunrise ; all things take the softly-blended hues that the sunset throws across the fields, tingeing the dusty roads with mellow light. If any should be bold enough to deny the influences of the fairest hour of the day, the very flowers would convict him of falsehood, intoxicating him with their subtlest scents, mingled with the tenderest sounds of insects the amorous faint twitter of birds.

Thin films of mist hovered above the " water-lanes" that furrowed the plain below the township. The poplars and acacias and sumach trees, planted in equal numbers along the roads, had grown so tall already that they shaded it, and in the wide fields on either side the large and celebrated herds of cattle were scattered about in groups, some still browsing, others chewing the cud. Men, women, and children were busy getting in the last of the hay, the most picturesque of all field-work. The evening air, less languid since the sudden breath of coolness after the storms, brought the wholesome scents of mown grass and swathes of hay. The least details in the beautiful landscape stood out perfectly sharp and clear.

There was some fear for the weather. The ricks were being finished in all haste ; men hurried about them with loaded forks, raked the heaps together, and loaded the carts. Out in the distance the scythes were still busy, the women were turning the long swathes that looked like hatched lines across the fields into dotted rows of haycocks.

Sounds of laughter came up from the hayfields, the workers frolicked over their work, the children shouted as they buried each other in the heaps. Every figure was distinct, the women's petticoats, pink, red, or blue, their kerchiefs, their bare arms and legs, the wide-brimmed straw hats of field-workers, the men's shirts, the white trousers that nearly all of them wore.

The last rays of sunlight fell like a bright dust over the long lines of poplar trees by the channels which divided up the plain into fields of various sizes, and lingered caressingly over the groups of men, women, and children, horses and carts and cattle. The shepherds and herdsmen began to gather their flocks together with the sound of their horns. The plain seemed so silent and so full of sound, a strange antithesis, but only strange to those who do not know the splendors of the fields. Loads of green fodder came into the township from every side. There was something indescribably somnolent in the influence of the scene, and Véronique, between the curé and Gérard, uttered no word.

At last they came to a gap made by a rough track that led from the houses ranged below the terrace to the parsonage house and the church; and, looking down into Montégnac, Gérard and M. Bonnet saw the upturned faces of the women, men, and children, all looking at them. Doubtless it was Mme. Graslin more particularly whom they followed with their eyes. And what affection and gratitude there were in their way of doing this! With what blessings did they not greet Véronique's appearance! With what devout intentness they watched the three benefactors of a whole countryside! It was as if man added a hymn of gratitude to all the songs of evening. While Mme. Graslin walked with her eyes set on the magnificent distant expanse of green, her dearest creation, the mayor and the curé watched the groups below. There was no mistake about their expression; grief, melancholy, and regret, mingled with hope, were plainly visible in them all. There was not a soul in Montégnac but knew how that M. Roubaud had gone to Paris to fetch some great doctors, and that the beneficent lady of the canton was nearing the end of a fatal illness. On market-days, in every place for thirty miles round, the peasants asked the Montégnac folk, "How is your mistress?" And so the great thought of death hovered over this countryside, amid the fair picture of the hayfields.

Far off in the plain, more than one mower sharpening his scythe, more than one girl leaning on her rake, or farmer among his stacks of hay, looked up and paused thoughtfully to watch Mme. Graslin, their great lady, the pride of the

Corrèze. They tried to discover some hopeful sign, or watched her admiringly, prompted by a feeling which put work out of their minds. "She is out of doors, so she must be better!" The simple phrase was on all lips.

Mme. Graslin's mother was sitting at the end of the terrace. Véronique had placed a cast-iron garden-seat in the corner, so that she might sit there and look down into the churchyard through the balustrade. Mme. Sauviat watched her daughter as she walked along the terrace, and her eyes filled with tears. She knew something of the preternatural effort which Véronique was making; she knew that even at that moment her daughter was suffering fearful pain, and that it was only a heroic effort of will that enabled her to stand. Tears, almost like tears of blood, found their way down among the sunburned wrinkles of a face like parchment, that seemed as if it could not alter one crease for any emotion any more. Little Graslin, standing between M. Ruffin's knees, cried for sympathy.

"What is the matter, child?" the tutor asked sharply.

"Grandmamma is crying——"

M. Ruffin's eyes had been fixed on Mme. Graslin, who was coming towards them; he looked at Mme. Sauviat; the Roman matron's face, stony with sorrow and wet with tears, gave him a great shock. That dumb grief had invested the old woman with a certain grandeur and sacredness.

"Madame, why did you let her go out?" asked the tutor.

Véronique was coming nearer. She walked like a queen, with admirable grace in her whole bearing. And Mme. Sauviat knew that she should outlive her daughter, and in the cry of despair that broke from her a secret escaped that revealed many things which roused curiosity.

"To think of it! She walks and wears a horrible hair shirt always pricking her skin!"

The young man's blood ran cold at her words; he could not be insensible to the exquisite grace of Véronique's move-

17

ments, and shuddered as he thought of the cruel, unrelenting mastery that the soul must have gained over the body. A Parisienne famed for her graceful figure, the ease of her carriage and bearing, might perhaps have feared comparison with Véronique at that moment.

"She has worn it for thirteen years, ever since the child was weaned," the old woman said, pointing to young Graslin. " She has worked miracles here ; and if they but knew her life, they might put her among the saints. Nobody has seen her eat since she came here, do you know why ? Aline brings her a bit of dry bread three times a day on a great platter full of ashes, and vegetables cooked in water without any salt, on a red earthenware dish that they put a dog's food in ! Yes. That is the way she lives who has given life to the canton. She says her prayers kneeling on the hem of her cilice. She says that if she did not practice these austerities she could not wear the smiling face you see. I am telling you this " (and the old woman's voice dropped lower) " for you to tell it to the doctor that M. Roubaud has gone to fetch from Paris. If he will prevent my daughter from continuing these penances, they might save her yet (who knows?), though the hand of death is on her head. Look ! Ah, I must be very strong to have borne all these things for fifteen years."

The old woman took her grandson's hand, raised it, and passed it over her forehead and cheeks as if some restorative balm communicated itself in the touch of the little hand ; then she set a kiss upon it, a kiss full of the love which is the secret of grandmothers no less than mothers. By this time Véronique was only a few paces distant, Clousier was with her, and the curé and Gérard. Her face, lit up by the setting sun, was radiant with awful beauty.

One thought, steadfast amid many inward troubles, seemed to be written in the lines that furrowed the sallow forehead in long folds piled one above the other, like clouds. The outlines of her face, now completely colorless, entirely white with the dead olive-tinged whiteness of plants grown without sunlight, were thin but not withered, and showed traces of great physical suffering produced by mental anguish. She had quelled the body through the soul, and the soul through the body. So completely worn out was she that she resembled her past self only as an old woman resembles her portrait painted in girlhood. The glowing expression of her eyes spoke of the absolute domination of a Christian will over a body reduced to the subjection required by religion, for in this woman the flesh was at the mercy of the spirit. As in profane poetry Achilles dragged the dead body of Hector, victoriously she dragged it over the stormy ways of life; and thus for fifteen years she had compassed the heavenly Jerusalem which she had hoped to enter, not as a thief, but amid triumphant acclamations. Never was anchorite amid the parched and arid deserts of Africa more master of his senses than Véronique in her splendid château in a rich land of soft and luxurious landscape, nestling under the mantle of the great forest where science, heir to Moses' rod, had caused plenty to spring forth and the prosperity and the welfare of a whole countryside. Véronique was looking out over the results of twelve years of patience, on the accomplishment of a task on which a man of ability might have prided himself; but with the gentle modesty which Pontorno's brush had depicted in the expression of his symbolical "Christian Chastity"—with her arms about the unicorn. Her two companions respected her silent mood when they saw that she was gazing over the vast plain, once sterile, and now fertile; the devout lady of the manor went with folded arms and eyes fixed on the point where the road reached the horizon.

Suddenly she stopped when but two paces away from Mme. Sauviat, who watched her as Christ's mother must have gazed at her Son upon the cross. Véronique raised her hand and pointed to the spot where the road turned off to Montégnac.

"Do you see that calèche and the four post-horses?" she asked, smiling. "That is M. Roubaud. He is coming back. We shall soon know now how many hours I have to live."

"*Hours!*" echoed Gérard.

"Did I not tell you that this was my last walk?" she said. "Did I not come to see this beautiful view in all its glory for the last time?"

She indicated the fair meadow land, lit up by the last rays of the sun, and the township below. All the village had come out and stood in the square in front of the church.

"Ah!" she went on, "let me think that there is God's benediction in the strange atmospheric conditions that have favored our hay-harvest. Storms all about us, rain and hail and thunder have laid waste pitilessly and incessantly, but not here. The people think so; why should not I follow their example? I need so much to find some good augury on earth for that which awaits me when my eyes shall be closed!"

Her child came to her, took his mother's hand, and laid it on his hair. The great eloquence of that movement touched Véronique; with preternatural strength she caught him up, held him on her left arm a moment as she used to hold him as a child at the breast, and kissed him. "Do you see this land, my boy?" she said. "You must go on with your mother's work when you are a man."

Then the curé spoke sadly: "There are a very few strong and privileged natures who are permitted to see death face to face, to fight a long duel with him, and to show courage and skill that strike others with admiration; this is the dreadful spectacle that you give us, madame; but, perhaps, you are somewhat wanting in pity for us. Leave us at least the hope that you are mistaken, that God will permit you to finish all that you have begun."

"I have done nothing save through you, my friend," said she. "It was in my power to be useful to you ; it is so no longer. Everything about us is green ; there is no desolate waste here now, save my own heart. You know it, dear curé, you know that I can only find peace and pardon *there*——"

She held out her hand over the churchyard. She had never said so much since the day when she first came to Montégnac and fainted away on that very spot. The curé gazed at his penitent ; and, accustomed as he had been for long to read her thoughts, he knew from those simple words that he had won a fresh victory. It must have cost Véronique a terrible effort over herself to break a twelve years' silence with such pregnant words ; and the curé clasped his hands with the devout fervor familiar to him, and looked with deep religious emotion on the family group about him. All their secrets had passed through his heart.

Gérard looked bewildered ; the words "peace and pardon" seemed to sound strangely in his ears ; M. Ruffin's eyes were fixed in a sort of dull amazement on Mme. Graslin. And meanwhile the calèche sped rapidly along the road, threading its way from tree to tree.

"There are five of them !" said the curé, who could see and count the travelers.

"Five !" exclaimed M. Gérard. "Will five of them know more than two ?"

"Ah !" murmured Mme. Graslin, who leaned on the curé's arm, "there is the public prosecutor. "What does he come to do here ?"

"And papa Grossetête too ! " cried Francis.

"Madame, take courage, be worthy of yourself," said the curé. He drew Mme. Graslin, who was leaning heavily on him, a few paces aside.

"What does he want ?" she said for all answer, and she went to lean against the balustrade. "Mother ! " she exclaimed, despairingly.

Mme. Sauviat sprang forward with an activity that belied her years.

"I shall see him again——" said Véronique.

"If he is coming with M. Grossetête," said the curé, "it can only be with good intentions, of course."

"Ah! sir, my daughter is dying!" cried Mme. Sauviat, seeing the change that passed over Mme. Graslin's face at the words. "How will she endure such cruel agitations?· M. Grossetête has always prevented that man from coming to see Véronique——"

Véronique's face flamed.

"So you hate him, do you?" the Abbé Bonnet asked, turning to his penitent.

"She left Limoges lest all Limoges should know her secrets," said Mme. Sauviat, terrified by that sudden change wrought in Mme. Graslin's drawn features.

"Do you not see that his presence will poison the hours that remain to me, when heaven alone should be in my thoughts? He is nailing me down to earth!" cried Véronique.

The curé took Mme. Graslin's arm once more, and constrained her to walk a few paces; when they were alone, he looked full at her with one of those angelic looks which calm the most violent tumult in the soul.

"If it is thus," he said, "I, as your confessor, bid you to receive him, to be kind and gracious to him, to lay aside this garment of anger, and to forgive him as God will forgive you. Can there be a taint of passion in the soul that I deemed purified? Burn this last grain of incense on the altar of penitence, lest all shall be one lie in you."

"There was still this last struggle to make, and it is made," she said, drying her eyes. "The evil one was lurking in the last recess in my heart, and doubtless it was God who put into M. de Granville's heart the thought that sends him here. How many times will He smite me yet?" she cried.

She stopped as if to put up an inward prayer; then she turned to Mme. Sauviat, and said in a low voice:

"Mother dear, be nice and kind to M. le Procureur général."

In spite of herself, the old Auvergnate shuddered feverishly.

"There is no hope left," she said, as she caught at the curé's hand.

As she spoke, the cracking of the postillion's whip announced that the calèche was climbing the avenue; the great gateway stood open, the carriage turned in the courtyard, and in another moment the travelers came out upon the terrace. Beside the public prosecutor and M. Grossetête, the archbishop had come (M. Dutheil was in Limoges for Gabriel de Rastignac's consecration as bishop), and M. Roubaud came arm in arm with Horace Bianchon, one of the greatest doctors in Paris.

"You are welcome," said Véronique, addressing her guests, "and *you*" (holding out a hand to the public prosecutor and grasping his) "especially welcome."

M. Grossetête, the archbishop, and Mme. Sauviat exchanged glances at this; so great was their astonishment that it overcame the profound discretion of old age.

"And I thank him who brought you here," Véronique went on, as she looked on the Comte de Granville's face for the first time in fifteen years. "I have borne you a grudge for a long time, but now I know that I have done you an injustice; you shall know the reason of all this if you will stay here in Montégnac for two days." She turned to Horace Bianchon—"This gentleman will confirm my apprehensions, no doubt." Then to the archbishop—"It is God surely who sends you to me, my lord," she said with a bow. "For our old friendship's sake you will not refuse to be with me in my last moments. By what grace, I wonder, have I all those who have loved me and sustained me all my life about me now?"

At the word " love " she turned with graceful, deliberate intent towards M. de Granville ; the kindness in her manner brought tears into his eyes.　There was a deep silence.　The two doctors asked themselves what witchcraft it was that enabled the woman before them to stand upright while enduring the agony which she must suffer.　The other three were so shocked at the change that illness had wrought in her that they could only communicate their thoughts by the eyes.

" Permit me to go with these gentlemen," she said, with her unvarying grace of manner ; " it is an urgent question." She took leave of her guests, and, leaning upon the two doctors, went towards the château so slowly and painfully that it was evident that the end was at hand.

The archbishop looked at the curé.

" M. Bonnet," he said, " you have worked wonders ! "

" Not I, but God, my lord," answered the other.

" They said that she was dying," exclaimed M. Grossetête ; " why, she is dead !　There is nothing left but a spirit——"

" A soul," said M. Gérard.

" She is the same as ever," cried the public prosecutor.

" She is a Stoic after the manner of the old Greek Zeno," said the tutor.

Silently they went along the terrace and looked out over the landscape that glowed a most glorious red color in the light shed abroad by the fires of the sunset.

" It is thirteen years since I saw this before," said the archbishop, indicating the fertile fields, the valley, and the hill above Montégnac, " so for me this miracle is as extraordinary as another which I have just witnessed ; for how can you let Mme. Graslin stand upright?　She ought to be lying in bed——"

" So she was," said Mme. Sauviat.　" She never left her bed for ten days, but she was determined to get up to see this place for the last time."

" I understand," said M. de Granville.　" She wished to

say farewell to all that she had called into being, but she ran the risk of dying here on the terrace.''

" M. Roubaud said that she was not to be thwarted,'' said Mme. Sauviat.

"What a marvelous thing!'' exclaimed the archbishop, whose eyes never wearied of wandering over the view. "She has made the waste into sown fields. But we know, monsieur,'' he added, turning to Gérard, "that your skill and your labors have been a great factor in this.''

" We have only been her laborers,'' the mayor said. "Yes; we are only the hands, she was the head.''

Mme. Sauviat left the group, and went to hear what the opinion of the doctor from Paris was.

" We shall stand in need of heroism to be present at this death-bed,'' said the public prosecutor, addressing the archbishop and the curé.

"Yes,'' said M. Grossetête ; " but for such a friend, great things should be dqne.''

While they waited and came and went, oppressed by heavy thoughts, two of Mme. Graslin's tenants came up. They had come, they said, on behalf of a whole township waiting in painful suspense to hear the verdict of the doctor from Paris.

" They are in consultation, we know nothing as yet, my friends,'' said the archbishop.

M. Roubaud came hurrying towards them, and at the sound of his quick footsteps the others hastened to meet him.

" Well?'' asked the mayor.

" She has not forty-eight hours to live,'' answered M. Roubaud. " The disease has developed while I was away. M. Bianchon cannot understand how she could walk. These seldom seen phenomena are always the result of great exaltation of mind. And so, gentlemen,'' he added, speaking to the churchmen, "she has passed out of our hands and into yours ; science is powerless ; my illustrious colleague thinks that there is scarcely time for the ceremonies of the church.''

"Let us put up the prayers appointed for times of great calamity," said the curé, and he went away with his parishioners. "His lordship will no doubt condescend to administer the last sacraments."

The archbishop bowed his head in reply; he could not say a word, his eyes were full of tears. The group sat down or leaned against the balustrade, and each was deep in his own thoughts. The church bells peeled mournfully, the sound of many footsteps came up from below, the whole village was flocking to the service. The light of the altar candles gleamed through the trees in M. Bonnet's garden, and then began the sounds of chanting. A faintly flushed twilight overspread the fields, the birds had ceased to sing, and the only sound in the plain was the shrill, melancholy, long-drawn note of the frogs.

"Let us do our duty," said the archbishop at last, and he went slowly towards the house, like a man who carries a burden greater than he can bear.

The consultation had taken place in the great drawing-room, a vast apartment which communicated with a state bedroom, draped with crimson damask. Here Graslin had exhibited to the full the self-made man's taste for display. Véronique had not entered the room half-a-dozen times in fourteen years; the great suite of apartments was completely useless to her; she had never received visitors in them, but the effort she had made to discharge her last obligations and to quell her revolted physical nature had left her powerless to reach her own rooms.

The great doctor had taken his patient's hand and felt her pulse, then he looked significantly at M. Roubaud, and the two men carried her into the adjoining room and laid her on the bed, Aline hastily flinging open the doors for them. There were, of course, no sheets on the state bed; the two doctors laid Mme. Graslin at full length on the crimson quilt, Roubaud opened the windows, flung back the Venetian shutters, and summoned help. La Sauviat and the servants came hurrying to the room; they lighted the wax-candles (yellow with age) in the sconces.

Then the dying woman smiled. "It is decreed that my death shall be a festival, as a Christian's death should be."

During the consultation she spoke again—

"The public prosecutor has done his work: I was going; he has despatched me sooner——"

The old mother laid a finger on her lips with a warning glance.

"Mother, I will speak now," Véronique said in answer. "Look! the finger of God is in all this; I shall die very soon in this room hung with red——"

La Sauviat went out in dismay at the words.

"Aline!" she cried, "she is speaking out!——"

"Ah! madame's mind is wandering," said the faithful waiting-woman, coming in with the sheets. "Send for M. le Curé, madame."

"You must undress your mistress," said Bianchon, as soon as Aline entered the room.

"It will be very difficult; madame wears a hair shirt next her skin."

"What?" the great doctor cried, "are such horrors still practiced in this nineteenth century?"

"Mme. Graslin has never allowed me to touch the stomach," said M. Roubaud. "I could learn nothing of her complaint save from her face and her pulse, and from what I could learn from her mother and her maid."

Véronique was laid on a sofa while they made the great bed ready for her at the farther end of the room. The doctors spoke together with lowered voices as La Sauviat and Aline made the bed. There was a look terrible to see in the two women's faces; the same thought was wringing both their hearts. "We are making her bed for the last time—this will be her bed of death."

The consultation was brief. In the first place, Bianchon insisted that Aline and La Sauviat must cut the patient out of the cilice and put her in a nightdress. The two doctors waited in the great drawing-room while this was done. Aline came out with the terrible instrument of penance wrapped in a towel. "Madame is just one wound," she told them.

"Madame, you have a stronger will than Napoleon had," said Bianchon, when the two doctors had come in again, and Véronique had given clear answers to the questions put to her. "You are preserving your faculties in the last stage of a disease in which the Emperor's brilliant intellect sank. From what I know of you, I feel that I owe it to you to tell you the truth."

"I implore you, with clasped hands, to tell it me," she said; "you can measure the strength that remains to me, and I have need of all the life that is in me for a few hours yet."

"You must think of nothing but your salvation," said Bianchon.

"If God grants that body and mind die together," she said, with a divinely sweet smile, "believe that the favor is vouchsafed for the glory of His Church on earth. My mind is still needed to carry out a thought from God, while Napoleon had accomplished his destiny."

The two doctors looked at each other in amazement; the words were spoken as easily as if Mme. Graslin had been in her drawing-room.

"Ah! here is the doctor who will heal me," she added, as the archbishop entered.

She summoned all her strength to sit upright to take leave of M. Bianchon, speaking graciously, and asking him to accept something beside money for the good news which he had just brought her; then she whispered a few words to her mother, who went out with the doctor. She asked the archbishop to wait until the curé should come, and seemed to wish to rest for a little while. Aline sat by her mistress' bedside.

At midnight Mme. Graslin woke and asked for the arch-bishop and the curé. Aline told her that they were in the room engaged in prayer for her. With a sign she dismissed her mother and the maid, and beckoned the two priests to her bed.

"Nothing of what I shall say is unknown to you, my lord, nor to you, M. le Curé. You, my lord archbishop, were the first to look into my conscience ; at a glance you read almost the whole past, and that which you saw was enough for you. My confessor, an angel sent by heaven to be near me, knows something more ; I have confessed all to him, as in duty bound. And now I wish to consult you—whose minds are enlightened by the spirit of the church ; I want to ask you how such a woman as I should take leave of this life as a true Christian. You, spirits holy and austere, do you think that if heaven vouchsafes pardon to the most complete and pro-found repentance ever made by a guilty soul, I shall have accomplished my whole task here on earth ? "

"Yes ; yes, my daughter," said the archbishop.

"No, my father, no ! " she cried, sitting upright, and lightnings flashed from her eyes. "Yonder lies an unhappy man in his grave, not many steps away, under the sole weight of a hideous crime ; here, in this sumptuous house, there is a woman crowned with the aureola of good deeds and a virtu-ous life. They bless the woman ; they curse him, poor boy. On the criminal they heap execrations, I enjoy the good opinion of all ; yet most of the blame of his crime is mine, and a great part of the good for which they praise me so and are grateful to me is his ; cheat that I am ! I have the credit of it, and he, a martyr to his loyalty to me, is covered with shame. In a few hours I shall die, and a whole canton will weep for me, a whole department will praise my good deeds, my piety, and my virtues ; and he died reviled and scorned, a whole town crowding about to see him die, for hate of the murderer ! You, my judges, are indulgent to me, but I hear

an imperious voice within me that will not let me rest.   Ah!
God's hand, more heavy than yours, has been laid upon me
day by day, as if to warn me that all was not expiated yet.
My sin shall be redeemed by public confession.   Oh! he was
happy, that criminal who went to a shameful death in the face
of earth and heaven!   But as for me, I cheated justice, and
I am still a cheat!   All the respect shown to me has been like
mockery, not a word of praise but has scorched my heart
like fire.   And now the public prosecutor has come here.   Do
you not see that the will of heaven is in accordance with this
voice that cries 'Confess?'''

Both priests, the prince of the church and the simple
country parson, the two great luminaries, remained silent, and
kept their eyes fixed on the ground.   So deeply moved
were the judges by the greatness and the submission of the
sinner that they could not pass sentence.   After a pause, the
archbishop raised his noble face, thin and worn with the daily
practice of austerity in a devout life.

"My child," he said, "you are going beyond the commandments of the church.   It is the glory of the church that she
adapts her dogmas to the conditions of life in every age; for
the church is destined to make the pilgrimage of the centuries
side by side with humanity.   According to the decision of
the church, private confession has replaced public confession.
This substitution has made the new rule of life.   The sufferings which you have endured suffice.   Depart in peace.   God
has heard you indeed."

"But is not this wish of a criminal in accordance with the
rule of the early church, which filled heaven with as many
saints and martyrs and confessors as there are stars in heaven?"
Véronique cried earnestly.   "Who was it that wrote 'Confess your faults one to another?'   Was it not one of our
Saviour's own immediate disciples?   Let me confess my
shame publicly upon my knees.   That will be an expiation
of the wrong that I have done to the world, and to a family

exiled and almost extinct through my sin. The world should
know that my good deeds are not an offering to God ; that
they are only the just payment of a debt—— Suppose that,
when I am gone, some finger should raise the veil of lies that
covers me ?—— Oh, the thought of it brings the supreme hour
nearer.''

"I see calculation in this, my child," the archbishop said
gravely. "There are still strong passions left in you; that
which I deemed extinguished is——"

"My lord," she cried, breaking in upon the speaker, turning her fixed horror-stricken eyes on him, "I swear to you that
my heart is purified so far as it may be in a guilty and repentant woman ; there is no thought left in me now but the thought
of God.''

"Let us leave heaven's justice take its course, my lord,"
the curé said, in a softened voice. "I have opposed this idea
for four years. It has caused the only differences of opinion
which have risen between my penitent and me. I have seen
the very depths of this soul ; earth has no hold left there.
When the tears, sighs, and contrition of fifteen years have
buried a sin in which two beings shared, do not think that
there is the least luxurious taint in the long and dreadful
remorse. For a long while memory has ceased to mingle
its flames in the most ardent repentance. Yes, many tears
have quenched so great a fire. I will answer," he said,
stretching his hand out above Mme. Graslin's head and raising
his tear-filled eyes, "I will answer for the purity of this archangel's soul. I used once to see in this desire a thought of
reparation to an absent family ; it seems as if God Himself
has sent one member of it here, through one of those acci-
dents in which His guidance is unmistakably revealed.''

Véronique took the curé's trembling hand and kissed it.

"You have often been harsh to me, dear pastor," she said ;
"and now, in this moment, I discover where your apostolic
sweetness lay hidden. You," she said, turning to the arch-

bishop, " you, the supreme head of this corner of God's earthly kingdom, be my stay in this time of humiliation. I shall prostrate myself as the lowest of women ; you will raise me, a forgiven soul, equal, it may be, with those who have never gone astray."

The archbishop was silent for a while, engaged, no doubt, in weighing the considerations visible to his eagle's glance.

" My lord," said the curé, "deadly blows have been aimed at religion. Will not this return to ancient customs, made necessary by the greatness both of the sin and the repentance, be a triumph which will redound to us ? "

" They will say that we are fanatics ! that we have insisted on this cruel scene ! " and the archbishop fell once more to his meditations.

Just at that moment Horace Bianchon and Roubaud came in without knocking at the door. As it opened, Véronique saw her mother, her son, and all the servants kneeling in prayer. The curés of the two neighboring parishes had come to assist M. Bonnet ; perhaps also to pay their respects to the great archbishop, in whom the church of France saw a cardinal-designate, hoping that some day the Sacred College might be enlightened by the advent of an intellect so thoroughly Gallican.

Horace Bianchon was about to start for Paris ; he came to bid farewell to the dying lady, and to thank her for her munificence. He approached the bed slowly, guessing from the manner of the two priests that the inward wound which had caused the disease of the body was now under consideration. He took Véronique's hand, laid it on the bed, and felt her pulse. The deepest silence, the silence of the fields in a summer-night, added solemnity to the scene. Lights shone from the great drawing-room, beyond the folding doors, and fell upon the little company of kneeling figures, the curés only were seated, reading their breviaries. About the crimson bed of state stood the archbishop, in his violet robes, the curé, and the two men of science.

" She is troubled even in death ! " said Horace Bianchon. Like many men of great genius, he not seldom found grand words worthy of the scenes at which he was present.

The archbishop rose, as if goaded by some inward impulse. He called M. Bonnet, and went towards the door. They crossed the chamber and the drawing-room, and went out upon the terrace, where they walked up and down for a few minutes. As they came in after a consideration of this point of ecclesiastical discipline, Roubaud went to meet them.

" M. Bianchon sent me to tell you to be quick ; Mme. Graslin is dying in strange agitation, which is not caused by the severe physical pain which she is suffering."

The archbishop hurried back, and in reply to Mme. Graslin's anxious eyes, he said, " You shall be satisfied."

Bianchon (still with his finger on the dying woman's wrist) made an involuntary start of surprise ; he gave Roubaud a quick look, and then glanced at the priests.

" My lord, this body is no longer our province," he said, " your words brought life in the place of death. You make a miracle credible."

" Madame has been nothing but soul this long time past," said Roubaud, and Véronique thanked him by a glance.

A smile crossed her face as she lay there, and, with the smile that expressed the gladness of a completed expiation, the innocent look of the girl of eighteen returned to her. The appalling lines traced by inward tumult, the dark coloring, the livid patches, all the details that but lately had contributed a certain dreadful beauty to her face, all alterations of all kinds, in short, had vanished ; to those who watched Véronique, it seemed as if she had been wearing a mask and had suddenly dropped it. The wonderful transfiguration by which the inward life and nature of this woman were made

18

visible in her features was wrought for the last time. Her whole being was purified and illuminated, her face might have caught a gleam from the flaming swords of the guardian angels about her. She looked once more as she used to look in Limoges when they called her " the little Virgin." The love of God manifestly was yet stronger in her than the guilty love had been; the earthly love had brought out all the forces of life in her; the love of God dispelled every trace of the inroads of death. A smothered cry was heard. La Sauviat appeared; she sprang to the bed. "So I see my child again at last!" she exclaimed.

Something in the old woman's accent as she uttered the two words, "my child," conjured up such visions of early childhood and its innocence, that those who watched by this heroic death-bed turned their heads away to hide their emotion. The great doctor took Mme. Graslin's hand, kissed it, and then went his way, and soon the sound of his departing carriage sent echoes over the countryside, spreading the tidings that he had no hope of saving the life of her who was the life of the country. The archbishop, curé, and doctor, and all who felt tired, went to take a little rest. Mme. Graslin herself slept for some hours. When she awoke the dawn was breaking; she asked them to open the windows, she would see her last sunrise.

At ten o'clock in the morning the archbishop, in pontifical vestments, came back to Mme. Graslin's room. Both he and M. Bonnet reposed such confidence in her that they made no recommendations as to the limits to be observed in her confession. Véronique saw other faces of other clergy, for some of the curés from neighboring parishes had come. The splendid ornaments which Mme. Graslin had presented to her beloved parish church lent splendor to the ceremony. Eight children, choristers in their red-and-white surplices, stood in a double row between the bed and the door of the great drawing-room, each of them holding one of the great candlesticks of gilded bronze which Véronique had ordered from Paris. A white-haired sacristan on either side of the daïs held the banner of the church and the crucifix. The servants, in their devotion, had removed the wooden altar from the sacristy and erected it near the drawing-room door; it was decked and ready for the archbishop to say mass. Mme. Graslin was touched by an attention which the church pays only to crowned heads. The great folding-doors that gave access to the dining-room stood wide open, so that she could see the hall of the château filled with people ; nearly all the village was there.

Her friends had seen to everything, none · but the people of the house stood in the drawing-room ; and before them, grouped about the door of her room, she saw her intimate friends and those whose discretion might be trusted. M. Grossetête, M. de Granville, Roubaud, Gérard, Clousier, and Ruffin stood foremost among these. All of them meant to stand upright when the time came, so that the dying woman's confession should not travel beyond them. Other things favored this design, for the sobs of those about her drowned her voice.

Two of these stood out dreadfully conspicuous among the rest. The first was Denise Tascheron. In her foreign dress, made with Quakerly simplicity, she was unrecognizable to any of the villagers who might have caught a glimpse of her. Not so for the public prosecutor ; she was a figure that he was not likely to forget, and with her reappearance a dreadful light began to dawn on him. Now he had a glimpse of the truth, a suspicion of the part which he had played in Mme. Graslin's life, and then the whole truth flashed upon him. Less over-awed than the rest by the religious influence, the child of the nineteenth century, the man of law felt a cruel sensation of dismay ; the whole drama of Véronique's inner life in the Hôtel Graslin during Tascheron's trial opened out before him. The whole of that tragic epoch reconstructed itself in his memory, lighted up by La Sauviat's eyes, which gleamed with hate of him not ten paces away; those eyes seemed to direct a double stream of molten lead upon him. The old woman had forgiven him nothing. The impersonation of man's justice felt shudders run through his frame. He stood there heart-stricken and pallid, not daring to turn his eyes to the bed where the woman he had loved was lying, lived beneath the shadow of death's hand, drawing strength from the very magnitude of her offense to quell her agony. Vertigo seized on him as he saw Véronique's shrunken profile, a white outline in sharp relief against the crimson damask.

The mass began at eleven o'clock. When the curé of Vizay had read the epistle, the archbishop divested himself of his dalmatic, and took up his station in the doorway—

"Christians here assembled to witness the administration of extreme unction to the mistress of this house, you who are uniting your prayers to those of the church to make intercession with God for the salvation of her soul, learn that she thinks herself unworthy to receive the holy viaticum until she has made, for the edification of others, a public confession of her greatest sin. We withstood her pious desire, although this act of contrition was long in use in the church in the earliest Christian times; but as the afflicted woman tells us that the confession touches on the rehabilitation of an unhappy child of this parish, we leave her free to follow the inspirations of repentance."

After these words, spoken with the benign dignity of a shepherd of souls, the archbishop turned and gave place to Véronique. The dying woman was seen, supported by her mother and the curé, two great and venerable symbols: did she not owe her double existence to the earthly mother who had borne her, and to the church, the mother of her soul? Kneeling on a cushion, she clasped her hands and meditated for a moment to gather up and concentrate the strength to speak from some source derived from heaven. There was something unspeakably awful in that silent pause. No one dared to look at his neighbor. All eyes were fixed on the ground. Yet when Véronique looked up, she met the public prosecutor's glance, and the expression of that white face sent the color to her own.

"I should not have died in peace," Véronique began, in a voice unlike her natural tone, "if I had left behind the false impression which each one of you who hears me speak has possibly formed of me. In me you see a great sinner, who beseeches your prayers, and seeks to merit pardon by the public confession of her sin. So deeply has she sinned, so fatal were the consequences of her guilt, that it may be that no repentance will redeem it. And yet the greater my humiliation on earth, the less, doubtless, have I to dread from God's anger in the heavenly kingdom whither I fain would go.

"It is nearly twenty years since my father, who had such great belief in me, recommended a son of this parish to my care ; he had seen in him a wish to live rightly, aptitude, and an excellent disposition. This young man was the unhappy Jean-François Tascheron, who thenceforward attached himself to me as his benefactress. How was it that my affection for him became a guilty one ? That explanation need not, I think, be required of me. Yet, perhaps, it might be thought that the purest possible motives were imperceptibly transformed by unheard-of self-sacrifice, by human frailty, by a host of causes which might seem to be extenuations of my guilt. But am I the less guilty because our noblest affections were my accomplices ? I would rather admit, in spite of the barriers raised by the delicacy natural to our sex between me and the young man whom my father intrusted to me, that I, who by my education and social position might regard myself as his protegé's superior, listened, in an evil hour, to the voice of the tempter. I soon found that my maternal position brought me into contact with him so close that I could not but be sensible of his mute and delicate admiration. He was the first and only creature to appreciate me at my just value.

Perhaps, too, I myself was led astray by unworthy considerations.   I thought that I could trust to the discretion of a young man who owed everything to me, whom chance had placed so far below me, albeit by birth we were equals.   In fact, I found a cloak to screen my conduct in my name for charity and good deeds.   Alas ! (and this is one of my worst sins) I hid my passion in the shadow of the altar.   I made everything conduce to the miserable triumph of a mad passion, the most irreproachable actions, my love for my mother, acts of a devotion that was very real and sincere and through so many errors—all these things were so many links in a chain that bound me.   My poor mother, whom I love so much, who hears·me even now, was unwittingly and for a long while my accomplice.   When her eyes were opened, I was too deeply committed to my dangerous way, and she found strength to keep my secret in the depths of her mother heart.   Silence in her has thus become the loftiest of virtues.   Love for her daughter overcame the love of God.   Ah ! now I solemnly relieve her of the load of secrecy which she has carried.   She shall end her days with no lie in her eyes and brow.   May her motherhood absolve her, may her noble and sacred old age, crowned with virtues, shine forth in all its radiance, now that the link which bound her indirectly to touch such infamy is severed——"

Here Véronique's sobs interrupted her words ; Aline made her inhale salts.

" Only one other has hitherto been in this secret, the faithful servant who does me this last service ; she has, at least, feigned not to know what she must have known, but she has been in the secret of the austerities by which I have broken this weak flesh.   So I ask pardon of the world for having lived a lie, drawn into that lie by the remorseless logic of the world.

" Jean-François Tascheron is not as guilty as men may have thought him.   Oh, all you who hear me ! I beg of you to

remember how young he was, and that his frenzy was caused
at least as much by the remorse which seized on *me*, as by the
spell of an involuntary attraction.   And more, far more, do
not forget that it was a sense of honor, if a mistaken sense of
honor, which caused the greatest disaster of all.   Neither of
us could endure that life of continual deceits.   He turned
from them to my own greatness, and, unhappy that he was,
sought to make our fatal love as little of a humiliation as
might be to me.   So I was the cause of his crime.   Driven
by necessity, the unhappy man, hitherto only guilty of too
great a love for his idol, chose of all evil actions the one most
irreparable.   I knew nothing of it until the very moment
when the deed was done.   Even as it was being carried out,
God overturned the whole fabric of crooked designs.   I
heard cries that ring even yet in my ears, and went into the
house again.   I knew that it was a struggle for life and death,
and that I, the object of this mad endeavor, was powerless to
interfere.   For Tascheron was mad; I bear witness that he
was mad ! ——''

Here Véronique looked at the public prosecutor, and a
deep audible sigh came from Denise.

" He lost his head when he saw his happiness (so he believed it to be) destroyed by unforeseen circumstances.   Love
led him astray, then fate dragged him from a misdemeanor to
a crime, and from a crime to a double murder.   At any rate,
when he left my mother's house he was an innocent man ;
when he returned, he was a murderer.   I, and I only in the
world, knew that the crime was not premeditated, nor accompanied by the aggravating circumstances which brought the
sentence of death on him.   A hundred times I determined to
give myself up to save him, and a hundred times a terrible
but necessary heroism outweighed all other considerations,
and the words died on my lips.   Surely my presence a few
steps away must have contributed to give him the hateful,
base, cowardly courage of a murderer.   If he had been

alone, he would have fled—— It was I who had formed his nature, who had given him loftier thoughts and a greater heart ; I knew him ; he was incapable of anything cowardly or base. Do justice to the innocent hand, do justice to him ! God in His mercy lets him sleep in the grave that you, guessing doubtless, the real truth, have watered with your tears ! Punish and curse the guilty thing here before you ! When once the deed was done, I was horror-struck ; I did all that I could to hide it. My father had left a charge to me, a childless woman ; I was to bring one child of God's family to God, and I brought him to the scaffold—— Oh, heap all your reproaches upon me ! The hour has come ! "

Her eyes glittered with fierce pride as she spoke. The archbishop, standing behind her, with his pastoral cross held out above her head, no longer maintained his impassive attitude ; he covered his eyes with his right hand, A smothered sound like a dying groan broke the silence, and two men—Gérard and Roubaud—caught Denise Tascheron in their arms. She had swooned away. The fire died down in Véronique's eyes; she looked troubled, but the martyr's serenity soon returned to her face.

" I deserve no praise, no blessings, for my conduct here, as you know now," she said. " In the sight of heaven I have led a life full of sharp penance, hidden from all other eyes, and heaven will value it at its just worth. My outward life has been a vast reparation of the evil that I have wrought ; I have engraved my repentance in characters ineffaceable upon this wide land, a record that will last for ever. It is written everywhere in the fields grown green, in the growing township, in the mountain streams turned from their courses into the plain, once wild and barren, now fertile and productive. Not a tree shall be felled here for a century but the peasants will tell the tale of the remorse to which they owe its shade. In these ways the repentant spirit which should have inspired a long and useful life will still make its influence felt among you for a long time to come. All that you should have owed to *his* talents and a fortune honorably acquired has been done for you by the executrix of his repentance, by her who caused his crime. All the wrong done socially has been repaired ; I have taken upon myself the work of a life cut short in its flower, the life intrusted to my guidance, the life for which I must shortly give an account——"

Here once more the burning eyes were quenched in tears. She paused.

"There is one among those present," she continued, "whom I have hated with a hate which I thought must be eternal, simply because he did no more than his duty. He was the first instrument of my punishment. I was too close to the deed, my feet were dipped too deep in blood, I was bound to hate justice. I knew that there was a trace of evil passion in my heart, so long as that spark of anger should trouble it; I have had nothing to forgive, I have simply purged the corner where the evil one lurked. Whatever the victory cost, it is complete."

The public prosecutor turned a tear-stained face to Véronique. It was as if man's justice was remorseful in him. Véronique, turning her face away to continue her story, met the eyes of an old friend; Grossetête, bathed in tears, stretched out his hands entreatingly towards her. "It is enough !" he seemed to say. The heroic woman heard such a chorus of sobs about her, received so much sympathy, that she broke down ; the balm of the general forgiveness was too much, weakness overcame her. Seeing that the sources of her daughter's strength were exhausted, the old mother seemed to find in herself the vigor of a young woman ; she held out her arms to carry Véronique.

"Christians," said the archbishop, "you have heard the penitent's confession ; it confirms the decree of man's justice ; it may lay all scruples and anxiety on that score to rest. In this confession you should find new reasons for uniting your

prayers to those of the church, which offers to God the holy
sacrifice of the mass to implore His mercy for the sinner after
so grand a repentance.''

The office was finished. Véronique followed all that was
said with an expression of such inward peace that she no
longer seemed to be the same woman. Her face wore a look
of frank innocence, such as it might have worn in the days
when, a pure and ingenuous girl, she dwelt under her father's
roof. Her brows grew white in the dawn of eternity, her face
glowed golden in the light of heaven. Doubtless she caught
something of its mystic harmonies; and in her longing to be
made one with God on earth for the last time, she exerted all
her powers of vitality to live. M. Bonnet came to the bedside and gave her absolution; the archbishop anointed her
with the holy oil, with a fatherly tenderness that revealed to
those who stood about how dear he held this sheep that had
been lost and was found. With that holy anointing the eyes
that had wrought such mischief on earth were closed to the
things of earth, the seal of the church was set on those two
eloquent lips, and the ears that had listened to the inspiration
of evil were closed for ever. All the senses, mortified by
penitence, were thus sanctified; the spirit of evil could have
no power over this soul.

Never had all the grandeur and deep meaning of a sacrament been apprehended more thoroughly than by those who
saw the church's care thus justified by the dying woman's
confession. After that preparation, Véronique received the
body of Christ with a look of hope and joy that melted the
icy barrier of unbelief at which the curé had so often knocked
in vain. Roubaud, confounded, became a Catholic from that
moment.

Awful as the scene was, it was no less touching; and in its
solemnity, as of the culminating-point of a drama, it might
have given some painter the subject of a masterpiece. When
the mournful episode was over, and the words of the Gospel

of St. John fell on the ears of the dying woman, she beckoned to her mother to bring Francis back again. (The tutor
had taken the boy out of the room.) When Francis knelt on
the step by the bedside, the mother whose sins had been forgiven felt free to lay her hands in blessing on his head, and so
she drew her last breath, La Sauviat standing at the post she
had filled for twenty years, faithful to the end. It was she, a
heroine after her manner, who closed the eyes of the daughter
who had suffered so much, and laid a kiss on them.

Then all the priests and assistants came round the bed, and
intoned the dread chant *De profundis* by the light of the
flaming torches; and from those sounds the people of the
whole countryside kneeling without, together with the friends
and all the servants praying in the hall, knew that the mother
of the canton had passed away. Groans and sobs mingled
with the chanting. The noble woman's confession had not
passed beyond the threshold of the drawing-room; it had
reached none but friendly ears. When the peasants came
from Montégnac, and all the district round about came in, each
with a green spray, to bid their benefactress a supreme farewell
mingled with tears and prayers, they saw a representative of
man's justice, bowed down with anguish, holding the cold
hand of the woman to whom all unwittingly he had meted out
such a cruel but just punishment.

Two days later and the public prosecutor, with Grossetête,
the archbishop, and the mayor, bore the pall when Mme.
Graslin was carried to her last resting-place. Amid deep
silence they laid her in the grave; no one uttered a word, for
no one had the heart to speak, and all eyes were full of tears.

"She is a saint!" Everywhere the words were repeated
along the roads which she had made, in the canton which
owed its prosperity to her. It was as if the words were sown
abroad across her fields to quicken the life in them. It struck
nobody as a strange thing that Mme. Graslin should be buried
beside Jean-François Tascheron. She had not asked this;

but a trace of pitying tenderness in the old mother prompted her to bid the sacristan put those together whom earth had separated by a violent death, whom one repentance should unite in purgatory.

Mme. Graslin's will fulfilled all expectations. She founded scholarships in the school at Limoges, and beds in the hospital, intended for the working classes only. A considerable sum (three hundred thousand francs in a period of six years) was left to purchase that part of the village called "Tascheron's," and for building an almshouse there. It was to serve as an asylum for the sick and aged poor of the district, a lying-in hospital for destitute women, and a home for foundling children, and was to be known by the name of Tascheron's Almshouse. Véronique directed that it was to be placed in the charge of the Franciscan Sisters, and fixed the salary of the head physician and house surgeon at four thousand francs. Mme. Graslin begged Roubaud to be the first head physician, and to superintend the execution of the sanitary arrangements and plans to be made by the architect, M. Gérard. She also endowed the commune of Montégnac with sufficient land to pay the taxes. A certain fund was put in the hands of the church to be used as determined in some exceptional cases; for the church was to be the guardian of the young; and if any of the children in Montégnac should show a special aptitude for art or science or industrial pursuits, the far-sighted benevolence of the testatrix provided thus for their encouragement.

The tidings of her death were received as the news of a calamity to the whole country, and no word that reflected on her memory went with it.

Gérard, appointed Francis Graslin's guardian, was required by the terms of the will to live at the château, and thither he went; but not until three months after Véronique's death did he marry Denise Tascheron, in whom Francis found, as it were, a second mother.

ALBERT SAVARON

(de Savarus).

To Madame Emile Girardin.

ONE of the few drawing-rooms where, under the Restoration, the archbishop of Besançon was sometimes to be seen, was that of the Baronne de Watteville, to whom he was particularly attached on account of her religious sentiments.

A word as to this lady, the most important lady of Besançon.

Monsieur de Watteville, a descendant of the famous Watteville, the most successful and illustrious of murderers and renegades—his extraordinary adventures are too much a part of history to be related here—this nineteenth-century Monsieur de Watteville was as gentle and peaceable as his ancestor of the *Grand Siècle* had been passionate and turbulent. After living in the *Comté** like a wood-louse in the crack of a wainscot, he had married the heiress of the celebrated house of Rupt. Mademoiselle de Rupt brought twenty thousand francs a year in the funds to add to the ten thousand francs a year in real estate of the Baron de Watteville. The Swiss gentleman's coat-of-arms (the Wattevilles are Swiss) was then borne as an escutcheon of pretense on the old shield of the Rupts. The marriage, arranged in 1802, was solemnized in 1815 after the second Restoration. Within three years of the birth of a daughter all Madame de Watteville's grandparents were dead and their estates wound up. Monsieur de Watteville's house was then sold, and they settled in the Rue de la Préfecture in the fine old mansion of the Rupts, with an immense garden stretching to the Rue du Perron. Madame de Watte-

* La Franche Comté.

ville, devout as a girl, became even more so after her marriage. She was one of the queens of the saintly brotherhood which gives the upper circles of Besançon a solemn air and prudish manners in harmony with the character of the town.

Monsieur le Baron de Watteville, a dry, lean man, devoid of intelligence, looked worn out without any one knowing whereby, for he enjoyed the profoundest ignorance ; but as his wife was a red-haired woman, and of a stern nature that became proverbial (we still say "as sharp as Madame de Watteville") some wits of the legal profession declared that he had been worn against that rock—*Rupt* is obviously derived from *rupes*. Scientific students of social phenomena will not fail to have observed that Rosalie was the only offspring of the union between the Wattevilles and the Rupts.

Monsieur de Watteville spent his existence in a handsome workshop with a lathe ; he was a turner ! As subsidiary to this pursuit, he took up a fancy for making collections. Philosophical doctors, devoted to the study of madness, regard this tendency toward collecting as a first degree of mental aberration when it is set on small things. The Baron de Watteville treasured shells and geological fragments of the neighborhood of Besançon. Some contradictory folk, especially women, would say of Monsieur de Watteville, "He has a noble soul ! He perceived from the first days of his married life that he would never be his wife's master, so he threw himself into a mechanical occupation and good living."

The house of the Rupts was not devoid of a certain magnificence worthy of Louis XIV., and bore traces of the nobility of the two families who had mingled in 1815. The chandeliers of glass cut in the shape of leaves, the brocades, the damask, the carpets, the gilt furniture, were all in harmony with the old liveries and the old servants. Though served in blackened family plate, round a looking-glass tray furnished with Dresden china, the food was exquisite. The wines selected by Monsieur de Watteville, who, to occupy his time and vary his employments, was his own butler, enjoyed a sort of fame throughout the department. Madame de Watteville's fortune was a fine one ; while her husband's, which consisted only of the estate of Rouxey, worth about ten thousand francs a year, was not increased by inheritance. It is needless to add that in consequence of Madame de Watteville's close intimacy with the archbishop, the three or four clever or remarkable abbés of the diocese who were not averse to good feeding were very much at home at her house.

At a ceremonial dinner given in honor of I know not whose wedding, at the beginning of September, 1834, when the women were standing in a circle round the drawing-room fire, and the men in groups by the windows, every one exclaimed with pleasure at the entrance of Monsieur l'Abbé de Grancey, who was announced.

"Well, and the lawsuit?" they all cried.

"Won!" replied the vicar-general. "The verdict of the court, from which we had no hope, you know why——"

This was an allusion to the members of the First Court of Appeal of 1830 ; the Legitimists had almost all withdrawn.

"The verdict is in our favor on every point, and reverses the decision of the lower court."

"Everybody thought you were done for."

"And we should have been, but for me. I told our advocate to be off to Paris, and at the crucial moment I was able to secure a new pleader, to whom we owe our victory, a wonderful man——"

"At Besançon?" said Monsieur de Watteville, guilelessly.

"At Besançon," replied the Abbé de Grancey.

"Oh yes, Savaron," said a handsome young man sitting near the Baroness, and named de Soulas.

"He spent five or six nights over it ; he devoured documents and briefs ; he had seven or eight interviews of several hours with me," continued Monsieur de Grancey, who had just reappeared at the Hôtel de Rupt for the first time in three weeks. " In short, Monsieur Savaron has just completely beaten the celebrated lawyer whom our adversaries had sent for from Paris. This young man is wonderful, the bigwigs say. Thus the chapter is twice victorious; it has triumphed in law and also in politics, since it has vanquished Liberalism in the person of the counsel of our municipality. ' Our adversaries,' so our advocate said, ' must not expect to find readiness on all sides to ruin the archbishoprics.' The president was obliged to enforce silence. All the townsfolk of Besançon applauded. Thus the possession of the buildings of the old convent remains with the Chapter of the Cathedral of Besançon. Monsieur Savaron, however, invited his Parisian opponent to dine with him as they came out of court. He accepted, saying, ' Honor to every conqueror,' and complimented him on his success without bitterness."

"And where did you unearth this lawyer?" said Madame de Watteville. "I never heard his name before."

" Why, you can see his windows from here," replied the vicar-general. " Monsieur Savaron lives in the Rue du Perron; the garden of his house joins on to yours."

" But he is not a native of the county," said Monsieur de Watteville.

" So little is he a native of any place, that no one knows where he comes from," said Madame de Chavoncourt.

" But who is he?" asked Madame de Watteville, taking the abbé's arm to go into the dining-room. " If he is a stranger, by what chance has he settled at Besançon? It is a strange fancy for a barrister."

" Very strange !" echoed Amédée de Soulas, whose biography is here necessary to the understanding of this tale.

In all ages France and England have carried on an exchange of trifles, which is all the more constant because it evades the tyranny of the custom-house. The fashion that is called English in Paris is called French in London, and this

is reciprocal. The hostility of the two nations is suspended
on two points—the uses of words and the fashion of dress.
"God save the King," the national air of England, is a tune
written by Lulli for the chorus of "Esther" or of "Athalie."
Hoops, introduced at Paris by an Englishwoman, were invented in London, it is known why, by a Frenchwoman, the
notorious Duchess of Portsmouth. They were at first so
jeered at that the first Englishwoman who appeared in them
at the Tuileries narrowly escaped being crushed by the crowd;
but they were adopted. This fashion tyrannized over the
ladies of Europe for half a century. At the peace of 1815,
for a year, the long waists of the English were a standing jest;
all Paris went to see Pothier and Brunet in "The Funny
Englishwomen;" but in 1816 and 1817 the belt of the
Frenchwoman, which in 1814 cut her across the bosom,
gradually descended till it reached the hips.

Within ten years England has made two little gifts to our
language. The *Incroyable*, the *Merveilleux*, the *Élégant*, the
three successors of the *petit-maître* of discreditable etymology,
have made way for the "dandy" and the "lion." The
lion is not the parent of the *lionne*. The *lionne* is due to the
famous song by Alfred de Musset—

" Have you seen in Barcelona   ⁞
       .   .   .   .   .

She that is my mistress and my lionne."

There has been a fusion—or, if you prefer it, a confusion—
of the two words and the leading ideas. When an absurdity
can amuse Paris, which devours as many masterpieces as absurdities, the provinces can hardly be deprived of them. So,
as soon as the *lion* paraded Paris with his mane, his beard
and mustaches, his waistcoats and his eyeglass, maintained in
its place, without the help of his hands, by the contraction .
of his cheek and eye-socket, the chief towns of some departments had their sub-lions, who protested by the smartness of

19

their trousers-straps against the untidiness of their fellow-townsmen.

Thus, in 1834, Besançon could boast of a *lion*, in the person of Monsieur Amédée-Sylvain de Soulas, spelt Souleyas at the time of the Spanish occupation. Amédée de Soulas is, perhaps, the only man in Besançon descended from a Spanish family. Spain sent men to manage her business in the Comté, but very few Spaniards settled there. The Soulas remained in consequence of their connection with Cardinal Granvelle.

Young Monsieur de Soulas was always talking of leaving Besançon, a dull town, church-going, and not literary, a military centre and garrison town, of which the manners and customs and physiognomy are worth describing. This opinion allowed of his lodging, like a man uncertain of the future, in three very scantily furnished rooms at the end of the Rue Neuve, just where it opens into the Rue de la Préfecture.

Young Monsieur de Soulas could not possibly live without a tiger. This tiger was the son of one of his farmers, a small servant aged fourteen, thick-set, and named Babylas. The lion dressed his tiger very smartly—a short tunic coat of iron-gray cloth, belted with patent leather, bright blue plush breeches, a red waistcoat, polished leather top-boots, a shiny hat with black lacing, and brass buttons with the arms of Soulas. Amédée gave this boy white cotton gloves and his washing, and thirty-six francs a month to keep himself—a sum that seemed enormous to the grisettes of Besançon: four hundred and twenty francs a year to a child of fifteen, without counting extras! The extras consisted in the price for which he could sell his turned clothes, a present when Soulas exchanged one of his horses, and the perquisite of the manure. The two horses, treated with sordid economy, cost, one with another, eight hundred a year. His bills for articles received from Paris, such as perfumery, cravats, jewelry, patent blacking, and clothes, ran to another twelve hundred francs. Add to this the groom, or tiger, the horses, a very superior style of dress, and six hundred francs a year for rent, and you will see a grand total of three thousand francs.

Now, Monsieur de Soulas' father had left him only four thousand francs a year, the income from some cottage farms in rather bad repair, which required keeping up, a charge which lent painful uncertainty to the rents. The lion had hardly three francs a day left for food, amusements, and gambling. He very often dined out, and breakfasted with remarkable frugality. When he was positively obliged to dine at his own cost, he sent his tiger to bring a couple of dishes from a cook-shop, never spending more than twenty-five sous.

Young Monsieur de Soulas was supposed to be a spendthrift, recklessly extravagant, whereas the poor man made the two ends meet in the year with a keenness and skill which would have done honor to a thrifty housewife. At Besançon in those days no one knew how great a tax on a man's capital were six francs spent in polish to spread on his boots or shoes, yellow gloves at fifty sous a pair, cleaned in the deepest secrecy to make them three times renewed, cravats costing ten francs, and lasting three months, four waistcoats at twenty-five francs, and trousers fitting close to the boots. How could he do otherwise, since we see women in Paris bestowing their special attention on simpletons who visit them, and cut out the most remarkable men by means of these frivolous advantages, which a man can buy for fifteen louis, and get his hair curled and a fine linen shirt into the bargain?

If this unhappy youth should seem to you to have become a *lion* on very cheap terms, you must know that Amédée de Soulas had been three times to Switzerland, by coach and in short stages, twice to Paris, and once from Paris to England. He passed as a well-informed traveler, and could say, "In England, where I went——" The dowagers of the town would say to him, "You, who have been in England——"

He had been as far as Lombardy, and seen the shores of the
Italian lakes. He read new books. Finally, when he was
cleaning his gloves, the tiger Babylas replied to callers,
"Monsieur is very busy." An attempt had been made to
withdraw Monsieur Amédée de Soulas from circulation by
pronouncing him "A man of advanced ideas." Amédée had
the gift of uttering with the gravity of a native the commonplaces that were in fashion, which gave him the credit of being one of the most enlightened of the nobility. His person
was garnished with fashionable trinkets, and his head furnished
with ideas hall-marked by the press.

In 1834 Amédée was a young man of five-and-twenty, of
medium height, dark, with a very prominent thorax, well-
made shoulders, rather plump legs, feet already fat, white
dimpled hands, a beard under his chin, mustaches worthy of
the garrison, a good-natured, fat, rubicund face, a flat nose,
and brown expressionless eyes; nothing Spanish about him.
He was progressing rapidly in the direction of obesity, which
would be fatal to his pretensions. His nails were well kept,
his beard trimmed, the smallest details of his dress attended to
with English precision. Hence Amédée de Soulas was looked
upon as the finest man in Besançon. A hairdresser who waited
upon him at a fixed hour—another luxury, costing sixty francs
a year—held him up as the sovereign authority in matters of
fashion and elegance.

Amédée slept late, dressed and went out towards noon, to
go to one of his farms and practice pistol-shooting. He
attached as much importance to this exercise as Lord Byron
did in his later days. Then at three o'clock he came home,
admired on horseback by the grisettes and the ladies who
happened to be at their windows. After an affectation of
study or business, which seemed to engage him till four, he
dressed to dine out, spent the evening in the drawing-rooms
of the aristocracy of Besançon playing whist, and went home
to bed at eleven. No life could be more above-board, more

prudent, or more irreproachable, for he punctually attended the services at church on Sundays and holy days.

To enable you to understand how exceptional is such a life, it is necessary to devote a few words to an account of Besançon. No town ever offered more deaf and dumb resistance to progress. At Besançon the officials, the employes, the military, in short, every one engaged in governing it, sent thither from Paris to fill a post of any kind, are all spoken of by the expressive general name of "The Colony." The colony is neutral ground, the only ground where, as in church, the upper rank and the townsfolk of the place can meet. Here, fired by a word, a look, or gesture, are started those feuds between house and house, between a woman of rank and a citizen's wife, which endure till death, and widen the impassable gulf which parts the two classes of society. With the exception of the Clermont-Mont-Saint-Jean, the Beauffremont, the de Scey, and the Gramont families, with a few others who come only to stay on their estates in the Comté, the aristocracy of Besançon dates no further back than a couple of centuries, the time of the conquest by Louis XIV. This little world is essentially of the *parlement,* and arrogant, stiff, solemn, uncompromising, haughty beyond all comparison, even with the Court of Vienna, for in this the nobility of Besançon would put the Viennese drawing-rooms to shame. As to Victor Hugo, Nodier, Fourier, the glories of the town, they are never mentioned, no one thinks about them. The marriages in these families are arranged in the cradle, so rigidly are the greatest things settled as well as the smallest. No stranger, no intruder, ever finds his way into one of these houses, and to obtain an introduction for the colonels or officers of title belonging to the first families in France when quartered there requires efforts of diplomacy which Prince Talleyrand would gladly have mastered to use at a congress.

In 1834 Amédée was the only man in Besançon who wore trousers-straps; this will account for the young man's being regarded as a lion.   And a little anecdote will enable you to understand the city of Besançon.

Some time before the opening of this story, the need arose at the préfecture for bringing an editor from Paris for the official newspaper, to enable it to hold its own against the little *Gazette*, dropped at Besançon by the great *Gazette*, and the *Patriot*, which frisked in the hands of the Republicans. Paris sent them a young man, knowing nothing about la ·Franche Comté, who began by writing them a leading article of the school of the *Charivari*.   The chief of the moderate party, a member of the municipal council, sent for the journalist and said to him, "You must understand, monsieur, that we are serious, more than serious—tiresome ; we resent being amused, and are furious at having been made to laugh.   Be as hard of digestion as the toughest disquisitions in the *Revue des Deux Mondes*, and you will hardly reach the level of Besançon."

The editor took the hint, and thenceforth spoke the most incomprehensible philosophical lingo.   His success was complete.

If young Monsieur de Soulas did not fall in the esteem of Besançon society, it was out of pure vanity on its part ; the aristocracy were happy to affect a modern air, and to be able to show any Parisians of rank who visited the Comté a young man who bore some likeness to them.

All this hidden labor, all this dust thrown in people's eyes, this display of folly and latent prudence, had an object, or the *lion* of Besançon would have been no son of the soil.   Amédée wanted to achieve a good marriage by proving some day that his farms were not mortgaged, and that he had some savings. He wanted to be the talk of the town, to be the finest and best-dressed man there, in order to win first the attention, and then the hand, of Mademoiselle Rosalie de Watteville.

In 1830, at the time when young Monsieur de Soulas was setting up in business as a dandy, Rosalie was but fourteen.

Hence, in 1834, Mademoiselle de Watteville had reached the
age when young persons are easily struck by the peculiarities
which attracted the attention of the town to Amédée. There
are many *lions* who become *lions* out of self-interest and speculation. The Wattevilles, who for twelve years had been drawing an income of fifty thousand francs, did not spend more
than four-and-twenty thousand francs a year, while receiving
all the upper circle of Besançon every Monday and Friday.
On Monday they gave a dinner, on Friday an evening party.
Thus, in twelve years, what a sum must have accumulated
from twenty-six thousand francs a year, saved and invested
with the judgment that distinguishes those old families! It
was very generally supposed that Madame de Watteville,
thinking she had land enough, had placed her savings in the
three per cents., in 1830. Rosalie's dowry would therefore,
as the best informed opined, amount to about twenty thousand
francs a year. So for the last five years Amédée had worked
like a mole to get into the highest favor of the severe Baroness,
while laying himself out to flatter Mademoiselle de Watteville's
conceit.

Madame de Watteville was in the secret of the devices by
which Amédée succeeded in keeping up his rank in Besançon,
and esteemed him highly for it. Soulas had placed himself
under her wing when she was thirty, and at that time had
dared to admire her and make her his idol ; he had got so far
as to be allowed—he alone in the world—to pour out to her
all the unseemly gossip which almost all very precise women
love to hear, being authorized by their superior virtue to look
into the gulf without falling, and into the devil's snares without being caught. Do you understand why the lion did not
allow himself the very smallest intrigue? He lived a public life,
in the street so to speak, on purpose to play the part of a lover
sacrificed to duty by the Baroness, and to feast her mind with
the sins she had forbidden to her senses. A man who is so
privileged as to be allowed to pour light stories into the ear of

a bigot is in her eyes a charming man. If this exemplary youth had better known the human heart, he might without risk have allowed himself some flirtations among the grisettes of Besançon who looked up to him as a king; his affairs might perhaps have been all the more hopeful with the strict and prudish Baroness. To Rosalie our Cato affected prodigality; he professed a life of elegance, showing her in perspective the splendid part played by a woman of fashion in Paris, whither he meant to go as Deputé.

All these manœuvres were crowned with complete success. In 1834 the mothers of the forty noble families composing the high society of Besançon quoted Monsieur Amédée de Soulas as the most charming young man in the town; no one would have dared to dispute his place as cock of the walk at the Hôtel de Rupt, and all Besançon regarded him as Rosalie de Watteville's future husband. There had even been some exchange of ideas on the subject between the Baroness and Amédée, to which the Baron's apparent nonentity gave some certainty.

Mademoiselle de Watteville, to whom her enormous prospective fortune at that time lent considerable importance, had been brought up exclusively within the precincts of the Hôtel de Rupt—which her mother rarely quitted, so devoted was she to her dear archbishop—and severely repressed by an exclusively religious education, and by her mother's despotism, which held her rigidly to principles. Rosalie knew absolutely nothing. It is knowledge to have learned geography from Guthrie, sacred history, ancient history, the history of France, and the four rules, all passed through the sieve of an old Jesuit? Dancing and music were forbidden, as being more likely to corrupt life than to grace it. The Baroness taught her daughter every conceivable stitch in tapestry and women's work—plain sewing, embroidery, knitting. At seventeen Rosalie had never read anything but the "Lettres édifiantes," and some works on heraldry. No newspaper had ever defiled her sight. She attended mass at the Cathedral every morning, taken there by her mother, came back to breakfast, did needlework after a little walk in the garden, and received visitors, sitting with the Baroness until dinner-time. Then, after dinner, excepting on Mondays and Fridays, she accompanied Madame de Watteville to other houses to spend the evening, without being allowed to talk more than the maternal rule permitted.

At eighteen Mademoiselle de Watteville was a slight, thin girl with a flat figure, fair, colorless, and insignificant to the last degree. Her eyes, of a very light blue, borrowed beauty from their lashes, which, when downcast, threw a shadow on her cheeks. A few freckles marred the whiteness of her forehead, which was shapely enough. Her face was exactly like those of Albert Dürer's saints, or those of the painters before Perugino ; the same plump, though slender modeling, the same delicacy saddened by ecstasy, the same severe guilelessness. Everything about her, even to her attitude, was suggestive of those virgins, whose beauty is only revealed in its mystical radiance to the eyes of the studious connoisseur. She had fine hands though red, and a pretty foot, the foot of an aristocrat.

She habitually wore simple checked cotton dresses ; but on Sundays and in the evenings her mother allowed her silk. The cut of her frocks, made at Besançon, also made her ugly, while her mother tried to borrow grace, beauty, and elegance from Paris fashions ; for through Monsieur de Soulas she procured the smallest trifles of her dress from there. Rosalie had never worn a pair of silk stockings or thin boots, but always cotton stockings and leather shoes. On high days she was dressed in a muslin frock, her hair plainly dressed, and had bronze kid shoes.

This education, and her own modest demeanor, hid in Rosalie a spirit of iron. Physiologists and profound observers will tell you, perhaps to your great astonishment, that tempers, characteristics, wit, or genius reappear in families at long intervals, precisely like what are known as hereditary diseases. Thus talent, like the gout, sometimes skips over two genera- tions. We have an illustrious example of this phenomenon in George Sand, in whom are resuscitated the force, the power, and the imaginative faculty of the Maréchal de Saxe, whose natural granddaughter she is.

The decisive character and romantic daring of the famous Watteville had reappeared in the soul of his grand-niece, reinforced by the tenacity and pride of blood of the Rupts. But these qualities—or faults, if you will have it so—were as deeply buried in this young girlish soul, apparently so weak and yielding, as the seething lavas within a hill before it be- comes a volcano. Madame de Watteville alone, perhaps, sus- pected this inheritance from two strains. She was so severe to her Rosalie that she replied one day to the archbishop, who blamed her for being too hard on the child, " Leave me to manage her, monseigneur. I know her! She has more than one Beelzebub in her skin ! ''

The Baroness kept all the keener watch over her daughter, because she considered her honor as a mother to be at stake. After all, she had nothing else to do. Clotilde de Rupt, at this time five-and-thirty, and as good as widowed, with a husband who turned egg-cups in every variety of wood, who set his mind on making wheels with six spokes out of iron- wood, and manufactured snuff-boxes for every one of his acquaintance, flirted in strict propriety with Amédée de Soulas. When this young man was in the house, she alternately dis- missed and recalled her daughter, and tried to detect symptoms of jealousy in that youthful soul, so as to have occasion to repress them. She imitated the police in its deal- ings with the Republicans; but she labored in vain. Rosalie showed no symptoms of rebellion. Then the arid bigot accused her daughter of perfect insensibility. Rosalie knew her mother well enough to be sure that if she had thought young Monsieur de Soulas *nice*, she would have drawn down

on herself a smart reproof. Thus, to all her mother's incite-
ment she replied merely by such phrases as are wrongly called
Jesuitical—wrongly, because the Jesuits were strong, and such
reservations are the spiked wall behind which weakness
takes refuge. Then the mother regarded the girl as a dissem-
bler. If by mischance a spark of the true nature of the Wattevilles and the Rupts blazed out, the mother armed herself with
the respect due from children to their parents to reduce Rosalie
to passive obedience.

This covert battle was carried on in the most secret seclusion
of domestic life, with closed doors. The vicar-general, the
dear Abbé Grancey, the friend of the late archbishop, clever
as he was in his capacity of the chief Father Confessor of the
diocese, could not discover whether the struggle had stirred
up some hatred between the mother and daughter, whether
the mother was jealous in anticipation, or whether the court
Amédée was paying to the girl through her mother had not
overstepped its due limits. Being a friend of the family,
neither mother nor daughter confessed to him. Rosalie, a
little too much harried, morally, about young de Soulas, could
not abide him, to use a homely phrase, and when he spoke to
her, trying to take her heart by surprise, she received him but
coldly. This aversion, discerned only by her mother's eye,
was a constant subject of admonition.·

" Rosalie, I cannot imagine why you affect such coldness
towards Amédée. Is it because he is a friend of the family,
and because we like him—your father and I ? "

" Well, mamma," replied the poor child one day, "if I
made him welcome, should I not be still more in the wrong ? "

" What do you mean by that ? " cried Madame de Watteville. " What is the meaning of such words? Your mother
is unjust, no doubt, and, according to you, would be so in any
case ! Never let such an answer pass your lips again to your
mother——" and so forth.

This quarrel lasted three hours and three-quarters. Rosalie

noted the time.   Her mother, pale with fury, sent her to her room, where Rosalie pondered on the meaning of this scene without discovering it, so guileless was she.   Thus young Monsieur de Soulas, who was supposed by every one to be very near the end he was aiming at, all neckcloths set, and by dint of pots of patent blacking—an end which required so much waxing of his mustaches, so many smart waistcoats, wore out so many horseshoes and stays—for he wore a leather vest, the stays of the *lion*—Amédée, I say, was farther away than any chance comer, although he had on his side the worthy and noble Abbé de Grancey.

"Madame," said Monsieur de Soulas, addressing the Baroness, while waiting till his soup was cool enough to swallow, and affecting to give a romantic turn to his narrative, "one fine morning the mail-coach dropped at the Hôtel National a gentleman from Paris, who, after seeking apartments, made up his mind in favor of the first floor in Mademoiselle Galard's house, Rue du Perron.   Then the stranger went straight to the Mairie, and had himself registered as a resident with all political qualifications.   Finally, he had his name entered on the list of barristers to the court, showing his title in due form, and he left his card on all his new colleagues, the ministerial officials, the councilors of the court and the members of the bench, with the name, 'ALBERT SAVARON.'"

"The name of Savaron is famous," said Mademoiselle de Watteville, who was strong in heraldic information.   "The Savarons of Savarus are one of the oldest, noblest, and richest families in Belgium."

"He is a Frenchman, and no man's son," replied Amédée de Soulas.   "If he wishes to bear the arms of the Savarons of Savarus, he must add a bar-sinister.   There is no one left of the Brabant family but a Mademoiselle de Savarus, a rich heiress, and unmarried."

"The bar-sinister is, of course, the badge of a bastard;

but the bastard of a Comte de Savarus is noble," answered Rosalie.

"Enough, that will do, mademoiselle!" said the Baroness.

"You insisted on her learning heraldry," said Monsieur de Watteville, "and she knows it very well."

"Go on, I beg, Monsieur de Soulas."

"You may suppose that in a town where everything is classified, known, pigeon-holed, ticketed, and numbered, as in Besançon, Albert Savaron was received without hesitation by the lawyers of the town. They were satisfied to say, 'Here is a man who does not know his Besançon. Who the devil can have sent him here? What can he hope to do? Sending his card to the judges instead of calling in person! What a blunder!' And so, three days after, Savaron had ceased to exist. He took as his servant old Monsieur Galard's man—Galard being dead—Jérôme, who can cook a little. Albert Savaron was all the more completely forgotten, because no one had seen him or met him anywhere."

"Then, does he not go to mass?" asked Madame de Chavoncourt.

"He goes on Sundays to Saint-Pierre, but to the early service, at eight in the morning. He rises every night between one and two in the morning, works till eight, has his breakfast, and then goes on working. He walks in his garden, going round fifty or perhaps sixty times; then he goes in, dines, and goes to bed between six and seven."

"How did you learn all that?" Madame de Chavoncourt asked Monsieur Soulas.

"In the first place, madame, I live in the Rue Neuve, at the corner of the Rue du Perron; I look out on the house where this mysterious personage lodges; then, of course, there are communications between my tiger and Jérôme."

"And you gossip with Babylas!" exclaimed Madame de Chavoncourt.

"What would you have me do out riding?"

"Well—and how was it that you engaged a stranger for your defense?" asked the Baroness, thus placing the conversation in the hands of the vicar-general.

"The president of the court played this pleader a trick by appointing him to defend at the assizes a half-witted peasant accused of forgery. But Monsieur Savaron procured the poor man's acquittal by proving his innocence and showing that he had been a tool in the hands of the real culprits. Not only did his line of defense succeed, but it led to the arrest of two of the witnesses, who were proved guilty and condemned. His speech struck the court and the jury. One of these, a merchant, placed a difficult case next day in the hands of Monsieur Savaron, and he won it. In the position in which we found ourselves, Monsieur Berryer finding it impossible to come to Besançon, Monsieur de Garcenault advised him to employ this Monsieur Albert Savaron, foretelling our success. As soon as I saw him and heard him, I felt faith in him, and I was not wrong."

"Is he then so extraordinary?" asked Madame de Chavoncourt.

"Certainly, madame," replied the vicar-general.

"Well, tell us about it," said Madame de Watteville.

"The first time I saw him," said the Abbé de Grancey, "he received me in his outer room next the ante-room—old Galard's drawing-room—which he has had painted like old oak, and which I found to be entirely lined with law-books, arranged on shelves also painted as old oak. The painting and the books are the sole decoration of the room, for the furniture consists of an old writing-table of carved wood, six old armchairs covered with tapestry, window curtains of gray stuff bordered with green, and a green carpet over the floor. The ante-room stove heats this library as well. As I waited there I did not picture my advocate as a young man. But this singular setting is in perfect harmony with his person; for Monsieur Savaron came out in a black merino dressing-

gown tied with a red cord, red slippers, a red flannel waistcoat, and a red smoking-cap.''

''The devil's colors!'' exclaimed Madame de Watteville.

'' Yes,'' said the abbé; '' but a magnificent head. Black
hair already streaked with a little gray, hair like that of Saint
Peter and Saint Paul in pictures, with thick shining curls,
hair as stiff as horsehair; a round white throat like a woman's;
a splendid forehead, furrowed by the strong median line which
great schemes, great thoughts, deep meditations stamp on a
great man's brow; an olive complexion marbled with red, a
square nose, eyes of flame, hollow cheeks, with two long lines
betraying much suffering, a mouth with a sardonic smile, and a
small chin, narrow, and too short; crows' feet on his temples;
deep-set eyes, moving in their sockets like burning balls; but,
in spite of all these indications of a violently passionate nature,
his manner was calm, deeply resigned, and his voice of pene-
trating sweetness, which surprised me in court by its easy
flow; a true orator's voice, now clear and appealing, sometimes insinuating, but a voice of thunder when needful, and
lending itself to sarcasm to become incisive.

'' Monsieur Albert Savaron is of middle height, neither
stout nor thin. And his hands are those of a prelate.

'' The second time I called on him he received me in his
bedroom, adjoining the library, and smiled at my astonishment when I saw there a wretched chest of drawers, a shabby
carpet, a camp-bed, and cotton window-curtains. He came
out of his private room, to which no one is admitted, as
Jérôme informed me; the man did not go in, but merely
knocked at the door.

'' The third time he was breakfasting in his library on the
most frugal fare; but on this occasion, as he had spent the
night studying our documents, as I had my attorney with me,
and as that worthy Monsieur Girardet is long-winded, I had
leisure to study the stranger. He certainly is no ordinary
man. There is more than one secret behind that face, at

once so terrible and so gentle, patient and yet impatient, broad and yet hollow. I saw, too, that he stooped a little, like all men who have some heavy burden to bear."

" Why did so eloquent a man leave Paris? For what purpose did he come to Besançon?" asked pretty Madame de Chavoncourt. " Could no one tell him how little chance a stranger has of succeeding here? The good folks of Besançon will make use of him, but they will not allow him to make use of them. Why, having come, did he make so little effort that it needed a freak of the president's to bring him forward?"

"After carefully studying that fine head," said the abbé, looking keenly at the lady who had interrupted him, in such a way as to suggest that there was something he would not tell, " and especially after hearing him this morning reply to one of the bigwigs of the Paris bar, I believe that this man, who may be five-and-thirty, will by-and-by make a great sensation."

" Why should we discuss him? You have gained your action, and paid him," said Madame de Watteville, watching her daughter, who, all the time the vicar-general had been speaking, seemed to hang on his lips.

The conversation changed, and no more was heard of Albert Savaron.

The portrait sketched by the cleverest of the vicars-general of the diocese had all the greater charm for Rosalie because there was a romance behind it. For the first time in her life she had come across the marvelous, the exceptional, which smiles on every youthful imagination, and which curiosity, so eager at Rosalie's age, goes forth to meet half-way. What an ideal being was this Albert—gloomy, unhappy, eloquent, laborious, as compared by Mademoiselle de Watteville to that chubby fat Count, bursting with health, paying compliments, and talking of the fashions in the very face of the splendor of the old Counts of Rupt. Amédée had cost her many quarrels and scoldings, and, indeed, she knew him only too well; while this Albert Savaron offered many enigmas to be solved.

"Albert Savaron de Savarus," she repeated to herself.

Now, to see him, to catch sight of him! This was the desire of the girl to whom desire was hitherto unknown. She pondered in her heart, in her fancy, in her brain, the least phrases used by the Abbé de Grancey, for all his words had told.

"A fine forehead?" said she to herself, looking at the head of every man seated at the table; "I do not see one fine one. Monsieur de Soulas' is too prominent; Monsieur de Grancey's is fine, but he is seventy, and has no hair, it is impossible to see where his forehead ends."

"What is the matter, Rosalie; you are eating nothing?"

"I am not hungry, mamma," said she. "A prelate's hands——" she went on to herself. "I cannot remember our handsome archbishop's hands, though he confirmed me."

Finally, in the midst of her coming and going in the labyrinth of her meditations, she remembered a lighted window she had seen from her bed, gleaming through the trees of the two adjoining gardens, when she had happened to wake in the night—— "Then that was his light!" thought she. "I might see him! I will see him."

"Monsieur de Grancey, is the chapter's lawsuit quite settled?" asked Rosalie point-blank of the vicar-general, during a moment of silence.

Madame de Watteville exchanged rapid glances with the vicar-general.

"What can that matter to you, my dear child?" she said to Rosalie, with an affected sweetness which made her daughter cautious for the rest of her days.

"It might be carried to the Court of Appeal, but our adversaries will think twice about that," replied the abbé.

"I never could have believed that Rosalie would think

20

about a lawsuit all through a dinner," remarked Madame de Watteville.

"Nor I either," said Rosalie, in a dreamy way that made every one laugh. "But Monsieur de Grancey was so full of it that I was interested."

The company rose from table and returned to the drawing-room. All through the evening Rosalie listened in case Albert Savaron should be mentioned again; but beyond the congratutations offered by each newcomer to the abbé on having gained his suit, to which no one added any praise of the advocate, no more was said about it. Mademoiselle de Watteville impatiently looked forward to bedtime. She had promised herself to wake at between two and three in the morning, and to look at Albert's dressing-room windows. When the hour came, she felt much pleasure in gazing at the glimmer from the lawyer's candles that shone through the trees, now almost bare of their leaves. By the help of the strong sight of a young girl, which curiosity seems to make longer, she saw Albert writing, and fancied she could distinguish the color of the furniture, which she thought was red. From the chimney above the roof rose a thick column of smoke.

"While all the world is sleeping, he is awake—like God!" thought she.

The education of girls brings with it such serious problems —for the future of a nation is in the mother—that the University of France long since set itself the task of having nothing to do with it. Here is one of these problems: Ought girls to be informed on all points? Ought their minds to be under restraint? It need not be said that the religious system is one of restraint. If you enlighten them, you make them demons before their time; if you keep them from thinking, you end in the sudden explosion so well shown by Molière in the character of Agnès, and you leave this suppressed mind, so fresh and clear-seeing, as swift and as logical as that of a savage, at the mercy of an accident. This inevitable crisis was brought on in Mademoiselle de Watteville by the portrait which one of the most prudent abbés of the Chapter of Besançon imprudently allowed himself to sketch at a dinner party.

Next morning, Mademoiselle de Watteville, while dressing, necessarily looked out at Albert Savaron walking in the garden adjoining that of the Hôtel de Rupt.

"What would have become of me," thought she, "if he had lived anywhere else? Here I can, at any rate, see him. What is he thinking about?"

Having seen this extraordinary man, though at a distance, the only man whose countenance stood forth in contrast with crowds of Besançon faces she had hitherto met with, Rosalie at once jumped at the idea of getting into his home, of ascertaining the reasons of so much mystery, of hearing that eloquent voice, of winning a glance from those fine eyes. All this she set her heart on, but how could she achieve it?

All that day she drew her needle through her embroidery with the obtuse concentration of a girl who, like Agnès, seems to be thinking of nothing, but who is reflecting on things in general so deeply that her artifice is unfailing. As a result of this profound meditation, Rosalie thought she would go to confession. Next morning, after mass, she had a brief interview with the Abbé Giroud at Saint-Pierre, and managed so ingeniously that the hour for her confession was fixed for Sunday morning at half-past seven, before eight o'clock mass. She committed herself to a dozen fibs in order to find herself, just for once, in the church at the hour when the lawyer came to mass. Then she was seized with an impulse of extreme affection for her father; she went to see him in his workroom, and asked him for all sorts of information on the art of turning, ending by advising him to turn larger pieces, columns. After persuading her father to set to work on some twisted pillars, one of the difficulties of the turner's art, she suggested that he should make use of a large heap of stones that lay in the middle of the garden to construct a sort of grotto on which he might erect a little temple or Belvedere in which his twisted pillars could be used and shown off to all the world.

At the climax of the pleasure the poor unoccupied man derived from this scheme, Rosalie said, as she kissed him, "Above all, do not tell mamma who gave you the notion; she would scold me."

"Do not be afraid!" replied Monsieur de Watteville, who groaned as bitterly as his daughter under the tyranny of the terrible descendant of the Rupts.

So Rosalie had a certain prospect of seeing ere long a charming observatory built, whence her eyes would command the lawyer's private room. And there are men for whose sake young girls can carry out such master-strokes of diplomacy, while, for the most part, like Albert Savaron, they know it not.

The Sunday so impatiently looked for arrived, and Rosalie dressed with such carefulness as made Mariette, the ladies' maid, smile.

"It is the first time I ever knew mademoiselle to be so fidgety," said Mariette.

"It strikes me," said Rosalie, with a glance at Mariette, which brought poppies to her cheeks, "that you too are more particular on some days than on others."

As she went down the steps, across the courtyard, and through the gates, Rosalie's heart beat, as everybody's does in anticipation of a great event. Hitherto she had never known what it was to walk in the streets; for a moment she had felt as though her mother must read her schemes on her brow, and forbid her going to confession, and she now felt new blood in her feet, she lifted them as though she trod on fire. She had, of course, arranged to be with her confessor at a quarter-past eight, telling her mother eight, so as to have about a quarter of an hour near Albert. She got to church before mass, and after a short prayer, went to see if the Abbé Giroud were in his confessional, simply to pass the time ; and she thus placed herself in such a way as to see Albert as he came into church.

The man must have been atrociously ugly who did not seem handsome to Mademoiselle de Watteville in the frame of mind produced by her curiosity. And Albert Savaron, who was really very striking, made all the more impression on Rosalie because his mien, his walk, his carriage, everything down to his clothing, had the indescribable stamp which can only be expressed by the word mystery.

He came in. The church, till now gloomy, seemed to Rosalie to be illuminated. The girl was fascinated by his slow and solemn demeanor, as of a man who bears a world on his shoulders, and whose deep gaze, whose very gestures, combine to express a devastating or absorbing thought. Rosalie now understood the vicar-general's words in their fullest extent. Yes, those eyes of tawny brown, shot with golden lights, covered an ardor which revealed itself in sudden flashes. Rosalie, with a recklessness which Mariette noted, stood in the lawyer's way, so as to exchange glances with him ; and this glance turned her blood, for it seethed and boiled as though its warmth were doubled.

As soon as Albert had taken a seat, Mademoiselle de Watteville quickly found a place whence she could see him perfectly during all the time the abbé might leave her. When Mariette said " Here is Monsieur Giroud," it seemed to Rosalie that the interval had lasted no more than a few minutes. By the time she came out from the confessional, mass was over. Albert had left the church.

"The vicar-general was right," thought she. "*He* is unhappy. Why should this eagle—for he has the eyes of an eagle—swoop down on Besançon? Oh! I must know everything! But how?"

Under the smart of this new desire Rosalie set the stitches

of her worsted-work with exquisite precision, and hid her meditations under a little innocent air, which shammed simplicity to deceive Madame de Watteville.

From that Sunday, when Mademoiselle de Watteville had met that look, or, if you please, received this baptism of fire— a fine expression of Napoleon's which may be well applied to love—she eagerly promoted the plan for the Belvedere.

"Mamma," said she one day when two columns were turned, "my father has taken a singular idea into his head; he is turning columns for a Belvedere he intends to erect on the heap of stones in the middle of the garden. Do you approve of it? It seems to me——"

"I approve of everything your father does," said Madame de Watteville drily, "and it is a wife's duty to submit to her husband even if she does not approve of his ideas. Why should I object to a thing which is of no importance in itself, if it only amuses Monsieur de Watteville?"

"Well, because from thence we shall see into Monsieur de Soulas' rooms, and Monsieur de Soulas will see us when we are there. Perhaps remarks may be made——"

"Do you presume, Rosalie, to guide your parents, and think you know more than they do of life and the proprieties?"

"I say no more, mamma. Besides, my father said that there would be a room in the grotto, where it would be cool, and where we can take coffee."

"Your father has had an excellent idea," said Madame de Watteville, who forthwith went to look at the columns.

She gave her entire approbation to the Baron de Watteville's design, while choosing for the erection of this monument a spot at the bottom of the garden, which could not be seen from Monsieur de Soulas' windows, but whence they could perfectly see into Albert Savaron's rooms. A builder was sent for, who undertook to construct a grotto, of which the top should be reached by a path three feet wide through the rock-work, where periwinkles would grow, iris, clematis, ivy, honeysuckle, and Virginia creeper. The Baroness desired that the inside should be lined with rustic woodwork, such as was then the fashion for flower-stands, with a looking-glass against the wall, an ottoman forming a box, and a table of inlaid bark. Monsieur de Soulas proposed that the floor should be of asphalt. Rosalie suggested a hanging chandelier of rustic wood.

"The Wattevilles are having something charming done in their garden," was rumored in Besançon.

"They are rich, and can afford a thousand crowns for a whim——"

"A thousand crowns!" exclaimed Madame de Chavon-court.

"Yes, a thousand crowns," cried young Monsieur de Soulas. "A man has been sent for from Paris to rusticate the interior, but it will be very pretty. Monsieur de Watteville himself is making the chandelier, and has begun to carve the wood."

"Berquet is to make a cellar under it," said an abbé.

"No," replied young Monsieur de Soulas, "he is raising the kiosk on a concrete foundation, that it may not be damp."

"You know the very least things that are done in that house," said Madame de Chavoncourt sourly, as she looked at one of her great girls waiting to be married for a year past.

Mademoiselle de Watteville, with a little flush of pride in thinking of the success of her Belvedere, discerned in herself a vast superiority over every one about her. No one guessed that a little girl, supposed to be a witless goose, had simply made up her mind to get a closer view of the lawyer Savaron's private study.

Albert Savaron's brilliant defense of the Cathedral Chapter was all the sooner forgotten because the envy of other lawyers was aroused. Also, Savaron, faithful to his seclusion, went nowhere. Having no friends to cry him up, and seeing no one, he increased the chances of being forgotten which are common to strangers in such a town as Besançon. Nevertheless, he pleaded three times at the commercial tribunal in three knotty cases which had to be carried to the superior court. He thus gained as clients four of the chief merchants of the place, who discerned in him so much good sense and sound legal discernment that they placed their claims in his hands.

On the day when the Watteville family inaugurated the Belvedere, Savaron also was founding a monument. Thanks to the connections he had obscurely formed among the upper class of merchants in Besançon, he was starting a fortnightly paper, called the *Eastern Review,* with the help of forty shares of five hundred francs each, taken up by his ten first clients, on whom he had impressed the necessity for promoting the interests of Besançon, the town where the traffic should meet between Mulhouse and Lyons, and the chief centre between Mulhouse and the Rhone.

To compete with Strasbourg, was it not needful that Besançon should become a focus of enlightenment as well as of trade? The leading questions relating to the interests of Eastern France could only be dealt with in a review. What a glorious task to rob Strasbourg and Dijon of their literary importance, to bring light to the East of France, and compete with the centralizing influence of Paris! These reflections, put forward by Albert, were repeated by the ten merchants, who believed them to be their own.

Monsieur Savaron did not commit the blunder of putting his name in front; he left the finances of the concern to his chief client, Monsieur Boucher, connected by marriage with one of the great publishers of important ecclesiastical works; but he kept the editorship, with a share of the profits as founder. The commercial interest appealed to Dôle, to Dijon, to Salins, to Neufchâtel, to the Jura, Bourg, Nantua, Lous-le-Saulnier. The concurrence was invited of the learning and energy of every scientific student in the districts of le Bugey, la Bresse, and Franche Comté. By the influence of commercial interests and common feeling, five hundred subscribers were booked in consideration of the low price : the *Review* cost eight francs a quarter.

To avoid hurting the conceit of the provincials by refusing their articles, the lawyer hit on the good idea of suggesting a desire for the literary management of this *Review* to Monsieur Boucher's eldest son, a young man of two-and-twenty, very eager for fame, to whom the snares and woes of literary responsibilities were utterly unknown. Albert quietly kept the upper hand, and made Alfred Boucher his devoted adherent. Alfred was the only man in Besançon with whom the king of the bar was on familiar terms. Alfred came in the morning to discuss the articles for the next number with Albert in the garden. It is needless to say that the trial number contained a " Meditation " by Alfred, which Savaron approved. In his conversations with Alfred, Albert would let drop some great ideas, subjects for articles of which Alfred availed himself. And thus the merchant's son fancied he was making capital out of the great man. To Alfred, Albert was a man of genius, of profound politics. The commercial world, enchanted at the success of the *Review*, had to pay up only three-tenths of their shares. Two hundred more subscribers, and the periodical would pay a dividend to the shareholders of five per cent., the editor remaining unpaid. This editing, indeed, was beyond price.

After the third number the *Review* was recognized for exchange by all the papers published in France, which Albert henceforth read at home. This third number included a tale signed " A. S.," and attributed to the famous lawyer. In spite of the small attention paid by the higher circle of Besançon to the *Review*, which was accused of liberal views, this, the first novel produced in the county, came under discussion that mid-winter at Madame de Chavoncourt's.

"Papa," said Rosalie, "a *Review* is published in Besançon ; you ought to take it in; and keep it in your room, for mamma would not let me read it, but you will lend it to me."

Monsieur de Watteville, eager to obey his dear Rosalie, who for the last five months had given him so many proofs of filial affection—Monsieur de Watteville went in person to subscribe for a year to the *Eastern Review* and loaned the four numbers already out to his daughter. In the course of the night Rosalie devoured the tale—the first she had ever read in her life—but she had only known life for two months past. Hence the effect produced on her by this work must not be judged by ordinary rules. Without prejudice of any kind as to the greater or less merit of this composition from the pen of a Parisian who had thus imported into the province the manner, the brilliancy, if you will, of the new literary school, it could not fail to be a masterpiece to a young girl abandoning all her intelligence and her innocent heart to her first reading of this kind.

Also, from what she had heard said, Rosalie had by intuition conceived a notion of it which strangely enhanced the interest of this novel. She hoped to find in it the sentiments, and perhaps something of the life of Albert. From the first pages this opinion took so strong a hold on her, that, after reading the fragment to the end, she was certain that it was no mistake. Here, then, is this confession, in which, according to the critics of Madame de Chavoncourt's drawing-room, Albert had imitated some modern writers, who, for lack of inventiveness, relate their private joys, their private griefs, or the mysterious events of their own life:

AMBITION FOR LOVE'S SAKE.

In 1823 two young men, having agreed as a plan for a holiday to make a tour through Switzerland, set out from Lucerne one fine morning in the month of July in a boat pulled by three oarsmen. They started for Fluelen, intending to stop at every notable spot on the lake of the four cantons. The views which shut in the waters on the way from Lucerne to Fluelen offer every combination that the most exacting fancy can demand of mountains and rivers, lakes and rocks, brooks, and pastures, trees, and torrents. Here are austere solitudes and charming headlands, smiling and trimly kept meadows, forests · crowning perpendicular granite cliffs like plumes, deserted but verdant reaches opening out, and valleys whose beauty seems the lovelier in the dreamy distance.

As they passed the pretty hamlet of Gersau, one of the friends looked for a long time at a wooden house which seemed to have been recently built, enclosed by a paling, and stand- ing on a promontory, almost bathed by the waters. As the boat rowed past, a woman's head was raised against the background of the room on the upper story of this house, to admire the effect of the boat on the lake. One of the young men met the glance thus indifferently given by the unknown fair one.

"Let us stop here," said he to his friend. "We meant to make Lucerne our headquarters for seeing Switzerland ; you will not take it amiss, Léopold, if I change my mind and stay here to take charge of our possessions. Then you can go where you please ; my journey is ended. Pull to land, men, and put us out at this village ; we will breakfast here. I will go back to Lucerne to fetch all our luggage, and before you leave you will know in which house I take a lodging, where you will find me on your return."

"Here or at Lucerne," replied Léopold, "the difference is not so great that I need hinder you from following your whim."

These two youths were friends in the truest sense of the word. They were of the same age ; they had learned at the same school ; and after studying the law, they were spending their holiday in the classical tour in Switzerland. Léopold,

by his father's determination, was already pledged to a place
in a notary's office in Paris. His spirit of rectitude, his gen-
tleness, and the coolness of his senses and his brain, guaranteed him to be a docile pupil. Léopold could see himself a
notary in Paris: his life lay before him like one of the high-
roads that cross the plains of France, and he looked along its
whole length with philosophical resignation.

The character of his companion, whom we will call Rodolphe, presented a strong contrast with Léopold's, and their
antagonism had no doubt had the result of tightening the
bond that united them. Rodolphe was the natural son of a
man of rank, who was carried off by a premature death before
he could make any arrangements for securing the means of
existence to a woman he fondly loved and to Rodolphe.
Thus cheated by a stroke of fate, Rodolphe's mother had re-
course to a heroic measure. She sold everything she owed to
the munificence of her child's father for a sum of more than
a hundred thousand francs, bought with it a life annuity for
herself at a high rate, and thus acquired an income of about
fifteen thousand francs, resolving to devote the whole of it to
the education of her son, so as to give him all the personal
advantages that might help to make his fortune, while saving,
by strict economy, a small capital to be his when he came of
age. It was bold ; it was counting on her own life ; but without this boldness the good mother would certainly have found
it impossible to live and to bring her child up suitably, and
he was her only hope, her future, the spring of all her joys.

Rodolphe, the son of a most charming Parisian woman,
and a man of mark, a nobleman of Brabant, was cursed with
extreme sensitiveness. From his infancy he had in everything shown a most ardent nature. In him mere desire became a guiding force and the motive power of his whole being,
the stimulus to his imagination, the reason of his actions.
Notwithstanding the pains taken by a clever mother, who
was alarmed when she detected this predisposition, Rodolphe

wished for things as a poet imagines, as a mathematician cal-
culates, as a painter sketches, as a musician creates melodies.
Tender-hearted, like his mother, he dashed with inconceivable
violence and impetus of thought after the object of his desires;
he annihilated time. While dreaming of the fulfillment of
his schemes, he always overlooked the means of attainment.
"When my son has children," said his mother, "he will
want them born grown up."

This fine frenzy, carefully directed, enabled Rodolphe to
achieve his studies with brilliant results, and to become what
the English call an accomplished gentleman. His mother
was then proud of him, though still fearing a catastrophe if
ever a passion should possess a heart at once so tender and so
susceptible, so vehement and so kind. Therefore, the judi-
cious mother had encouraged the friendship which bound
Léopold to Rodolphe and Rodolphe to Léopold, since she
saw in the cold and faithful young notary a guardian, a comrade, who might to a certain extent take her place if by some
misfortune she should be lost to her son. Rodolphe's mother,
still handsome at three-and-forty, had inspired Léopold with
an ardent passion. This circumstance made the two young
men even more intimate.

So Léopold, knowing Rodolphe well, was not surprised to
find him stopping at a village and giving up the projected
journey to Saint-Gothard, on the strength of a single glance
at the upper window of a house. While breakfast was prepared for them at the Swan Inn, the friends walked round the
hamlet and came to the neighborhood of the pretty new house;
here, while gazing about him and talking to the inhabitants,
Rodolphe discovered the residence of some decent folk, who
were willing to take him as a boarder, a very frequent custom
in Switzerland. They offered him a bedroom looking over
the lake and the mountains, and whence he had a view of one
of those immense sweeping reaches which, in this lake, are
the admiration of every traveler. This house was divided by

a roadway and a little creek from the new house, where Rodolphe had caught sight of the unknown fair one's face.

For a hundred francs a month Rodolphe was relieved of all thought for the necessaries of life. But, in consideration of the outlay the Stopfer couple expected to make, they bargained for three months' residence and a month's payment in advance. Rub a Swiss ever so little, and you find the usurer. After breakfast, Rodolphe at once made himself at home by depositing in his room such property as he had brought with him for the journey to the Saint-Gothard, and he watched Léopold as he set out, moved by the spirit of routine, to carry out the excursion for himself and his friend. When Rodolphe, sitting on a fallen rock on the shore, could no longer see Léopold's boat, he turned to examine the new house with stolen glances, hoping to see the fair unknown. Alas! he went in without its having given a sign of life. During dinner, in the company of Monsieur and Madame Stopfer, retired coopers from Neufchâtel, he questioned them as to the neighborhood, and ended by learning all he wanted to know about the lady, thanks to his hosts' loquacity; for they were ready to pour out their budget of gossip without any pressing.

The fair stranger's name was Fanny Lovelace. This name (pronounced *Loveless*) is that of an old English family, but Richardson has given it to a creation whose fame eclipses all others! Miss Lovelace had come to settle by the lake for her father's health, the physicians having recommended him the air of Lucerne. These two English people had arrived with no other servant than a little girl of fourteen, a dumb child, much attached to Miss Fanny, on whom she waited very intelligently, and had settled, two winters since, with Monsieur and Madame Bergmann, the retired head-gardeners of his excellency Count Borromeo of Isola Bella and Isola Madre in the Lago Maggiore. These Swiss, who were possessed of an income of about a thousand crowns a year, had let the top story of their house to the Lovelaces for three years, at a rent of two hundred francs a year. Old Lovelace, a man of ninety, and much broken, was too poor to allow himself any gratifications, and very rarely went out; his daughter worked to maintain him, translating English books, and writing some herself, it was said. The Lovelaces could not afford to hire boats to row on the lake, or horses and guides to explore the neighborhood.

Poverty demanding such privation as this excites all the greater compassion among the Swiss, because it deprives them of a chance of profit. The cook of the establishment fed the three English boarders for a hundred francs a month inclusive. In Gersau it was generally believed, however, that the gardener and his wife, in spite of their pretensions, used the cook's name as a screen to net the little profits of this bargain. The Bergmanns had made beautiful gardens round their house, and had built a hothouse. The flowers, the fruit, and the botanical rarities of this spot were what had induced the young lady to settle on it as she passed through Gersau. Miss Fanny was said to be nineteen years old ; she was the old man's youngest child, and the object of his adulation. About two months prior she had hired a piano from Lucerne, for she seemed to be crazy about music, his hosts informed him.

"She loves flowers and music, and she is unmarried ! " thought Rodolphe ; " what good luck ! "

The next day Rodolphe went to ask leave to visit the hothouses and gardens, which were beginning to be somewhat famous. The permission was not immediately granted. The retired gardeners asked, strangely enough, to see Rodolphe's passport ; it was sent to them at once. The paper was not returned to him till next morning, by the hands of the cook, who expressed her master's pleasure in showing him their place. Rodolphe went to the Bergmanns, not without a certain trepidation, known only to persons of strong feelings, who go through as much passion in a moment as some men experience in a whole lifetime.

After dressing himself carefully to gratify the old gardeners of the Borromean Islands, whom he regarded as the warders of his treasure, he went all over the grounds, looking at the house now and again, but with much caution ; the old couple treated him with evident distrust.   But his attention was soon attracted by the little English deaf-mute, in whom his discern-ment, though young as yet, enabled him to recognize a girl of African, or at least of Sicilian origin.   The child had the golden-brown color of a Havana cigar, eyes of fire, Armenian eyelids with lashes of very un-British length, hair blacker than black ; and under this almost olive skin, sinews of extraordi-nary strength and feverish alertness.   She looked at Rodolphe with amazing curiosity and effrontery, watching his every movement.

"To whom does that little Moresco belong?" he asked worthy Madame Bergmann.

" To the English," Monsieur Bergmann replied.

" But she never was born in England ! "

"They may have, perhaps, brought her from the Indies," said Madame Bergmann.

" I have been told that Miss Lovelace is fond of music.   I should be delighted if, during the residence by the lake to which I am condemned by my doctor's orders, she would allow me to join her."

"They receive no one, and will not see anybody," said the old gardener.

Rodolphe bit his lips and went away, without having been invited into the house, or taken into the part of the garden that lay between the front of the house and the shore of the little promontory.   On that side the house had a balcony above the first floor, made of wood, and covered by the roof, which projected deeply like the roof of a chalet on all four sides of the building, in the Swiss fashion.   Rodolphe had loudly praised the elegance of this arrangement, and talked of the view from that balcony, but all in vain. When he had taken leave of the Bergmanns it struck him that he was a simpleton, like any man of spirit and imagination disappointed of the result of a plan which he had believed would succeed.

In the evening he, of course, went out in a boat on the lake, round and about the spit of land, to Brunnen and to Schwytz, and came in at nightfall. From afar he saw the window open and brightly. lighted ; he heard the sound of a piano and the tones of an exquisite voice. He made the boatmen stop, and gave himself up to the pleasure of listening to an Italian air delightfully sung. When the singing ceased, Rodolphe landed and sent away the boat and rowers. At the cost of wetting his feet, he went to sit down under the water-worn granite shelf crowned by a thick hedge of thorny acacia, by the side of which ran a long lime avenue in the Berg-manns' garden. By the end of an hour he heard steps and voices just above him, but the words that reached his ears were all Italian, and spoken by two women.

He took advantage of the moment when the two speakers were at one end of the walk to slip noiselessly to the other. After half an hour of struggling he got to the end of the avenue, and there took up a position whence, without being seen or heard, he could watch the two women without being observed by them as they came towards him. What was Rodolphe's amazement on recognizing the deaf-mute as one of them ; she was talking to Miss Lovelace in Italian.

It was now eleven o'clock at night. The stillness was so perfect on the lake and around the dwelling that the two women must have thought themselves safe ; in all Gersau there could be no eyes open but theirs. Rodolphe supposed that the girl's dumbness. must be a necessary deception. From the way in which they both spoke Italian, Rodolphe suspected that it was the mother tongue of both girls, and concluded that the English name also hid some disguise.

21

"They are Italian refugees," said he to himself, "outlaws
in fear of the Austrian or Sardinian police. The young lady
waits till it is dark to walk and talk in security."

He lay down by the side of the hedge, and crawled like a
snake to find a way between two acacia shrubs. At the risk
of leaving his coat behind him, or tearing deep scratches in
his back, he got through the hedge when the so-called Miss
Fanny and her pretended deaf-and-dumb maid were at the
other end of the path; then, when they had come within
twenty yards of him without seeing him, for he was in the
shadow of the hedge, and the moon was shining brightly, he
suddenly rose.

"Fear nothing," said he in French to the Italian girl, "I
am not a spy. You are refugees, I have guessed that. I am
a Frenchman whom one look from you has fixed at Gersau."

Rodolphe, startled by the acute pain caused by some steel
instrument piercing his side, fell like a log.

"*Nel lago con pietra !*" said the terrible dumb girl.

"Oh, Gina!" exclaimed the Italian.

"She has missed me," said Rodolphe, pulling from the
wound a stiletto, which had been turned by one of the false
ribs. "But a little higher up it would have been deep in my
heart. I was wrong, Francesca," he went on, remembering
the name he had heard little Gina repeat several times; "I
owe her no grudge, do not scold her. The happiness of
speaking to you is well worth the prick of a stiletto. Only
show me the way out; I must get back to the Stopfers' house.
Be easy; I shall tell nothing."

Francesca, recovering from her astonishment, helped Rodolphe to rise, and said a few words to Gina, whose eyes filled
with tears. The two girls made him sit down on a bench and
take off his coat, his waistcoat, and his cravat. Then Gina
opened his shirt and sucked the wound strongly. Francesca,
who had left them, returned with a large piece of sticking-
plaster, which she applied to the wound.

"You can walk now as far as your house," she said.

Each took an arm, and Rodolphe was conducted to a side gate, of which the key was in Francesca's apron pocket.

"Does Gina speak French?" said Rodolphe to Francesca.

"No. But do not excite yourself," replied Francesca with some impatience.

"Let me look at you," said Rodolphe pathetically, "for it may be long before I am able to come again——"

He leaned against one of the gate-posts contemplating the beautiful Italian, who allowed him to gaze at her for a moment under the sweetest silence and the sweetest night that ever, perhaps, shone on this lake, the king of these beautiful Swiss lakes.

Francesca was quite of the classic Italian type, and such as imagination supposes or pictures, or, if you will, dreams, that Italian women are. What first struck Rodolphe was the grace and elegance of a figure evidently powerful, though so slender as to appear fragile. An amber paleness overspread her face, betraying sudden interest, but it did not dim the voluptuous glance of her liquid eyes of velvety blackness. A pair of hands as beautiful as ever a Greek sculptor added to the polished arms of a statue grasped Rodolphe's arm, and their whiteness gleamed against his black coat. The rash Frenchman could but just discern the long, oval shape of her face, and a melancholy mouth showing brilliant teeth between the parted lips, full, fresh, and brightly red. The exquisite lines of this face guaranteed to Francesca permanent beauty ; but what most struck Rodolphe was the adorable freedom, the Italian frankness of this woman, wholly absorbed as she was in her pity for him.

Francesca said a word to Gina, who gave Rodolphe her arm as far as the Stopfers' door, and fled like a swallow as soon as she had rung.

"These patriots do not play at killing!" said Rodolphe to himself as he felt his sufferings when he found himself in his bed. "'*Nel lago!*' Gina would have pitched me into the lake with a stone tied to my neck."

Next day he sent to Lucerne for the best surgeon there, and when the surgeon came, enjoined on him absolute secrecy, giving him to understand that his honor strictly depended on such observance.

Léopold returned from his excursion on the day when his friend first got out of bed. Rodolphe made up a story, and begged him to go to Lucerne to fetch their luggage and letters. Léopold brought back the most fatal, the most dreadful news : Rodolphe's mother was dead. While the two friends were on their way from Bâle to Lucerne, the fatal letter, written by Léopold's father, had reached Lucerne the day they left for Fluelen.

In spite of Léopold's utmost precautions, Rodolphe fell ill of a nervous fever. As soon as Léopold saw his friend out of danger, he set out for France with a power of attorney, and Rodolphe could thus remain at Gersau, the only place in the world where his grief could grow calmer. The young Frenchman's position, his despair, the circumstances which made such a loss worse for him than for any other man, were known, and secured him the pity and interest of every one at Gersau. Every morning the pretended dumb girl came to see him and bring him news of her mistress.

As soon as Rodolphe could go out he went to the Bergmanns' house, to thank Miss Fanny Lovelace and her father for the interest they had taken in his sorrow and his illness. For the first time since he had lodged with the Bergmanns the old Italian admitted a stranger to his room, where Rodolphe was received with the cordiality due to his misfortunes and to his being a Frenchman, which excluded all distrust of him. Francesca looked so lovely by candlelight that first evening that she shed a ray of brightness on his grieving heart. Her smiles flung the roses of hope on his woe. She sang, not indeed gay songs, but grave and solemn melodies suited to the state of Rodolphe's heart, and he observed this touching care.

At about eight o'clock the old man left the young people without any sign of uneasiness, and went to his room. When Francesca was tired of singing, she led Rodolphe on to the balcony, whence they perceived the sublime scenery of the lake, and signed to him to be seated by her on a rustic wooden bench.

"Am I very indiscreet in asking how old you are, cara Francesca?" said Rodolphe.

"Nineteen," said she, "well past."

"If anything in the world could soothe my sorrow," he went on, "it would be the hope of winning you from your father, whatever your fortune may be. So beautiful as you are, you seem to me richer than a prince's daughter. And I tremble as I confess to you the feelings with which you have inspired me; but they are deep—they are eternal."

"*Zitto!*" said Francesca, laying a finger of her right hand on her lips. "Say no more; I am not free. I have been married these three years."

For a few minutes utter silence reigned. When the Italian girl, alarmed at Rodolphe's stillness, went close to him, she found that he had fainted.

"*Povero!*" she said to herself. "And I thought him cold." She fetched some salts, and revived Rodolphe by making him smell at them.

"Married!" said Rodolphe, looking at Francesca. And then his tears flowed freely.

"Child!" said she. "But there still is hope. My husband is——"

"Eighty?" Rodolphe put in.

"No," said she with a smile, "but sixty-five. He has disguised himself as much older to mislead the police."

"Dearest," said Rodolphe, "a few more shocks of this kind and I shall die. Only when you have known me twenty years will you understand the strength and power of my heart, and the nature of its aspirations for happiness. This plant," he went on, pointing to the yellow jasmine which covered the balustrade, " does not climb more eagerly to spread itself in the sunbeams than I have clung to you for this month past. I love you passionately. That love will be the secret fount of my life—I may possibly die of it."

"Oh! Frenchman, Frenchman!" said she, emphasizing her exclamation with a little incredulous grimace.

"Shall I not be forced to wait, to accept you at the hands of time?" said he gravely. "But know this; if you are in earnest in what you have allowed to escape you, I will wait for you faithfully, without suffering any other attachment to grow up in my heart."

She looked at him doubtfully.

"None," said he, "not even a passing fancy. ' I have my fortune to make ; you must have a splendid one, nature created you a princess——"

At this word Francesca could not repress a faint smile, which gave her face the most bewitching expression, something subtle, like what the great Leonardo has so well depicted in the *Gioconda*. This smile made Rodolphe pause. "Ah, yes!" he went on, "you must suffer much from the destitution to which exile has brought you. Oh, if you would make me happy above all men, and consecrate my love, you would treat me as a friend. Ought I not to be your friend? My poor mother has left sixty thousand francs of savings; take half."

Francesca looked steadily at him. This piercing gaze went to the bottom of Rodolphe's soul.

"We want nothing ; my work amply supplies our luxuries," she replied in a grave voice.

"And can I endure that a Francesca should work?" cried he. "One day you will return to your country and find all you left there." Again the Italian girl looked at Rodolphe.

"And you will then repay me what you may have condescended to borrow," he added, with an expression full of
delicate feeling.

"Let us drop this subject," said she, with incomparable
dignity of gesture, expression, and attitude. "Make a splendid fortune, be one of the remarkable men of your country;
that is my desire. Fame is a drawbridge which may serve to
cross a deep gulf. Be ambitious, if you must. I believe you
have great and powerful talents, but use them rather for the
happiness of mankind than to deserve me; you will be all the
greater in my eyes."

In the course of this conversation, which lasted two hours,
Rodolphe discovered that Francesca was an enthusiast for
liberal ideas, and for that worship of liberty which had led to
the three revolutions in Naples, Piédmont, and Spain. On
leaving, he was shown to the door by Gina, the so-called
mute. At eleven o'clock no one was astir in the village,
there was no fear of listeners; Rodolphe took Gina into a
corner, and asked her in a low voice and bad Italian, "Who
are your master and mistress, child? Tell me, I will give
you this fine new gold-piece."

"Monsieur," said the girl, taking the coin, "my master is
the famous bookseller Lamporani of Milan, one of the leaders of
the revolution, and the conspirator of all others whom Austria
would most like to have in the Spielberg."

"A bookseller's wife! Ah, so much the better," thought
he; "we are on an equal footing. And what is her family?"
he added, "for she looks like a queen."

"All Italian women do," replied Gina proudly. "Her
father's name is Colonna."

Emboldened by Francesca's modest rank, Rodolphe had an
awning fitted to his boat and cushions in the stern. When
this was done, the lover came to propose to Francesca to come
out on the lake. The Italian accepted, no doubt to carry out
her part of a young English miss in the eyes of the villagers,

but she brought Gina with her.   Francesca Colonna's lightest
actions betrayed a superior education and the highest social
rank.   By the way in which she took her place at the end of
the boat Rodolphe felt himself in some sort cut off from her,
and, in the face of a look of pride worthy of an aristocrat,
the familiarity he had intended fell dead.   By a glance Francesca made herself a princess, with all the prerogatives she
might have enjoyed in the middle ages.   She seemed to have
read the thoughts of this vassal who was so audacious as to
constitute himself her protector.

Already, in the furniture of the room where Francesca had
received him, in her dress, and in the various trifles she made
use of, Rodolphe had detected indications of a superior character and a fine fortune.   All these observations now recurred
to his mind; he became thoughtful after having been trampled
on, as it were, by Francesca's dignity.   Gina, her half-grown-up
confidante, also seemed to have a mocking expression as she
gave a covert or side glance at Rodolphe.   This obvious disa-
greement between the Italian lady's rank and her manners was
a fresh puzzle to Rodolphe, who suspected some further trick
like Gina's assumed dumbness.

" Where would you go, Signora Lamporani ? " he asked.

" Towards Lucerne," replied Francesca in French.

" Good ! " said Rodolphe to himself, " she is not startled
by hearing me speak her name; she had, no doubt, foreseen
that I should ask Gina—she is so cunning.   What is your
quarrel with me ? " he went on, going at last to sit down by
her side, and asking her by a gesture to give him her hand,
which she withdrew.   " You are cold and ceremonious ; what,
in colloquial language, we should call *short*."

" It is true," she replied with a smile.   "I am wrong.   It
is not good manners ; it is vulgar.   In French you would call it
inartistic.   It is better to be frank than to harbor cold or
hostile feelings towards a friend, and you have already proved
yourself my friend.   Perhaps I have gone too far with you.

You must have taken me to be a very ordinary woman." Rodolphe made many signs of denial. "Yes," said the bookseller's wife, going on without noticing this pantomime, which, however, she plainly saw. "I have detected that, and naturally I have reconsidered my conduct. Well! I will put an end to everything by a few words of deep truth. Understand this, Rodolphe : I feel in myself the strength to stifle a feeling if it were not in harmony with my ideas or anticipation of what true love is. I could love—as we can love in Italy, but I know my duty. No intoxication can make me forget it. Married without my consent to that poor old man, I might take advantage of'the liberty he so generously gives me; but three years of married life imply acceptance of its laws. Hence the most vehement passion would never make me utter, even involuntarily, a wish to find myself free.

"Emilio knows my character. He knows that without my heart, which is my own, and which I might give away, I should never allow any one to take my hand. That is why I have just refused it to you. I desire to be loved and waited for with fidelity, nobleness, ardor, while all I can give is infinite tenderness of which the expression may not overstep the boundary of the heart, the permitted neutral ground. All this being thoroughly understood. Oh!" she went on with a girlish gesture, " I will be as coquettish, as gay, as glad, as a child who knows comparatively nothing of the dangers of familiarity."

This plain and frank declaration was made in a tone, an accent, and supported by a look which gave it the deepest stamp of truth.

"A Princess Colonna could not have spoken better," said Rodolphe, smiling.

"Is that," she answered with some haughtiness, "a reflection on the humbleness of my birth? Must your love flaunt a coat-of-arms? At Milan the noblest names are written over shop-doors: Sforza, Canova, Visconti, Trivulzio, Ursini;

there are Archintos apothecaries ; but, believe me, though I keep a shop, I have the feelings of a duchess."

"A reflection !   Nay, madame, I meant it for praise."

"By comparison ? " she said archly.

"Ah, once for all," said he, "not to torture me if my words should ill express my feelings, understand that my love is perfect ; it carries with it absolute obedience and respect."

She bowed as a woman satisfied, and said, "Then monsieur accepts the treaty ? "

"Yes," said he.   "I can understand that in a rich and powerful feminine nature the faculty of loving ought not to be wasted, and that you, out of delicacy, wished to restrain it. Ah ! Francesca, at my age tenderness requited, and by so sublime, so royally beautiful a creature as you are—why, it is the fulfillment of all my wishes.   To love you as you desire to be loved—is not that enough to make a young man guard himself against every evil folly ?   Is it not to concentrate all his powers in a noble passion, of which in the future he may be proud, and which can leave none but lovely memories? If you could but know with what hues you have clothed the chain of Pilatus, the Rigi, and this superb lake——"

"I want to know," said she, with the Italian artlessness which has always a touch of artfulness.

"Well, this hour will shine on all my life like a diamond on a queen's brow."

Francesca's only reply was to lay her hand on Rodolphe's.

"Oh dearest ! for ever dearest !   Tell me, have you never loved ? "

"Never."

"And you allow me to love you nobly, looking to heaven for the utmost fulfillment ? " he asked.

She gently bent her head.   Two large tears rolled down Rodolphe's cheeks.

"Why ! what is the matter ? " she cried, abandoning her imperial manner.

"I have now no mother whom I can tell of my happiness; she left this earth without seeing what would have mitigated her agony——"

"What?" said she.

"Her tenderness replaced by an equal tenderness——"

"*Povero mio!*" exclaimed the Italian, much touched. "Believe me," she went on after a pause, "it is a very sweet thing, and to a woman, a strong element of fidelity to know that she is all in all on earth to the man she loves; to find him lonely, with no family, with nothing in his heart but his love—in short, to have him wholly to herself."

When two lovers thus understand each other, the heart feels delicious peace, supreme tranquillity. Certainty is the basis for which human feelings crave, for it is never lacking to religious sentiment; man is always certain of being fully repaid by God. Love never believes itself secure but by this resemblance to divine love. And the raptures of that moment must have been fully felt to be understood; it is unique in life; it can never return again, alas! than the emotions of youth. To believe in a woman, to make her your human religion, the fount of life, the secret luminary of all your least thoughts!—is not this a second birth? And a young man mingles with this love a little of the feeling he had for his mother.

Rodolphe and Francesca for some time remained in perfect silence, answering each other by sympathetic glances full of thoughts. They understood each other in the midst of one of the most beautiful scenes of nature, whose glories, interpreted by the glory in their hearts, helped to stamp on their minds the most fugitive details of that unique hour. There had not been the slightest shade of frivolity in Francesca's conduct. It was noble, large, and without any second thought. This magnanimity struck Rodolphe greatly, for in it he recognized the difference between the Italian and the Frenchwoman. The waters, the land, the sky, the woman, all were grandiose and suave, even their love in the midst of this picture, so vast in its expanse, so rich in detail, where the sternness of the snowy peaks and their hard folds standing clearly out against the blue sky reminded Rodolphe of the circumstances which limited his happiness: a lovely country shut in by snows.

This delightful intoxication of soul was destined to be disturbed. A boat was approaching from Lucerne; Gina, who had been watching it attentively, gave a joyful start, though faithful to her part as a mute. The bark came nearer; when at length Francesca could distinguish the faces on board, she exclaimed, "Tito!" as she perceived a young man. She stood up and remained standing at the risk of being drowned. "Tito! Tito!" cried she, impulsively waving her handkerchief.

Tito desired the boatmen to slacken, and the two boats pulled side by side. The Italian and Tito talked with such extreme rapidity, and in a dialect unfamiliar to a man who hardly knew even the Italian of books, that Rodolphe could neither hear nor guess the drift of this conversation. But Tito's handsome face, Francesca's familiarity, and Gina's expression of delight, all aggrieved him. And indeed no lover can help being ill pleased at finding himself neglected for another, whoever he may be. Tito tossed a little leather bag to Gina, full of gold, no doubt, and a packet of letters to Francesca, who began to read them, with a farewell wave of the hand to Tito.

"Get quickly back to Gersau," she said to the boatmen. "I will not let my poor Emilio pine ten minutes longer than he need."

"What has happened?" asked Rodolphe, as he saw Francesca finish reading the last letter.

"Liberty!" she exclaimed, with an artist's enthusiasm.

"And money," added Gina, like an echo, for she had found her tongue.

"Yes," said Francesca, "no more poverty! For more

than eleven months have I been working, and I was beginning to be tired of it. I am certainly not a literary woman."

" Who is this Tito ? " asked Rodolphe.

" The secretary of state to the financial department of the humble shop of the Colonnas, in other words the son of our *ragionato*. Poor boy ! he could not come by the Saint-Gothard, nor by the Mont-Cenis, nor by the Simplon ; he came by sea, by Marseilles, and had to cross France. Well, in three weeks we shall be in Geneva, and living at our ease. Come, Rodolphe," she added, seeing sadness overspread the Parisian's face, " is not the Lake of Geneva quite as good as the Lake of Lucerne ? "

" But allow me to bestow a regret on the Bergmanns' delightful house," said Rodolphe, pointing to the little promontory.

" Come and dine with us to add to your associations, *povero mio*," said she. " This is a great day ; we are out of danger. My mother writes that within a year there will be an amnesty. Oh ! *la cara patria !* "

These three words made Gina weep. " Another winter here," said she, " and I should have been dead ! "

" Poor little Sicilian kid ! " said Francesca, stroking Gina's head with an expression and an affection which made Rodolphe long to be so caressed, even if it were without love.

The boat grounded ; Rodolphe sprang on to the sand, offered his hand to the Italian lady, escorted her to the door of the Bergmanns' house, and went to dress and return as soon as possible.

When he joined the bookseller and his wife, who were sitting on the balcony, Rodolphe could scarcely repress an exclamation of surprise at seeing the prodigious change which the good news had produced in the old man. He now saw a man of about sixty, extremely well preserved, a lean Italian, as straight as an I, with hair still black though thin and showing a white skull, with bright eyes, a full set of white teeth, a face like Cæsar, and on his diplomatic lips a sardonic smile, the almost false smile under which a man of good breeding hides his real feelings.

"Here is my husband under his natural form," said Francesca gravely.

"He is quite a new acquaintance," replied Rodolphe, bewildered.

"Quite," said the bookseller; "I have played many a part, and know well how to make up. Ah! I played one in Paris under the Empire, with Bourrienne, Madame Murat, Madame d'Abrantis *e tuttè quanti.* Everything we take the trouble to learn in our youth, even the most futile, is of use. If my wife had not received a man's education—an unheard-of thing in Italy—I should have been obliged to chop wood to get my living here. *Povera* Francesca! who would have told me that she would some day maintain me!"

As he listened to this worthy bookseller, so easy, so affable, so hale, Rodolphe scented some mystification, and preserved the watchful silence of a man who has been duped.

"*Che avete, signor?*" Francesca asked with simplicity. "Does our happiness sadden you?"

"Your husband is a young man," he whispered in her ear.

She broke into such a frank, infectious laugh that Rodolphe was still more puzzled.

"He is but sixty-five, at your service," said she; "but I can assure you that even that is something—to be thankful for!"

"I do not like to hear you jest about an affection so sacred as this, of which you yourself prescribed the conditions."

"*Zitto!*" said she, stamping her foot, and looking whether her husband were listening. "Never disturb the peace of mind of that dear man, as simple as a child, and with whom I can do what I please. He is under my protection," she added. "If you could know with what generosity he risked his life and fortune because I was a Liberal! for he does not share my political opinions. Is not that love, Monsieur Frenchman? But they are like that in his family. Emilio's younger brother was deserted for a handsome youth by the woman he loved. He thrust his sword through his own heart ten minutes after he had said to his servant, ' I could of course kill my rival, but it would grieve the *Diva* too deeply.' "

This mixture of dignity and banter, of haughtiness and playfulness, made Francesca at this moment the most fascinating creature in the world. The dinner and the evening were full of cheerfulness, justified, indeed, by the relief of the two refugees, but depressing to Rodolphe.

"Can she be fickle?" he asked himself as he returned to the Stopfers' house. " She sympathized in my sorrow, and I cannot take part in her joy 1 "

He blamed himself, justifying this girl-wife.

"She has no taint of hypocrisy, and is carried away by impulse," thought he, " and I want her to be like a Parisian woman."

Next day and the following days—in fact, for twenty days after—Rodolphe spent all his time at the Bergmanns', watching Francesca without having determined to watch her. In some souls admiration is not independent of a certain penetration. The young Frenchman discerned in Francesca the imprudence of girlhood, the true nature of a woman as yet unbroken, sometimes struggling against her love, and at other moments yielding and carried away by it. The old man certainly behaved to her as a father to his daughter, and Francesca treated him with a deeply felt gratitude which roused her instinctive nobleness. The situation and the woman were to Rodolphe an impenetrable enigma, of which the solution attracted him more and more.

These last days were full of secret joys, alternating with melancholy moods, with tiffs and quarrels even more delightful than the hours when Rodolphe and Francesca were of one mind. And he was more and more fascinated by this tenderness apart from wit, always and in all things the same, an affection that was jealous of mere nothings—already!

"You care very much for luxury?" said he one evening to Francesca, who was expressing her wish to get away from Gersau, where she missed many things.

"I!" cried she. "I love luxury as I love the arts, as I love a picture by Raphael, a fine horse, a beautiful day, or the Bay of Naples. Emilio," she went on, "have I ever complained here during our days of privation?"

"You would not have been yourself if you had," replied the old man gravely.

"After all, is it not in the nature of plain folks to aspire to grandeur?" she asked, with a mischievous glance at Rodolphe and at her husband. "Were my feet made for fatigue?" she added, putting out two pretty little feet. "My hands"—and she held one out to Rodolphe—"were those hands made to work? Leave us," she said to her husband; "I want to speak to him."

The old man went into the drawing-room with sublime good faith; he was sure of his wife.

"I will not have you come with us to Geneva," she said to Rodolphe. "It is a gossiping town. Though I am far above the nonsense the world talks, I do not choose to be calumniated, not for my own sake, but for his. I make it my pride to be the glory of that old man, who is, after all, my only protector. We are leaving; stay here a few days. When you come on to Geneva, call first on my husband, and let him introduce you to me. Let us hide our great and unchangeable affection from the eyes of the world. I love you; you know it; but this is how I will prove it to you— you shall never discern in my conduct anything whatever that may arouse your jealousy."

She drew him into a corner of the balcony, kissed him on the forehead, and fled, leaving him in amazement.

Next day Rodolphe heard that the lodgers at the Berg-manns' had left at daybreak. It then seemed to him intoler-able to remain at Gersau, and he set out for Vevay by the longest route, starting sooner than was necessary. Attracted to the waters of the lake where the beautiful Italian awaited him, he reached Geneva by the end of October. To avoid the discomforts of the town he took rooms in a house at Eaux-Vives, outside the walls. As soon as he was settled, his first care was to ask his landlord, a retired jeweler, whether some Italian refugees from Milan had not lately come to reside at Geneva.

"Not so far as I know," replied the man. "Prince and Princess Colonna of Rome have taken Monsieur Jeanrenaud's place for three years; it is one of the finest on the lake. It is situated between the Villa Diodati and that of Monsieur Lafin-de-Dieu, let to the Vicomtesse de Beauséant. Prince Colonna has come to see his daughter and his son-in-law, Prince Gandolphini, a Neapolitan, or if you like, a Sicilian, an old adherent of King Murat's, and a victim of the last revolution. These are the last arrivals at Geneva, and they are not Milanese. Serious steps had to be taken, and the pope's interest in the Colonna family was invoked, to obtain permission from the foreign powers and the King of Naples for the Prince and Princesse Gandolphini to live here. Geneva is anxious to do nothing to displease the Holy Alliance to which it owes its independence. *Our* part is not to ruffle foreign courts: there are many foreigners here, Russians and English."

"Even some Genevese?"

"Yes, monsieur, our lake is so fine! Lord Byron lived here about seven years at the Villa Diodati, which every one goes to see now, like Coppet and Ferney."

"You cannot tell me whether within a week or so a book-seller from Milan has come with his wife—named Lamporani, one of the leaders of the last revolution?"

22

"I could easily find out by going to the Foreigners' Club," said the jeweler.

Rodolphe's first walk was very naturally to the Villa Diodati, the residence of Lord Byron, whose recent death added to its attractiveness: for is not death the consecration of genius?

The road to Eaux-Vives follows the shore of the lake, and, like all the roads in Switzerland, is very narrow; in some spots, in consequence of the configuration of the hilly ground, there is scarcely space for two carriages to pass each other.

At a few yards from the Jeanrenauds' house, which he was approaching without knowing it, Rodolphe heard the sound of a carriage behind him, and, finding himself in a sunken road, he climbed to the top of a rock to leave the road free. Of course he looked at the approaching carriage—an elegant English phaeton, with a splendid pair of English horses. He felt quite dizzy as he beheld in this carriage Francesca, beautifully dressed, by the side of an old lady as hard as a cameo. A servant blazing with gold lace stood behind. Francesca recognized Rodolphe, and smiled at seeing him like a statue on a pedestal. The carriage, which the lover followed with his eyes as he climbed the hill, turned in at the gate of a country house, towards which he ran.

"Who lives here?" he asked of the gardener.

"Prince and Princess Colonna, and Prince and Princess Gandolphini."

"Have they not just driven in?"

"Yes, sir."

In that instant a veil fell from Rodolphe's eyes; he saw clearly the meaning of the past.

"If only this is her last piece of trickery!" thought the thunder-stricken lover to himself.

He trembled lest he should have been the plaything of a whim, for he had heard what a *capriccio* might mean in an

Italian. But what a crime had he committed in the eyes of a woman—in accepting a born princess as a citizen's wife! in believing that a daughter of one of the most illustrious houses of the middle ages was the wife of a bookseller! The consciousness of his blunders increased Rodolphe's desire to know whether he would be ignored and repelled. He asked for Prince Gandolphini, sending in his card, and was immediately received by the false Lamporani, who came forward to meet him, welcomed him with the best possible grace, and took him to walk on a terrace whence there was a view of Geneva, the Jura, the hills covered with villas, and below them a wide expanse of the lake.

"My wife is faithful to the lakes, you see," he remarked, after pointing out the details to his visitor. "We have a sort of concert this evening," he added, as they returned to the splendid Villa Jeanrenaud. "I hope you will do me and the Princess the pleasure of seeing you. Two months of poverty endured in intimacy are equal to years of friendship."

Though he was consumed by curiosity, Rodolphe dared not ask to see the Princess; he slowly made his way back to Eaux-Vives, looking forward to the evening. In a few hours his passion, great as it had already been, was augmented by his anxiety and by suspense as to future events. He now understood the necessity for making himself famous, that he might some day find himself, socially speaking, on a level with his idol. In his eyes Francesca was made really great by the simplicity and ease of her conduct at Gersau. Princess Colonna's haughtiness, so evidently natural to her, alarmed Rodolphe, who would find enemies in Francesca's father and mother—at least, so he might expect; and the secrecy which Princess Gandolphini had so strictly enjoined on him now struck him as a wonderful proof of affection. By not choosing to compromise the future, had she not confessed that she loved him?

At last nine o'clock struck; Rodolphe could get into a carriage and say with an emotion that is very intelligible, " To the Villa Jeanrenaud—to Prince Gandolphini's.''

At last he saw Francesca, but without being seen by her. The Princess was standing quite near the piano.   Her beautiful hair, so thick and long, was bound with a golden fillet. Her face, in the light of wax-candles, had the brilliant pallor peculiar to Italians, and which looks its best only by artificial light.   She was in full evening dress, showing her fascinating shoulders, the figure of a girl and the arms of an antique statue.   Her sublime beauty was beyond all possible rivalry, though there were some charming English and Russian ladies present, the prettiest women of Geneva, and other Italians, among them the dazzling and illustrious Princess Varese, and the famous singer Tinti, who was at that moment engaged in singing.

Rodolphe, leaning against the door-post, looked at the Princess, turning on her the fixed, tenacious, attracting gaze, charged with the full, insistent will which is concentrated in the feeling called desire, and thus assumes the nature of a vehement command.   Did the flame of that gaze reach Francesca ?   Was Francesca expecting each instant to see Rodolphe ? In a few minutes she stole a glance at the door, as though magnetized by this current of love, and her eyes, without reserve, looked deep into Rodolphe's.   A slight thrill quivered through that superb face and beautiful body ; the shock to her spirit reacted : Francesca blushed !   Rodolphe felt a whole life in this exchange of looks, so swift that it can only be compared to a lightning flash.   But to what could his happiness compare ?   He was loved.   The lofty Princess, in the midst of her world, in this handsome villa, kept the pledge given by the disguised exile, the capricious beauty of Bergmanns' lodgings.   The intoxication of such a moment enslaves a man for life !   A faint smile, refined and subtle, candid and triumphant, curled Princess Gandolphini's lips, and at a moment when she did not feel herself observed she looked at

Rodolphe with an expression which seemed to ask his pardon for having deceived him as to her rank.

When the song was ended Rodolphe could make his way to the Prince, who graciously led him to his wife. Rodolphe went through the ceremonial of a formal introduction to Princess and Prince Colonna, and to Francesca. When this was over, the Princess had to take part in the famous quartette, *Mi manca la voce*, which was sung by her with Tinti, with the famous tenor Genovese, and with a well-known Italian prince then in exile, whose voice, if he had not been a prince, would have made him one of the princes of art.

"Take that seat," said Francesca to Rodolphe, pointing to her own chair. "*Oimè!* I think there is some mistake in my name; I have for the last minute been Princess Ro-dolphini."

It was said with an artless grace which revived, in this avowal hidden beneath a jest, the happy days at Gersau. Rodolphe reveled in the exquisite sensation of listening to the voice of the woman he adored, while sitting so close to her that one cheek was almost touched by the stuff of her dress and the gauze of her scarf. But when, at such a moment, *Mi manca la voce* is being sung, and by the finest voices in Italy, it is easy to understand what it was that brought the tears to Rodolphe's eyes.

In love, as perhaps in all else, there are certain circum- stances, trivial in themselves, but the outcome of a thousand little previous incidents, of which the importance is immense, as an epitome of the past and as a link with the future. A hundred times already we have felt the preciousness of the one we love; but a trifle—the perfect touch of two souls united during a walk perhaps by a single word, by some unlooked-for proof of affection—will carry the feeling to its supremest pitch. In short, to express this truth by an image which has been pre-eminently successful from the earliest ages of the world, there are in a long chain points of attachment

needed where the cohesion is stronger than in the intermediate
loops of rings. This recognition between Rodolphe and
Francesca, at this party, in the face of the world, was one of
those intense moments which join the future to the past, and
rivet a real attachment more deeply in the heart. It was
perhaps of these incidental rivets that Bossuet spoke when he
compared to them the rarity of happy moments in our lives—
he who had such a living and secret experience of love.

Next to the pleasure of admiring the woman we love comes
that of seeing her admired by every one else. Rodolphe was
enjoying both at once. Love is a treasury of memories, and
though Rodolphe's was already full, he added to it pearls of
great price ; smiles shed aside for him alone, stolen glances,
tones in her singing which Francesca addressed to him alone,
but which made Tinti pale with jealousy, they were so much
applauded. All his strength of desire, the special expression
of his soul, was thrown over the beautiful Roman, who became
unchangeably the beginning and the end of all his thoughts
and actions. Rodolphe loved as every woman may dream of
being loved, with a force, a constancy, a tenacity, which
made Francesca the very substance of his heart ; he felt her
mingling with his blood as purer blood, with his soul as a
more perfect soul ; she would henceforth underlie the least
efforts of his life as the golden sand of the Mediterranean lies
beneath the waves. In short, Rodolphe's lightest aspiration
was now a living hope.

At the end of a few days, Francesca understood this boundless love ; but it was so natural, and so perfectly shared by
her, that it did not surprise her. She was worthy of it.

"What is there that is strange ? " said she to Rodolphe, as
they walked on the garden terrace, when he had been betrayed
into one of those outbursts of conceit which come so naturally to Frenchmen in the expression of their feelings—"what
is extraordinary in the fact of your loving a young and beautiful woman, artist enough to be able to earn her living like

Tinti, and of giving you some of the pleasures of vanity? What lout but would then become an Amadis? This is not in question between you and me. What is needed is that we both love faithfully, persistently; at a distance from each other for years, with no satisfaction but that of knowing that we are loved."

"Alas!" said Rodolphe, "will you not consider my fidelity as devoid of all merit when you see me absorbed in the efforts of devouring ambition? Do you imagine that I can wish to see you one day exchange the fine name of Gandolphini for that of a man who is a nobody? I want to become one of the most remarkable men of my country, to be rich, great—that you may be as proud of my name as of your own name of Colonna."

"I should be grieved to see you without such sentiments in your heart," she replied, with a bewitching smile. "But do not wear yourself out too soon in your ambitious labors. Remain young. They say that politics soon make a man old."

One of the rarest gifts in women is a certain gaiety which does not detract from tenderness. This combination of deep feeling with the lightness of youth added an enchanting grace at this moment to Francesca's charms. This is the key to her character; she laughs and she is touched; she becomes enthusiastic, and returns to arch raillery with a readiness, a facility, which make her the charming and exquisite creature she is, and for which her reputation is known outside Italy. Under the graces of a woman she conceals vast learning, thanks to the excessively monotonous and almost monastic life she led in the castle of the old Colonnas.

This rich heiress was at first intended for the cloister, being the fourth child of Prince and Princess Colonna; but the death of her two brothers, and of her elder sister, suddenly brought her out of her retirement, and made her one of the most brilliant matches in the papal states. Her elder sister had been betrothed to Prince Gandolphini, one of the richest landowners in Sicily; and Francesca was married to him instead, so that nothing might be changed in the position of the family. The Colonnas and Gandolphinis had always intermarried.

From the age of nine till she was sixteen, Francesca, under the direction of a cardinal of the family, had read all through the library of the Colonnas, to make weight against her ardent imagination by studying science, art, and letters. But in these studies she acquired the taste for independence and liberal ideas, which threw her, with her husband, into the ranks of the revolution. Rodolphe had not yet learned that, besides five living languages, Francesca knew Greek, Latin, and Hebrew. The charming creature perfectly understood that, for a woman, the first condition of being learned is to keep it deeply hidden.

Rodolphe spent the whole winter at Geneva. This winter passed like a day. When spring returned, notwithstanding the infinite delights of the society of a clever woman, wonderfully well informed, young and lovely, the lover went through cruel sufferings, endured indeed with courage, but which were sometimes legible in his countenance, and betrayed themselves in his manners or speech, perhaps because he believed that Francesca shared them. Now and again it annoyed him to admire her calmness. Like an English-woman, she seemed to pride herself on expressing nothing in her face; its serenity defied love; he longed to see her agitated; he accused her of having no feeling, for he believed in the tradition which ascribes to Italian women a feverish excitability.

"I am a Roman!" Francesca gravely replied one day when she took quite seriously some banter on this subject from Rodolphe.

There was a depth of tone in her reply which gave it the appearance of scathing irony, and which set Rodolphe's pulses throbbing. The month of May spread before them the treasures of her fresh verdure ; the sun was sometimes as powerful as at midsummer. The two lovers happened to be at a part of the terrace where the rock rises abruptly from the lake, and where leaning over the stone parapet that crowns the wall above a flight of steps leading down to a landing-stage. From the neighboring villa, where there is a similar stairway, a boat presently shot out like a swan, its flag flaming, its crimson awning spread over a lovely woman comfortably reclining on red cushions, her hair wreathed with real flowers ; the boatman was a young man dressed like a sailor, and rowing with all the more grace because he was under the lady's eye.

"They are happy!" exclaimed Rodolphe, with bitter emphasis. "Claire de Bourgogne, the last survivor of the only house which could ever vie with the royal family of France——"

"Oh ! of a bastard branch, and that a female line."

"At any rate, she is Vicomtesse de Beauséant ; and she did not——"

"Did not hesitate, you would say, to bury herself here with Monsieur Gaston de Nueil," replied the daughter of the Colonnas. "She is only a Frenchwoman ; I am an Italian, my dear sir ! "

Francesca turned away from the parapet, leaving Rodolphe, and went to the farther end of the terrace, whence there is a wide prospect of the lake. Watching her as she slowly walked away; Rodolphe suspected that he had wounded her soul, at once so simple and so wise, so proud and so humble. It turned him cold ; he followed Francesca, who signed to him to leave her to herself. But he did not heed the warning, and detected her wiping away her tears. Tears ! in so strong a nature.

"Francesca," said he, taking her hand, "is there a single regret in your heart ? "

She was silent, disengaged her hand which held her embroidered handkerchief, and again dried her eyes.

"Forgive me!" he said.   And with a rush, he kissed her eyes to wipe away the tears.

Francesca did not seem aware of his passionate impulse, she was so violently agitated.   Rodolphe, thinking she consented, grew bolder; he put his arm round her, clasped her to his heart, and snatched a kiss.   But she freed herself by a dignified movement of offended modesty, and, standing a yard off, she looked at him without anger, but with firm determination.

"Go this evening," she said.   "We meet no more till we meet at Naples."

The order was stern, but it was obeyed, for it was Francesca's will.

On his return to Paris, Rodolphe found in his rooms a portrait of Princess Gandolphini painted by Schinner, as Schinner can paint.   The artist had passed through Geneva on his way to Italy.   As he had positively refused to paint the portraits of several women, Rodolphe did not believe that the Prince, anxious as he was for a portrait of his wife, would be able to conquer the great painter's objections; but Francesca, no doubt, had bewitched him, and obtained from him—which was almost a miracle—an original portrait for Rodolphe, and a duplicate for Emilio.   She told him this in a charming and delightful letter, in which the mind indemnified itself for the reserve required by the worship of the proprieties.   The lover replied.   Thus began, never to cease, a regular correspondence between Rodolphe and Francesca, and which was the only indulgence that they allowed themselves through the many years following.

Rodolphe, possessed by an ambition sanctified by his love, set to work.   First he longed to make his fortune, and risked his all in an undertaking to which he devoted all his faculties as well as his capital; but he, an inexperienced youth, had to contend against duplicity, which won the day.   Thus three years were lost in a vast enterprise, three years of struggling and courage.

The Villèle ministry fell just when Rodolphe was ruined. The valiant lover thought he would seek in politics what commercial industry had refused him ; but before braving the storms of this career, he went, all wounded and sick at heart, to have his bruises healed and his courage revived at Naples, where the Prince and Princess had been reinstated in their place and rights on the King's accession. This, in the midst of his warfare, was a respite full of delights ; he spent three months at the Villa Gandolphini, rocked in hope.

Rodolphe then began again to construct his fortune. His talents were already known ; he was about to attain the desires of his ambitions ; a high position was promised him as the reward of his zeal, his devotion, and his past services, when the storm of July, 1830, broke, and again his bark was swamped.

She, and God ! These are the only witnesses of the brave efforts, the daring attempts of a young man gifted with fine qualities, but to whom, so far, the protection of luck—the god of fools—has been denied. And this indefatigable wrestler, upheld by love, comes back to fresh struggles, lighted on his way by an always friendly eye, an ever-faithful heart.

Lovers ! Pray for him !

———

As she finished this narrative, Mademoiselle de Watteville's cheeks were on fire ; there was a fever in her blood. She was crying—but with rage. This little novel, inspired by the literary style then in fashion, was the first reading of the kind that Rosalie had ever had the chance of devouring. Love was depicted in it, if not by a master-hand, at any rate by a man who seemed to give his own impressions ; and truth, even if unskilled, could not fail to touch a virgin soul. Here lay the secret of Rosalie's terrible agitation, of her fever and her tears ; she was jealous of Francesca Colonna.

She never for an instant doubted the sincerity of this poetical flight; Albert had taken pleasure in telling the story of his passion, while changing the names of persons and perhaps of places. Rosalie was possessed by infernal curiosity. What woman but would, like her, have wanted to know her rival's name—for she too loved! As she read these pages, to her really contagious, she had said solemnly to herself, "I love him!" She loved Albert, and felt in her heart a gnawing desire to fight for him, to snatch him from this unknown rival. She reflected that she knew nothing of music, and that she was not beautiful.

"He will never love me!" thought she.

This conclusion aggravated her anxiety to know whether she might not be mistaken, whether Albert really loved an Italian princess, and was loved by her. In the course of this fateful night, the power of swift decision, which had characterized the famous Watteville, was fully developed in his descendant. She devised those whimsical schemes, round which hovers the imagination of most young girls when, in the solitude to which some injudicious mothers confine them, they are aroused by some tremendous event which the system of repression to which they are subjected could neither foresee nor prevent. She dreamed of descending by a ladder from the kiosk into the garden of the house occupied by Albert; of taking advantage of the lawyer being asleep to look through the window into his private room. She thought of writing to him, or of bursting the fetters of Besançon society by introducing Albert to the drawing-room of the Hôtel de Rupt. This enterprise, which to the Abbé de Grancey even would have seemed the climax of the impossible, was a mere passing thought.

"Ah!" said she to herself, "my father has a dispute pending as to his land at les Rouxey. I will go there! If there is no lawsuit, I will manage to make one, and *he* shall come into our drawing-room!" she cried, as she sprang out of bed and to the window to look at the fascinating gleam which shone through Albert's lights. The clock struck one ; he was still asleep.

" I shall see him when he gets up ; perhaps he will come to his window.''

At this instant Mademoiselle de Watteville was witness to an incident which promised to place in her power the means of knowing Albert's secrets. By the light of the moon she saw a pair of arms stretched out from the kiosk to help Jérôme, Albert's servant, to get across the coping of the wall and step into the little building. In Jérôme's accomplice Rosalie at once recognized Mariette the lady's maid.

"Mariette and Jérôme ! " said she to herself. "Mariette, such an ugly girl ! Certainly they must be ashamed of themselves.''

Though Mariette was horribly ugly and six-and-thirty, she had inherited several plots of land. She had been seventeen years with Madame de Watteville, who valued her highly for her bigotry, her honesty, and long service, and she had no doubt saved money and invested her wages and perquisites. Hence, earning about ten louis a year, she probably had by this time, including compound interest and her little inheritance, not less than ten thousand francs.

In Jérôme's eyes ten thousand francs could alter the laws of optics ; he saw in Mariette a neat figure ; he did not perceive the pits and seams which virulent smallpox had left on her flat, parched face ; to him the crooked mouth was straight ; and ever since Savaron, by taking him ·into his service, had brought him so near to the Wattevilles' house, he had laid siege systematically to the maid, who was as prim and sanctimonious as her mistress, and who, like every ugly old maid, was far more exacting than the handsomest.

If the night-scene in the kiosk is thus fully accounted for to all perspicacious readers, it was not so to Rosalie, though she derived from it the most dangerous lesson that can be given, that of a bad example. A mother brings her daughter up strictly, keeps her under her wing for seventeen years, and then, in one hour, a servant-girl destroys the long and painful work, sometimes by a word, often indeed by a gesture! Rosalie got into bed again, not without considering how she might take advantage of her discovery.

Next morning, as she went to mass accompanied by Mariette —her mother was not well—Rosalie took the maid's arm, which surprised the country wench not a little.

"Mariette," said she, "is Jérôme in his master's confidence?"

"I do not know, mademoiselle."

"Do not play the innocent with me," said Mademoiselle de Watteville drily. "You let him kiss you last night under the kiosk; I no longer wonder that you so warmly approved of my mother's ideas for the improvements she planned."

Rosalie could feel how Mariette was trembling by the shaking of her arm.

"I wish you no ill," Rosalie went on. "Be quite easy; I shall not say a word to my mother, and you can meet Jérôme as often as you please."

"But, mademoiselle," replied Mariette, "it is perfectly respectable; Jérôme honestly means to marry me——"

"But then," said Rosalie, "why meet at night?"

Mariette was completely dumfounded, and could make no reply.

"Listen, Mariette; I am in love too! In secret and without any return. I am, after all, my father's and mother's only child. You have more to hope for from me than from any one else in the world——"

"Certainly, mademoiselle, and you may count on us for life or death," exclaimed Mariette, rejoiced at the unexpected turn of affairs.

"In the first place, silence for silence," said Rosalie. "I will not marry Monsieur de Soulas; but one thing I will have, and must have ; my help and favor are yours on one condition only."

" What is that ? "

" I must see the letters which Monsieur Savaron sends to the post by Jérôme."

" But what for? " said Mariette in alarm.

" Oh ! merely to read them, and you yourself shall post them afterwards. It will cause a little delay; that is all."

At this moment they went into church, and each of them, instead of reading the order of mass, fell into her own train of thought.

" Dear, dear, how many sins are there in all that ? " thought Mariette.

Rosalie, whose soul, brain, and heart were completely upset by reading the story, by this time regarded it as history, written for her rival. By dint of thinking of nothing else, like a child, she ended by believing that the *Eastern Review* was no doubt forwarded to Albert's ladylove.

" Oh ! " said she to herself, her head buried in her hands in the attitude of a person lost in prayer; " Oh ! how can I get my father to look through the list of people to whom the *Review* is sent ? "

After breakfast she took a turn in the garden with her father, coaxing and cajoling him, and brought him to the kiosk.

" Do you suppose, my dear little papa, that our *Review* is ever read abroad? "

" It is but just started——"

" Well, I will wager that it is."

" It is hardly possible."

" Just go and find out, and note the names of any subscribers out of France."

Two hours later Monsieur de Watteville said to his daughter—

"I was right; there is not one foreign subscriber as yet. They hope to get some at Neufchâtel, at Berne, and at Geneva. One copy is, in fact, sent to Italy, but it is not paid for—to a Milanese lady at her country house at Belgirate, on Lago Maggiore."

"What is her name?"

"The Duchesse d'Argaiolo."

"Do you know her, papa?"

"I have heard about her. She was by birth a Princess Soderini, a Florentine, a very great lady, and quite as rich as her husband, who has one of the largest fortunes in Lombardy. Their villa on the Lago Maggiore is one of the sights of Italy."

Two days after, Mariette placed the following letter in Mademoiselle de Watteville's hands:

Albert Savaron to Léopold Hannequin.

"Yes, 'tis so, my dear friend; I am at Besançon, while you thought I was traveling. I would not tell you anything till success should begin, and now it is dawning. Yes, my dear Léopold, after so many abortive undertakings, over which I have shed the best of my blood, have wasted so many efforts, spent so much courage, I have made up my mind to do as you have done—to start on a beaten path, on the highroad, as the longest but the safest. I can see you jump with surprise in your lawyer's chair!

"But do not suppose that anything is changed in my personal life, of which you alone in the world know the secret, and that under the reservations *she* insists on. I did not tell you, my friend; but I was horribly weary of Paris. The outcome of the first enterprise, on which I had founded all my hopes, and which came to a bad end in consequence of the utter rascality of my two partners, who combined to cheat and fleece me—me, though everything was done by my energy

—made me give up the pursuit of a fortune after the loss of three years of my life. One of these years was spent in the law courts, and perhaps I should have come worse out of the scrape if I had not been made to study law when I was twenty.

"I made up my mind to go into politics solely, to the end that I may some day find my name in a list for promotion to the Senate under the title of Comte Albert Savaron de Savarus, and so revive in France a good name now extinct in Belgium—though indeed I am neither legitimate nor legitimized."

"Ah! I knew it! He is of noble birth!" exclaimed Rosalie, dropping the letter.

"You know how conscientiously I studied, how faithful and useful I was as an obscure journalist, and how excellent a secretary to the statesman who, on his part, was true to me in 1829. Flung to the depths once more by the revolution of July, just when my name was becoming known, at the very moment when, as master of appeals, I was about to find my place as a necessary wheel in the political machine, I committed the blunder of remaining faithful to the fallen, and fighting for them, without them. Oh! why was I but three-and-thirty, and why did I not apply to you to make me eligible? I concealed from you all my devotedness and my dangers. What would you have? I was full of faith. We should not have agreed.

"Ten months ago, when you saw me so gay and contented, writing my political articles, I was in despair; I foresaw my fate, at the age of thirty-seven, with two thousand francs for my whole fortune, without the smallest fame, just having, failed in a noble undertaking, the founding, namely, of a daily paper, answering only to a need of the future instead of appealing to the passions of the moment. I did not know which way to turn, and I felt my own value! I wandered about, gloomy and hurt, through the lonely places of Paris—

23

Paris which had slipped through my fingers—thinking of my
crushed ambitions, but never giving them up. Oh, what
frantic letters I wrote at that time to *her*, my second conscience, my other self ! Sometimes, I would say to myself,
'Why did I sketch so vast a programme of life? Why
demand everything? Why not wait for happiness while
devoting myself to some mechanical employment.'

' "I then looked about me for some modest appointment by
which I might live. I was about to get the editorship of a
paper under a manager who did not know much about it, a
man of wealth and ambition, when I took fright. 'Would
she ever accept as her husband a man who had stooped so
low ?' I wondered.

"This reflection made me two-and-twenty again. But, oh,
my dear Léopold, how the soul is worn by these perplexities !
What must not caged eagles suffer, and imprisoned lions !
They suffer what Napoleon suffered, not at Saint Helena, but
on the Quay of the Tuileries, on the 10th of August, when
he saw Louis XVI. defending himself so badly while he could
have quelled the insurrection ; as he actually did, on the same
spot, a little later, in Vendémiaire. Well, my life has been
a torment of that kind, extending over four years. How
many a speech to the Chamber have I not delivered in the
deserted alleys of the Bois de Boulogne ! These wasted
harangues have at any rate sharpened my tongue and accustomed my mind to formulate its ideas in words. And while
I was undergoing this secret torture, you were getting married,
you had paid for your business, you were made law-clerk to
the mayor of your district, after gaining the cross for a wound
at Saint-Merri.

"Now, listen. When I was a small boy and tortured cock-
chafers, the poor insects had one form of struggle which used
almost to put me in a fever. It was when I saw them making
repeated efforts to fly but without getting away, though they
could spread their wings. We used to say, 'They are mark-

ing time.' Now, was this sympathy? Was it a vision of my own future? Oh! to spread my wings and yet be unable to fly! That has been my predicament since that fine undertaking by which I was disgusted, but which has now made four families rich.

"At last, seven months ago, I determined to make myself a name at the Paris bar, seeing how many vacancies had been left by the promotion of several lawyers to eminent positions. But when I remembered the rivalry I had seen among men of the press, and how difficult it is to achieve anything of any kind in Paris, the arena where so many champions meet, I came to a determination painful to myself, but certain in its results, and perhaps quicker than any other. In the course of our conversations you had given me a picture of the society of Besançon, of the impossibility for a stranger to get on there, to produce the smallest effect, to get into society, or to succeed in any way whatever. It was there that I determined to set up my flag, thinking, and rightly, that I should meet with no opposition, but find myself alone to canvass for the election. The people of the Comté will not meet the outsider? The outsider will not meet them! They refuse to admit him to their drawing-rooms, he will never go there! He never shows himself anywhere, not even in the streets! But there is one class that elects the deputies—the commercial class. I am going especially to study commercial questions, with which I am already familiar ; I will gain their lawsuits, I will effect compromises, I will be the greatest pleader in Besançon. By-and-by I will start a *Review*, in which I will defend the interests of the country, will create them, or preserve them, or resuscitate them. When I shall have won a sufficient number of votes, my name will come out of the urn. For a long time the unknown barrister will be treated with contempt, but some circumstance will arise to bring him to the front—some unpaid defense, or a case which no other pleader will undertake.

"Well, my dear Léopold, I packed up my books in eleven cases, I bought such law-books as might prove useful, and I sent everything off, furniture and all, by carrier to Besançon. I collected my diplomas, and I went to bid you good-bye. The mail-coach dropped me at Besançon, where, in three days' time, I chose a little set of rooms looking out over some gardens. I sumptuously arranged the mysterious private room where I spend my nights and days, and where the portrait of my divinity reigns—of her to whom my life is dedicated, who fills it wholly, who is the mainspring of my efforts, the secret of my courage, the cause of my talents. Then, as soon as the furniture and books had come, I engaged an intelligent man-servant, and there I sat for five months like a hibernating marmot.

"My name had, however, been entered on the list of lawyers in the town. At last I was called one day to defend an unhappy wretch at the assizes, no doubt in order to hear me speak for once! One of the most influential merchants of Besançon was on the jury; he had a difficult task to fulfill; I did my utmost for the man, and my success was absolute and complete. My client was innocent; I very dramatically secured the arrest of the real criminals, who had come forward as witnesses. In short, the court and the public were united in their admiration. I managed to save the examining magistrate's pride by pointing out the impossibility of detecting a plot so skillfully planned.

"Then I had to fight a case for my merchant, and won his suit. The Cathedral Chapter next chose me to defend a tremendous action against the town, which had been going on for four years; I won that. Thus after three trials, I had become the most famous advocate of Franche-Comté.

"But I bury my life in the deepest mystery, and so hide my aims. I have adopted habits which prevent my accepting any invitations. I am only to be consulted between six and eight in the morning; I go to bed after my dinner, and work at night. The vicar-general, a man of parts, and very influential, who placed the chapter's case in my hands after they had lost it in the lower court, of course professed their gratitude. 'Monsieur,' said I, 'I will win your suit, but I want no fee ; I want more ' (start of alarm on the abbé's part). 'You must know that I am a great loser by putting myself forward in antagonism to the town. I came here only to leave the place as deputy. I mean to engage only in commercial cases, because commercial men return the members ; they will distrust me if I defend " the priests "—for to them you are simply the priests. If I undertake your defense, it is because I was, in 1828, private secretary to such a minister ' (again a start of surprise on the part of my abbé), 'and master of appeals, under the name of Albert de Savarus ' (another start). ' I have remained faithful to monarchical opinions ; but, as you have not the majority of votes in Besançon, I must gain votes among the citizens. So the fee I ask of you is the votes you may be able secretly to secure for me at the opportune moment. Let us each keep our own counsel, and I will defend, for nothing, every case to which a priest of this diocese may be a party. Not a word about my previous life, and we will be true to each other.'

" When he came to thank me afterwards, he gave me a note for five hundred francs, and said in my ear, ' The votes are a bargain all the same.' I have in the course of five interviews made a friend, I think, of this vicar-general.

" Now I am overwhelmed with business, and I understand no cases but those brought me by merchants, saying that commercial questions are my specialty. This line of conduct attaches business men to me, and allows me to make friends with influential persons. So all goes well. Within a few months I shall have found a house to purchase in Besançon, so as to secure a qualification. I count on your lending me the necessary capital for this investment. If I should die, if I should fail, the loss would be too small to be any considera-

tion between you and me. You will get the interest out of
the rental, and I shall take good care to lookout for something cheap, so that you may lose nothing by this mortgage,
which is indispensable.

"Oh! my dear Léopold, no gambler with the last remains
of his fortune in his pocket, bent on staking it at the Cercle
des Etrangers for the last time one night, when he must come
away rich or ruined, ever felt such a perpetual ringing in his
ears, such a nervous moisture on his palms, such a fevered
tumult in his brain, such inward qualms in his body as I go
through every day now that I am playing my last card in the
game of ambition. Alas! my dear and only friend, for
nearly ten years now have I been struggling. This battle
with men and things, in which I have unceasingly poured out
my strength and energy, and so constantly worn the springs
of desire, has, so to speak, undermined my vitality. With
all the appearance of a strong man of good health, I feel
myself a wreck. Every day carries with it a shred of my inmost life. At every fresh effort I feel that I should never be
able to begin again. I have no power, no vigor left but for
happiness; and if it should never come to crown my head
with roses, the *me* that is really me would cease to exist, I
should be a ruined thing. I should wish for nothing more in
the world. I should want to cease from living. You know
that power and fame, the vast moral empire that I crave, is
but secondary; it is to me only a means to happiness, the
pedestal for my idol.

"To reach the goal and die, like the runner of antiquity!
To see fortune and death stand on the threshold hand in
hand! To win the beloved woman just when love is extinct!
To lose the faculty of enjoyment after earning the right to be
happy! Of how many men has this been the fate!

"But there surely is a moment when Tantalus rebels, crosses
his arms, and defies hell, throwing up his part of the eternal
dupe. That is what I shall come to if anything should thwart

my plan ; if, after stooping to the dust of provincial life, prowl-
ing like a starving tiger round these tradesmen, these electors,
to secure their votes; if, after wrangling in these squalid
cases, and giving them my time—the time I might have spent
on Lago Maggiore, seeing the waters she sees, basking in her
gaze, hearing her voice—if, after all, I failed to scale the
tribune and conquer the glory that should surround the name
that is to succeed to that of Argaiolo! Nay, more than this,
Léopold ; there are days when I feel a heavy languor ; deep
disgust surges up from the depths of my soul, especially when,
abandoned to long day-dreams, I have lost myself in anticipation of the joys of blissful love ! May it not be that our desire has only a certain modicum of power, and that it perishes,
perhaps, of a too lavish effusion of its essence? For, after
all, at this present, my life is fair, illuminated by faith, work,
and love.

"Farewell, my friend ; I send love to your children, and
beg you to remember me to your excellent wife. Yours,

"ALBERT."

Rosalie read this letter twice through, and its general purport
was stamped on her heart. She suddenly saw the whole of
Albert's previous existence, for her quick intelligence threw
light on all the details, and enabled her to take it all in. By
adding this information to the little novel published in the
Review, she now fully understood Albert. Of course, she
exaggerated the greatness, remarkable as it was, of this lofty
soul and potent will, and her love for Albert thenceforth
became a passion, its violence enhanced by all the strength of
her youth, the weariness of her solitude, and the unspent
energy of her character. Love is in a young girl the effect
of a natural law ; but when her craving for affection is centred
in an exceptional man, it is mingled with the enthusiasm
which overflows in a youthful heart. Thus Mademoiselle de
Watteville had in a few days reached a morbid and very

dangerous stage of enamored infatuation. The Baroness was much pleased with her daughter, who, being under the spell of her absorbing thoughts, never resisted her will, seemed to be devoted to feminine occupations, and realized her mother's ideal of a docile daughter.

The lawyer was now engaged in court two or three times a week. Though he was overwhelmed with business he found time to attend the trials, call on litigious merchants, and conduct the *Review;* keeping up his personal mystery, from the conviction that the more covert and hidden was his influence, the more real it would be. But he neglected no means of success, reading up the list of electors of Besançon, and finding out their interests, their characters, their various friendships and antipathies. Did ever a cardinal hoping to be made pope give himself more trouble?

One evening Mariette, on coming to dress Rosalie for an evening party, handed to her, not without many groans over this treachery, a letter of which the address made Mademoiselle de Watteville shiver and redden and turn pale again as she read the address:

To Madame la Duchesse d' Argaiolo
(*née Princesse Soderini*),
At Belgirate,
Lago Maggiore,   *Italy.*

In her eyes this direction blazed as the words *Mene, Mene, Tekel, Upharsin,* did in the eyes of Belshazzar. After concealing the letter, Rosalie went downstairs to accompany her mother to Madame de Chavoncourt's; and as long as the endless evening lasted, she was tormented by remorse and scruples. She had already felt shame at having violated the secrecy of Albert's letter to Léopold; she had several times asked herself whether, if he knew of her crime, infamous inasmuch as it necessarily goes unpunished, the high-minded Albert could esteem her. Her conscience answered an uncompromising "No."

She had expiated her sin by self-imposed penances; she fasted; she mortified herself by remaining on her knees, her arms outstretched for hours, and repeating prayers all the time. She had compelled Mariette to similar acts of repentance; her passion was mingled with genuine asceticism, and was all the more dangerous.

"Shall I read that letter, shall I not?" she asked herself, while listening to the Chavoncourt girls. One was sixteen, the other seventeen and a half. Rosalie looked upon her two friends as mere children because they were not secretly in love. "If I read it," she finally decided, after hesitating for an hour between yes and no, "it shall, at any rate, be the last. Since I have gone so far as to see what he wrote to his friend, why should I not know what he says to *her?* If it is a horrible crime, is it not a proof of love? Oh, Albert! am I not your love?"

When Rosalie was in bed she opened the letter, dated from day to day, so as to give the Duchess a faithful picture of Albert's life and feelings.

"*25th.*

"My dear Soul, all is well. To my other conquests I have just added an invaluable one: I have done a service to one of the most influential men who work the elections. Like the critics, who make other men's reputations but can never make their own, he makes deputies though he can never become one. The worthy man wanted to show his gratitude without loosening his purse-strings by saying to me, 'Would you care to sit in the Chamber? I can get you returned as deputy.'

"'If I ever made up my mind to enter on a political career,' replied I hypocritically, 'it would be to devote myself to the Comté, which I love, and where I am appreciated.'

"'Well,' he said, 'we will persuade you, and through you

we shall have weight in the Chamber, for you will distinguish
yourself there.'

"And so, my beloved angel, say what you will, my perseverance will be rewarded.   Ere long I shall, from the high-
place of the French Tribune, come before my country, before
Europe.   My name will be flung to you by the hundred voices
of the French press.

"Yes, as you tell me, I was old when I came to Besançon,
and Besançon has aged me more ; but, like Sixtus V., I shall
be young again the day after my election.   I shall enter on
my true life, my own sphere.   Shall we not then stand in the
same line ?   Count Savaron de Savarus, ambassador I know
not where, may surely marry a Princess Soderini, the widow
of the Duc d'Argaiolo !   Triumph restores the youth of men
who have been preserved by incessant struggles.   Oh, my
Life ! with what gladness did I fly from my library to my
private room, to tell your portrait of this progress before
writing to you !   Yes, the votes I can command, those of
the vicar-general, of the persons I can oblige, and of this
client, make my election already sure.

"*26th.*

"We have entered on the twelfth year since that blest
evening when, by a look, the beautiful Duchess sealed the
promises made by the exile Francesca.   You, dear, are thirty-
two, I am thirty-five ; the dear Duke is seventy-seven—that is
to say, ten years more than yours and mine put together, and
he still keeps well !   My patience is almost as great as my
love, and indeed I need a few years yet to rise to the level of
your name.   As you see, I am in good spirits to-day, I can
laugh ; that is the effect of hope.   Sadness or gladness, it all
comes to me through you.   The hope of success always carries
me back to the day following that on which I saw you for
the first time, when my life became one with yours as the
earth turns to the light.   *Qual pianto* are these eleven years,
for this is the 26th of December, the anniversary of my arrival

at your villa on the Lake of Geneva. For eleven years have I been crying to you, while you shine like a star set too high for man to reach it.

" *27th.*

" No, dearest, do not go to Milan; stay at Belgirate. Milan terrifies me. I do not like that odious Milanese fashion of chatting at the Scala every evening with a dozen persons, among whom it is hard if no one says something sweet. To me solitude is like the lump of amber in whose heart an insect lives for ever in unchanging beauty. Thus the heart and soul of a woman remain pure and unaltered in the form of their first youth. Is it the *Tedeschi* that you regret ?

" *28th.*

" Is your statue never to be finished? I should wish to have you in marble, in painting, in miniature, in every pos-sible form, to beguile my impatience. I still am waiting for the view of Belgirate from the south, and that of the balcony ; these are all that I now lack. I am so extremely busy that to-day I can only write you nothing—but that nothing is everything. Was it not of nothing that God made the world ? That nothing is a word, God's word : I love you !

" *30th.*

" Ah ! I have received your journal. Thanks for your punctuality. So you found great pleasure in seeing all the details of our first acquaintance thus set down ? Alas ! even while disguising them I was sorely afraid of offending you. We had no stories, and a *Review* without stories is a beauty without hair. Not being inventive by nature, and in sheer despair, I took the only poetry in my soul, the only adventure in my memory, and pitched it in the key in which it would bear telling ; nor did I ever cease to think of you while writing the only literary production that will ever come from my heart, I cannot say from my pen. Did not the trans-formation of your fierce Sormano into Gina cause you to laugh ?

"You ask after my health. Well, it is better than in Paris. Though I work enormously, the peacefulness of the surroundings has its effect on the mind. What really tries and ages me, dear angel, is the anguish of mortified vanity, the perpetual friction of Paris life, the struggle of rival ambitions. This peace is a balm.

"If you could imagine the pleasure your letter gives me!—the long, kind letter in which you tell me the most trivial incidents of your life. No! you women can never know to what a degree a true lover is interested in these trifles. It was an immense pleasure to see the pattern of your new dress. Can it be a matter of indifference to me to know what you wear? If your lofty brow is knit? If our writers amuse you? If Canalis' songs delight you? I read the books you read. Even to your boating on the lake; every incident touched me. Your letter is as lovely, as sweet as your soul! Oh! flower of heaven, perpetually adored, could I have lived without those dear letters, which for eleven years have upheld me in my difficult path like a light, like a perfume, like a steady chant, like some divine nourishment, like everything which can soothe and comfort life.

"Do not fail me! If you knew what anxiety I suffer the day before they are due, or the pain a day's delay can give me! Is she ill? Is *he?* I am midway between hell and paradise.

"*O mia cara diva*, keep up your music, exercise your voice, practice. I am enchanted with the coincidence of employments and hours by which, though separated by the Alps, we live by precisely the same rule. The thought charms me and gives me courage. The first time I undertook to plead here—I forgot to tell you this—I fancied that you were listening to me, and I suddenly felt the flash of inspiration which lifts the poet above mankind. If I am returned to the Chamber—oh! you must come to Paris to be present at my first appearance there!

"Good heavens, how I love you! Alas! I have intrusted too much to my love and my hopes. An accident
which should sink that overloaded bark would end my life!
For three years now I have not seen you, and at the thought
of going to Belgirate my heart beats so wildly that I am
forced to stop. To see you, to hear that girlish caressing
voice! To embrace in my gaze that ivory skin, glistening
under the candlelight, and through which I can read your
noble mind! To admire your fingers playing on the keys,
to drink in your whole soul in a look, in the tone of an *Oimè*
or an *Alberto!* To walk by the blossoming orange trees, to
live a few months in the bosom of that glorious scenery!
That is life. What folly it is to run after power, a name,
fortune! But at Belgirate there is everything; there is poetry,
there is glory! I ought to have made myself your steward,
or, as that dear tyrant whom we cannot hate proposed to me,
live there as *cavaliere servente*, only our passion was too fierce
to allow of it.

"Farewell, my angel, forgive me my next fit of sadness in
consideration of this cheerful mood; it has come as a beam
of light from the torch of Hope, which has hitherto seemed
to me a will-o'-the-wisp."

"How he loves her!" cried Rosalie, dropping the letter,
which seemed heavy in her hand. "After eleven years, to
write like this!"

"Mariette," said Mademoiselle de Watteville to her maid
next morning, "go and post this letter. Tell Jérôme that I
know all I wished to know, and that he is to serve Monsieur
Albert faithfully. We will confess our sins, you and I, without
saying to whom the letters belonged, nor to whom they were
going. I was in the wrong ; I alone am guilty."

"Mademoiselle has been crying?" said Mariette, noticing
Rosalie's eyes.

" Yes, but I do not want that my mother should perceive it ; give me some very cold water."

In the midst of the storms of her passion Rosalie ofteñ listened to the voice of conscience. Touched by the beautiful fidelity of these two hearts, she had just said her prayers, telling herself that there was nothing left to her but to be resigned, and to respect the happiness of two beings worthy of each other, submissive to fate, looking to God for everything, without allowing themselves any criminal acts or wishes. She felt a better woman, and had a certain sense of satisfaction after coming to this resolution, inspired by the natural rectitude of youth. And she was confirmed in it by a girl's idea : She was sacrificing herself for *him.*

" She does not know how to love," thought she. "Ah ! if it were I—I would give up everything to a man who loved me so. To be loved ! When, by whom shall I be loved ? That little Monsieur de Soulas only loves my money; if I were poor, he would not even look at me."

" Rosalie, my child, what are you thinking about ? You are working beyond the outline," said the Baroness to her daughter, who was making worsted-work slippers for the Baron.

Rosalie spent the winter of 1834–35 torn by secret tumult ; but in the spring, in the month of April, when she reached the age of nineteen, she sometimes thought that it would be a fine thing to triumph over a Duchesse d'Argaiolo. In silence and solitude the prospect of this struggle had fanned her passion and her evil thoughts. She encouraged her romantic daring by making plan after plan. Although such characters are an exception, there are, unfortunately, too many Rosalies in the world, and this story contains a moral which ought to serve them as a warning.

In the course of this winter Albert Savaron had quietly made considerable progress in Besançon. Most confident of success, he now impatiently awaited the dissolution of the

Chamber. Among the men of the moderate party he had won the suffrages of one of the makers of Besançon, a rich contractor, who had very wide influence.

Wherever they settled the Romans took immense pains, and spent enormous sums to have an unlimited supply of good water in every town of their empire. At Bensaçon they drank the water from Arcier, a hill at some considerable distance from Besançon. The town stands in a horseshoe circumscribed by the river Doubs. Thus, to restore an aqueduct in order to drink the same water that the Romans drank, in a town watered by the Doubs, is one of those absurdities which only succeed in a country place where the most exemplary gravity prevails. If this whim could be brought home to the hearts of the citizens, it would lead to considerable outlay, and this expenditure would benefit the influential contractor.

Albert Savaron de Savarus opined that the water of the river was good for nothing but to flow under a suspension bridge, and that the only drinkable water was that from Arcier. Articles were printed in the *Review* which merely expressed the views of the commercial interest of Besançon. The nobility and the citizens, the moderates and the legitimists, the government party and the opposition, everybody, in short, was agreed that they must drink the same water as the Romans, and boast of a suspension bridge. The question of the Arcier water was the order of the day at Besançon. At Besançon—as in the matter of the two railways to Versailles—as for every standing abuse—there were private interests unconfessed which gave vital force to this idea. The reasonable folk in opposition to this scheme, who were indeed but few, were regarded as old women. No one talked of anything but of Savaron's two projects. And thus, after eighteen months of underground labor, the ambitious lawyer had succeeded in stirring to its depths the most stagnant town in France, the most unyielding to foreign influence, in finding the length of its foot, to use a vulgar phrase, and exerting a preponderant influence without stirring from his own room. He had solved the singular problem of how to be powerful without being popular.

In the course of this winter he won seven lawsuits for various priests of Besançon. At moments he could breathe freely at the thought of his coming triumph. This intense desire, which made him work so many interests and devise so many springs, absorbed the last strength of his terribly overstrung soul. His disinterestedness was lauded, and he took his clients' fees without comment. But this disinterestedness was, in truth, moral usury; he counted on a reward far greater to him than all the gold in the world.

In the month of October, 1834, he had bought, ostensibly to serve a merchant who was in difficulties, with money loaned him by Léopold Hannequin, a house which gave him a qualification for election. He had not seemed to seek or desire this advantageous bargain.

"You are really a remarkable man," said the Abbé de Grancey, who, of course, had watched and understood the lawyer. The vicar-general had come to introduce to him a canon who needed his professional advice. "You are a priest who has taken the wrong turning." This observation struck Savaron.

Rosalie, on her part, had made up her mind, in her strong girl's head, to get Monsieur de Savaron into the drawing-room and acquainted with the society of the Hôtel de Rupt. So far she had limited her desires to seeing and hearing Albert. She had compounded, so to speak, and a composition is often no more than a truce.

Les Rouxey, the inherited estate of the Wattevilles, was worth just ten thousand francs a year; but in other hands it would have yielded a great deal more. The Baron in his indifference—for his wife was to have, and in fact had, forty thousand francs a year—left the management of Les Rouxey to a sort of factotum, an old servant of the Wattevilles named

Modinier. Nevertheless, whenever the Baron and his wife wished to go out of the town, they went to Les Rouxey, which is very picturesquely situated. The château and the park were, in fact, created by the famous Watteville, who in his active old age was passionately attached to this magnificent spot.

Between two precipitous hills—little peaks with bare summits known as the great and the little Rouxey—in the heart of a ravine where the torrents from the heights, with the Dent de Vilard at their head, come tumbling to join the lovely upper waters of the Doubs, Watteville had a huge dam constructed, leaving two cuttings for the overflow. Above this dam he made a beautiful lake, and below it two cascades; and these, uniting a few yards below the falls, formed a lovely little river to irrigate the barren, uncultivated valley, hitherto devastated by the torrent. This lake, this valley, and these two hills he enclosed in a ring fence, and built himself a retreat on the dam, which he widened to two acres by accumulating above it all the soil which had to be removed to make a channel for the river and the irrigation canals.

When the Baron de Watteville thus obtained the lake above his dam he was owner of the two hills, but not of the upper valley thus flooded, through which there had been at all times a right-of-way to where it ends in a horseshoe under the Dent de Vilard. But this ferocious old man was so widely dreaded, that so long as he lived no claim was urged by the inhabitants of Riceys, the little village on the farther side of the Dent de Vilard. When the Baron died, he left the slopes of the two Rouxey hills joined by a strong wall, to protect from inundation the two lateral valleys opening into the valley of Rouxey, to the right and left at the foot of the Dent de Vilard. Thus he died the master of the Dent de Vilard.

His heirs asserted their protectorate of the village of Riceys, and so maintained the usurpation. The old assassin, the old renegade, the old Abbé Watteville, ended his career

24

by planting trees and making a fine road over the shoulder of one of the Rouxey hills to join the high-road. The estate belonging to this park and house was extensive, but badly cultivated; there were chalets on both hills and neglected forests of timber. It was all wild and deserted, left to the care of nature, abandoned to chance growths, but full of sublime and unexpected beauty. You may now imagine Les Rouxey.

It is unnecessary to complicate this story by relating all the prodigious trouble and the inventiveness stamped with genius by which Rosalie achieved her end without allowing it to be suspected. It is enough to say that it was in obedience to her mother that she left Besançon in the month of May, 1835, in an antique traveling carriage drawn by a pair of sturdy hired horses, and accompanied her father to Les Rouxey.

To a young girl love lurks in everything. When she rose, the morning after her arrival, Mademoiselle de Watteville saw from her bedroom window the fine expanse of water, from which the light mists rose like smoke, and were caught in the firs and larches, rolling up and along the hills till they reached the heights, and she gave a cry of admiration.

"They loved by the lakes! *She* lives by a lake! A lake is certainly full of love!" she thought.

A lake fed by snows has opalescent colors and a translucency that make it one huge diamond; but when it is shut in like that of Les Rouxey, between two granite masses covered with pines, when silence broods over it like that of the Savannahs or the Steppes, then every one must exclaim as Rosalie did.

"We owe that," said her father, "to the notorious Watteville."

"On my word," said the girl, "he did his best to earn forgiveness. Let us go in a boat to the farther end; it will give us an appetite for breakfast."

The Baron called two gardener lads who knew how to row, and took with him his prime minister, Modinier. The lake was about six acres in breadth, in some places ten or twelve, and four hundred in length. Rosalie soon found herself at the upper end shut in by the Dent de Vilard, the Jungfrau of that little Switzerland.

" Here we are, Monsieur le Baron," said Modinier, signing to the gardeners to tie up the boat ; " will you come and look ? "

" Look at what ? " asked Rosalie.

" Oh, nothing ! " exclaimed the Baron. " But you are a sensible girl ; we have some little secrets between us, and I may tell you what ruffles my mind. Some difficulties have arisen since 1830 between the village authorities of Riceys and me, on account of this very Dent de Vilard, and I want to settle the matter without your mother knowing anything about it, for she is stubborn ; she is capable of flinging fire and flames broadcast, particularly if she should hear that the mayor of Riceys, a Republican, got up this action as a sop to his people."

Rosalie had presence of mind enough to disguise her delight, so as to work more effectually on her father.

" What action ? " said she.

" Mademoiselle, the people of Riceys," said Modinier, " have long enjoyed the right of grazing and cutting fodder on their side of the Dent de Vilard. Now Monsieur Chantonnit, the mayor since 1830, declares that the whole Dent belongs to his district, and maintains that a hundred years ago, or more, there was a way through our grounds. You understand that in that case we should no longer have them to ourselves. Then this barbarian would end by saying, what the old men in the village say, that the ground occupied by the lake was appropriated by the Abbé de Watteville. That would be the end of Les Rouxey ; what next ? "

" Indeed, my child, between ourselves, it is the truth," said Monsieur de Watteville simply. " The land is an usurpation, with no title-deed but lapse of time. And, therefore, to

avoid all worry, I should wish to come to a friendly understanding as to my border-line on this side of the Dent de
Vilard, and I will then raise a wall."

"If you give way to the municipality, it will swallow you
up. You ought to have threatened Riceys."

"That is just what I told the master last evening," said
Modinier. "But in confirmation of that view I proposed
that he should come to see whether, on this side of the Dent
or on the other, there may not be, high or low, some traces
of an enclosure."

For a century the Dent de Vilard had been used by both
parties without coming to extremities; it stood as a sort of
party wall between the communes of Riceys and Les Rouxey,
yielding little profit. Indeed, the object in dispute, being
covered with snow for six months in the year, was of a nature
to cool their ardor. Thus it required all the hot blast by
which the revolution of 1830 inflamed the advocates of the
people to stir up this matter, by which Monsieur Chantonnit,
the mayor of Riceys, hoped to give a dramatic turn to his
career on the peaceful frontier of Switzerland, and to immor-
talize his term of office. Chantonnit, as his name shows, was
a native of Neufchâtel.

"My dear father," said Rosalie, as they got into the boat
again, "I agree with Modinier. If you wish to secure the
joint possession of the Dent de Vilard, you must act with
decision and get a legal opinion which will protect you against
this enterprising Chantonnit. Why should you be afraid?
Get the famous lawyer Savaron—engage him at once, lest
Chantonnit should place the interests of the village in his
hands. The man who won the case for the chapter against
the town can certainly win that of Watteville *versus* Riceys!
Besides," she added, "Les Rouxey will some day be mine—
not for a long time yet, I trust. Well, then, do not leave me
with a lawsuit on my hands. I like this place; I shall often live
here, and add to it as much as possible. On those banks," and

she pointed to the feet of the two hills, "I shall cut flower-beds and make the loveliest English gardens. Let us go to Besançon and bring back with us the Abbé de Grancey, Monsieur Savaron, and my mother, if she cares to come. You can then make up your mind ; but in your place I should have done so already. Your name is Watteville, and you are afraid of a fight ! If you should lose your case—well, I will never reproach you by a word ! "

" Oh, if that is the way you take it," said the Baron, " I am quite ready ; I will see the lawyer."

" Besides, a lawsuit is really great fun. It brings some interest into life, with coming and going and raging over it. You will have a great deal to do before you can get hold of the judges. We did not see the Abbé de Grancey for three weeks, he was so busy ! "

" But the very existence of the chapter was involved," said Monsieur de Watteville ; " and then the archbishop's pride, his conscience, everything that makes up the life of the priesthood, were at stake. That Savaron does not know what he did for the chapter ! He saved it ! "

" Listen to me," said his daughter in his ear, " if you secure Monsieur de Savaron, you will gain your suit, won't you ? Well, then, let me advise you. You cannot get at Monsieur Savaron excepting through Monsieur de Grancey. Take my word for it, and let us together talk to the dear abbé, without my mother's presence at the interview, for I know a way of persuading him to bring the lawyer to us."

" It will be very difficult to avoid mentioning it to your mother ! "

" The Abbé de Grancey will settle that afterwards. But just make up your mind to promise your vote to Monsieur Savaron at the next election, and you will see ! "

" Go to the election ! take the oath ? " cried the Baron de Watteville.

" What then ? " said she.

"And what will your mother say?"

"She may even desire you to do it," replied Rosalie, knowing as she did from Albert's letter to Léopold how deeply the vicar-general had pledged himself.

Four days after, the Abbé de Grancey called very early one morning on Albert de Savaron, having announced his visit the day before. The old priest had come to win over the great lawyer to the house of the Wattevilles, a proceeding which shows how much tact and subtlety Rosalie must have employed in an underhand way.

"What can I do for you, Monsieur le Vicaire-Général?" asked Savaron.

The abbé, who told his story with admirable frankness, was coldly heard by Albert.

"Monsieur l'Abbé," said he, "it is out of the question that I should defend the interests of the Wattevilles, and you shall understand why. My part in this town is to remain perfectly neutral. I will display no colors; I must remain a mystery till the eve of my election. Now, to plead for the Wattevilles would mean nothing in Paris, but here! Here, where everything is discussed, I should be supposed by every one to be an ally of your Faubourg Saint-Germain."

"What! do you suppose that you can remain unknown on the day of the election, when the candidates must oppose each other? It must then become known that your name is Savaron *de Savarus*, that you have held the appointment of master of appeals, that you supported the Restoration!"

"On the day of the election," said Savaron, "I will be all I am expected to be; and I intend to speak at the preliminary meetings."

"If you have the support of Monsieur de Watteville and his party, you will get a hundred votes in a mass, and far more to be trusted than those on which you rely. It is always possible to produce division of interests; convictions are inseparable."

" The deuce is in it ! " said Savaron. " I am attached to you, and I could do a great deal for you, father ! Perhaps we may compound with the devil. Whatever Monsieur de Watteville's business may be, by engaging Girardet, and prompting him, it will be possible to drag the proceedings out till the elections are over. I will not undertake to plead till the day after I am returned."

" Do this one thing," said the abbé. " Come to the Hôtel de Rupt : there is a young person of nineteen there who, one of these days, will have a hundred thousand francs a year, and you can seem to be paying your court to her——"

" Ah ! the young lady I sometimes see in the kiosk ? "

" Yes, Mademoiselle Rosalie," replied the Abbé de Grancey. " You are ambitious. If she takes a fancy to you, you may be everything an ambitious man can wish—who knows? A minister perhaps. A man can always be a minister who adds a hundred thousand francs a year to your amazing talents."

" Monsieur l'Abbé, if Mademoiselle de Watteville had three times her fortune, and adored me into the bargain, it would be impossible that I should marry her——"

" You are married ? " exclaimed the abbé.

" Not in church nor before the mayor, but morally speaking," said Savaron.

" That is even worse when a man cares about it as you seem to care," replied the abbé. " Some things that are done can be undone. Do not stake your fortune and your prospects on a woman's liking, any more than a wise man counts on a dead man's shoes before starting on his way."

" Let us say no more about Mademoiselle de Watteville," said Albert gravely, " and agree as to the facts. At your desire—for I have a regard and respect for you—I will appear for Monsieur de Watteville, but after the elections. Until then Girardet must conduct the case under my instructions. That is the utmost I can do."

"But there are questions involved which can only be settled after careful inspection of the localities," said the vicar-general.

"Girardet can go," said Savaron. "I cannot allow myself, in the face of a town I know so well, to take any step which might compromise the supreme interests that lie beyond my election."

The abbé left Savaron after giving him a keen look, in which he seemed to be laughing at the young athlete's uncompromising politics, while admiring his firmness.

"Ah! I would have dragged my father into a lawsuit—I would have done anything to get him here!" cried Rosalie to herself, standing in the kiosk and looking at the lawyer in his room, the day after Albert's interview with the abbé, who had reported the result to her father. "I would have committed any mortal sin, and you will not enter the Wattevilles' drawing-room; I may not hear your fine voice! You make conditions when your help is required by the Wattevilles and the Rupts! Well, God knows, I meant to be content with these small joys; with seeing you, hearing you speak, going with you to Les Rouxey, that your presence might to me make the place sacred. That was all I asked. But now—now I mean to be your wife. Yes, yes; look at *her* portrait, at *her* drawing-room, *her* bedroom, at the four sides of *her* villa, the points of view from *her* gardens. You expect her statue? I will make her marble herself towards you! After all, the woman does not love. Art, science, books, singing, music, have absorbed half her senses and her intelligence. She is old, too; she is past thirty; my Albert will not be happy!"

"What is the matter that you stay here, Rosalie?" asked her mother, interrupting her reflections. "Monsieur de Soulas is in the drawing-room, and he observed your attitude, which certainly betrays more thoughtfulness than is due at your age."

"Then is Monsieur de Soulas a foe to thought?" asked Rosalie.

"Then you were thinking?" said Madame de Watteville.

"Why, yes, mamma."

"Why, no! you were not thinking. You were staring at that lawyer's window with an attention that is neither becoming nor decent, and which Monsieur de Soulas, of all men, ought never to have observed."

"Why?" said Rosalie.

"It is time," said the Baroness, "that you should know what our intentions are. Amédée likes you, and you will not be unhappy as Comtesse de Soulas."

Rosalie, as white as a lily, made no reply, so completely was she stupefied by contending feelings. And yet, in the presence of the man she had this instant begun to hate vehemently, she forced the kind of smile which a ballet-dancer puts on for the public. Nay, she could even laugh; she had the strength to conceal her rage, which presently subsided, for she was determined to make use of this fat simpleton to further her designs.

"Monsieur Amédée," said she, at a moment when her mother was walking ahead of them in the garden, affecting to leave the young people together, "were you not aware that Monsieur Albert Savaron de Savarus is a Legitimist?"

"A Legitimist?"

"Until 1830 he was master of appeals to the Council of State, attached to the Supreme Ministerial Council, and in favor with the Dauphin and Dauphiness. It would be very good of you to say nothing against him, but it would be better still if you would attend the election this year, carry the day, and hinder that poor Monsieur de Chavoncourt from representing the town of Besançon."

"What sudden interest have you in this Savaron?"

"Monsieur Albert Savaron de Savarus, the natural son of the Comte de Savarus—pray keep the secret of my indis-

cretion—if he is returned deputy, will be our advocate in the
suit about Les Rouxey. Les Rouxey, my father tells me, will be
my property; I intend to live there, it is a lovely place! I
should be broken-hearted at seeing that fine piece of the great
de Watteville's work destroyed."

"The devil!" thought Amédée, as he left the house.
"The heiress is not such a fool as her mother thinks her."

Monsieur de Chavoncourt is a Royalist, of the famous 221.
Hence, from the day after the revolution of July, he always
preached the salutary doctrine of taking the oaths and resist-
ing the present order of things, after the pattern of the
Tories against the Whigs in England. This doctrine was not
acceptable to the Legitimists, who, in their defeat, had the
wit to divide in their opinions, and to trust to the force of
inertia, and to Providence. Monsieur de Chavoncourt was
not wholly trusted by his own party, but seemed to the
Moderates the best man to choose; they preferred the triumph
of his half-hearted opinions to the acclamation of a Republican who should combine the votes of the enthusiasts and
the patriots.

Monsieur de Chavoncourt, highly respected in Besançon,
was the representative of an old parliamentary family; his
fortune, of about fifteen thousand francs a year, was not an
offense to anybody, especially as he had a son and three
daughters. With such a family, fifteen thousand francs a year
are a mere nothing. Now when, under these circumstances,
the father of the family is above bribery, it would be hard if
the electors did not esteem him. Electors wax enthusiastic
over a *beau idéal* of parliamentary virtue, just as the audience
in the pit do at the representation of the generous sentiments
they so little practice.

Madame de Chavoncourt, at this time a woman of forty,
was one of the beauties of Besançon. While the Chamber
was sitting, she lived meagrely in one of their country places
to recoup herself by economy for Monsieur de Chavoncourt's

expenses in Paris. In the winter she received very creditably once a week, on Tuesdays, understanding her business as mistress of the house. Young Chavoncourt, a youth of two-and-twenty, and another young gentleman, named Monsieur de Vauchelles, no richer than Amédée and his school-friend, were his intimate allies. They made excursions together to Granvelle, and sometimes went out shooting; they were so well-known to be inseparable that they were invited to the country together.

Rosalie, who was intimate with the Chavoncourt girls, knew that the three young men had no secrets from each other. She reflected that if Monsieur de Soulas should repeat her words, it would be to his two companions. Now, Monsieur de Vauchelles had his matrimonial plans, as Amédée had his; he wished to marry Victoire, the eldest of the Chavoncourts, on whom an old aunt was to settle an estate worth seven thousand francs a year, and a hundred thousand francs in hard cash, when the contract should be signed. Victoire was this aunt's god-daughter and favorite niece. Consequently, young Chavoncourt and his friend Vauchelles would be sure to warn Monsieur de Chavoncourt of the danger he was in from Albert's candidature.

But this did not satisfy Rosalie. She sent the préfet of the department a letter written with her left hand, signed "*A friend to Louis Philippe,*" in which she informed him of the secret intentions of Monsieur Albert Savaron, pointing out the serious support a Royalist orator might give to Berryer, and revealing to him the deeply artful course pursued by the lawyer during his two years' residence at Besançon. The préfet was a capable man, a personal enemy of the Royalist party, devoted by conviction to the government of July—in short, one of those men of whom, in the Rue de Grenelle, the Minister of the Interior could say, "We have a capital préfet at Besançon." The préfet read the letter, and, in obedience to its instructions, he burnt it.

Rosalie aimed at preventing Albert's election, so as to keep him five years longer at Besançon.

At that time an election was a fight between parties, and in order to win, the ministry chose its ground by choosing the moment when it would give battle. The elections were therefore not to take place for three months yet. When a man's whole life depends on an election, the period that elapses between the issuing of the writs for convening the electoral bodies and the day fixed for their meetings is an interval during which ordinary vitality is suspended. Rosalie fully understood how much latitude Albert's absorbed state would leave her during these three months. By promising Mariette —as she afterwards confessed—to take both her and Jérôme into her service, she induced the maid to bring her all the letters Albert might send to Italy, and those addressed to him from that country. And all the time she was pondering these machinations, the extraordinary girl was working slippers for her father with the most innocent air in the world. She even made a greater display than ever of candor and simplicity, quite understanding how valuable that candor and innocence would be to her ends.

"My daughter grows quite charming!" said Madame de Watteville.

Two months before the election a meeting was held at the house of Monsieur Boucher senior, composed of the contractor who expected to get the work for the acqueduct for the Arcier waters; of Monsieur Boucher's father-in-law; of Monsieur Granet, the influential man for whom Savaron had done a service, and who was to nominate him as a candidate; of Girardet the lawyer; of the printer of the *Eastern Review;* and of the president of the Chamber of Commerce. In fact, the assembly consisted of twenty-seven persons in all, men who in the provinces are regarded as bigwigs. Each man represented on an average six votes, but in estimating their value they said ten, for men always begin by exaggerating their own influence. Among these twenty-seven was one who was wholly devoted to the préfet, one false brother who secretly looked for some favor from the ministry, either for himself or for some one belonging to him.

At this preliminary meeting, it was agreed that Savaron the lawyer should be named as candidate, a motion received with such enthusiasm as no one looked for from Besançon. Albert, waiting at home for Alfred Boucher to fetch him, was chatting with the Abbé de Grancey, who was interested in this absorbing ambition. Albert had appreciated the priest's vast political capacities; and the priest, touched by the young man's entreaties, had been willing to become his guide and adviser in this culminating struggle. The chapter did not love Monsieur de Chavoncourt, for it was his wife's brother-in-law, as president of the Tribunal, who had lost the famous suit for them in the lower court.

"You are betrayed, my dear fellow," said the shrewd and worthy abbé, in that gentle, calm voice which old priests acquire.

"Betrayed!" cried the lawyer, struck to the heart.

"By whom I know not at all," the priest replied. "But at the préfecture your plans are known, and your hand read like a book. At this moment I have no advice to give you. Such affairs need consideration. As for this evening, take the bull by the horns, anticipate the blow. Tell them all your previous life, and thus you will mitigate the effect of the discovery on the good folks of Besançon."

"Oh, I was prepared for it," said Albert in a broken voice.

"You would not benefit by my advice; you had the opportunity of making an impression at the Hôtel de Rupt; you do not know the advantage you would have gained——"

"What?"

"The unanimous support of the Royalists, an immediate readiness to go to the election—in short, above a hundred votes. Adding to these what, among ourselves, we call the ecclesiastical vote, though you were not yet nominated, you were master of the votes by ballot. Under such circumstances, a man may temporize, may make his way——"

Alfred Boucher when he came in, full of enthusiasm, to announce the decision of the preliminary meeting, found the vicar-general and the lawyer cold, calm, and grave.

"Good-night, Monsieur l'Abbé," said Albert. "We will talk of your business at greater length when the elections are over."

And he took Alfred's arm, after pressing Monsieur de Grancey's hand with meaning. The priest looked at the ambitious man, whose face at that moment wore the lofty expression which a general may have when he hears the first gun fired for a battle. He raised his eyes to heaven, and left the room, saying to himself, "What a priest he would make!"

Eloquence is not at the bar. The pleader rarely puts forth the real powers of his soul; if he did, he would die of it in a few years. Eloquence is, nowadays, rarely in the pulpit; but it is found on certain occasions in the Chamber of Deputies, when an ambitious man stakes all to win all, or, stung by a myriad of darts, at a given moment bursts into speech. But it is still more certainly found in some privileged beings, at the inevitable hour when their claims must either triumph or be wrecked, and when they are forced to speak. Thus at this meeting, Albert Savaron, feeling the necessity of winning himself some supporters, displayed all the faculties of his soul and the resources of his intellect. He entered the room well, without awkwardness or arrogance, without weakness, without cowardice, quite gravely, and was not dismayed at finding himself among twenty or thirty men. The news of the meeting and of its determination had already brought a few docile sheep to follow the bell.

Before listening to Monsieur Boucher, who was about to deluge him with a speech announcing the decision of the Boucher Committee, Albert begged for silence, and, as he shook hands with Monsieur Boucher, tried to warn him, by a sign, of an unexpected danger.

"My young friend, Alfred Boucher, has just announced to me the honor you have done me. But before that decision is irrevocable," said the lawyer, "I think that I ought to explain to you who and what your candidate is, so as to leave you free to take back your word if my declarations should disturb your conscience!"

This exordium was followed by profound silence. Some of the men thought it showed a noble impulse.

Albert gave a sketch of his previous career, telling them his real name, his action under the Restoration, and revealing himself as a new man since his arrival at Besançon, while pledging himself for the future. This address held his hearers breathless, it was said. These men, all with different interests, were spellbound by the brilliant eloquence that flowed at boiling heat from the heart and soul of this ambitious spirit. Admiration silenced reflection. Only one thing was clear—the thing which Albert wished to get into their heads—

Was it not far better for the town to have one of those men who are born to govern society at large than a mere voting-machine? A statesman carries power with him. A common-place deputy, however incorruptible, is but a conscience. What a glory for Provence to have found a Mirabeau, to return the only statesman since 1830 that the revolution of July had produced!

Under the pressure of this eloquence, all the audience believed it great enough to become a splendid political instrument in the hands of their representative. They all saw in Albert Savaron, Savarus the great Minister. And, reading the secret calculations of his constituents, the clever candidate gave them to understand that they would be the first to enjoy the right of profiting by his influence.

This confession of faith, this ambitious programme, this retrospect of his life and character was, according to the only man present who was capable of judging of Savaron (he has since become one of the leading men of Besançon), a master-piece of skill and of feeling, of fervor, interest, and fascination. This whirlwind carried away the electors. Never had any man had such a triumph. But, unfortunately, speech, a weapon only for close warfare, has only an immediate effect. Reflection kills the word when the word ceases to overpower reflection. If the votes had then been taken, Albert's name would undoubtedly have come out of the ballot-box. At the moment, he was conqueror. But he must conquer every day for two months.

Albert went home quivering. The townsfolk had applauded him, and he had achieved the great point of silencing before-hand the malignant talk to which his early career might give rise. The commercial interest of Besançon had unanimously nominated the lawyer, Albert Savaron de Savarus, as its candidate.

Alfred Boucher's enthusiasm, at first infectious, presently became blundering.

The préfet, alarmed by this success, set to work to count the ministerial votes, and contrived to have a secret interview with Monsieur de Chavoncourt, so as to effect a coalition in their common interests. Every day, without Albert being able to discover how, the voters in the Boucher Committee diminished in number.

Nothing could resist the slow grinding of the préfecture. Three or four clever men would say to Albert's clients, " Will the deputy defend you and win your lawsuits? Will he give you advice, draw up your contracts, arrange your compromises? He will be your slave for five years longer, if, instead of returning him to the Chamber, you only hold out the hope of his going there five years hence.''

This calculation did Savaron all the more mischief, because the wives of some of the merchants had already made it. The parties interested in the matter of the bridge and that of the water from Arcier could not hold out against a talking-to from a clever ministerialist, who proved to them that their safety lay at the préfecture, and not in the hands of an ambitious man. Each day was a check for Savaron, though each day the battle was led by him and fought by his lieutenants— a battle of words, speeches, and proceedings. He dared not go to the vicar-general, and the vicar-general never showed himself. Albert rose and went to bed in a fever, his brain on fire.

At last the day dawned of the first struggle, practically the show of hands ; the votes are counted, the candidates estimate their chances, and clever men can prophesy their failure or success. It is a decent hustings, without the mob, but formidable ; agitation, though it is not allowed any physical display, as it is in England, is not the less profound. The English fight these battles with their fists, the French with hard words. Our neighbors have a scrimmage, the French try their fate by cold combinations calmly worked out. This particular political business is carried out in opposition to the character of the two nations.

The Radical party named their candidate ; Monsieur de Chavoncourt came forward ; then Albert appeared, and was accused by the Chavoncourt Committee and the Radicals of being an uncompromising man of the Right, a second Berryer. The ministry had their candidate, a stalking-horse, useful only to receive the purely ministerial votes. The votes, thus divided, gave no result. The Republican candidate had twenty, the Ministry got fifty, Albert had seventy, Monsieur de Chavoncourt obtained sixty-seven. But the préfet's party had perfidiously made thirty of its most devoted adherents vote for Albert, so as to deceive the enemy. The votes for Monsieur de Chavoncourt, added to the eighty votes—the real number—at the disposal of the préfecture would carry the election, if only the préfet could succeed in gaining over a few of the Radicals. A hundred and sixty votes were not

25

recorded : those of Monsieur de Grancey's following and the Legitimists.

The show of hands at an election, like a dress rehearsal at a theatre, is the most deceptive thing in the world. Albert Savaron came home, putting a brave face on the matter, but half-dead. He had had the wit, the genius, or the good-luck to gain, within the last fortnight, two staunch supporters— Girardet's father-in-law and a very shrewd old merchant to whom Monsieur de Grancey had sent him. These two worthy men, his self-appointed spies, affected to be Albert's most ardent opponents in the hostile camp. Towards the end of the show of hands they informed Savaron, through the medium of Monsieur Boucher, that thirty voters, unknown, were secretly working against him in his party, playing the same sharp trick that they were playing for his benefit on the other side.

A criminal marching to execution could not suffer as Albert suffered as he went home from the hall where his fate was at stake. The despairing lover could endure no companionship. He walked through the streets alone, between eleven o'clock and midnight. At one in the morning, Albert, to whom sleep had been unknown for the past three days, was sitting in his library in a deep armchair, his face as pale as if he were dying, his hands hanging limp, in a forlorn attitude worthy of the Magdalen. Tears hung on his long lashes, tears that dim the eyes, but do not fall ; fierce thought drinks them up, the fire of the soul consumes them. Alone, he might weep. And then, under the kiosk, he saw a white figure, which reminded him of Francesca.

"And for three months I have had no letter from her ! What has become of her ? I have not written for two months, but I warned her. Is she ill ? Oh my love ! My life ! Will you ever know what I have gone through ? What a wretched constitution is mine ! Have I an aneurism ?" he asked himself, feeling his heart beat so violently that its pulses seemed

"SHE WAS ONE OF THOSE WOMEN WHO ARE BORN TO REIGN!"

audible in the silence like little grains of sand dropping on a big drum,

At this moment three distinct taps sounded on his door; Albert hastened to open it, and almost fainted with joy at seeing the vicar-general's cheerful and triumphant mien. Without a word, he threw his arms round the Abbé de Grancey, held him fast, and clasped him closely, letting his head fall on the old man's shoulder. He was a child again; he cried as he had cried on hearing that Francesca Soderini was a married woman. He betrayed his weakness to no one but to this priest, on whose face shone the light of hope. The priest had been sublime, and as shrewd as he was sublime.

"Forgive me, dear abbé, but you come at one of those moments when the man vanishes, for you are not to think me vulgarly ambitious."

"Oh! I know," replied the abbé. "You wrote *'Ambition for love's sake!'* Ah! my son, it was love in despair that made me a priest in 1786, at the age of two-and-twenty. In 1788 I was in charge of a parish. I know life. I have refused three bishoprics already; I mean to die at Besançon."

"Come and see her!" cried Savaron, seizing a candle, and leading the abbé into the handsome room where hung the portrait of the Duchess d'Argaiolo, which he lighted up.

"She is one of those women who are born to reign!" said the vicar-general, understanding how great an affection Albert showed him by this mark of confidence. "But there is pride on that brow; it is implacable; she would never forgive an insult! It is the Archangel Michael, the angel of execution, the inexorable angel. 'All or nothing' is the motto of this type of angel. There is something divinely pitiless in that head."

"You have guessed well," cried Savaron. "But, my dear abbé, for more than twelve years now she has reigned over my life, and I have not a single thought for which to blame myself——"

"Ah! if you could only say the same of God!" said the priest with simplicity. "Now, to talk of your affairs. For ten days I have been at work for you. If you are a real politician, this time you will follow my advice. You would not be where you are now if you would have gone to the Wattevilles when I first told you. But you must go there to-morrow; I will take you in the evening. The Rouxey estates are in danger; the case must be defended within three days. The election will not be over in three days. They will take good care not to appoint examiners the first day. There will be several voting days, and you will be elected by ballot——"

"How can that be?" asked Savaron.

"By winning the Rouxey lawsuit you will gain eighty Legitimist votes; add them to the thirty I can command, and you have a hundred and ten. Then, as twenty remain to you of the Boucher Committee, you will have a hundred and thirty in all."

"Well," said Albert, "we must get seventy-five more."

"Yes," said the priest, "since all the rest are ministerial. But, my son, you have two hundred votes, and the préfecture no more than a hundred and eighty."

"I have two hundred votes?" said Albert, standing stupid with amazement, after starting to his feet as if shot up by a spring.

"You have those of Monsieur de Chavoncourt," said the abbé.

"How?" said Albert.

"You will marry Mademoiselle Sidonie de Chavoncourt."

"Never!"

"You will marry Mademoiselle Sidonie de Chavoncourt," the priest repeated coldly.

"But you see—she is inexorable," said Albert, pointing to Francesca.

"You will marry Mademoiselle Sidonie de Chavoncourt," said the abbé calmly for the third time.

This time Albert understood. The vicar-general would not be implicated in the scheme which at last smiled on the despairing politician. A word more would have compromised the priest's dignity and honor.

"To-morrow evening at the Hôtel de Rupt you will meet Madame de Chavoncourt and her second daughter. You can thank her beforehand for what she is going to do for you, and tell her that your gratitude is unbounded, that you are hers body and soul, that henceforth your future is that of her family. You are quite disinterested, for you have so much confidence in yourself that you regard the nomination as deputy as a sufficient fortune.

"You will have a struggle with Madame de Chavoncourt; she will want you to pledge your word. All your future life, my son, lies in that evening. But, understand clearly, I have nothing to do with it. I am answerable only for the Legitimist voters; I have secured Madame de Watteville, and that means all the aristocracy of Besançon. Amédée de Soulas and Vauchelles, who will both vote for you, have won over the young men ; Madame de Watteville will get the old ones. As to my electors, they are infallible."

"And who on earth has gained over Madame de Chavoncourt?" asked Savaron.

"Ask me no questions," replied the abbé. "Monsieur de Chavoncourt, who has three daughters to marry, is not capable of increasing his wealth. Though Vauchelles marries the eldest without anything from her father, because her old aunt is to settle something on her, what is to become of the two others? Sidonie is sixteen, and your ambition is as good as a gold mine. Some one has told Madame de Chavoncourt that she will do better by getting her daughter married than by sending her husband to waste his money in Paris. That some one manages Madame de Chavoncourt, and Madame de Chavoncourt manages her husband."

"That is enough, my dear abbé. I understand. When

once I am returned as deputy, I have somebody's fortune to make, and by making it large enough I shall be released from my promise. In me you have a son, a man who will owe his happiness to you. Great heavens! what have I done to deserve so true a friend?"

"You won a triumph for the chapter," said the vicar-general, smiling. "Now, as to all this, be as secret as the tomb. We are nothing, we have done nothing. If we were known to have meddled in election matters, we should be eaten up alive by the Puritans of the Left—who do worse—and blamed by some of our own party, who want everything. Madame de Chavoncourt has no suspicion of my share in all this. I have confided in no one but Madame de Watteville, whom we may trust as we trust ourselves."

"I will bring the Duchess to you to be blessed!" cried Savaron.

After seeing out the old priest, Albert went to bed in the swaddling-clothes of power.

Next evening, as may well be supposed, by nine o'clock Madame la Baronne de Watteville's rooms were crowded by the aristocracy of Besançon in convocation extraordinary. They were discussing the exceptional step of going to the poll, to oblige the daughter of the de Rupts. It was known that the former master of appeals, the secretary of one of the most faithful ministers under the elder branch, was to be presented that evening. Madame de Chavoncourt was there with her second daughter Sidonie, exquisitely dressed, while her elder sister, secure of her lover, had not indulged in any of the arts of the toilet. In country towns these little things are re-marked. The Abbé de Grancey's fine and clever head was to be seen moving from group to group, listening to every-thing, seeming to be apart from it all, but uttering those incisive phrases which sum up a question and direct the issue.

"If the elder branch were to return," said he to an old

statesman of seventy, "what politicians would they find?"
"Berryer, alone on his bench, does not know which way to
turn ; if he had sixty votes, he would often scotch the wheels
of the government and upset ministries!"   "The Duc de
Fitz-James is to be nominated at Toulouse."   "You will
enable Monsieur de Watteville to win his lawsuit."   "If you
vote for Monsieur Savaron, the Republicans will vote with you
rather than with the Moderates ! " etc., etc.

At nine o'clock Albert had not arrived.   Madame de
Watteville was disposed to regard such delay as an imperti-
nence.

"My dear Baroness," said Madame de Chavoncourt, "do
not let such serious issues turn on such a trifle.   The varnish
on his boots is not dry—or a consultation, perhaps, detains
Monsieur de Savaron."

Rosalie shot a side glance at Madame de Chavoncourt.

"She is very lenient to Monsieur de Savaron," she whispered to her mother.

"You see," said the Baroness, with a smile, "there is a
question of a marriage between Sidonie and Monsieur de
Savaron."

Mademoiselle de Watteville hastily went to a window looking out over the garden.

At ten o'clock Albert de Savaron had not yet appeared.
The storm that threatened now burst.   Some of the gentlemen
sat down to cards, finding the thing intolerable.   The Abbé
de Grancey, who did not know what to think, went to the
window where Rosalie was hidden, and exclaimed aloud in
his amazement, "He must be dead ! "

The vicar-general stepped out into the garden, followed
by Monsieur de Watteville and his daughter, and they all
three went up to the kiosk.   In Albert's rooms all was dark ;
not a light was to be seen.

"Jérôme ! " cried Rosalie, seeing the servant in the yard
below.   The abbé looked at her with astonishment.   "Where

in the world is your master?" she asked the man, who came
to the foot of the wall.

"Gone—in a post-chaise, mademoiselle."

"He is ruined !" exclaimed the Abbé de Grancey, " or he
is happy ! "

The joy of triumph was not so effectually concealed on
Rosalie's face that the vicar-general could not detect it.   He
affected to see nothing.

" What can this girl have had to do with this business ? "
he asked himself.

They all three returned to the drawing-room, where Monsieur de Watteville announced the strange, the extraordinary,
the prodigious news of the lawyer's departure, without any
reason assigned for his evasion.   By half-past eleven only
fifteen persons remained, among them Madame de Chavan-
court and the Abbé de Godenars, another vicar-general, a
man of about forty, who hoped for a bishopric ; the two Chavoncourt girls and Monsieur de Vauchelles, the Abbé de
Grancey, Rosalie, Amédée de Soulas, and a retired magistrate, one of the most influential members of the upper circle
of Besançon, who had been very eager for Albert's election.
The Abbé de Grancey sat down by the Baroness in such a
position as to watch Rosalie, whose face, usually pale, wore a
feverish flush.

" What can have happened to Monsieur de Savaron ? " said
Madame de Chavoncourt.

At this moment a servant in livery brought in a letter for
the Abbé de Grancey on a silver tray.

" Pray read it," said the Baroness de Watteville, with
manifest interest.

The vicar-general read the letter ; he saw Rosalie suddenly
turn as white as her kerchief.

" She recognizes the writing," said he to himself, after
glancing at the girl over his spectacles.   He folded up the
letter, and calmly put it in his pocket without a word.   In

three minutes he had met three looks from Rosalie which were enough to make him guess everything.

"She is in love with Albert Savaron!" thought the vicar-general.

He rose and took leave. He was going towards the door when, in the next room, he was overtaken by Rosalie, who said—

"Monsieur de Grancey, it was from Albert!"

"How do you know that it was his writing, to recognize it from so far?"

The girl's reply, caught as she was in the toils of her impatience and rage, seemed to the abbé sublime.

"I love him! What is the matter?" she said after a pause.

"He gives up the election."

Rosalie put her finger to her lip.

"I ask you to be as secret as if it were a confession," said she before returning to the drawing-room. "If there is an end of the election, there is an end of the marriage with Sidonie."

In the morning, on her way to mass, Mademoiselle de Watteville heard from Mariette some of the circumstances which had prompted Albert's disappearance at the most critical moment of his life.

"Mademoiselle, an old gentleman from Paris arrived yesterday morning at the Hôtel National; he came in his own carriage with four horses, and a courier in front, and a servant. Indeed, Jérôme, who saw the carriage returning, declares he could only be a prince or a *milord*."

"Was there a coronet on the carriage?" asked Rosalie.

"I do not know," said Mariette. "Just as two was striking he came to call on Monsieur Savaron, and sent in his card; and when he saw it, Jérôme says Monsieur turned as pale as a sheet, and said he was to be shown in. As he himself locked the door, it is impossible to tell what the old gentleman and the lawyer said to each other; but they were together above an hour, and then the old gentleman, with the lawyer, called up his servant. Jérôme saw the servant go out again with an immense package, four feet long, which looked like a great painting on canvas. The old gentleman had in his hand a large parcel of papers. Monsieur Savaron was paler than death, and he, so proud, so dignified, was in a state to be pitied. But he treated the old gentleman so respectfully that he could not have been politer to the king himself. Jérôme and Monsieur Albert Savaron escorted the gentleman to his carriage, which was standing with the horses in. The courier started on the stroke of three.

"Monsieur Savaron went straight to the préfecture, and from that to Monsieur Gentillet, who sold him the old traveling carriage that used to belong to Madame de Saint-Vier before she died; then he ordered post-horses for six o'clock. He went home to pack; no doubt he wrote a lot of letters; finally, he settled everything with Monsieur Girardet, who went to him and stayed till seven. Jérôme carried a note to Monsieur Boucher, with whom his master was to have dined; and then, at half-past seven, the lawyer set out, leaving Jérôme with three months' wages, and telling him to find another place.

"He left his keys with Monsieur Girardet, whom he took home, and at his house, Jérôme says, he took a plate of soup, for at half-past seven Monsieur Girardet had not yet dined. When Monsieur Savaron got into the carriage again he looked like death. Jérôme, who, of course, saw his master off, heard him tell the postillion 'The Geneva Road!'"

"Did Jérôme ask the name of the stranger at the Hôtel National?"

"As the old gentleman did not mean to stay, he was not asked for it. The servant, by his orders no doubt, pretended not to speak French.'"

"And the letter which came so late to the Abbé de Grancey?" said Rosalie.

"It was Monsieur Girardet, no doubt, who ought to have delivered it; but Jérôme says that poor Monsieur Girardet, who was much attached to lawyer Savaron, was as much upset as he was. So he who came so mysteriously, as Mademoiselle Galard says, is gone away just as mysteriously."

After hearing this narrative, Mademoiselle de Watteville fell into a brooding and absent mood, which everybody could see. It is useless to say anything of the commotion that arose in Besançon on the disappearance of Monsieur Savaron. It was understood that the préfect had obliged him with the greatest readiness by giving him at once a passport across the frontier, for he was thus quit of his only opponent. Next day Monsieur de Chavoncourt was carried to the top by a majority of a hundred and forty votes.

"Jack is gone by the way he came," said an elector on hearing of Albert Savaron's flight.

This event lent weight to the prevailing prejudice at Besançon against strangers; indeed, two years previously they had received confirmation from the affair of the Republican newspaper. Ten days later Albert de Savaron was never spoken of again. Only three persons—Girardet the attorney, the vicar-general, and Rosalie—were seriously affected by his disappearance. Girardet knew that the white-haired stranger was Prince Soderini, for he had seen his card, and he told the vicar-general; but Rosalie, better informed than either of them, had known for three months past that the Duc d'Argaiolo was dead.

In the month of April, 1836, no one had had any news from or of Albert de Savaron. Jérôme and Mariette were to be married, but the Baroness confidentially desired her maid to wait till her daughter was married, saying that the two weddings might take place at the same time.

"It is time that Rosalie should be married," said the

Baroness one day to Monsieur de Watteville. "She is nineteen, and she is fearfully altered in these last months."

"I do not know what ails her," said the Baron.

"When fathers do not know what ails their daughters, mothers can guess," said the Baroness; "we must get her married."

"I am quite willing," said the Baron. "I shall give her Les Rouxey now that the court has settled our quarrel with the authorities of Riceys by fixing the boundary line at three hundred feet up the side of the Dent de Vilard. I am having a trench made to collect all the water and carry it into the lake. The village did not appeal, so the decision is final."

"It has never yet occurred to you," said Madame de Watteville, "that this decision cost me thirty thousand francs handed over to Chantonnit. That peasant would take nothing else; he sold us peace. If you give away Les Rouxey, you will have nothing left," said the Baroness.

"I do not need much," said the Baron; "I am breaking up."

"You eat like an ogre!"

"Just so. But however much I may eat, I feel my legs get weaker and weaker——"

"It is from working the lathe," said his wife.

"I do not know," said he.

"We will marry Rosalie to Monsieur de Soulas; if you give her Les Rouxey, keep the life interest. I will give them fifteen thousand francs a year in the funds. Our children can live here; I do not see that they are much to be pitied."

"No. I shall give them Les Rouxey out and out. Rosalie is fond of Les Rouxey."

"You are a queer man with your daughter! It does not occur to you to ask me if I am fond of Les Rouxey."

Rosalie, at once sent for, was informed that she was to marry Monsieur de Soulas one day early in the month of May.

"I am very much obliged to you, mother, and to you too, father, for having thought of settling me ; but I do not mean to marry ; I am very happy with you."

" Mere speeches ! " said the Baroness. " You are not in love with Monsieur de Soulas, that is all."

" If you insist on the plain truth, I will never marry Monsieur de Soulas——"

" Oh ! the *never* of a girl of nineteen ! " retorted her mother, with a bitter smile.

" The *never* of Mademoiselle de Watteville," said Rosalie with firm decision. " My father, I imagine, has no intention of making me marry against my wishes ? "

" No, indeed no ! " said the poor Baron, looking affectionately at his daughter.

" Very well ! " said the Baroness, sternly controlling the rage of a bigot startled at finding herself unexpectedly defied, " you yourself, Monsieur de Watteville, may take the responsibility of settling your daughter. Consider well, Mademoiselle, for if you do not marry to my mind you will get nothing out of me ! "

The quarrel thus begun between Madame de Watteville and her husband, who took his daughter's part, went so far that Rosalie and her father were obliged to spend the summer at Les Rouxey ; life at the Hôtel de Rupt was unendurable. It thus became known in Besançon that Mademoiselle de Watteville had positively refused the Comte de Soulas.

After their marriage Mariette and Jérôme came to Les Rouxey to succeed Modinier in due time. The Baron restored and repaired the house to suit his daughter's taste. When she heard that these improvements had cost about sixty thousand francs, and that Rosalie and her father were building a conservatory, the Baroness understood that there was a leaven of spite in her daughter. The Baron purchased various outlying plots, and a little estate worth thirty thousand francs. Madame de Watteville was told that, away from her,

Rosalie showed masterly qualities, that she was taking steps to
improve the value of Les Rouxey, that she had treated herself
to a riding-habit and rode about; her father, whom she made
very happy, who no longer complained of his health, and who
was growing fat, accompanied her in her expeditions.   As the
Baroness' name-day drew near—her name was Louise—the
vicar-general came one day to Les Rouxey, deputed, no doubt,
by Madame de Watteville and Monsieur de Soulas, to negotiate a peace between the mother and daughter.

"That little Rosalie has a head on her shoulders," said the
folk of Besançon.

After handsomely paying up the ninety thousand francs
spent on Les Rouxey, the Baroness allowed her husband a thousand francs a month to live on ; she would not put herself in
the wrong.   The father and daughter were perfectly willing
to return to Besançon for the 15th of August, and to remain
there till the end of the month.

When, after dinner, the vicar-general took Mademoiselle de
Watteville apart, to open the question of the marriage, by
explaining to her that it was vain to think any more of
Albert, of whom they had had no news for a year past, he
was stopped at once by a sign from Rosalie.   The strange girl
took Monsieur de Grancey by the arm, and led him to a seat
under a clump of rhododendrons, whence there was a view of
the lake.

"Listen, dear abbé," said she.   "You whom I love as
much as my father, for you had an affection for my Albert, I
must at last confess that I committed crimes to become his
wife, and he must be my husband.   Here ; read this."

She held out to him a number of the *Gazette* which she had
in her apron pocket, pointing out the following paragraph
under the date of Florence, May 25th :

"The wedding of Monsieur le Duc de Rhétoré, eldest son
of the Duc de Chaulieu, the former ambassador, to Madame la
Duchesse d'Argaiolo, *née* Princess Soderini, was solemnized

with great splendor. Numerous entertainments given in honor of the marriage are making Florence gay. The Duchess' fortune is one of the finest in Italy, for the late Duke left her everything."

"The woman he loved is married," said she. "I divided them."

"You? How?" asked the abbé.

Rosalie was about to reply, when she was interrupted by a loud cry from two of the gardeners, following on the sound of a body falling into the water; she started, and .ran .off screaming, "Oh! father!" The Baron had disappeared.

In trying to reach a piece of granite on which he fancied he saw the impression of a shell, a circumstance which would have contradicted some system of geology, Monsieur de Watteville had gone down the slope, lost his balance, and slipped into the lake, which, of course, was deepest close under the roadway. The men had the greatest difficulty in enabling the Baron to catch hold of a pole pushed down at the place where the water was bubbling, but at last they pulled him out, covered with mud, in which he had sunk; he was getting deeper and deeper in, by dint of struggling. Monsieur de Watteville had dined heavily, digestion was in progress, and was thus checked.

When he had been undressed, washed, and put to bed, he was in such evident danger that two servants at once set out on horseback: one to ride to Besançon, and the other to fetch the nearest doctor and surgeon. When Madame de Watteville arrived, eight hours later, with the first medical aid from Besançon, they found Monsieur de Watteville past all hope, in spite of the intelligent treatment of the Rouxey doctor. The fright had produced serious effusion on the brain, and the shock to the digestion was helping to kill the poor man.

This death, which would never have happened, said Madame de Watteville, if her husband had stayed at Besançon, was ascribed by her to her daughter's obstinacy. She took an

aversion for Rosalie, abandoning herself to grief and regrets
that were evidently exaggerated. She spoke of the Baron as
" her dear lamb ! ''

The last of the Wattevilles was buried on an island in the
lake at Les Rouxey, where the Baroness had a little Gothic
monument erected of white marble, like that called the tomb
of Héloïse at Père-Lachaise.

A month after this catastrophe the mother and daughter had
settled in the Hôtel de Rupt, where they lived in savage silence.
Rosalie was suffering from real sorrow, which had no visible
outlet ; she accused herself of her father's death, and she
feared another disaster, much greater in her eyes, and very
certainly her own work ; neither Girardet the attorney nor
the Abbé de Grancey could obtain any information concerning Albert. This silence was appalling. In a paroxysm
of repentance she felt that she must confess to the vicar-general
the horrible machinations by which she had separated Francesca and Albert. They had been simple, but formidable.
Mademoiselle·de Watteville had intercepted Albert's letters to
the Duchess as well as that in which Francesca announced
her husband's illness, warning her lover that she could write
to him no more during the time while she was devoted, as was
her duty, to the care of the dying man. Thus, while Albert
was wholly occupied with election matters, the Duchess had
written him only two letters ; one in which she told him that
the Duc d'Argaiolo was in danger, and one announcing her
widowhood—two noble and beautiful letters, which Rosalie
kept back.

After several nights' labor she succeeded in imitating
Albert's writing very perfectly. She had substituted three
letters of her own writing for three of Albert's, and the rough
copies which she showed to the old priest made him shudder
—the genius of evil was revealed in them to such perfection.
Rosalie, writing in Albert's name, had prepared the Duchess
for a change in the Frenchman's feelings, falsely representing

him as faithless, and she had answered the news of the Duc d'Argaiolo's death by announcing the marriage ere long of Albert and Mademoiselle de Watteville. The two letters, intended to cross on the road, had, in fact, done so. The infernal cleverness with which the letters were written so much astonished the vicar-general that he read them a second time. Francesca, stabbed to the heart by a girl who wanted to kill love in her rival, had answered the last in these four words: "You are free. Farewell."

"Purely moral crimes, which give no hold to human justice, are the most atrocious and detestable," said the abbé severely. "God often punishes them on earth; herein lies the reason of the terrible catastrophes which to us seem inexplicable. Of all secret crimes buried in the mystery of private life, the most disgraceful is that of breaking the seal of a letter, or of reading it surreptitiously. Every one, whoever it may be, and urged by whatever reason, who is guilty of such an act has stained his honor beyond retrieving.

"Do you not feel all that is touching, that is heavenly in the story of the youthful page, falsely accused, and carrying the letter containing the order for his execution, who sets out without a thought of ill, and whom Providence protects and saves—miraculously, we say! But do you know wherein the miracle lies? Virtue has a glory as potent as that of innocent childhood.

"I say these things not meaning to admonish you," said the old priest, with deep grief. "I, alas! am not your spiritual director; you are not kneeling at the feet of God; I am your friend, appalled by dread of what your punishment may be. What has become of that unhappy Albert? Has he, perhaps, killed himself? There was tremendous passion under his assumption of calm. I understand now that old Prince Soderini, the father of the Duchess d'Argaiolo, came here to take back his daughter's letters and portraits. This was the thunderbolt that fell on Albert's head, and he went off, no doubt, to try to justify himself. But how is it that in fourteen months he has given us no news of himself? "

" Oh! if I marry him, he will be so happy ! "

" Happy? He does not love you. Besides, you have no great fortune to give him. Your mother detests you; you made her a fierce reply which rankles, and which will be your ruin. When she told you yesterday that obedience was the only way to repair your errors, and reminded you of the need for marrying, mentioning Amédée—' If you are so fond of him, marry him yourself, mother ! '—Did you, or did you not, fling these words in her teeth? "

" Yes," said Rosalie.

" Well, I know her," Monsieur de Grancey went on. " In a few months she will be Comtesse de Soulas ! She will be sure to have children ; she will give Monsieur de Soulas forty thousand francs a year ; she will benefit him in other ways, and reduce your share of her fortune as much as possible. You will be poor as long as she lives, and she is but eight-and-thirty ! Your whole estate will be the land of Les Rouxey, and the small share left to you after your father's legal debts are settled, if indeed, your mother should consent to forego her claims on Les Rouxey. From the point of view of material advantages, you have done badly for yourself; from the point of view of feeling, I imagine you have wrecked your life. Instead of going to your mother——" Rosalie shook her head fiercely.

" To your mother," the priest went on, " and to religion, where you would, at the first impulse of your heart, have found enlightenment, counsel and guidance, you chose to act in your own way, knowing nothing of life, and listening only to passion ! "

These words of wisdom terrified Mademoiselle de Watteville.

" And what ought I to do now? " she asked after a brief pause.

"To repair your wrongdoing, you must ascertain its extent," said the abbé.

"Well, I will write to the only man who can know anything of Albert's fate, Monsieur Léopold Hannequin, a notary in Paris, his friend from childhood."

"Write no more, unless to do honor to truth," said the vicar-general. "Place the real and the false letters in my hands, confess everything in detail as though I were the keeper of your conscience, asking me how you may expiate your sins, and doing as I bid you. I shall see—for, above all things, restore this unfortunate man to his innocence in the eyes of the woman he had made his divinity on earth. Though he has lost his happiness, Albert must still hope for justification."

Rosalie promised to obey the abbé, hoping that the steps he might take would perhaps end in bringing Albert back to her.

Not long after Mademoiselle de Watteville's confession a clerk came to Besançon from Monsieur Léopold Hannequin, armed with a power of attorney from Albert; he called first on Monsieur Girardet, begging his assistance in selling the house belonging to Monsieur Savaron. The attorney undertook to do this out of friendship for Albert. The clerk from Paris sold the furniture, and with the proceeds could repay some money owed by Savaron to Girardet, who, on the occasion of his inexplicable departure, had lent him five thousand francs while undertaking to collect his assets. When Girardet asked what had become of the handsome and noble pleader, to whom he had been much attached, the clerk replied that no one knew but his master, and that the notary had seemed greatly distressed by the contents of the last letter he had received from Monsieur Albert de Savaron.

On hearing this, the vicar-general wrote to Léopold. This was the worthy notary's reply:

"To Monsieur l'Abbé de Grancey, Vicar-General of the Diocese of Besançon.

"PARIS.

"Alas, monsieur, it is in nobody's power to restore Albert to the life of the world; he has renounced it. He is a novice in the monastery of the Grande Chartreuse near Grenoble. You know, better than I who have but just learned it, that on the threshold of that cloister everything dies. Albert, foreseeing that I should go to him, placed the general of the order between my utmost efforts and himself. I know his noble soul well enough to be sure that he is the victim of some odious plot unknown to us ; but everything is at an end. The Duchesse d'Argaiolo, now Duchesse de Rhétoré, seems to me to have carried severity to an extreme. At Belgirate, which she had left when Albert flew thither, she had left instructions leading him to believe that she was living in London. From London Albert went in search of her to Naples, and from Naples to Rome, where she was now engaged to the Duc de Rhétoré. When Albert succeeded in seeing Madame d'Argaiolo, at Florence, it was at the ceremony of her marriage.

"Our poor friend swooned in church, and even when he was in danger of death he could never obtain any explanation from this woman, who must have had I know not what in her heart. For seven months Albert had traveled in pursuit of a cruel creature who thought it sport to escape him ; he knew not where or how to catch her.

"I saw him on his way through Paris ; and if you had seen him, as I did, you would have felt that not a word might be spoken about the Duchess, at the risk of bringing on an attack which might have wrecked his reason. If he had known what his crime was, he might have found means to justify himself; but being falsely accused of being married !—what could he do? Albert is dead, quite dead to the world. He longed for rest ; let us hope that the deep silence and prayer into which he has thrown himself may give him happiness in another

guise. You, monsieur, who have known him, must greatly
pity him ; and pity his friends also.

"Yours, etc."

As soon as he received this letter the good vicar-general
wrote to the general of the Carthusian order, and this was the
letter he received from Albert Savaron :

"Brother Albert to Monsieur l'Abbé de Grancey, Vicar-
General of the Diocese of Besançon.

" LA GRANDE CHARTREUSE.

"I recognized your tender soul, dear and well-beloved
vicar-general, and your still youthful heart, in all that the
reverend father general of our order has just told me. You
have understood the only wish that lurks in the depths of my
heart so far as the things of the world are concerned—to get
justice done to my feelings by her who has treated me so
badly ! But before leaving me at liberty to avail myself of
your offer, the general wanted to know that my vocation was
sincere ; he was so kind as to tell me his idea, on finding that
I was determined to preserve absolute silence on this point.
If I had yielded to the temptation to rehabilitate the man
of the world, the friar would have been rejected by this monastery. Grace has certainly done her work ; but, though short,
the struggle was not the less keen or the less painful. Is not
this enough to show you that I could never return to the
world.

" Hence my forgiveness, which you ask for the author of so
much woe, is entire and without a thought of vindictiveness.
I will pray to God to forgive that young lady as I forgive her,
and as I shall beseech Him to give Madame de Rhétoré a life
of happiness. Ah ! whether it be death, or the obstinate
hand of a young girl madly bent on being loved, or one of the
blows ascribed to chance, must we not all obey God ? Sorrow
in some souls makes a vast void through which the Divine
voice rings. I learned too late the bearings of this life on

that which awaits us ; all in me is worn out ; I could not serve in the ranks of the church militant, and I lay the remains of an almost extinct life at the foot of the altar.

" This is the last time I shall ever write. You alone, who loved me, and whom I loved so well, could make me break the law of oblivion I imposed on myself when I entered these headquarters of Saint Bruno, but you are always especially named in the prayers of

" BROTHER ALBERT.

" *November*, 1836."

" Everything is for the best, perhaps," thought the Abbé de Grancey.

When he showed this letter to Rosalie, who with a pious impulse kissed the lines which contained her forgiveness, he said to her—

" Well, now that he is lost to you, will you not be reconciled to your mother and marry the Comte de Soulas ? "

" Only if Albert should order it," said she.

" But you see it is impossible to consult him. The general of the order would not allow it."

" If I were to go to see him ? "

" No Carthusian sees any visitor. Besides, no woman but the Queen of France may enter a Carthusian monastery," said the abbé. " So you have no longer any excuse for not marrying young Monsieur de Soulas."

" I do not wish to destroy my mother's happiness," retorted Rosalie.

" Satan ! " exclaimed the vicar-general.

Towards the end of that winter the worthy Abbé de Grancey died. This good friend no longer stood between Madame de Watteville and her daughter, to soften the impact of those two iron wills.

The event he had foretold took place. In the month of August, 1837, Madame de Watteville was married to Monsieur de Soulas in Paris, whither she went by Rosalie's advice, the

girl making a show of kindness and sweetness to her mother.
Madame de Watteville believed in this affection on the part
of her daughter, who simply desired to go to Paris to give
herself the luxury of a bitter revenge ; she thought of nothing
but avenging Savaron by torturing her rival.

Mademoiselle de Watteville had been declared legally of
age ; she was, in fact, not far from one-and-twenty. Her
mother, to settle with her finally, had resigned her claims on
Les Rouxey, and the daughter had signed a release for all the
inheritance of the Baron de Watteville. Rosalie encouraged
her mother to marry the Comte de Soulas and settle all her
own fortune on him.

" Let us each be perfectly free," she said.

Madame de Soulas, who had been uneasy as to her daughter's intentions, was touched by this liberality, and made her
a present of six thousand francs a year in the funds as conscience money. As the Comtesse de Soulas had an income
of forty-eight thousand francs from her own lands, and was
quite incapable of alienating them in order to diminish
Rosalie's share, Mademoiselle de Watteville was still a fortune
to marry, of eighteen hundred thousand francs ; Les Rouxey,
with the Baron's additions, and certain improvements, might
yield twenty thousand francs a year, besides the value of the
house, rents, and preserves. So Rosalie and her mother, who
soon adopted the Paris style and fashions, easily obtained
introductions to the best society. The golden key—eighteen
hundred thousand francs—embroidered on Mademoiselle de
Watteville's stomacher, did more for the Comtesse de Soulas
than her pretentions *à la* de Rupt, her inappropriate pride, or
even her rather distant great connections.

In the month of February, 1838, Rosalie, who was eagerly
courted by many young men, achieved the purpose which had
brought her to Paris. This was to meet the Duchesse de
Rhétoré, to see this wonderful woman, and to overwhelm her
with perennial remorse. Rosalie gave herself up to the most

bewildering elegance and vanities in order to face the Duchess on an equal footing.

They first met at a ball given annually after 1830 for the benefit of the pensioners on the old Civil List. A young man, prompted by Rosalie, pointed her out to the Duchess, saying—

"There is a very remarkable young person, a strong-minded young lady too! She drove a clever man into a monastery —the Grande Chartreuse—a man of immense capabilities, Albert de Savaron, whose career she wrecked. She is Mademoiselle de Watteville, the famous Besançon heiress——"

The Duchess turned pale. Rosalie's eyes met hers with one of those flashes which, between woman and woman, are more fatal than the pistol-shots of a duel. Francesca Soderini, who had suspected that Albert might be innocent, hastily quitted the ball-room, leaving the speaker at his wits' end to guess what terrible blow he had inflicted on the beautiful Duchesse de Rhétoré.

"If you want to hear more about Albert, come to the opera ball on Tuesday with a marigold in your hand."

This anonymous note, sent by Rosalie to the Duchess, brought the unhappy Italian to the ball, where Mademoiselle de Watteville placed in her hand all Albert's letters, with that written to Léopold Hannequin by the vicar-general, and the notary's reply, and even that in which she had written her own confession to the Abbé de Grancey.

"I do not choose to be the only sufferer," she said to her rival, "for one has been as ruthless as the other."

After enjoying the dismay stamped on the Duchess' beautiful face, Rosalie went away; she went out no more, and returned to Besançon with her mother.

Mademoiselle de Watteville, who lived alone on her estate of Les Rouxey, riding, hunting, refusing two or three offers a year, going to Besançon four or five times in the course of the winter, and busying herself with improving her land, was regarded as a very eccentric personage. She was one of the celebrities of the Eastern provinces.

Madame de Soulas has two children, a boy and a girl, and she has grown younger; but young Monsieur de Soulas has aged a good deal.

"My fortune has cost me dear," said he to young Chavoncourt. "Really to know a bigot it is unfortunately necessary to marry her!" .

Mademoiselle de Watteville behaves in the most extraordinary manner. "She has vagaries," people say. Every year she goes to gaze at the walls of the Grande Chartreuse. Perhaps she dreams of imitating her grand-uncle by forcing the walls of the monastery to find a husband, as Watteville broke through those of his monastery to recover his liberty.

She left Besançon in 1841, intending, it was said, to get married; but the real reason of this expedition is still unknown, for she returned home in a state which forbids her ever appearing in society again. By one of those chances of which the Abbé de Grancey had spoken, she happened to be on the Loire in a steamboat of which the boiler burst. Mademoiselle de Watteville was so severely injured that she lost her right arm and her left leg; her face is marked with fearful scars, which have bereft her of her beauty; her health, cruelly upset, leaves her few days free from suffering. In short, she now never leaves the Chartreuse of Les Rouxey, where she leads a life wholly devoted to religious practices.

PARIS, *May*, 1842.